Sherry Cole

Phillip's WAR

Published by Rachel D. Muller and Timeline Press™
www.racheldmuller.com
www.timelinepress.net

Printed in the United States of America

Timeline Press is a trademark of Rachel D. Muller filed with the state of Maryland.

ISBN 10: 0-9993809-4-X (e-book)
     13: 978-0-9993809-4-9 (e-book)
ISBN10: 0-9993809-5-8 (pbk)
     13: 978-0-9993809-5-6 (pbk)

Cover art by Roseanna White Designs, 2015, 2017
All scripture taken from the King James Version Bible
All photos purchased through **www.Shutterstock.com**

LOVE & WAR
Book Three

RACHEL MULLER

DEDICATION

For Wayne Weeks Jr.—the person who inspired the start of this series and my true life pen pal.
Wayne, thank you for the friendship we shared and the correspondence that helped to bring both of us through lonely times. Who knew it would spark the beginning of a
book?
Also for Sarah, Wayne's wife—the woman who helped bridge a reunion 13 years in the making.
Sarah, your friendship has been nothing short of a blessing. I thank the Lord for placing you and Wayne in my life. May the blessings continue to rain down on you
and your growing family.
My love to both of you.
~Rachel

PROLOGUE

Saipan, Marianas Islands
July 1944

If he ever lived to see the end of this war, Phillip Johnson knew he would never be the same again.

Waiting soldiers eyed the Marpi Point Cliffs as a native to the islands pleaded over a loudspeaker. All eyes focused on the cliffs, just waiting, hoping, the islanders would emerge from their caves and put their trust in the American Army.

Phillip could hear the desperation in the Filipino's voice as he spoke in his native tongue to his people. The tension hung so thick in the air, it was as if one could smell the anxiety of the situation. But maybe it was the stench of cigarette smoke, instead, as nervous soldiers waited out the drama by pulling a drag on their ciggies.

The soldiers' eyes were heavy with exhaustion. Cheeks pulled taught against each man's face. Unshaven stubble shadowed their jaws where dirt and mud hadn't caked to their skin. The Marines' khakis hung loosely from their bodies, revealing how little they'd eaten in the past few weeks. If exhaustion and heat didn't claim them, starvation probably would.

Phillip looked back at the cliff known as Marpi Point. Frightened faces peered over the lush foliage of Saipan's ridge. He saw apprehension in their eyes, desperation the Japanese Army had etched into the minds. He was the enemy on this turf.

The natives hid themselves, and their children, in the caves of the cliffs. Afraid, despondent, because the Americans were savage beasts.

Phillip's heart knocked against his chest. The slight twinge of a headache pulsed within his temples. The day was hot, humid, just like any other day. He'd become dehydrated in the heat, the stress of today's altercation not help matters. For hours they'd been pleading, trying to extricate and save the lives of a people mistreated by the

Japanese Army. So far, they had not been successful.

To Phillip's right, the rustling of combat boots against mountainous rock and tropical grass aroused his trained senses. His head swiveled around and found his fellow brothers standing to their feet, picking up their rifles, and dousing their cigarettes. No longer standing as still as statues, movement of soldiers livened the hillside.

"Over there."

Phillip turned his gaze to the spot where a fellow Marine had pointed. Just beyond the next valley of rock, small, dirty faces moved toward them. He spotted a man, then two. They were soon followed by mostly women and children—the same women and children who feared them most of all. They were so few in number, he could have counted them on all ten fingers and all ten toes.

"It's about time," Phillip grumbled to the soldier beside him.

"They couldn't hide up there forever. We just had to wait them out."

The boys' squad leader motioned for them to follow. As soon as the natives moved down from the cliffs, the squad would scale the hills for Japanese artillery. The enemy liked to hide in concealed areas. The cliffs at Marpi Point proved to be the best high ground on this island. Surely enemy soldiers would be waiting, ready for the kill.

"Hey! Hey! What are they all doing?"

All eyes shifted to the alarming shriek of one soldier's voice.

In the distance, the detonation of a grenade popped and echoed off the cliff.

The rush of Marines to the crags sent an eerie chill down Phillip's spine. He, too, hurried to the rock face. His knees bent with the incline of the rocky edge, stressing his already tired legs. He gripped his rifle a little closer, a little tighter, in the event that a Japanese sniper slit the air with a bullet.

When he reached the cliff's edge, a group of Marines were already standing at the bluffs, staring down into the mouth of the Pacific Ocean.

"What is it?" he asked as he drew closer. "We got a rogue native on our hands?"

The air stood still around him. No one glanced up at him. No one spoke. Eyes, wide with dismay and disbelief, stared blankly at the shoreline below.

"What's the deal, fella?" he tried again.

"You'd never believe it if you saw it with your own eyes." The corporal answering him choked on his words.

With hesitation, Phillip treaded carefully to the edge. He was ready for anything. His forefinger extended to the trigger of his rifle, ready if need be. His heart beat a little harder in his chest. Deeply, he breathed as he took that last step to the cliff's overlook. What he saw next would scar his mind and haunt him viciously for the days to come.

ONE

Arbor Springs Station
8 January 1946

Never before had Libby experienced so many emotions at one time. Should she be happy that her long lost love was finally coming home to her? Should she be angry at him for leaving and breaking his promise to love and cherish her? Or would her nerves get the best of her and she would collapse under the pressure and scrutiny of all those who now surrounded her on the train platform?

From beneath the veil of her hat, she glanced toward her mother-in-law, hoping she hadn't worn the weight of her inner thoughts for all to see.

The skin of her hands burned from the constant wringing of her fingers against her palms. For the first time in nearly four years she would finally see the man she married. The man she'd waited for since her new life began.

She fixed the small pillbox hat that adorned her head, adjusting it just so the red veil didn't obstruct her view of the rail line. She wanted to look her best for the moment when Phillip's eyes would meet hers. What woman wouldn't want to impress her beau after his long journey around the world?

She glanced at her watch.

1:57 p.m.

The afternoon 2:10 would be chugging down the tracks in just a little over ten minutes, placing her beloved Phillip in her arms—this time for good.

As her eyes scanned the tracks, anxious and excited patrons continued to hinder her view of the rail line. Women sat nervously on benches situated on the platform against the paneled walls. Older gentlemen—she presumed awaiting fathers of soldiers—with pipes wedged between their lips and smoke curling around their graying heads, paced alongside the tracks as if destined to wear a foot trail along the aged wood beneath their feet.

Watching them stride back and forth only intensified her nervous energy. She felt like a young school girl once again, waiting impatiently for her sweetheart to arrive for her.

With nothing else to do but wait, her mind stayed with Phillip. What would he look like now? Would she even recognize him when he stepped off the train? Four years apart was a long time, and much could change a person in the stretch since Phillip's departure. She'd already seen what the aftermath of war could do to a man just returning home from the battlefront.

Mrs. Johnson patted Libby's knee, as if saying she understood Libby's anxiety. Perhaps she *had* exhibited all her conflicting thoughts on the outside, but no words were spoken between them. Libby cast an anxious glance at the older woman and attempted a smile. The gleam in Mrs. Johnson's eyes made Libby's stomach turn ill.

Could she do this?

Her last moments with Phillip had been strained. Beyond her tears, anger had built a wall around her heart. And Phillip knew it. So letters were far and few.

It was easier not knowing what type of danger her husband was in than it was to love him unconditionally and lose him on the battlefield. Now that the war was over, she just wanted Phillip home.

Her heart pounded beneath her cotton dress, and her palms became increasingly moist. It was like revisiting her wedding day all over again. Only this time is wasn't Phillip who was waiting for her, she was the one waiting anxiously for her groom to roll down an isle of steel and wood.

She subtly pressed a fist into her stomach. Unable to sit any longer, Libby stood. "I'll be right back," she told her mother-in-law as she started down the platform. The faint smell of carnation petals lifted to her nose from the pink corsage she wore on the lapel of her ladies suit, reminding her of the carnations she held in her hand the day of her marriage ceremony.

"Hey, kiddo, you hanging in there all right?" Maggie's bold, yet caring, voice sang behind her.

"Yes, of course. Just have the jitters, I guess. You know…the first time seeing him and all."

"Trust me, Libby, you have nothing to worry about. As soon as my brother steps off that train and gets a load of you, all fears and jitters will be put to rest."

"I hope you're right. Right now, I'm feeling quite ill."

"You did take my advice and eat breakfast and lunch today?"

"Yes, of course."

"Good thing. Don't need you fainting on us here at the depot now, do we?"

Maggie winked an eye in her teasing way, but on the inside, the banter didn't calm Libby's nerves in the slightest. If anything, it only fueled her anxiety.

She needed to break away. To do this on her own. Part of her wanted Phillip all to herself and not share any moment of the day with his parents and sister, but that would be selfish and rude. Yet part of her claimed that she deserved those first few precious moments with the man she loved, especially after their new life together ended so brusquely, cheating her out of a normal life as a young, married woman. Why, one would think after nearly four years of marriage she'd at least have one child to show for it.

For nearly four solid years she'd fought back those demons, battling back and forth inside her own mind whether she should hate Phillip for leaving her alone or forgive him because he made it through the war alive. Truth was, the matter still wasn't settled—even as she stood at the station knowing Phillip was within mere miles of her arms. She hoped and prayed that as soon as she caught a glimpse of his handsome face all past regrets and annoyances would just fall away and fade into the background. Yes, that's all it would take. Just one look at his tender eyes and easy smile.

The faint shriek of a train whistle jerked her eyes down the tracks. It must've had that effect on everyone because every head on the platform lifted and strained to stare at the railroad tracks. The northbound 2:10 was right around the corner!

Feeling a light hold on her arm, Libby glanced down to see Phillip's mother and Maggie, standing at her side. Their misty-eyed smiles gave away what she already felt...

Anticipation. Joy. Relief.

"Look, Libby." Mrs. Johnson pointed down the tracks. "Your husband is coming home."

Libby's heart pounded harder, faster. The train's wheels screeched to a stop and people flooded the platform as they rushed to catch a glimpse of their own loved ones. Passengers emerged from the coaches. Libby's breath quickened as her eyes darted through the crowd of people. Through eager eyes, she searched the train cars and passengers' faces for a glimpse of Phillip.

This was it.

For the first time in four years she'd finally hold him in her arms. To touch his face, look into his brown eyes, and hear his masculine voice.

Her steps carried her down each train car as she watched and waited. Her hands clasped together and she craned her neck to look above the crowd.

There was still no sign of him.

A smidge of disappointment entered her chest. Maybe he was delayed and wouldn't be on this train after all. Her heart began to ache, and tears sprang to her eyes. He had to be here. She looked frantically. There were still three more cars left on this line.

She hoped. She prayed.

Then...

Her chest lifted and she held her breath as she spotted a dark-haired Marine step off the very last coach. Libby's wavering hand came to her lips and tears pooled in her eyes. Through a watery canvas, the dark-haired fellow looked like...stood like...

"Phillip!" His name exploded from her mouth like a canon ball. She knew her voice reached his ears because his head turned sharply in her direction. It was his face. That handsome, dreamy face! Weaving through the crowd of passengers, she hurried to meet him, her eyes never leaving his. From the urgent expression on his face, he was just as overjoyed to see her. Oh, he was a beautiful sight. He was here. He was home. And he was reaching for her.

"Phillip, oh Phillip, you're home, you're home." Strong arms enclosed around her and lifted her body from the ground, clinging tightly to her.

It all seemed like a dream. Her breath left her body, and she fell limp into his embrace.

"Libby. Are you real, darling? Oh, I missed you so much." His hands smoothed back her hair and cradled her head against his chest.

"It's me, dear. I can't believe you're home. I couldn't live another day without you." Her arms squeezed his middle a little tighter and a silent tear slipped from her eye.

"I know, darling. It's okay. You don't have to anymore." He pulled back slightly and tipped her chin upward as his face lowered to hers. He placed gentle kisses on her cheeks, her forehead, her nose, and finally her lips.

Her skin pricked with shivers and a warm sensation boiled from deep within. She couldn't break away from his kiss. She didn't care if they stood in public with everyone watching them. She was finally holding the man who was the center of her life. The man she loved with every morsel and fiber within her.

Her hands touched his scruffy face, not caring if he hadn't shaved in a week. Her fingers glided through his short, oily, dark hair. It felt like silk compared to the years of stroking his photograph. Finally, he was hers to have and hold.

Inhaling the spice of his cologne, she nuzzled her head into his chest, all the while thanking God from within. As light, salty tears seeped from her eyelashes, she knew...

Today, so much would end. Today, so much would begin.

TWO

Soft, wintry moonlight slanted through the bedroom curtains. Snuggled in the warmth of clean blankets and a beautiful woman, Phillip glanced down at his sleeping bride. How could he feel annoyed with the inability to sleep if it meant he got to watch his wife's peaceful form lying next to him? It was a privilege he'd been cheated out of for four long years.

The moment was surreal to him. For well over one thousand nights, he'd been away from Libby. Slept in a bed separated by a country and a whole ocean from her. And now, after so many nights of longing, of waiting, of fighting, he was back where he belonged.

A mix of emotions he hadn't allowed himself to experience flooded into his mind. His throat tightened and he swallowed hard. A shaky breath left his lungs. Libby stirred and snuggled deeper into his chest, a light sigh escaping her. A sense of devotion and protectiveness overcame him. He cradled her against him, holding her close, and placed a gentle kiss against Libby's forehead.

Her hand slid up his chest and caught his dog tags, which he hadn't removed from his neck. Closing his eyes, he rested his hand on hers, cupping not just her delicate hand but his tags as well.

But like countless nights before, sleep was nowhere to be found, and remnants of his time at war invaded places of his mind he wished were forgotten.

Like those nights he survived, hidden beneath the canvas of jungle darkness, he scolded himself for leaving Libby and rushing off to war. What sort of man left his new bride within months of their marriage? Then again, he remembered so many of his compatriots who'd married just days before being deployed into battle.

Nights in the jungle grew morbidly dark and lonesome. Sometimes the stench of decaying bodies drifted under his nose, reminding him of the danger he faced both day and night. If it wasn't enough to worry about the enemy, it was the environment. Harmful mosquitoes and lethal snakes lurked in the shadows of his encampment.

He'd been far from the safety of home. Far from Libby. At times, he could almost feel her warm skin beneath his fingertips. If he imagined hard enough, he could faintly hear the soft ring of her beautiful, soprano voice calling his name. Of course, it was only his imagination—and possibly starvation—that caused those mirages and noises to flit through his mind. But one thing was for sure, he'd never forget the look on Libby's face when he came home that day to tell her he'd joined the Marines. The memory often visited him in the form of ghastly dreams while at war. His conscience cried out in the dark of night, placing layers of guilt over his aching heart. Guilt over the hurt he'd caused Libby by making such a hasty decision. That's when her image came to visit him in the shadows.

Her look of utter devastation reminded him how he felt when he'd learned his best friend, Jack Gregory, had perished in the attack on Pearl Harbor. Was that how Libby had viewed his enlistment? Had Phillip signed his own death certificate in her mind? Sure, he'd encountered a close call, but he made a full recovery and outsmarted the enemy.

Without warning, Phillip's mind travelled on. Across the plains. Across the ocean. The miles behind him now caught up with him. He may have left Saipan and the Pacific Theatre without a second glance, but his mind refused to allow him closure. Grizzly images abruptly flashed in front of him. They came in spells, like droves of bombers dropping their bombs, one after the other.

Saipan had left its brand on the forehead of Phillip Johnson. Although he was safe in the company of family and tucked securely beside Libby, it didn't erase the horrible images that were scorched into his mind's eye. With every blink of his eye, one dismantled body after another flashed through his mind.

Nights had become increasingly difficult to find slumber. Phillip hoped that once he made it home, his world would right itself.

Before his mind could torture him further, the squeeze of Libby's hand brought him back to the present. He glanced down and was met by her diamond gaze. Silvery moonlight cast specks of sparkles into her eyes. Welcoming the beautiful image to his mind, he smiled and smoothed back her chocolate locks. She returned his attention by snuggling close to his shoulder and hugging his middle.

"I missed you so much," she softly whispered. It was just enough for him to hear—the sweet sound of affection and devotion in her voice.

Arching his neck, Phillip tipped her chin up and leaned in to place a kiss on her tender lips.

"You won't have to miss me again. I'm never leaving you. Ever."

As soon as he said the words, a sting pricked at his heart.

Libby's love-laden eyes fluttered closed as she drifted back to sleep.

There he was once again. A feeling of hollowness burrowing its way into his heart, this time corrupting his quiet moment with his wife. His thoughts painfully reverted back to Saipan. Back to the cliffs. Back to...*her*.

❦❧

A sharp and thunderous detonation aroused Phillip from his slumber, causing him to awake with a jolt and search frantically for the enemy. His breath came quick and his heart thrust into his chest with incredible force. His ears ticked with each heartbeat as it had whenever the enemy was within hearing distance.

He blinked, then glanced around him.

Working to catch his breath, he wiped perspiration from his neck and face, his fingers catching the chain still hanging down his chest.

His hand clasped his dog tags and tightened. When would the nightmares cease? When would those ghastly images fade just as those sweet images of Libby and his mother had? Why was it so difficult to picture his family, but the terrors of war were so easily vivid?

His nerves had reached their height of anxiety. It wasn't the first time he'd experienced nights like this. In fact, they were coming more frequent. He'd hoped that once he came home to Arbor Springs the joy of being reunited with his wife and family would take over and push out all other horrid memories from his war-torn mind.

Finally, his surroundings became clear. When his eyes adjusted to dawn's early light, he remembered where he was. Cheery walls surrounded him. Soft curtains hung in the windows. Buffets adorned with photos, crocheted doilies, and Libby's lipstick greeted him. His robe hung from the hook on the back of the closet door. The scene was a picture of tranquility. Phillip relaxed into his soft mattress and pillows and willed his spirit to still.

Both his hands rubbed over his face, trying to force out those bad dreams. His eyes reopened. Phillip pulled the quilt back from his legs and feet and swung them over the side of the bed. He smiled when his foot bumped against something soft on the floor. Libby had placed his bedroom slippers at his bedside. She was always thinking of him. After slipping them on, he ambled to the window and pulled back the curtains.

How long had it been since he'd seen the existence of modern civilization? Months? Years? Phillip leaned closer to the window and peered out the glass that separated him from the outside world.

Home.

It all seemed so strange to him. He'd grown accustomed to dense jungles, thick and lush bamboo trees, marsh lands, and extreme heat.

Looking out the window to the gentle roll of Arbor Springs, it didn't seem right. There should be trees, and bushes so thick he shouldn't be able to see for as far as he could. There should be Japanese snipers camouflaged and hiding behind every rock, every home, every single tree that stood. Even now, his eyes squinted against the morning's rays and peered into bare trees. He'd grown accustomed to searching the tree tops for danger. But here, the trees were so different. There were no palms to block the sun and enemy snipers. He could see right through the skeletons of dormant oaks and maples. There was no threat here.

He wiped a calloused hand over his weary eyes to swab away the memories flooding into his mind all over again. He'd worked so hard the last few days to convince himself that the war was over. He was going home. No more dense cover of tank fire. No more screaming Japanese soldiers ramming their bayonets in his direction. No more death. No more caves of terrified and dying civilians. No more wide-eyed children staring up into his dirt-stained face. No more...

Enough! His fist landed against the window trim with enough force that it shook the window pane. The sudden reflex surprised even him. Where had it come from?

Phillip's eyes squeezed closed. He needed to stop that. He needed to stop revisiting the place of torment and put the war behind him.

Coffee.

He needed something to neutralize his overactive brain. If he'd had anything stronger in the house to grab, he would have given in to it— just as he had many times before in the jungle.

But he was home now. Libby wouldn't have any of that, he was sure. For now he'd have to settle for black coffee and hope it would do the job of calming his nerves.

However, before he did anything, there was one thing he needed to take care of.

Phillip's War

Phillip scurried back to his army green duffel bag he had yet to unpack. No matter how hard he tried to forget the war and what he'd left behind, there was still one reminder that would forever tie him to that wretched island. And to be a man of his word, that one reminder would be the gateway to his undoing.

THREE

One name and one address filled the distance between Phillip's thumbs. He blankly stared down into that crumbled piece of scrap paper. A great weight pressed onto the walls of his heart.

Painful tears sprung to the corners of his eyes, blurring the quiet landscape before him. His throat burned and he swallowed back the lump that constricted it. He'd left so much behind as he made his long journey home. So many friends. Friends as close as brothers died before his eyes. Deaths so horrible that he couldn't comprehend them. But he'd witnessed so much more. Scared civilians begging for their lives on the Marianas as if they thought the American troops were there to torture them as the Japanese had.

Phillip made his way into the bathroom and leaned against the sink basin. His head hung below his shoulders, exhaustion and apprehension weighing heavily on them.

Too many images resurfaced their ugly heads in the dark of night. Images such as a young, starving mother in hiding with her sickly baby girl.

Phillip splashed cold water onto his face, shocking away those horrid recollections.

Why couldn't he shake those memories? Why did they insist on plaguing him with every blink of his eye?

There were still so many unanswered questions left open in his mind. Why did good men like Jack Gregory have to die? Where were his buddies now? Were they all home to their wives and families? Were they sitting at their breakfast table reading the newspaper or staring intently at their beautiful brides? Did they, too, have vivid recollections of the war in the same way that continued to plague Phillip's mind? And what about—about all those victims on the Marianas? What had happened to those he'd come to create friendships with? Those he…cared about.

He stared into the mirror fastened above the sink. The redness in his eyes was all but gone, and his hollow, dark sockets were fading and filling out. The months of foreign dirt that had caked onto his skin, neck, and face was gone, leaving the man in the mirror looking like a familiar old friend. One who hadn't been visited in almost four years.

So why didn't he feel delight to revisit the man he once was? Why did his chest suddenly feel heavy with regrets?

He turned the faucet on and listened to the trickle of running water for several seconds. It was so different from the sound of streams he'd crossed countless times in the bush. So different than the water he used to clean himself up with while on the front lines. He cupped his hands under the cool, clean water and splashed it onto his face. He repeated the action until he felt good and awake. Then he brushed his teeth shaved the stubble from his jawline and neck, and patted them down with a towel. He grabbed a clean and freshly pressed shirt from the wire hanger on the back of the bathroom door and dressed himself.

Those few minutes of cleaning himself up helped relieve the tension in his muscles and the burden from his weary mind.

Shuffling from downstairs captured his attention. Quietly he made his way down the upstairs hall and toward the staircase. The sounds of an iron skillet clanging against the stove echoed to his ears followed by the crack of an eggshell.

Libby.

A smile spread over his lips and his footsteps became more confident as he started down the staircase. He rolled up his shirt sleeves and sniffed. Bacon tinted the air around him, enticing him to the kitchen—as if the knowledge that Libby was home wasn't enough already.

The smell of eggs and bacon grew stronger as he neared the kitchen. Food he hadn't eaten in years made his stomach grumble and mouth water. His taste buds couldn't wait to get a lick of freshly cut meats and dairy, prepared by the hands of his loving Libby.

As he entered the kitchen, the small, round table for two was already set. Blue and white print china plates sat at each chair with a butter knife and fork in their appropriate places. Two mugs, waiting to be filled with steaming hot coffee, also rested on the old, oak table. He could smell it now, the flavor of freshly brewed coffee coming off the stove.

Libby's back was turned to him as she stirred the eggs and turned over the bacon. His feet came to an easy stop as he leaned against the doorway's wood trim and watched Libby in her white apron hurry about the kitchen. He could see by the way her hands gripped the pan handles and stirred the spatulas that she was eager to surprise him with a farmhouse breakfast. His lip curled upward. She looked so cute in her blue cotton house dress and large bow tied around her waist to keep her apron in place. She'd even taken time to fix her hair so each strand was not out of place. The toast popped from the toaster and she rushed to put it onto another china plate. He stifled a laugh when he saw her bare feet come out from around the other side of the table.

The beautiful scene of a wife cooking for her husband tenderly stirred his soul. He wanted to awaken to this every morning. How he'd missed so many years.

For a moment, he regretted his wistful actions of running off to win a war so hastily. Especially when it seemed his life was about to take off in a most pleasant way. But he couldn't do anything to change the past.

Libby turned at that moment and startled when she caught a glimpse of him watching her.

"Phillip! Good morning." After setting the plate of toast onto the table, she rushed into his arms and held him tightly. Then her face tilted upward to catch his morning kiss, which he gave freely. "It was all I could do to not wake you. I missed you, even while you slept safely in our bed."

Phillip's arms squeezed her tightly, not wanting to let her go. Let his breakfast get cold and spoil. This was where he belonged.

"How did you sleep?" she asked.

He hugged her tighter. "Much better with you by my side."

It wasn't completely true. He hadn't slept well at all, but the truth of his statement was her presence lying next to him made the night bearable.

Her chin pressed into his neck as he held her. Her lips were so close to his ear he could hear her slight breaths.

"Do you want to know how my night was?"

"Tell me." He pulled back just enough to lean his forehead against hers and look into her eyes.

"It was the happiest night of my life. It was warm and peaceful. I don't ever recall a better night's rest. I spent too many dreadful nights away from you. Just to feel you next to me and know you're alive and well—it's the best feeling in the world."

Phillip had no words. He'd known the loneliness of the last four years. He knew the ache in his chest from being away from the person he loved most. But he hadn't taken into consideration that Libby had endured the same misfortune. Guilt settled into that place where loneliness once occupied. But as he had learned to do with every other hurt he'd felt over the last few years, he shoved that sense of guilt deep, deep down into a place where he'd never find it.

In a matter of moments, Phillip had recovered from the threat of falling into a place he didn't want to be—*feeling*.

Just like in war, if he allowed himself to feel, he would be letting his defenses down. He would be unguarded. He would be exposed. And exposing himself to the unnecessary elements of his deepest sentiments would ultimately control and crumble his soul.

The thought of it caused his pulse to race and muscles to tense. He drew in a shaky breath and released Libby.

"I'm going out to find work today." He knew it was an abrupt change in subject, but it was the closest thing he could reach out to in order to restrain his emotions.

"Find work?"

Although her voice rose a few notes, he sensed her disappointment.

"I'll keep working my job at the factory until you're fit enough to go ba—"

He held his finger to her lips to hush her. "Shh. I won't have my girl working herself to the bone. You've done more than your share already. It's time for me to be the man and take care of you and our needs. That's just how it has to be, Libby."

Her eyes cast downward, but her hands still clung tightly to the back of his shirt.

"Libby, I know it all seems rushed, but I plan to go out today to find work. I'll most likely be gone all day. And if I don't find anything today, then I'll do the same tomorrow, and the day after that. Until someone hires me."

"Must you go so soon?"

"I must."

Her beautiful brown eyes glanced up at him and his chest fell heavy. How he loved her so.

"All right. If you insist. I know it sounds selfish, but I just want you all to myself. But I know if we are to get on with our life together, it must be done. On the other hand, we can't support a family without a good job. And I so desperately want to start a family."

Family.

Everything in Phillip's present world came to an abrupt halt.

His hands fell at his sides, and his jaw hinged open as if Libby had just betrayed him.

"Phillip?" Her eyes now searched his with concern.

How could he tell her? He couldn't. There was no way on this green earth she would understand.

He tried to swallow, but his mouth had dried and his tongue stuck like paste to the roof of his mouth. He attempted to speak, but he only stuttered instead.

"N—now—now, Li—Libby. Don't you think a f—family is a little premature? I mean…" Nervously, his hands rubbed over his brow and to the back of his neck.

"Phillip, what's got you all in a tizzy all of a sudden?"

"More than you know," he mumbled under his breath. "It's just—" He turned and gently gripped her shoulders. "Well, look at us, Libby. I've barely been home twenty-four hours and I have no job lined up of any sorts. Raising a family takes money. Hard-earned money. As it is now, I can't pay for nill. Don't you think all this family talk is a little premature?"

Libby's eyes had softened and a quaint smile spread on her lips. "Phillip, all will be fine. God will provide. He always has. I believe that. Don't you?"

"Sure. Of course I do. But we can't be hasty and foolish." He winced after he'd said those words, hoping he hadn't come across as too brash. But Libby only shrugged.

"I've waited this long. What's a little longer?" She pushed past him. "Oh! Breakfast! It's probably burnt. Are you hungry for burnt bacon and eggs?"

"Starving."

FOUR

With a gleam in her eye, Libby stood sideways, glancing into the mirror that adorned her bureau. Her fingers gently pressed against the flat lining of her stomach. Her eyes stared down at the imaginary bump she longed to see protruding from her thin body.

Now that Phillip was home and on the hunt for a suitable job, her dream of becoming a mother was now closer than ever. She could finally hang up her coveralls and boots and exchange them for bottles and booties.

She giggled at her musings as she imagined cradling a tiny baby—*her* tiny baby—in her arms. She could hear her voice now, singing a lullaby to her precious child as she rocked him or her to sleep.

Just the thought of the new possibilities awaiting her created a deeper yearning for her very own family. A family she could grow and share with her husband.

So many other women in town were starting their own families now that their husbands had returned home. She only wondered just how much longer it would be before she gained knowledge of her own little person growing inside her.

The shear anticipation racing through her mind stole her breath. She needed something to keep her busy and take her thoughts off her obsessive hopes and dreams. Maybe she could bury herself in her housework, clean Phillip's laundry, make him a savory meal.

With a bounce in her step, Libby scurried toward the closet door where Phillip had dropped his army green duffel. Her fingers wrapped around the heavy cotton material and she lifted it to her chest. Staring at his bag, she envisioned where this duffel had traveled. Like Phillip, it'd been half-way around the world. It'd seen exotic places. Perhaps changed hands with exotic people.

Lowering her nose to the rough fabric, Libby inhaled. Perhaps, she could catch hint of what a tropical island smelled like. Its musky scent nearly choked her. A strange aroma was stained to the fibers of the cloth. It certainly didn't smell like tropical flowers or anything close to gardenia. Instead, it smelled of dirt, sulfur, sweat, and...blood?

Goose bumps scurried down her arms and a shiver tickled down her spine. This particular item was in dire need of a good washing. But as she gathered Phillip's things together, the odor of his duffel lingered below her nose. Its peculiar stench troubled her, and for the first time, she wondered if she'd just been introduced to a smidge of Phillip's life *over there*. If so, it was far from the tropical paradise she'd imagined in her dreams.

∽◛⌇∾

For the rest of the morning, Libby busied herself with her house work. She'd taken the day off from the cannery to help ease Phillip back into life, into their marriage. It was the role she'd wanted since the day they wed.

Once buried in her tasks, she soon forgot about Phillip's duffel and sweet thoughts of her future family invaded the chambers of her mind.

Her housework had not distracted her from those thrilling musings. Instead, it had only fueled her desire to plunge into the only role she so desperately coveted.

Her gentle steps carried her up the staircase to the second floor. Her arms were heavy laden with Phillip's laundry, but as she passed by the guest room, her feet came to a halt and her eyes shifted to their corners, catching a glimpse of a cozy room. She carefully set down the pile of laundry and stood in the doorway.

With a soft touch, her hand rested against the door jam and she gazed into the floral room. She could see it now—a baby's cradle in the far right corner. A small dresser, adorned with photos, and a lamp, across the way. Baby blue curtains with flowing ruffles hanging from the back window. And a wooden rocking chair set perfectly in the corner, just inviting her to sit with her baby in her arms.

Libby found herself involuntarily running her fingers along the wooden dresser. The picture coming into view was quite different from the picture she saw in her mind. As her eyes focused on the room as it stood now, it was a painful reminder of what wasn't. This room *wasn't* a nursery. And she *didn't* have a forthcoming baby to hold fast to.

Phillip hadn't so much as left her a child as a parting gift when he shipped out for the West Coast. Libby hadn't felt such a void since before Phillip returned home. That void had festered, now re-opening that lonesome hole in her heart.

A sigh escaped her chest and the slightest of tears formed in her eyes.

"One day...Lord willing."

It was the prayer she muttered to herself throughout these last four years. The prayer that held promise to get her through the war.

The scene was impeccable in her mind. Not at all marred by difficulty or misgiving. She imagined a more abundant and fulfilling life for herself and Phillip as they ventured into parenthood. Only good times could await her. Until then, she would pray and continue to hope that God would grant her request.

"Hello? Anyone home?"

Maggie's voice rising from downstairs interrupted those contesting thoughts, and at the right time, too.

Libby swiped tears from her eyes and squared her shoulders as she called from the guest room. "I'm here, Maggie. I'll be right down."

◦⋦⋧◦

"Sorry, for keeping you, Maggie. Let me just take this laundry to the kitchen."

"Take your time. I just came to say hello on my day off."

From the kitchen, Libby called back, "Oh, a day off, you say? How lovely."

"Yes. There are still plenty of fellas flooding the hospital. Many of them are being sent to a convalescent home. But it's my job to be there until they're moved. It's my first day off in six days."

That Maggie, always the one to think of others. Libby chided herself once again for pushing her sister-in-law away so many years ago. If she had only trusted others then as she did now, she wouldn't feel such guilt in her heart. She'd blamed her father for that. If he'd only been the kind of father to love her...to love mother...

She stopped herself from thinking back to that mess of her life and brought the conversation back to Maggie. "You'd think with the war ended and all we'd stop hearing of those cases rolling through the hospital doors."

"You'd think, dear sister, but not all wounds are skin deep and not all who survived the war can come home."

Libby's brows furrowed in consideration of Maggie's statement. Emerging from the kitchen, she asked, "What do you mean by that, Maggie?"

"I'm sure you've heard the rumors traveling around town."

Libby's curiosity sparked and she lowered herself onto the couch cushions. "No. I'm not sure what you're speaking of."

Maggie straightened and peered at Libby in disbelief. "Why, I'm talking about all those fellas affected by shell shock."

"Shell shock." Libby repeated it under her breath. It wasn't something people spoke of every day. In fact, it was more of a subject snubbed by most townsfolk.

"Yes. Extremely debilitating, if not more so than a bullet to the chest."

Libby clasped her hands together and breathed a sigh of commiseration. "So what happens to them?"

"Not much, I'm afraid. In fact, in most cases, those poor fellas become non-existent. There are some that just can't be reasoned with. Others have lost their minds completely. Looking at them today, it's hard to believe they were once strong, unmovable soldiers. The breakdown of the mind is a very complex thing. Nothing like I've ever seen, that's for sure."

"I'm glad it hasn't affected Phillip. How awful it is for those poor men and their families."

Maggie tossed her dark curls over her shoulder and crossed one knee over the other. "Speaking of my brother, where is he on this chilly January day?"

"You just missed him, I'm afraid. He's off in search of work."

"Yup. That sounds just like my brother, all right. Always the go-getter, looking for the next thing in life. That doesn't surprise me one bit."

Libby smiled. "Yes, that's the Phillip we all know, isn't it? He wants me to quit my job at the cannery. So he headed out right early this morning to get a head start on the job hunt."

"Well then, I'll leave the message with you. Mother is wanting to make over Phillip like no one's business. She's throwing a welcoming home party in his honor. My job is to see that he and you get there on time."

Libby straightened and a smile leaked from her mouth. "She is? Well, that's wonderful. I'll see to it that we make it on time."

"Mother says to be at her house promptly at seven o'clock on Saturday night. No need to bring anything. Says she'll take care of all the food and fixin's. And she's planning on having everyone we've ever encountered at this shindig. Well, everyone within reason, that is." Maggie winked.

"Sounds more like Danny's mother is planning this social."

Laughter bellowed from Maggie's chest and Libby soon chimed in.

"I can't say Mother hasn't learned a few things from Mama Russo since Danny and I married."

Once the laughter subsided, Libby's eyes turned to her sister-in-law. "How does it feel, Maggie?"

Maggie regarded her with a quizzical expression.

"You've been across the ocean and back, surviving attacks, explosions, gunfire, and disease, and married the one fella that almost didn't come back. What's that like?"

For the first time since Libby had known Maggie, she witnessed something cross her eyes she'd never seen before. Maggie's eyes stiffened slightly. Sadness and relief revealed a side of her that usually remained concealed.

Libby was almost sorry she asked and was about to say as much, but then Maggie surprised her by answering without hesitation.

"In all honesty, Libby, I feel as if it all never happened. In some ways it seems like it was a dream. That one day I just woke up and I was snuggled safely in my own bed. It doesn't mean those memories and images are erased from my mind. It just feels as though all the bad times were nightmares I lived through, then I simply woke up. As for nearly losing Danny three times, well, I prefer to not think about that. But I thank the good Lord every day that I didn't lose him to war or my own stubbornness." Maggie paused and took in a shaky breath. "But as for marriage, Libby, I couldn't be happier. It's everything and so much more than I could have hoped for."

Libby sighed with longing in her heart. Looking back on the events of the war and the last few years—and now that the danger had passed—it sounded all too romantic to her ears. Maggie and Grace both had lived out a storybook ending to the darkest chapters of their lives. They'd overcome steep obstacles and found true love in the center of destruction.

In a way, Libby envied them. Both women had braved very different elements and beaten the odds dealt to them. Libby hadn't so much as braved anything besides the move to Arbor Springs without Phillip. Her in-laws had handed her the money to purchase the home in which she now lived. Her father-in-law also saw to it that she found a suitable job in the cannery to help make ends meet. Even Grace, Luke, Maggie, and Danny pitched in to help her renovate the broken down house and make it into a warm and inviting home for her and Phillip. Without the help of everyone around her, she wasn't so sure she would've made it on her own.

She was weak. One in need of a shepherd, guiding her along life's pathway. She wasn't at all strong and capable like Maggie, who ventured into Germany's hostile territory all alone. Or resilient like Grace, who found strength to bounce back after a devastating loss.

She was simply, Libby. Elizabeth. The poor girl from York County who needed a safe harbor and an escape.

FIVE

Chilling winds nipped at Phillip's nose and stung his cheeks. It'd been so long since he'd experienced winter that he nearly forgot how dreadful those northeasterly winds could blow. Ever since stepping foot outside his new abode, Phillip's bones had absorbed every drop in the temperature. One would think the cold, January air had everything to do with the chill that penetrated his skin, but it was not so. The air biting at him was only a small portion of the cold that had settled over his heart.

For twenty minutes he walked the mile down the street toward the post office. Each breath of air he took cooled his heart even more.

His fingers were tucked securely inside his coat pockets. His one hand rested comfortably in its warmth, but the other—the other hand perspired and twisted its fingers around that dreadful, yet critical, letter he'd stuffed into his coat just before leaving the house.

He had to place it inside his pocket unnoticed. It was one of many promises he to keep. Above all, this one was the most important.

Phillip's stomach churned and growled as if angry with him for concealing his secret from Libby. He had no choice. There was no possible way she would understand. He'd put her through too much already. She didn't need to have this piece of information hanging around her neck either.

As his hand gripped the letter, his teeth clenched together. Why did he, of all the people there on that forsaken island, have to stumble upon *this*? Why had he been the one to discover that dark cave? Why had he ventured into it? Why did he have to care so much?

Too many questions. Questions like, why did the all-powerful God choose to take his best friend, Jack, away from him and away from the girl Jack was to marry? Why did war have to tear apart so many families and relationships? Why did so many good people die? And why—why did God allow him to survive when men standing not eighteen inches from him fell dead to the ground?

Phillip's breath came quicker. Hot air now exited his flared nostrils and his heart beat with panic. This was what happened when he allowed himself to feel. If he would just learn to heed the advice his commanding officers gave him. *Look straight ahead, and feel nothing.*

It hadn't been enough. All those days and nights he told himself to stop thinking, to stop feeling...it wasn't enough.

The small town of Arbor Springs came into view. As he rounded the corner, he glanced at the name in the shop's window to his left.

Oscar's

He didn't have to strain his eyes to see what the place was about. As the door opened and a burlesque man staggered out the entryway, Phillip didn't have to second guess his presumption. Instead of turning his head and holding his nose like any God-fearing citizen would do, his eyes deliberated. That small voice from deep within was urging him to go in. It was a voice he'd suppressed until now. Libby wouldn't approve. Mother and Pop certainly wouldn't hear of it. But some bad habits couldn't be stifled for the duration. Not when those bad habits had become the saving grace he needed to get through one more day in the bush. Before long, that one sip to ease tensions and forget all atrocities had turned from need to want, triggered by all those random flashbacks that kept recurring in his mind.

As Phillip stood outside in the bitter cold contemplating his inward struggle, he remembered the letter inside his coat pocket and wrapped his fingers around it tightly.

This first, Sergeant. This is more important.

With that resolve, he put his feet back in motion toward the post office, but mentally, he made note of *Oscar's* at Main and Liberty Streets.

❧❧

As he expected, the post office was busy with patrons sending their packages and letters. Not everyone was home from the war, so it only seemed right that cookies and love letters still littered the post office counters.

Phillip found a partially clear counter and pulled the letter from his pocket. He glanced around his surroundings once, then began addressing his envelope:

Miss Adaline Howard
2300 Parkton

His heart pounded as he wrote out the address. He hoped the contents of the letter would reach Miss Howard in time. For the time being, Phillip's hands were tied. He'd made a promise. And while his promise had got him as far as San Francisco, guilt still plagued his heart. He could do more, but then again, it seemed impossible.

Maybe he was a fool for making such a hasty decision. What else could he do in that dire situation? It was a matter of life and death. He'd witnessed too much death. To allow it to happen when he had the power to stop it would have sent him into shell shock for sure. It was the only way to keep the war ghosts at bay. He *had* to do this.

He only hoped Libby would one day understand.

❧ ❧

His body was unaccustomed to the biting cold of the northern winds. Over three years in the tropics seemed to have taken away his tolerance of the northeastern winters.

Onward, Phillip trudged through downtown Arbor Springs, passing the brewery's smoke stack, crossing the railroad tracks, and finally finding himself standing in the doorway of a warm diner. Removing his fedora and loosening his overcoat, he made his way to the café bar and took a seat on the barstool.

"Right nippy out there, hey fella?" the waitress called. "What'll it be on a cold day like this?"

"Just a good cup of hot coffee. Black," Phillip sniffed.

He stole a glance at the gentleman alongside him who sipped on his own cup of coffee. A bowl of steaming chicken and dumplings soup sat in front of him.

"Say, that looks right appetizing," Phillip said in the man's direction.

"Beats K-rations, that's for sure."

Phillip crossed his arms and leaned against the counter. "I hear you there, fella." After even a month of K-rations, the worst meal tasted like silky goodness to the tongue. "Pacific or Europe?"

The man beside him, slurped a spoonful of soup then answered, "Europe. Twenty-ninth infantry."

Phillip nodded. "Seems quite a few of the home boys were attached to the Twenty-ninth."

"Mostly. Unless you enlisted with another branch, most who were summoned got a free ticket to England and France. Dreary and cold most of the year. Rain and mud, snow and ice. Days much like today when the wind blew."

"I never thought much of it before now, but I think I'll take the tropic heat and humidity over this." Phillip thumbed over his shoulder to the doorway.

The gentleman sipping his coffee twisted on his stool and leered at Phillip. "Pacific theatre then?"

"Compliments of the United States Marines." A smirk crept onto Phillip's face, proud to have the chance to boast about his patriotic duty to another comrade in service.

"Whereabouts? Man, I hear all sorts of horrific stories about the Pacific ops. They all true?"

"Your coffee, sir." The waitress appeared with his order and set it down in front of him.

"Depends on who you talk to and what they say."

It didn't matter whether Phillip said one way or another. No matter which way the military sent them in the Pacific, any confrontation with a Japanese soldier was an unpleasant one, to put it gently.

But he didn't have to disclose all that. Phillip put out his hand. "Phillip Johnson, and my last mission was on Iwo Jima."

"Pete Glowaski. As I mentioned earlier, boots on the ground in England and France."

They both nodded in acknowledgement. Then Peter went back to his soup and Phillip sipped on his coffee.

"So, did Uncle Sam set you up good upon arrival in the States?"

"I'm not sure I know what you mean." Phillip said quizzically.

"You know, fella, military housing, schooling, a good paying job?"

"Obviously, I've been away too long. But I don't need any handouts. My wife and I will be just fine. In fact, I just put in for two jobs down at the courthouse."

They weren't glamorous jobs, of course—a jailor for one and paperwork filer for the other. But Peter didn't have need of knowing details.

"The courthouse? Man, get a grip on yourself. Get into the trades, work with your hands. Me and the fellas found work at the city limits. Good payin' jobs, too. We all took advantage of the government handouts. Got decent houses, food on the table, and money in our pockets. We deserve no less for what we done went through over there. As a matter of fact, I bet I could take ya down to the boss right now and get ya started working tomorrow morning. Are you in?"

"Gee, I don't know, fella. What type of work are you talkin'?"

"Construction. With the new government subsidies, new housing projects are being erected just outside of town. It's enough work for several years." Pete half chuckled, "With the production of plastics exploding in industry, I daresay we'll see quite a boost in the economy—one like we haven't seen in our lifetime. So, whaddya say, man?"

The man was right. Phillip had read the articles in the newspaper about the industry's leap into plastics, a new invention that seemed promising for the future. Changes were taking place and the war had somehow thrust the country into an industrial boom. Work was needed for the returning soldiers as many women were still holding on to the jobs they'd taken at factories and warehouses. With the return of men to the States, that meant they and their families needed places to stay, confirming Pete's statement that military and government housing were becoming more and more a necessity.

But could Phillip do the work? He'd surely experienced the pains of hard labor while in the bush of the jungle. How much more difficult could housing construction be? At least he wouldn't have to worry about dodging bullets while he worked in the open, exposed and vulnerable to the outside conditions.

And Libby? Why, he could provide for her, allowing her the freedom to quit her job at the cannery and go back to her wifely duties in their own home. Dirty warehouse jobs were no place for a woman anyhow. Besides, he was sure she would rather work in the garden or can vegetables in the comfort of her own home. With the wages he acquired, maybe he could buy Libby a new dancing dress or a clothes washer instead of the old scrub board.

He rolled the possibilities around in his mind before his final resolve.

"All right." He put out his hand. "I'm in. Put 'er there."

The two men shook on the agreement, and within the hour, Pete had taken Phillip down to the agency and cinched a spot with Davenport Construction Company.

The whole way home, Phillip walked with anticipation to tell Libby the good news. She could finally quit her job. Phillip could take control of his household finances once again and be the man he promised he'd be. Wouldn't Libby be giddy with joy when he came home to announce his good fortune.

"You what?" Libby gasped. Her eyes grew wide with amazement. "But you only started your search today."

"I know. Call it a miracle. Some fella down at the diner hooked me up with the agency and next thing I knew, Davenport Construction hired me right there in his office."

"Why, Phillip, that's—that's absolutely wonderful."

Her smile gave away the joy bursting inside her. She reached out to him and wrapped her tender arms around his neck. Shudders of attraction inched down his spine as he stood in her embrace.

"I'm so proud of you." The spark in her eyes...how they shone with such alluring power. But the elation he perceived in them was almost too much to bear. Oh, how he loved this woman. How wonderful it was to relish in her tantalizing embrace and stare fervently into her round, brown eyes.

"You know what this means, don't you, Libby?" He waited for her brows to shift upward. "You don't have to work at that smelly ol' cannery anymore. You can stay here, at home, working in your gardens, sewing up things, washing our clothes with your new clothes washer, and whatever else you womenfolk do during the day."

"Oh, Phillip, it sounds like a dream come true! I hoped and prayed to God that this day would come. I just had no idea that it would come all at once. You've made me the happiest girl in all of Arbor Springs."

SIX

9 January 1946
The Russo Home

No other feeling in the world compared to how Maggie felt right now. As she rested comfortably in the arms of the man she loved, and cuddled close against him on the sofa, she couldn't remember a time in the history of her life that could parallel this moment. Everything was so right. So perfect. So complete.

Those first few weeks of marriage had come easy. The meshing of two souls into one body was so natural that it seemed her life had always been this way. She could hardly remember what singleness was before reciting her vows to Danny.

"Are you comfortable, peaches?" Danny pressed his lips against the silkiness of her hair.

"It beats the trenches by a landslide," she teased, and snuggled deeper in his embrace.

Secretly, in a place only known in her mind, she thought back to the night Danny rescued her from the rubble of the bombed-out hospital. That night, she fell asleep in the warmth of his arms, so familiar, yet so unfamiliar. But even now as she lay gently in those same arms, she felt the familiarity of a man once emaciated and broken.

Her forefinger traced the veins on his arm. Small scars dotted his skin, a morbid souvenir the war had awarded to the both of them. Although the site of Danny's scars still brought shivers to her body, they also reminded her how blessed she was to have him home with her. So many women didn't have the same promise God had bestowed on her.

In the quiet and comfort of this cold, winter night, Maggie whispered from her heart a prayer of thanksgiving to God, her Savior, for allowing her a second chance at life and love. The war had almost stolen away her hopes, dreams, and her very self. It also threatened to take away Danny, her life's true love. How terrible their situation had been just a short year ago. How badly her heart ached when the Army assumed Danny's death. How bittersweet was their reunion...then how wonderful was their homecoming.

Some nights—quiet nights such as this one—her thoughts travelled back across the Atlantic. At times, it was as if she could hear the constant shelling or *rat-a-tat-tat* of gunfire or smell the stench of sulfur hanging in the air. At other times, her dreams would awaken her—dreams that had taken her right back to the OR of the 238th. It was then that her mind forced her to relive the accounts of the war that she wanted to forget...

The wounded.

The dying.

The screams of those, whose wounds would cut deeper than the surface of their skin, leaving a lasting scar that would not soon heal over.

Consequently, in her own futile attempts to save the lives of those whose battle would end prematurely, she also received the same battle scars that many had returned home with. Thankfully, the arousal of those painful memories only plagued her once in a while—usually when her mind was fatigued.

Maggie's eyelids pressed closed and she buried herself into Danny's chest, chasing away the dark shadows that attempted to creep back into her mind. Instinctively, Danny's arms cradled her in a tighter grip and she allowed her being to relax into the gentleness of his core.

Danny's chest rose then fell, before rising again as he sucked in a breath. "You know, I thought nothing could get my heart pumping harder than the rush of jumping from a plane...but I've come to the conclusion that this beats freefalling. And you're the bee's knees of parachutes if I ever had one."

Maggie's head slanted up toward him and her brows furrowed as if contemplating his quirky compliment.

"Is that so? I didn't know I was even competing against such a thing, Daniel Russo."

"Well, it takes something daring to get this Joe's adrenaline going." Danny held his hands palm up as if weighing out two objects. "Let's see, jumping out of a cargo plane at fifteen hundred feet above the ground with German bullets whizzing at my head or loving the most beautiful girl in the world?" He weighed the thought in his hands, teasingly eyeing Maggie all the while with a taunting grin spread across his face.

"Ha-ha. Always the jokester. I certainly hope you come to the correct verdict. It may cost you dearly if you don't," she jested back.

"I don't believe you, Margaret Russo. I doubt there is one rancorous bone in your small body."

Maggie sat up and rested her fists on her hip. "But you forget, Lieutenant, I'm highly trained in the war zone and can put up one feisty fight."

"Maybe you forget. I am also carefully trained in the game of war. I'm especially experienced in hand to hand combat." Danny's arms reached around her trim waist as he pulled himself closer to her and placed a kiss against her warm cheek.

"No fair trying to bribe the enemy." But Maggie didn't mind at all. Instead she allowed herself to be overtaken by Danny's charm—the same charm that had won her heart in the first place. "You know, *Joe*, it's really late. Why don't we continue this battle in the comfort of our bedroom?"

Maggie pulled away, grasping Danny's hands and tugging him up with her. As she led the way out of the living room and down the hall, Danny's hand released and she sensed the absence of her husband. When she glanced back over her shoulder, she caught Danny staring somberly into the glass of one particular picture frame.

Without hesitation, without having to wonder which photograph caught his attention, she knew. It was the only photograph from the war that Danny requested a frame for—the picture of him standing in full gear alongside his closest buddies.

Maggie's hand came to rest on the door jam and she leaned her head against the wood trim. She knew what he was thinking. Many times he had expressed his wonder and concern over the men he left behind. Those who had returned home before him. And those whose whereabouts were still unknown.

One man's name in particular always came to mind—Abe.

The sickly soldier who was abandoned by Danny's German captors, left in a barn on the German countryside while he suffered from a serious case of pneumonia. Maybe even left to die by those Danny hoped would take care of him.

She'd heard the story…many times. She'd seen the sheen in Danny's eyes while he recounted the horrid ordeal. They'd come so far together only to be torn apart, never knowing the fate the other met.

She'd been in Danny's very shoes. She'd known the emptiness that dwelled in her heart as she searched for Danny while he remained an

MIA casualty. The fear of never knowing where he was or what had happened was far too difficult for her to comprehend at times. But yet, she remained hopeful that Major Walter Radford would find Danny for her. At least until that fateful day when Walt delivered the devastating blow that Danny had been declared dead by the United States Army.

Her mind shook the awful memory away, but then she froze as a new one took its place.

Not just a memory, but an evolving idea was forming in her thoughts...

Walter! Yes, Walter!

∽৯ৎৈ∾

10 January 1946

Soft, imaginary kisses left Maggie's hand as she blew them in Danny's direction from the front porch. He was off to work at the gas and electric company. She was always sad to see him off for the day—especially on the days she had off from the hospital—but today was different.

Today, she had plans.

After Danny's car left the driveway and drove out of sight, Maggie hurried back inside the house. She rubbed her hands up and down her arms, warming them from winter's chill.

Without wasting any time, Maggie sat down at the wooden desk she'd moved from the apartment she'd shared with Grace. A sense of familiarity washed over her as she pulled out a sheet of stationery from the top drawer and placed it atop the desk.

From here, this very desk, so many letters had been fashioned. It was the place where she wrote her first correspondence letter to Danny. And it was here that Grace had penned so many letters to Luke.

Maggie glanced across the desk and her eyes rested on her beloved souvenir from Germany—a photograph snapped just before the hospital bombing. Her eyes swept over the faces of four young women. All smiling with their arms slung around one another's shoulders.

Maggie's fingers grasped the frame and gently lifted it for a closer look.

She remembered that day so well, yet somehow, that day—which was roughly eighteen months earlier—seemed like a lifetime ago. She examined each woman's face, noting how much the war had changed them in the time since their enlistment.

They stood tall, wearing naïve, unaware smiles on their lips and ready to charge into battle without knowledge of what true life and death were really all about. Vera, to the far left, wore her usual coy grin with her glamorous blonde hair pinned closely to her head in victory curls. Next to Vera was Maggie, standing proud with her lieutenant's badge pinned securely to her lapel. She recalled the heightened jubilance of the day. The day they would leave the 238th and attach to the 39th Evacuation Hospital. A new start and a new day for each woman pictured.

Her eyes moved to Bonnie, that precious, petite girl who grew in valor and stature, and one who so bravely stared death in the face and refused to succumb to its perilous fate. The frightful *pat-a-tat-tat* of German fighter ammo still rattled in the confines of Maggie's mind. Sometimes the sounds of war would find her and bring to mind the horrors she was forced to face.

Opening her eyes from the memory, her gaze slid to Helen. Dear, sweet Helen.

Tiny prickles stung Maggie's nose as she pressed her fingers over Helen's photographic form. Why, it seemed only a few days had passed since she last sat with the girl for a pork and biscuit breakfast. Or shared a horrible cup of bland coffee with her.

Poor Helen.

A beautiful life that ended all too quickly. A life taken by the enemy. A life that couldn't be recovered.

She brushed at a fallen tear and sniffed. Sometimes reminiscing was good for the soul. Sometimes a shed tear helped alleviate the bottled up pain time had preserved.

Those days may be far behind, but lingering remnants of war still peppered their lives. There were many things that they would soon not forget.

Maggie sucked in a cleansing breath and set the photograph back at its place on the desk.

Some things may still be an open wound unable to heal, but today's particular area was something in need of closure.

Grasping her pen in hand, Maggie began her letter...

Dear Walter,

I do hope married life is treating you and Peggy well. My thoughts are with the two of you most days, mostly wondering how you both are doing and praying the Army hasn't sent you back to Germany.

Danny and I are situated nicely back in Arbor Springs. We are very happy and adjusting to marriage quite nicely. However, I must confess I have an ulterior motive for sending you this letter.

You see, there is a certain soldier Danny talks about from time to time. There are days when I catch him staring at some of the photographs he brought back from Germany, and I know, in his mind, he is wondering what-ever became of the fellow.

I only know part of the story, but from what Danny has told me, the man's name is Abe. Abe Stewart. PoW from the same Stalag Danny was initially imprisoned. Best Danny can remember, Abe was left behind on their march from Poland in a barn on the German countryside. From what Danny could gather, Abe may not have survived, considering he was suffering from a serious case of pneumonia at the time.

I know my effort may turn up nothing at all, and you certainly owe me nothing, but I am going to ask anyway. Would you somehow be able to locate Abe Stewart for me? If anything, just to give Danny some sense of closure to the whereabouts of a close friend.

I wish to thank you in advance and hope this letter finds you and Peggy well. I look forward to your response.

Your friend,
Maggie Russo

SEVEN

12 January 1946

"Libby, what am I supposed to wear to this charade?" Phillip emerged from the bathroom with a hand towel draped over his bare shoulder and specks of shaving cream dotted on his face.

Weariness etched crevices below his eyes, but tonight's homecoming party meant so much to Libby and his mother. He tried to act as though his mood was light, but in truth, the thought of acting the guest of honor was enough to drive him to exhaustion.

So here he stood, getting cleaned up and shaved so his wife and mother could show him off to their small world. He only hoped the conversations that were bound to happen didn't turn to his participation in the war—but they probably would anyway.

"Libby!" he called again. "Will a shirt and tie be sufficient for the party?"

Breathless, Libby scurried from behind their bedroom door, her arms twisted behind her back attempting to zip up her dress.

She gave him a quick glance then wrinkled her nose. "Actually, Phillip, I was hoping you'd wear your formal. You know, sport the Marines' colors. I do think you look awfully handsome in the formal uniform."

He was afraid of that. Would his service in the military always be on display for all to see?

Then again, he tried to remind himself, it'd been almost four years since his wife last saw him. Only two times before had she seen him dressed in the uniform. What was once more?

But only once.

Then he could retire the get-up into his foot locker and never wear it again.

Pulling the hand towel from his shoulder, he patted down his face and neck, wiped off his hands, and strode to Libby's aid.

"Here, let me help you."

She stopped and pulled her hands from her back as he approached.

"Oh. All right. I guess I'm so used to doing things on my own, I forget I have you to help me."

She nervously laughed, and he wasn't sure if it was in response to his helping her or her own insecurity.

"I'll wear the uniform. But only for you." With ease, his fingers gently zipped up her dress. How delicate her shoulders looked. Somehow he'd forgotten how petite and small her frame really was. Had she lost weight? In a way, her thin form seemed smaller than he remembered. No matter, she was perfect in his eyes.

His hands slid up her arms and rested on her shoulders. Gently, he gave them a squeeze and moved his head closer to hers. He inhaled the scent of her flowered perfume then kissed her cheek from behind.

"You look beautiful, Elizabeth."

She turned to face him, a look of shock registering on her face. Her eyes pierced his, sending a jolt of exhilaration to his chest.

"You used my name."

"Yeah, I guess I did."

She slipped her arms around his waist and rested her head against his chest. That familiar feeling of protectiveness overcame him and he pulled her closer to him.

"Phillip, it's been so long. So long since I've heard your voice say my full name. I'd nearly forgotten how much I've missed that."

She sighed and relaxed into him. How good it was to be home.

"How did I endure so many years away from you, Elizabeth? Missing so many moments like this? Never again. I promise."

"You don't know how much I needed to hear that, Phillip. There were days and nights I wondered if I'd ever see you again. It seemed as if the war would just rage on and on."

He smoothed his hand over her soft, chocolate curls. "I know. At times I wondered the same thing. But I'm here now."

The two of them lingered there in the doorway of their bedroom for a few moments longer, lost in each other's embrace. But the clock on the living room wall chimed the half hour, rushing those precious moments along.

"Come now," Phillip reluctantly pulled away. "Let's get ourselves ready before we miss our own party altogether."

If life were a bed of roses, he'd certainly find the thistles lying beneath its surface.

The pit of his stomach roiled in unrest. He wouldn't let on to Libby just how much he was dreading tonight's festivities.

He'd tried his best to put on a good performance in front of her, but after they started on the road toward his parents' house, those feelings of dread bubbled within.

He hated crowds.

All the voices ringing at once. All the dizzying conversations that would be gabbing all around him. He wouldn't be able to focus. It had happened so many times as he travelled home.

The train stations were the worst. Hundreds of people circled him, buzzed past him, bumped into him. He'd nearly lost all sense of direction. At one point while in San Francisco, he wished he was back in the Marianas with his small group of compatriots. At least there he knew everyone and the company was only a small crowd to keep track of. It was nothing like the bustle of a large city where people seemed to pop out of every nook and cranny.

His knuckles paled as his fingers twisted the steering wheel. He shifted in his seat as he tried to push away the uncomfortable thoughts.

But one thought only led to another.

Lost memories pricked at his soul like tiny needles threading through his skin. Only instead of mending the break in his heart, it only inflicted pain and sorrow. Things he'd tried so hard to forget would all come rushing back to him tonight, he was sure of it. Perhaps the most difficult memory to face...

Seeing Grace Campbell, err make that *Brady*, for the first time since Jack's funeral.

EIGHT

Phillip's quiet disposition made Libby nervous. All day his head seemed to be floating somewhere above the clouds. Now that they sat in the silence of their vehicle, she'd hoped that maybe he'd start a lively conversation with her as he once did. But as she stole glances at him from the corner of her eye, she realized that his mind truly was somewhere else. But perhaps that's how it would be the first few days of his homecoming. He was surely exhausted. Instead of interrupting his thoughts, she recalled her own. She remembered the way her heart fluttered when Phillip entered their bedroom just moments earlier...

From her vanity table across the bedroom, Libby stole a glance in Phillip's direction. A sense of peace and contentment calmed her soul. Ever since Phillip's arrival home, she felt as giddy as the day their hearts first connected. With that thought, her love-laden eyes glazed over and the memory of younger days appeared before her.

Phillip had been the most handsome boy in high school. Of course, there weren't too many to choose from as most boys had dropped out by sixth grade to work on the family farm or to find jobs of their own to help support their families. Not Phillip Johnson though. No, his father thought very strongly of education and wouldn't let his son drop out until he'd graduated with honors. That gave Libby four long and beautiful years to admire her crush.

His gentle spirit. His quiet disposition. His thin-lipped smile...all qualities she'd noticed right off the bat about him. They wrapped together around her heart and penetrated its thick walls. Soon she'd realized she'd fallen in love.

She didn't know how he'd done it. For those first three years she'd warned herself not to fall for him. It wasn't easy suppressing her attraction to him, especially when he was the finest of four boys in the class. But she wasn't about to let her guard down as her mother did and allow pain and hurt and suffering to be the product of desire and longing. By her senior year of high school, however, Libby found herself pining for him. And she remembered the exact day it happened.

Not every girl in school had hopes of attending the spring cotillion. With so few boys to pick from, it was nearly impossible for every gal in the school to show up with a date. And no one wanted to go alone. As time drew nearer to the dance, Libby was one of those girls expecting to stay home that night. Unbeknownst to her, Phillip had other plans.

As she stood on a small wooden ladder stringing up a green and white banner in the gymnasium, she'd heard her name called from behind her. When she peered over her shoulder, she startled at the sight of Phillip, his big brown eyes gazing at her. The sudden start caused her to lose her balance. Before she could let out a scream, she was sitting in Phillip's arms. It was then she first felt something more stir in her chest. Something in his eyes told her that this man would be her's forever, whether she wanted him or not.

"You caught me," she said daftly.

"I couldn't very well let you break an ankle before the dance, now could I?"

"I wasn't planning to go." Her eyes had cast downward and her cheeks had grown warm with embarrassment.

"May I ask why not?" Phillip still hadn't let go of her. He stood there in the school gymnasium with her in his arms as if she were no more than a small kitten in his brawny hands.

Then she realized her own hands had curled around his neck. Warmth made her cheeks rosier than they already were.

"I—I hadn't been asked yet," she dared say. Libby now hoped that he'd come for a reason. That he came with her in mind. And since he didn't seem in any hurry to right her up on her own two feet, she had the slightest inkling that maybe, just maybe, her notion was right.

"Is that a fact, Libby Taylor?" His eyes bounced off hers and dipped to her lips and back again.

The pit of her stomach twisted and her toes curled inside her pumps.

Her mouth had dried up of all words. All she could do was roll her lips under her teeth and nod.

"Well, a pretty gal like you should have someone to go with. Can't waste all that prettiness at home."

He'd been testing her. She knew that. He was purposely drawing out his request at her expense. From somewhere, she'd found nerve to finally say what she wanted, yet shouldn't. "Phillip Johnson, are you here to ask me to the dance or to flatter me until I can no longer walk on legs of butter?"

A hard laugh bellowed from his mouth. Instead of going along with him, however, it angered her. She wriggled out of his hands and stood with flames in her eyes.

"How dare you find humor with my feelings!" Her hands, clenched in fists, stiffened at her sides. Her back, ramrod straight, gave off the false façade that she was stronger than she felt.

But then, Phillip became serious and reached out for her hands. She jerked away, but she didn't turn and run like she wished she had. And for that she would be glad.

"I'm sorry, Libby. I didn't mean to embarrass you. Truth is, I'm not real good at this sort of thing."

His right hand rubbed the back of his neck. And for the first time that day, she noticed slight beads of moisture gathering at the base of his hairline. He was actually more nervous than she was.

"I know I haven't said more than two words to you in the past, but truthfully, I always choke up when I do find the courage to confront you. Until now. This is our last dance of the year. After that, we'll all break off and go our separate ways. I can't leave high school not knowing what might have happened. That's why I'm here." He paused and gulped down a hard swallow. "Would—would you be my date for the dance this Friday night?"

There, cradled in a mix of sensations and sentiments, her heart had fallen hard. Of course she'd said yes, and they *did* go to the dance together. It was the first of many dances to come.

The vision had dissipated as she stared into her vanity at his reflection, and Libby found herself smiling at the precious memory.

Phillip tossed his tunic over his shoulders and buttoned up the front. How tall and erect he stood—a slight difference of how he used to carry himself. His chin held level with the floor, his eyes locked straight ahead. Libby assumed the Marines had engrained that into his way of living so that now it was habit.

He reached for his white belt and slid it around his waist.

Libby watched in awe as her husband transformed in front of her eyes. When Phillip's handsome uniformed self turned to face her, every morsel of her being melted. Her breath stole. It was almost like courting her beau all over again. That flutter in her stomach and breathless sensation overcame all her senses, and she felt more in love today than she had ever before.

The last time she saw Phillip dress in his Marine's best was the day he boarded a train bound for the west coast. Broken fragments of that memory flashed before her and misted her eyes.

The urge to go to him escalated and she dropped her compact onto her vanity table as she rose to be near him. His cap rested on their bed quilt and she spotted it. Reaching out her hand, she swiped his white military cap from their bed and stood in front of Phillip, a proud and engaging smile grew across her face.

Her chin tipped upward as she stared up into his eyes. How handsome he looked with his ensemble almost complete.

"Well? How do I look?" he asked with slight sarcasm.

Libby let out a quaint giggle, and her smile broadened. "Sergeant Johnson, you are the most handsome Marine I ever did lay eyes on. But you're missing one thing."

She took a step closer to him and his hands rested around her waist.

"What might that be, Mrs. Johnson?"

"Your cap and a kiss from your gal."

Phillip bent down to meet her lips. Her eyes rolled beneath her lids. It was a moment's satisfaction that sent electrifying shivers through her veins. If only time would allow them a few moments longer.

Pulling away, slowly, her eyelids lifted and she held up his Marine cap. In an attempt to place it atop his head, she was stopped short by Phillip's hands.

A questionable look furrowed her brows.

"Allow me," he explained, then took the visor hat from her grasp. He turned away and ducked to catch his reflection in the mirror over their dresser and carefully placed the hat over his neatly combed hair. "Have to place it just right, or the boss gets bent out of shape."

"Oh. I see."

She didn't understand why, but disappointment and a sense of awkwardness invaded her calm. It shouldn't bother her, but it did. Why had he stopped her short? And why should he care how perfect his cap was placed? He was no longer on active duty. His superiors wouldn't be present at his parents' home.

But Libby kept all those feelings quiet and to herself. Instead of voicing her questions and insecurities, she'd do as she'd always done—pretend she paid no mind to it and move on.

∽⌘∾

"I feel like a silly school girl again," Libby said as Phillip escorted her from their vehicle.

Winter's chill couldn't suppress the butterflies that fluttered in Libby's stomach.

"And why is that, darling?"

Libby lovingly glanced up at him. "Because I feel as if the Prince is taking me to the ball tonight."

Smile lines creased Phillip's cheeks and she giggled before adding, "My, you are handsome tonight. I'm the luckiest girl in all of Arbor Springs right now."

"Not as lucky as I. I have the prettiest gal in all the globe standing next to me. And I can say that in truth. I've traveled half-way around it."

She clung a little tighter to his side, indulging in the feel of his form next to hers. His strength, his towering height, even the development of his erect posture gave her a sense of protection and providence.

"This new side of you is going to take some getting used to, but I do think I like it."

She felt his eyes question her.

"What do you mean by that, darling?"

"It's little things I've noticed since you got back. For one, I'm not accustomed to how stiff and rigid you're walking right now. It's as if you're marching before your commanding officer." A slight laugh accentuated her last words.

"Perhaps I've picked up military protocol, but without discipline and uniformity one can't win a war."

Had her simple remark struck a nerve? There was tension in his voice.

"I didn't mean anything by it, Phillip. It was just a simple observation."

"I just think proper changes should be expected after returning home from a costly war."

He *was* cross with her.

"As I said, Phillip, I meant nothing by it. I like it. I truly do." She glanced up at him, hoping to catch his eye. When he returned her gaze, she offered up her sweet smile.

The muscles in his arm relaxed, and she wondered why a small observation would rile him. Then again, maybe her remark did *sound* more like a complaint rather than a compliment. She'd have to be more careful how she worded her opinion in the future. But she wouldn't let a slight misunderstanding ruin her evening, and she hoped Phillip felt the same. So as he opened the door for her, she gracefully strolled into the foyer of the senior Mr. and Mrs. Johnson's home, stopping only once to wait for Phillip to return to her side.

NINE

He knew he shouldn't be irritated, but for some unknown reason, Libby's comment bothered him. Thankfully, the Marines had taught him how to wrangle his feelings and reel them back.

What had everyone expected of him? One simply did not go to war for four years and return the same person. After all the horrific sights and butchering that he fell witness to, it was a wonder that he returned with a sane mind at all. He'd watched so many brave soldiers crumble in front him, losing not just their mental state, but losing their soul to the confines of war. It seemed impossible for the human brain to process the atrocities without some sort of scarring. Those men, although survivors of warfare, were never coming home. At least, not in the same way they left.

However, Phillip pushed those sentiments away. Stuffed them deeply into an internal box that remained in a darkened corner of his soul. There, those harsh memories could be forgotten, allowing him to push forward and give Libby the night she deserved.

He loved her, and he wouldn't let a small squabble affect their evening.

Mother and Pop's house was bustling with activity as he and Libby stepped inside. Jazz and swing music emanated from the small radio as the band played a lively number over the air waves. Must have been something new from Tommy Dorsey. Fresh music didn't travel across the Pacific, putting him behind on the latest in entertainment.

His eyes scanned his surroundings—something also learned from the Marines. Couples stood in group circles talking and laughing among one another. Mother had hung a large banner from the ceiling that read, *Welcome Home Phillip*. The aroma of warm apple pie, homemade cookies, and pot luck soup tickled his nose.

"Oh!" a voice squealed from the kitchen. "Our guest of honor has arrived!" Like a mad woman, Mother came rushing from the kitchen, pulling off her apron as she neared. Her arms were outstretched wide and the broadest smile he'd ever seen spread across her weathered face.

"My boy! Welcome, welcome." Her aging hands pressed against his cheeks and Phillip lowered himself to her height as she placed a kiss on his cheek.

"Hello, Mother. It's awfully good to see you."

"The pleasure is mine." She turned to Libby. "Libby dear, come here and let me squeeze you."

Phillip side-stepped as his wife and mother embraced. My, how quickly they'd come to love each other in the time he was away. It was another reminder of how much things had changed since he'd been gone.

"Well, don't just stand there, darkening the doorway. Come in, come in. Everyone will want to say hello to their hometown hero."

Phillip shook his head as his mother scurried away tapping guests on their shoulders and pointing him out to the crowd. How happy she seemed though. There was a gleam in her eye that he'd never seen before.

What had happened to everyone while he was away?

One by one, guests greeted him and Libby. Warm hands firmly embraced his and strong pats on his back relayed everything words couldn't say. Hugs surrounded Libby and cheerful chatter filled the room as they mingled in the center of the living room.

"How does it go there, brother?" Maggie sidled up beside him, bumping his side in playful banter. Her timing was impeccable as a slight lull gave him a few free moments to himself.

"I do believe this is easier than I anticipated."

"Is that a fact?" Maggie crossed her arms and side-glanced at him.

"It's been sometime since I was surrounded by a room full of people."

"Eh. You'll get used to it. Give it some time. Here—" Maggie turned and dipped a spoonful of punch into a mug. "Have something to drink. That'll keep your hands busy for the time being."

Taking the glass from her, he muttered his thanks and sipped heavily on his glass. He leaned against the sofa, tossing his cap onto the empty chair beside him and gazing into nothing as he settled.

"Did everything seem strange to you when you first came home, Maggie?"

He felt her eyes consider him a moment before answering. "Things didn't seem the same, if that's what you mean. But now, well, I think things haven't been better." She cast a glance in Danny's direction.

Of course, she would think that. Maggie was only newly married. The newness of matrimony had yet to wear off.

Things *did* seem different, at least to him. His family had transformed before his eyes into caring, loving people he didn't expect to encounter. Why, it appeared as though the relationship between Maggie and his parents had in some manner mended, creating a bond he'd never seen within his own family. Ah, but there was more. More to his melancholy, more changes he had yet to pinpoint.

Those feelings stirred within his soul until he heard Libby greet someone from across the way, but another guest intercepted him before he could turn to see who had just arrived. As Mr. Thompson, his old grade school teacher, went on about life in Arbor Springs since the Johnsons had left, Danny called out Phillip's name from the foyer. His eyes wandered across the room until they fell upon a familiar face, suddenly choking back every word that he was about to say.

Nothing could have prepared him for what he was about to face. Libby had already met their guests at the door and cheery voices filled his parents' living room. But all air deflated from his lungs as the image of a familiar, blonde-haired woman stood with her back to him. He started for her, and as his footsteps slowed, she turned and faced him, a smile spreading over her glowing face.

All at once his body froze. Then before he knew what was coming, it all came back to him…like a mortar round to his chest.

For the first time since the *incident*, he was staring at Grace Campbell. Make that, Grace *Brady*.

TEN

Grace Brady knew this moment would one day happen. She'd taken the last few weeks to prepare herself for this meeting.

As she and Luke stood with the Russos and Libby, a slight flutter pitted in her stomach as Danny called over his shoulder for Phillip. Grace placed a hand over her protruding middle, but it wasn't the baby's movements that fluttered about inside her. No, her nerves were on edge about something else. Something that she'd long forgotten until recently.

"How good to see all of you! Grace! Hello, my friend. Please come inside and make yourself comfortable." Libby's warm welcome helped take away the edge of her slight unease...at least for the moment.

Luke strolled up beside her to help with her overcoat.

"Thank you, dear."

"You know I never mind," he replied with a wink of his eye.

Nervously, Grace's eyes darted around the room.

No matter how many years had passed that she'd lived in complete peace, she knew she would be faced with one final burden to bury.

Just as her mind raced through all those grievances, her eyes collided with those of a man she hadn't seen since...since Jack's funeral.

Phillip Johnson.

His tall, dark form emerged from the shadows of gathered guests, and she couldn't break her eyes away from his. As he drew closer, he paused, seeming just as overcome with sentiment as she was. That's when the past unsheathed its sharp blade.

Jack and Phillip had been best friends. Chums. Nearly brothers. At the time of Phillip's enlistment, a few weeks after the news of Jack's death had reached them, Grace had been inconsolable. The pain was too great for her to see another young man off to potentially meet the same fate as her fiancé.

Life and time had marched on since then. The stress of war and worry had left their scar, making the last four years seem as if they were a lifetime ago. With much help from her family and friends, and her faith in God, she was able to overcome her agony and fears and live the life God intended her to live.

Now, as she took in the sight of Phillip, her heart didn't ache with that throbbing sting as it once had. Above all, she could look at him, her last tie to Jack, and rejoice with the Johnson family that another one had returned home safely. Her heart still held that solemn respect for her deceased loved one, but her soul was no longer chained to the grave Jack slept in. That's why she was able to move on with ease and peace in her wonderful, new life with Luke Brady.

Although she could examine her own self and see the healing God had brought her, she saw something different in Phillip's eyes as he took that final step and stood eye level with her.

"Hello, Grace."

His deep, baritone voice was so familiar, but the rigid cut of his posture was not.

"Hello, Phillip." For a moment, her tongue lodged in her throat, but she gave him a genuine smile.

As she did the day of Jack's funeral, she held her arms out for a comforting embrace and he accepted. His lips pecked her cheek, just as they had at Jack's graveside.

"It's good to see you. Welcome home."

"Thank you. You're looking well."

She retracted from his grasp. "As well as can be expected, I guess." Her cheeks filled with warmth as she glanced down at her swollen belly. A moment's pause rested on her tongue as she pondered her next phrase. "It's been a long time…"

"Yes. Yes, it has. And it's always good to reunite with an old friend. But I don't think I've had the pleasure of meeting the replacement." He glanced at Luke, who stood at Grace's side.

Phillip's consideration of Luke darkened his eyes.

"Pardon?" Grace wondered if she heard correctly as all banter quieted within their circle. Maggie appeared behind Phillip, her eyes clouded with confusion and surprise.

Phillip reached out his hand to Luke. "You must be Jack's replacement—"

Maggie's gasp sliced through the tension. "Phillip! What an awful thing to say."

Grace's shock distorted her own understanding. As always,

Maggie's quick response came to her aid in time of need, allowing Grace to gather her thoughts.

"Relax, dear sister. I mean nothing by it."

A questionable Luke reached out his left hand—his only hand—catching Phillip off guard.

Grace tensed.

With a bit of hesitation on Phillip's part, he withdrew his right hand and met Luke's left-handed shake.

"Luke Brady. And you must be the brother I've heard so much about."

"Sergeant Phillip Johnson. United States Marines. Looks like you fell on some hard times." Phillip motioned to Luke's missing arm.

"D-Day advancement. Only I didn't exactly advance much past the beach. Mortar shell. Took out nearly all my men, but spared me."

"They shoulda had more Marines to back you guys up. Probably would've cut the casualty rate in half."

Grace blinked at Phillip's abrasive tone. In fact, it seemed everyone did. Never before had she known sweet, gentle Phillip to be so smug and full of himself. She half wondered if they were talking to the same man. But one look at Libby's mortified expression confirmed that this behavior was not at all normal for him.

At that moment, Maggie decided to intercede. "All right, Phillip, this isn't some war contest. Some of us would rather leave those instances behind us. Let's not ruin a perfectly wonderful evening with war talk."

As if a storm had passed, the clouds in Phillip's eyes rolled away. "You're right, sis. Time to put the past behind us. As some of us already have." His eyes shot Grace a threatening glance, his point made. "Let's not all stand around crowding the door when there's food and fellowship to be had."

Grace didn't understand what had just happened. Never before had she felt so scrutinized, so belittled, so...threatened.

Her heart pounded beneath her cotton dress as she tried to take deep, even breaths.

The air between them was still and silent, awkward and uneasy. Grace glanced at Libby whose face bore worry lines. Her hands wrung together, revealing white knuckles. And Maggie shook her head and shrugged her shoulders in confusion. Grace couldn't bring herself to look at Luke. What must he be thinking right about now? Sure, he'd survived a whole war and barking officers, but this wasn't the battlefield.

"So, Luke, time's a'gettin' close. Not too long and you'll be an ol' man." Danny jabbed at Luke's good arm, all in good fun as usual.

Thankfully, Danny's humor had not been affected. Call it excellent timing or Danny's close comradery, he'd come to Grace's rescue not a moment too late.

Breathing a sigh of relief, Grace was glad for Danny's presence. The two men had been friends for years, joining up together, serving together, and now living in the same town. Grace wasn't sure she'd know what to do without Maggie and Danny's close companionship.

Luke pointed to himself. "This boy can survive a mortar round to the body, but I'm not so sure he'll survive the anticipation of a baby."

"Oh, stop," Grace forced her laugh. "You'll do just fine, and you'll be a great *ol' man*." She flashed Luke a bat of her eye.

Maggie chimed in. "Don't take anything Danny says to heart. When that day comes for us, he'll be no good at all." Maggie paused to glance up at Danny's thick head of dark Italian hair, then she ruffled her fingers through it. "That'll be the day you start losing all this."

"Hey, hey!" Danny swatted at her hand then combed back his carefully placed hair while the rest of them bellowed with laughter. "No one messes with the hair, and I ain't gonna be going bald anytime soon."

"Yes, dear." Through her giggles, Maggie placed a kiss against Danny's puckered lips.

Oh, how the Russos were just the people Grace needed to take her mind off other things. Especially when she caught Phillip glancing in her direction. The night wasn't over yet, and Grace knew Phillip wasn't over Jack's death. When Maggie's hand gently pulled her aside, Grace also knew Maggie wasn't over Phillip's curt attitude.

"I'm so sorry, Grace. I don't know what came over him."

Grace blinked hard and held up a palm. "Now, now, Maggie, let's just forget the whole thing."

"No. I can't just let it go. You're my best friend. I don't want anything coming between us."

"Simmer down, Maggie. Nothing is going to come between us. I love you like my own sister. Don't be silly."

"I'm going to talk with Phillip and straighten this whole thing out. Please apologize to Luke for me." Maggie's knuckles warmed against her cheeks. "How frightfully awkward that must have been for him."

Yes, Grace thought just the same. But Luke hadn't batted an eye. Either he was better at masking his astonishment or he didn't catch Phillip's low jabs at all. Grace hoped for the latter, but she knew Luke was no fool. No…likely, Luke was the better man. He wouldn't allow a few harsh comments to ruin this evening.

But as for Jack…well, that may be a hurdle Luke had yet to clear.

ELEVEN

"Your father is ready to make a toast...to you."

Phillip glanced around the room. To his surprise, all the guests had gathered into the large living room. All were holding glasses in their hand. Some stood with their eyes on him, grins and smiles spread across their faces. Others peered at his father, the senior Mr. Johnson, who stood with authority and intent and smiled proudly down at him.

Remembering his manners, Phillip slowly stood to his feet and Dad handed him his glass.

In the next moment, the start of Dad's speech left Phillip nearly dumbstruck...

"I want to thank everyone here for braving the weather and coming out tonight to celebrate a very special homecoming. My wife and I cannot truly express the joy in our hearts as we are able to welcome home my boy from a ghastly and grueling time away from us while fighting the enemy. We feel most fortunate to not only welcome home Margaret and her new husband, Danny, after so many months apart, but now we have the blessing of bringing home our son...alive."

Dad's gaze faltered then dropped to his glass. Was he actually...choked up? It was a side of his father that Phillip had never seen. A side not at all unyielding and harsh, but soft and tender. How much more had changed while he was away?

After a moment of gathering his thoughts, Dad glanced back up, this time staring Phillip in the eyes as he continued...

"Phillip, I know I never coddled you as a boy, or outwardly mentioned the fact that I'm proud of you, but I'm saying it now. I'm...proud...of you. When we received the telegram stating that you went missing in action, we thought our world had ended, and we couldn't bear that loss. Later, we'd learned of Maggie's injuries and we were left to wonder if we would have the chance to ever see or welcome either of our children home again. That's when we realized it. We realized the error of our ways and knew a change was in order.

"We let both you and Maggie down and for that, we are truly sorry. But we also found that the love we lacked could be filled through our Savior, Jesus. So we prayed. Ohh...we prayed ever so persistently every night that the good Lord would grant our desire. Do you know what that desire was, Phillip?"

Still unable to fully comprehend the words filtering into his ears, Phillip shook his head.

"It was for you. And for Maggie. That your mother and I would have the chance to welcome you into our arms once more and to tell you that we love you."

The quiver in Dad's voice was enough to send a shiver down Phillip's spine. These were words he wasn't accustomed to hearing. Words that had never come easy to an overbearing father. Was he just supposed to sit here and forget the past? Forget how demanding his father was or how many times he was berated and ordered to become a better person? While his father had many good qualities as a man, and while Phillip knew he was favored over Maggie for a multitude of varying reasons, it was still hard to swallow the seemingly hypocritical speech his father was making. How was he to untangle this mixed up web of deceit while sitting in front of a roomful of guests?

Guests.

Although his irritation was building, Phillip knew he had to be mindful of all the people standing around them, lest he make another abrasive outburst. Shoving aside all conflicting thoughts, he managed a weak smile and gave his father a nod.

"So to you, Phillip," Dad went on. "I propose this toast for your brave service in combat and in life. For facing the enemy amid all the dangers and uncertainty that soldiering had to offer. For saving the lives of men, women, and children. And for coming home to us alive."

With that, Dad raised his glass of cider to which the rest of room echoed, "Here, here," and sipped.

But Phillip's stomach churned. Even more so than after confronting Grace and Luke Brady. Everything was different now. Everyone had changed, in one way or another. His parents' entire demeanor was unfamiliar to him since the day he arrived home. Their sudden change of housing preference had also been a surprise to him. Now to hear these strange and heartfelt words from his father, a man that knew nothing of tenderheartedness. It was all too much for him to take in at once.

The laughter of happy guests filled the room. Even Libby, who sat beside him, chattered along in perky conversation with the other women. Yet, here he was sitting in the center of all this happy attention, and still, he sat alone, empty, and completely detached from the rest of the world around him.

That moment of truth transported him back to a black night where a screen of smoke shrouded the stars from sight. The lack of even the smallest light from those tiny stars made the darkness close in on him.

He and his fellow Marines had barricaded themselves in the thicket of jungle, lying with their faces against damp, rich soil on Japanese-infested ground. Sleep had not come for two days and the enemy's attack had not ceased. Bullets whistled toward them from places unknown and unseen. The dense dark of the forest prevented them from locating snipers hidden in the jungle's trees.

He knew who surrounded him on the ground—the brotherhood of his compatriots. They'd spent every waking day together. They knew their part. They had one another's backs. They each had their own directive. As long as every man in his squad executed his target, they would survive.

So they waited. In the cold, sticky mud, they lay flat, unmoving, and listened intently for the slightest sound—a snapping twig, the rustling of jungle leaves against twill uniforms, the cock of a rifle. They'd taught themselves to fine tune their ears to listen for any sign of the approaching enemy.

The Marines had done a fine job of training him for hand-to-hand combat. They'd taught him how to handle weapons, how to fight with his hands, how to kill, and ultimately, how to *not* feel. Because caring may lead to his own death and the death of his military brothers. So any and all emotion had to be locked away in a place where not even he had access to it.

Out here it was survival of the fittest. And through living the last year in Pacific waters, he'd also learned the lay of the land. As long as he could keep from contracting Malaria through the island's infected mosquitoes, he may come home alive...

Then it happened. The deafening burst of a sniper's rifle, and the burn of a bullet ripping into his side...

Blinking hard, Phillip squinted at his unexpected memories. His hand reached to his side where the bullet had left its mark. How did it happen? How did he get from his parents' living room to an island half a world away?

For the remainder of the evening, Phillip retreated to a corner of the house. From there he observed everyone. He'd become good at hiding and keeping a low profile. Especially when observing his target.

TWELVE

I f anyone knew Phillip Johnson inside and out, it was Maggie.
Ever since his rogue remark in the foyer about Luke, Maggie
had stood from a distance and watched her brother.

Something wasn't quite right. Could it be he hadn't had enough
time to settle in? Possibly. Was it probable that tensions between
brotherhoods, the Army and Marines, had increased since the war's
end? Potentially. But that didn't explain Phillip's strange behavior.

Maggie set down her glass of punch with purpose. Just like old
times, the only way to figure out her brother's odd mood was to charm
him into talking.

She found him near a corner close to the front door. His eye caught
hers and he excused himself from his conversation with his old
elementary teacher.

"I guess I should thank you for that rescue," he whispered under
his breath. "I forgot how the man could go on and on..."

Maggie gave his arm a smack. "Phillip, don't be simple."

"Simple or not, the man's a bore." He took a long sip on his drink
as he rested his backside against the wall. "It's awfully warm in here,"
he said as he tugged at the collar of his suit.

"I would assume so in that getup."

Maggie joined him in his small corner away from everyone else,
and for the first time since his return, they were somewhat alone.

"It was Libby's idea. She wanted to see the Marines' colors one
last time, I suppose."

Maggie nodded in understanding. "There always was something
about a man in uniform...but you pull it off well enough. Not quite as
handsome as the Airborne's uniform—particularly that one right
there," she teased as she pointed to Danny.

Phillip's familiar, easy smile played across his face and his head
bobbed as he identified with her jesting.

"So my little sister's in love."

"She is."

"And happy?"

Maggie turned and met his eyes. "She is. *I* am. Very much so."

His gaze broke away from hers and fell across the room. My, how different Phillip seemed. The spark, the joy in his eyes had fizzled. But hadn't they all returned home with some tarnish to their souls? Perhaps like she and the others who'd returned home from the war, time needed to heal certain wounds.

"It's good to have you back, Phillip. I was so frightened for you when—when your status had come back MIA."

His quick side glance considered her a mere moment as his brow quirked. "It's good to be back."

"Is it really?" Maggie turned, probing deeper as her eyes penetrated him.

"What's that supposed to mean?"

"I can't help but notice you've been a little off kilter tonight, is all."

Phillip's palms turned upward. "Look at all this, Maggie," he whispered. "I didn't ask for a King's Ball in my honor."

"No, but Mother wanted to make it special for you."

He kept his voice lowered. "Speaking of Mother…what's with her and Dad? Why is everyone acting so strange all of a sudden?"

"What do you mean?" Maggie asked, not sure what he was inquiring of.

"Why the tender speech, the spiritual talk, and Dad getting all choked up and the like? They are not the same people I left."

Maggie's mouth hinged open and she mouthed the word, *oh*. "Phillip, a lot has changed since you left—since *I* left. I don't know how to explain it other than their eyes have been opened by the Holy Spirit. I think they've finally found peace and have come to accept us for who we are. More importantly, they've found who God is."

"And you?" Phillip's gaze landed on her.

"What about me?"

"Have you forgiven them?"

"I have." She could say it with a clear conscience and without hesitation because she had.

Maggie had finally found peace with her own tainted past and disapproving parents. Mother and Dad had come to her with open arms and tearful regrets seeking her forgiveness. Maggie had witnessed their bitterness and harsh attitude melt away into something beautiful. Only God Almighty could have taken a disaster and turned it into promise and blessing.

"That's it? Two words. *I have.* You were able to take years of Mother's nit-picking, her criticism, and Dad's overbearing rules and back lashings and just say *all is forgiven*? I don't know who this family is anymore."

Maggie gave off a slight giggle. "Give it time, Phillip. You'll find they're easy to love."

Phillip raked his hand through his hair and blew out a long breath. "It seems nothing is the same as I left it."

Whether he knew it or not, Maggie watched as Phillip's glance landed on Grace. Maggie followed the path his eyes took and when they hovered over Grace's form as she sat at Luke's side, Maggie realized that maybe her brother hadn't yet buried *his* past.

THIRTEEN

The evening had not gone as Grace expected.

She hoped her first reunion with Jack's best friend would go smoothly. That all past influences would be buried—where she'd left them. Life had gone on now. Her heart had healed, was made new, and she couldn't imagine her life without Luke in it. However, it seemed, Phillip had not met the same understanding.

Occasionally, she caught his thoughtful stares pointed at her. But as their eyes met, he didn't back down. It was as if he was sizing her up, trying to make an assumption of her. Finally, she was the one to look away and act as though she hadn't paid any mind to his perusal.

"How are you holding up, Sweetheart?" Luke's voice tickled Grace's ear as he bent down and whispered to her, taking her hand in his own.

"I'm fine, honey. Really." She met his eyes then spotted Maggie heading into the kitchen. Some of the guests had taken their leave and the house was quieting. "Now, you go in there and have your man talk with the fellas while the girls and I start cleaning up."

Luke smiled down at her and gave a nod of his head. "All right, doll. But the moment you start to feel weary, let me know, and I'll get you home to rest."

"Always the hero, Luke Brady," she teased.

"Must be in my blood." With the wink of his eye, he turned and joined Danny and the fellas.

"You're too lucky, Grace." Libby matched Grace's steps as she walked toward the kitchen with a tray of glasses in her hands.

"Lucky? Blessed is more like it." Grace giggled quietly and turned to the gals. "Who knew a man could be so attentive when his wife is expecting a child? It's amazing what he's done around the house since we learned the news of the baby. One would never guess he had an incapability."

Grace glanced over her shoulder, finding Luke in the adjoining room and resting her eyes on his striking form.

"Speaking of which…" Maggie set herself down at the now cleared table and tilted her head in Luke's direction. "Has he said anymore about the possibility of a prosthesis?"

Grace's eyes slid to her husband's tall form—a man still ever so handsome today as he was the first night she met him. Even considering he'd lost an arm in the span of their absence from each other. But it pained her to think of him learning how to live life without the complete use of one arm and with the total loss of another.

A lump formed in her throat and she worked hard to swallow back the pity that ached in her chest for him.

"We've visited the topic a few times. And the doctors are pushing for sooner rather than later to fit him for a prosthetic arm, but…" Her hand rested against her swollen abdomen. "I think he worries about the baby and wonders what his child will think of having a father with a phony limb."

"But, Grace, he can't let all those what-ifs interfere with his livelihood." Maggie interjected. "I've worked with plenty of combat veterans who have taken the prosthetic arm. It gives them so much more freedom…and help."

Grace lowered herself onto the dining room chair and rested her hands in her lap. In a soft voice she replied, "I know. But I won't ask anymore of him. He's given and lost so much—I don't want to be the one to ask him to give up his dignity also, if that's how he views wearing a prosthesis."

Her throat tightened and Grace searched her mind for a change of subject. Out of habit, she glanced back toward Luke, but instead of her eyes falling on her husband, they were met once again by Phillip's intense gaze.

It unsettled her.

Tiny prickles of goose bumps dotted her arms and slid down her back. Turning away, once more, she warmed her hands on her tea cup and sipped from it.

"Tell me, Libby, how is Phillip doing? Due to my not feeling well, we haven't had the chance to welcome him home until now."

Grace decided to take the plunge. To test the waters and see if she could figure out the cause of Phillip's strange behavior.

"Aw, you know. He's still coping with the time change, and I think he's still adjusting to getting back to normal life." Libby took pause and dropped her hands into the sink full of sudsy dish water. Her gaze stared aimlessly out the kitchen window into the dark of night. After a moment's silence, she resumed washing the dishes. "Phillip, as *manly* as he is, won't tell you that, though. Always the strong type, you know. Won't talk much about the war, so I don't mention it. Come to think of it, he hasn't said much at all."

It was possible Phillip still suffered from the time zone change. Or rotten war reminders. Grace knew all the men who returned from *over there* did not return the same as when they left.

"Luke still has a difficult time of things. Not just the fact that he lost his arm in the France invasion, but well, mental scars. Flashbacks. Nightmares. Those sort of things. When we were first married, it was hard for me to see him wake up in a sweat at night, all shaking and clammy. Over time, I adjusted and came to expect it, but he's spoken with the pastor a few times and I think Luke's strengthening of his faith is what has brought him through and this far."

Maggie's eyes took on a far-away look then she offered up her own reminders.

"Sometimes I can still hear the whistling of bombs dropping. Or the sound of a machine gun firing into the night. But the most vivid of memories are the wounded and dying laying on the table in front of me, screaming at me to save them. And in those awful dreams, I can't do anything. I just stand there staring at them. There's nothing I can do for them."

Grace reached out a hand and rested it on Maggie's. "I can't imagine what you went through over there, Maggie, but I do know you answered God's call and did your best for all those poor souls. You're a right, good nurse."

"Thank you, Grace. No matter how many times I've put all that behind me, it's still good to hear those reassuring words." Droplets of moisture dotted Maggie's cheeks and she quickly swept them away. "Now, that's enough of that. This is a party, isn't it? Why aren't we laughing?"

"My thoughts exactly, Maggie. I'm either a terrible guest or we are a bunch of sentimental fools." Libby turned with a tray of coffee and coffee cups in her hand. "I'll just be a minute. I'll take this in to the fellas."

∽⤐∽

"Thank you for a wonderful evening," Grace said as Luke slipped her overcoat onto her shoulders.

"The pleasure is ours," Libby replied with a smile cracking through her weary façade. "I'm grateful the two of you came."

Libby awkwardly stepped forward to embrace Grace in a warm hug. But from over Libby's shoulder, Phillip's gaze speared Grace. Something unsettling pinched in her stomach. She knew it wasn't just the pregnancy causing her belly to turn, yet she couldn't quite determine what it was she saw in Phillip's eyes.

Grace stepped back, breaking her gaze from Phillip, and clung a little tighter to Luke's good arm. Giving Phillip a slight smile of acknowledgement, she turned her attention to Luke and inhaled the scent of his cologne—something she often did when she needed to settle her mind. Her gaze shifted to Luke's face. "Well? Shall we?"

Luke reached out his hand to Phillip.

Grace's muscles stiffened. Part of her hoped Phillip wouldn't make another smug comment about her husband. But another part of her believed he was a better man than that. She watched as the two men exchanged words, but their discussion fell deaf on her ears as she admired Luke, thanking God all over again for the exemplary man he was and for the precious life He'd given to the two of them. Nothing could mar the perfect union of their two hearts.

Good-byes were said. Luke held open the door for her and bid everyone a goodnight, but Phillip wasn't through. He turned to Grace, stepped forward and placed a betraying kiss on her cheek. His shrewd smile ended abruptly with his final statement. "It was good to see you again. I'm sure Jack would be very happy for the two of you."

With that, he turned and left the room.

Suddenly, a great wall of nausea built up in Grace's abdomen and she knew at that moment what Phillip's dark glances had meant.

FOURTEEN

"Honestly, Phillip, what was that back there?" The hiss in Maggie's controlled tone echoed not only through the hallway, but through Phillip's ears as well.

After speaking his peace with Grace, he'd retreated through the living room, Maggie close on his heels. From the sound of her direct steps, she was angry with him.

"I don't know, Maggie. I don't know what came over me." Phillip rubbed his fingers across his brow. He needed to clear the unfamiliar fog from his eyes, his mind.

"Well, whatever it is, get over it. Really, I've never felt so humiliated."

"I'm sorry, Maggie."

But she had already stormed off, muttering to herself as she did. "Try to make a fella feel loved and welcomed home and he insults the company..."

After his exchange with Grace and Luke, the dizzying conversations surrounding him sent his mind into a spiraling whirlwind. His eyes, his thoughts, were unable to focus on one subject. There were too many people crowding him. Too many voices coming from all directions. Not one voice seemed familiar to him. And to add to his sudden confusion, he was outside the confines of his home, or his tropical tent, thousands of miles from the place he left it. Where could he find his escape? The walls seemed to close in on him as he searched for any opening, any hole to flee to.

With each quickening breath, his heart pounded against his chest. In an attempt to recalibrate his mind, he shut his eyes and opened them again. Tiny beads of sweat formed at his hairline and he quickly brushed at his forehead. His hands, clammy with anxiety, shook. His eyes squeezed shut.

What was happening to him?

Why did it seem so hard to find tranquility in a place where he knew he was safe from the enemy's hand?

"Phillip?"

A soft, feminine hand rested against his wrist and he flinched.

When he opened his eyes, they immediately focused on the beautiful dark-haired woman he'd married.

Libby, his heart skipped. Maybe just what he needed to calm his pulse.

Her eyes were questioning, but she went on...

"Honey, was everything all right back there? I—it's not like you to make such a...well, a rudimentary remark."

"Would everyone stop asking if I'm *all right*? I made one little slip up and everyone gets their feathers ruffled."

"Well, I hardly call insulting your best friend's old fiancée and her now husband a minor slip up."

"So I got a little defensive. How else would you address the person who stole your best friend's fiancée away from them?"

"Phillip..." Libby's pause lasted long enough to catch his attention. "Jack's gone. He and Grace were never married. Did you really expect her to become a spinster and live alone the rest of her life? She *needed* Luke, and he needed her. It all worked out the way it was supposed to."

Phillip's mood simmered and the blinding fog began to clear. "I know," he painfully admitted. "But Jack was over the moon for Grace. Everyone knew that. His world revolved around her. You have to remember, Libby, the last time I saw either of them, they were together...even at his funeral service. She was by his side. Seeing her without him doesn't seem right."

"But that's all in the past now."

The past.

Just another painful reminder that life wasn't going to be the same post-war.

"Come on, Libby, we're going home."

Libby

Phillip grabbed his suit coat from his chair and swung it over his arm.

Libby couldn't help but hesitate at Phillip's abrupt announcement.

"But honey, not all the guests have left yet. You'll be expected to say something. After all, your parents intended for this party to be in your honor." Her efforts were cut short when Phillip's hands rested against her elbows, leading her toward the doorway.

"I've said my peace for the night. I'm ready to go home."

His actions had been so mysterious this evening. And for some unknown reason, his mood seemed to be particularly irritated today. Of all days, this evening's festivities.

"All right, I'm coming." Not given the chance to say an appropriate good-bye to the remaining friends and family, Phillip rushed her off. His swift strides made it difficult for her to keep up with as she nearly trotted in her heels. "Really, Phillip, won't you slow down a little? This isn't the Kentucky Derby and I'm no jockey."

"Libby, must you argue with me? It's been a long day. I'm tired and ready to be in the comfort of my own home, in my own bed."

"That's fine, dear. I just thought you'd want to see everyone. It's been so long since anyone has had the chance to see you. It seems rude to cut out early when your family went through all the trouble of buying food and laying it all out."

"They'll understand, and besides, the night is practically over anyhow." With haste, Phillip opened her passenger side door and waited for her to step inside. Once both of them were seated, he started the ignition and backed out of the driveway.

Libby glanced over at him quizzically.

"What is it?" he asked flatly.

"I…was just wondering what has you flustered all of a sudden."

"I'm not flustered."

"Then something is irritating you."

"Libby, right now your questions and accusations are irritating me."

His sharp reply halted anymore rebuttal from escaping her mouth. She sat in quiet surprise at his sudden reprimand of her.

For several minutes they sat in silence. Phillip, with his dark eyes glued to the road ahead, and she, with her confused thoughts.

Remember, Libby, he's just returned from war. He's tired. He's weakened. And you should be more sensitive to his needs right now. He doesn't mean what he's saying. This isn't who he is.

It was the truth. This wasn't who Phillip truly was on the inside. Not the Phillip she'd sent off to war. It only seemed logical that the years at war had worn him down and he was in dire need of recuperation—just like the mounting stress he'd endured after Jack's death. She was his wife, it was her duty to see that he was as comfortable as possible and happy—even if that meant a few weeks of inconvenience for her. Soon he would feel better. Once he fell into the habit of his old routine and socialized with his family and friends, life would return to normal again.

A slight smile spread across her lips and she shot another glance at her husband...this time a tender glance.

"You know what? You're right, dear. I've been selfish. I'm just so happy to have you home. I guess I want to show you off to everyone now that you're here. But I forget sometimes that you've traveled halfway around the world and back. You deserve some quiet time." She paused, and he looked at her from the corner of his eye. Her gloved hand patted his knee. "I promise, from now on I'll try to be a little more understanding and considerate of how you're feeling. I love you."

His right eyebrow arched as he glanced down at her for a mere moment. The slightest hint of a smile turned the corner of his lips upward. "I'm sorry too, darling. I don't know what's wrong with me. I'll try to do better too."

∽৯৶৹

Phillip

Through the silence of the evening, the water faucet seemed to scream at Phillip as he cupped his hands and splashed cool water over his face. He repeated the act several times, until he could no longer bear to hear the hiss of the faucet any longer.

As droplets of water dripped from his chin, he grasped the sink bowl and stared down into its porcelain face. His thoughts had tortured him ever since his confrontation with Grace. It was the first time he'd seen her since...since the funeral.

His hand jerked and rubbed moisture from his eyes. Using his hand towel, he wiped down his taut face and neck, catching everything he could to rid himself of his own filth. That is, everything except the filth on the inside. It didn't matter how hard he tried. Those things were branded into his soul and had somehow attached to his whole being.

Grace.

How could he have known that seeing her would kindle such a burning in his soul? How could her form alongside someone else infuriate him to no end? And yet, what gave him the right to taunt her like he did?

He knew his words were vile. He tasted their bitter sting. But how could she just move on like nothing had ever happened? How could she forget so quickly? And how could she smile and act like nothing was wrong?

Maybe he had her figured wrong. Maybe Grace Campbell Brady wasn't the girl he thought she was.

Reflecting back on her words and promises of years past made him believe they were all empty promises. Promises made in vain. Promises that were never meant to be kept—

And that angered him further.

Jack Gregory was a good man. An honest man. And he would have made good on his commitment to Grace. How could she tromp on Jack's memory and marry the next fella who came along?

He splashed another handful of cold water onto his face to erase all those conflicting thoughts from his mind.

Why didn't he have control of his own inner thoughts and feelings? Why should he care so much about what Grace did with her life? Why should standing in a room full of friends and family affect him in adverse ways? Why did he feel claustrophobic? Why did it seem that all the walls were closing in on him? And why couldn't he erase Jack from his past as Grace had so easily done?

Jack...

A friend who was more like a brother. A man who had so much to look forward to in life. A man too young to die.

Phillip had gone to war to avenge his best friend's death. But had he succeeded? Had he heard bells tolling in Jack's honor the day the Japanese surrendered? Had those brutal enemies come crawling on their knees begging for forgiveness and apologizing for all their wrongdoings?

No.

There were no tolling bells. Not where he was. Oh, yes, there were cries for joy when they learned the war was over. But not one person had remembered or heard of the name, Jack Gregory.

In an instant, it was as if all those who were lost were now forgotten. So had Phillip really avenged his friend's death? Or had it all been in vain?

It couldn't have been for nothing.

Phillip refused to believe that his service was a dishonor to Jack. Or a vain attempt to bring back was what lost.

Is that what he was doing? Was Phillip trying to bring Jack back to Arbor Springs?

Then it hit him, knocking the breath from his lungs—

Jack wasn't coming back.

Jack would never return to Arbor Springs.

Phillip raked his fingers through his dampened hair then patted dry his face with the towel that was slung over his shoulder.

That familiar urge was calling out to him. The habit he'd picked up on the islands had finally chased him down. It wasn't supposed to find him. It was meant to stay far behind him, stranded on that awful island in the middle of the Pacific. Under the thick of bush, the shade of palm trees, the covering of sand, and the ash of ruins, it was supposed to stay buried where no one—not even he—could find it. But here it was, knocking on his soul's door.

Glancing down the hallway to his bedroom, he spotted Libby sitting at her vanity, combing out her hair and wearing her favorite, blue silk nightgown. Although he knew he should go to her, the urge to rummage through his foot locker in search of his remedy was stronger than his will.

It wouldn't take long.

Quietly, he made his way to the guest bedroom where his foot locker was tucked away behind the closet door. He winced when the old doorknob squeaked as he turned it. After opening the door, he knelt down and ran his hand over the smooth texture of the army green paint.

SGT. Johnson

His rank and name was stenciled across the top in black lettering.

Gently, he lifted the lid and removed the top insert, revealing the attire and artifacts inside. His old uniform, caked with dirt and smudged with grease and oil still held that familiar, tropic smell of sea salt, coconuts, and mechanic's grease. Oddly, visions didn't corrupt his mind nor did the smell of the island trigger grizzly flashbacks. Nor did the aura of stale alcohol filter through his lungs.

Phillip continued hunting through his foot locker.

There had to be something here. Even just a few remaining droplets. Anything to kill the anxiety and chase away any threat of fitful sleep and nightmares.

The clank of a bottle hitting against wood brought his hand to the corner where his fingers rubbed against smooth glass.

"That's it," he breathed to himself.

Pulling the flask from deep inside, Phillip eyed it in the dark and swished its contents.

"Only a sipper left, but you'll have to do," he spoke to the bottle as if speaking to an old friend.

Uncorking the flask, Phillip tossed the liquid into his mouth. The burn of alcohol scraped down his throat. It was only the tiniest bit compared to the rounds the boys had shared at camp, but it was enough to quench his desire for the time-being.

"Phillip?"

Libby's voice caused him to throw the bottle back into its rightful place—buried in a deep, dark corner.

"I'll be right out, darling."

With haste, he closed his foot locker and the closet door, leaving the guest room altogether. Sighing deeply, he made his way down the hall and walked through their bedroom doorway.

Libby stood in the middle of the room. The soft glow of lamplight bounced off her silk nightgown, adding a becoming radiance to her beautiful face.

She was waiting for him. Not just tonight, but for years she'd been lying in wait.

Guilt entered his heart.

Once again, he'd put his own selfish needs in front of hers. He should have run straight for Libby instead of running to his addictions.

But he could run to her now.

He took soft, slow steps in her direction and reached out for her waist. Libby stepped into his arms and with a smile spreading on her lips, she tipped her chin upwards and met his kiss.

Suddenly, all his depravities and demons faded away somewhere in the dark of night and behind the image of his beautiful wife.

FIFTEEN

Too many nights had she been robbed of sleep, but tonight was different. Grace's restlessness ended with a sharp jerk as her eyes fluttered open to a moonlit room. Her sleepy eyes fought to stay open. A good night's rest seemed to escape her these last few weeks, making it harder for her to muster up the strength to roll over and check what had awakened her.

Instinctively, she knew to reach for Luke. It seemed lately his sleep was just as disturbed as hers. As her hand stretched across the bed to a warm, empty space, she lifted her head and peered across it. A few heartbeats passed before her eyes adjusted to her surroundings. When they focused, she saw Luke's masculine form standing at the window.

Like so many nights before, Luke stood in a place completely cut off from the living and withdrawn from the world.

As his wife, and knowing what evils plagued his mind, Grace's heart broke for him. And suddenly her own discomfort of carrying a small bundle of joy didn't seem of great inconvenience.

Her slender fingers rested against her swollen abdomen, reminding her all over again how much she loved and adored her husband.

She swept the bed quilt from her legs and swung her feet off the bed. With care, she pushed off the mattress, her pink nightgown falling over her belly and sweeping against her ankles as she stood.

Luke stood vigil at the bedroom window, his left hand leaning against the window frame. As she stepped closer, beads of sweat that had formed on his shoulders glistened in the moonlight—an indication that his dreams were once again interrupted by a haunting reminder of war.

"Luke?" she called out in a soft voice, careful not to startle him.

With a jerk of his head, he swung around. "Sweetheart. You shouldn't be out of bed. You need your rest." His arm reached out and cradled her waist.

"Don't trouble yourself. I'm fine," she answered and stretched a finger to his lips. Her arms encircled his middle. "But you're not. I'm sorry, honey. I keep praying the nightmares will go away. Is it Tommy again?"

His eyes peered past her line of sight and out the window. He gazed deep into the starry night sky. His chest lifted and exhaled as if he fought against a great weight.

"What is it?" she pressed.

His jaws tensed and she knew he was trying to put his thoughts into words.

"Am I—am I good enough for you, Grace?"

"What?" Surprise sent a jolt straight through her heart. "Luke, why would you even ask such a thing?"

"Just answer. Please. I need to know." His gaze penetrated her skin and bore a hole into her core. Why was he questioning his worth to her?

"First, I want to know what brought this question on. Luke, haven't I made it clear how much you mean to me? How much I love you?"

His gentle touch smoothed over her hand and he kissed her fingers. "I've been doing some thinking."

"About the war?"

"About Jack."

Grace's heart stilled. "Jack?" Confusion now replaced curiosity and concern. What on earth was going through Luke's mind? And why now? "What about Jack?"

"If…Jack was still alive and he came home right now, would you be sorry you married me?"

Utter dismay prevented Grace from comprehending Luke's words. Her jaw hung open, her heart pierced with a sharp prick. After a moment of unscrambling her thoughts, she finally found her voice.

"Darling, Jack was part of my life for a season. I was never meant to have a life with him. Most importantly, I was able to let him go completely. It's you I love and you that I want to spend the rest of my life with. I couldn't regret any of my decisions. Never."

She watched for assurance to register on his face. Although he regarded her with his dimpled smile, that reassurance never reached his eyes.

He turned back to the window and she traced the outline of his profile against the moonlight. Reaching up on her tip toes, she gently kissed his cheek.

"Won't you come back to bed? It gets awfully lonely when you're away from me."

His adoring eyes, now scarred by war and hurt, gazed down upon her. She returned his adoration by squeezing his waist and pressing her head into his chest. "I love you, Luke Brady," she whispered.

She only hoped and prayed that he believed she meant every word. Because she could never live without him.

❧❧

How could reminders of the past plague the mind so fiercely that it stole all comfort and peace from the night?

Luke had come back to bed nearly two hours ago and here she was still lying awake. At least her husband had finally found peace of mind and drifted off into a solid slumber. But now her reminders of the war had somehow resurfaced and pushed up into the places of her mind where her new memories should be residing instead. She wished she could pretend she didn't know what disturbed Luke, but in truth, she knew exactly where the source had stemmed from.

Phillip.

For the remainder of the evening, after leaving the Johnsons' home, Grace put on a brave face and acted as though Phillip's awkward introduction didn't phase her. But her heart had ached the whole ride home. She only hoped that Luke didn't take offense to Phillip's strange behavior. But after Jack's name was brought up by Luke tonight as they stood by the window, she knew the subject of her late fiancé had indeed bothered her husband.

Jack may have been part of her life for a season, but Luke had been sent by God to stand beside her for the rest of her days on earth. She'd buried her old hopes and dreams for good the day she visited Jack's grave for the last time. It was the day she laid to rest one vow and whole-heartedly committed to a new one.

Now, as she lay awake staring at a blank ceiling, she wondered if Phillip had intended to hurt her, to challenge Luke. To make her unearth a darkened time in her life that would cause harm to her relationship with Luke.

She wasn't about to let that happen.

SIXTEEN

26 February 1946

Libby shifted the old Ford into PARK and turned the key, killing the engine. Before she exited her car, her eyes swept across the lawn to the front porch.

There he sat…in the same chair, in the same position, the same time as yesterday—and the day before. And the day before that.

He had a look in his eye—a look that she'd never noticed during their courting years, nor the first few months of their marriage even. But something was there and yet, something was missing. It was like he was watching an old movie reel replaying in his mind. His body positioned in such a way that although he sat relaxed, his posture was tense.

He's still adjusting. Just tired from the years of deprived sleep and gruesome sights.

That's all it was. Phillip needed time for his body to adapt to his new surroundings. After all, he had moved from York, Pennsylvania to California to the Philippines and back to Arbor Springs, Maryland in a span of almost four years.

Libby slid from the Ford's bench seat and retrieved her bag of groceries from the back. The closing of the car door seemed to jar Phillip's thoughts. He stood to his feet.

His inviting smile reassured her uneasy mind that he was all right. "There's my girl. What have you here?"

"Just some groceries. Thought I'd fix you up a nice meal."

"Darling, I could eat biscuits and jelly for a month and feel it's a grand occasion."

The screen door closed behind them as they made their way into the kitchen. Libby set the bag on the counter and began placing the groceries in the cupboards. But then she stopped, hesitated, and cautiously asked, "Phillip, what *did* they feed you over there?"

His eyes clouded over and his head swiveled to stare out the kitchen window.

She watched his muscles tense in his back. The set of his jawbone also stiffened, but she didn't understand why.

"To put in perspective, it amounted to nothing. Nothing at all."

That was all he said. He'd shut down on her and was now making his way back to the porch...to his wicker chair.

After Phillip had returned to his solemn mood and favorite resting spot, Libby silently walked to the screen door and peered around the door frame at her husband. He sat with military posture. Both hands rested on each of the chair arms and his line of vision pointed directly across the street at a red brick house with black shutters. It almost looked as though he was standing watch...for something, or someone.

For the past few days she wondered what it was his eyes were seeing that she couldn't. Had some childhood memory revisited him and he was relishing in that moment? Was he thinking of the war? She wasn't familiar with this side of him. She expected an exuberant, rambling husband who couldn't wait to tell her of his tales in the jungle, and his outsmarting tactics while serving in the bush. She expected him to pick up where he left off, finding peace in his job, and joy in getting along with their life together. But no, instead, Phillip Johnson had kept to himself and hardly made mention of what happened to him in the four years he was absent from her. Instead of coming home and greeting her with a kiss, he sat in the wicker chair for hours at a time, staring...just staring.

Libby was about to step away from the screen door and finish her task of putting groceries away when Phillip reached into his pocket and unfolded a letter.

Her brows furrowed together as she hadn't remembered a missive being delivered to him. Now curiosity and questions entered her mind. She watched as he read along. Her eyes bounced off his face and to the letter. What could it be? A note from an old war buddy? One of her love letters that she'd sent him while in the Pacific? Her heart warmed at the thought of Phillip keeping one of her letters so close to him. Perhaps it was one of his favorites that he kept near so that he could pull it out and read it anytime he needed to feel close to her.

Suddenly, Phillip cleared his throat and quickly folded the letter back up and stuffed it down into his pocket. Once again, his eyes fixated on the house across the way and he sat cold as stone. He was never aware of her close proximity. Of her eyes on him. And oh, how she longed for him to look at her once again with heartfelt love and adoration—much like the way he just read that letter.

❧❦

26 March 1946

Phillip was growing distant from her. She sensed it and in her heart, she knew it. The last four weeks had been difficult as Libby questioned herself and her abilities. Had she done something to displease her husband?

He hadn't said much since the day she'd asked him about his time across seas. Now, here she stood once again, in the same kitchen, with the same pile of groceries waiting to be put away. Only this time, Phillip had not followed her into the house. This time, he barely glanced her way as she fumbled with the grocery bags and the door knob.

She couldn't suppress her disappointment.

With the last of the food stuffs put away, the cabinet door closed with a thud. Libby leaned against the counter, thinking. What else could she do to please him? To show Phillip just how much she loved and needed him? What could she do to turn his head as she had five years ago?

So she did what any loving wife would do. She fixed some lightly sweetened coffee and served it to her husband. It's what Mother would have done when Daddy came home in one his moods.

"It's nippy out today. I thought you might like something warm to drink."

She purposely stood in front of him, obstructing his view of the house across the way, and held his mug out to him. It seemed to do the trick. He broke free of his fixation and stared up into her eyes.

Without a word, he took the mug and sipped from it. After setting the cup down on the side table next to him, he reached for her hand and pulled her onto his knee. But the gesture seemed flat.

"Thank you, darling." His chin stubble nuzzled her neck.

For a moment she closed her eyes and relished in it. The aroma of his cologne lifted just beneath her nose, causing her insides to melt.

She ached to ask him the questions on her heart, but she feared it would only upset him. So she sat for a quiet moment, enjoying the time spent on his lap, wrapped in his embrace with his face so near hers. Then she decided to plunge—finally ask him the burning question.

"Are you happy, Phillip?"

SEVENTEEN

L ike a lightning bolt striking him, Phillip's insides burned. He couldn't understand why, but Libby's sudden and accusing query annoyed him.

"Why, for heaven's sake, would you ask such nonsense?" He pulled back from Libby and she hopped from his lap to her feet.

"Y—you've just seemed so morose lately. You hardly speak to me, and you sit out here nearly all evening in the cold. What else am I to think?"

"A man has his reasons for the things he does. It's a woman's place to keep quiet on such matters."

His words were crisp and sharp. He knew it. But he couldn't stop them. Even so, why had she attempted to pry in the first place? She couldn't understand the thoughts running through his head, the things that weighed him down.

Aware of the heavy weight that lay in his right pocket, his hand came to rest against the outline of the letter. Only moments before had he pulled it from its concealed place and read its contents. He'd read it with his guard down. If Libby had seen him reading the missive, he wouldn't know what to do. He'd have to be more careful in the future.

Several stone silent moments passed between him and Libby. With his eyes downcast, purposely averted from hers, he caught sight of her black pumps turning and briskly retreating from him. A few steps had put her inside their home. The screen door banged shut, followed by the thud of the inner door.

His chest heaved and sighed.

She would just have to learn to understand. She would have to learn there were some places he could not allow her passage.

With that, Phillip pushed himself out of the wicker chair and tromped down the steps. With long, even strides, he made his way around the side of the house and entered the old dilapidated shed in the backyard. From there, he could close the door behind him, light the lantern, and think privately. From here, he could sit, without anyone else knowing he was inside, and hoard his privacy. From here, he could...

Phillip pulled the letter from his pocket.

From here, Phillip could continue to hide his secret.

❧❧

6 April 1946

Phillip's irritation was growing with each passing day. Libby was pressuring him about a family, Mother was mulling over him like he was some sort of war hero, and Maggie kept insisting he get a physical done after spending so much time in the mosquito-infested jungle. To make matters worse, Libby was questioning his happiness.

Of course he was happy. Happy to be home.

So why did he feel so melancholy? Like a member of his family had just passed on. Like he'd lost his best friend.

But...he *had* lost his best friend.

Although the rain was falling at a steady pace from the clouded sky, Phillip still sat in his white wicker chair staring at the brick house across the street. Libby, nor his parents, had ever mentioned the fact that the house they'd bought was situated directly across from the place he did half his growing up in—the Gregory's.

At first, he welcomed his boyhood recollections, reminiscing on the stories that old brick house retained. But then flashbacks tarnished the beautiful landscape, propelling billows of black smoke and explosive mines over the peak of the house, fogging Phillip's eyesight. Jack was somewhere in the chaos, lost in the lethal smokescreen.

Beads of sweat formed on Phillip's brow, and all at once, his hands pressed against both sides of his temples.

He needed to escape.

He needed to hide in his safe house.

In a huff, he lunged himself out of his chair and scurried down the porch steps into the falling rain. The small wood shed behind the house had proven to be his safe harbor. A place of peace and quiet where he could hide on a dirt floor, smell the same earthy aroma he'd grown accustomed to.

But halfway past the house, his eyes squeezed shut against the agonizing vista of morbid war visions, and he tried to force the violence from his mind, taking one deep breath after another. His legs, no longer able to carry the weight of his body, collapsed to the soggy ground. On his knees, Phillip squeezed his eyes shut. His body rocked back and forth, and a moan rumbled in his chest. Just a few more moments and the spell would pass.

Rain soaked into the fibers of his shirt and dripped from the locks of hair of that hung over his forehead, but he didn't care. He'd spent many a day and night walking through tropical rainfalls. This was nothing more than a sprinkle compared to it.

"Phillip? Phillip, what's wrong?"

The unexpected sound of Libby's voice immediately drowned out the lingering thoughts followed by the skittering of her heels down the porch steps and sloshing through the thawing ground.

She'd emerged from inside the house. Embarrassment flooded his cheeks when he realized how foolish he must look bent over, covering his head with his hands in the rain and mud.

Recovering from his *spell*, his eyelids lifted and he pressed his hands to the ground as if looking for something.

"Uh...I..." His lungs deflated. "Nothing. I'm fine. I dropped a nail, but I can't find it."

Finding his pride, he pushed up off the ground, not unaware of Libby's probing eye or the touch of her hand against his drenched elbow.

"Phillip, dear, are you sure everything's all right? Are you well? Did you faint—"

"No," he snapped. "I didn't *faint*. Men do not simply faint. Everything is fine. I noticed that there shutter was crooked, but..." He let his words hang in mid-air.

Libby glanced at the shutter quizzically, then back at him. "In the rain?"

He ignored her question as if she were daft. As he made his way back to the porch, his back rested against his wicker chair and he wiped his sweaty and soggy palms along his pant leg, trying to act as though nothing was amiss. But Libby regarded him with uncertainty.

To prove he was all right, he straightened his back and cleared his throat. "I was just thinking I might run into town for a few errands."

She stood with her arms crossed and her brows creased together. Droplets of rain dripped from the tendrils of hair that hung over her shoulder. She did look awfully cute in the rain, but the frown tugging her lips downward tugged at his heart. She was unhappy and disapproving.

"Darling, don't look at me like that." He pushed himself out off the seat and planted his feet in front of her, taking her arms in his hands.

"Have I upset you?"

"I'm just wondering why you spend so much time out here on the porch, in that chair. It's Saturday and raining, and I thought maybe you'd want to spend it with me."

It was Saturday already? Somehow that small detail seemed to slip his mind. A lot of things seemed to slip his mind recently.

Libby went on. "Not to mention the fact that you nearly passed out in the front yard."

"I didn't pass out or nearly faint," he said through clenched teeth. "I'm sorry, darling. I didn't realize how quickly time got away from me. Will you be all right if I went into town for a few hours? I promise I'll make it up to you. We'll have dinner in the city, or we'll spend the day in the park, or I'll take you to see a picture next week."

Her arms crossed over her chest and her eyes averted his as she stared down at his shoes in contemplation.

"Well, there is that new Bob Hope movie. The one with Bing Crosby called *Road to Utopia*. It just released at the theater and I would like to see it."

In one swoop, Phillip stepped toward her and gave her shoulders a loving squeeze.

"Then we'll do it. It's a date, huh, sweetheart?"

Her chocolate eyes peered up at him with such innocence and trust. "It's a date, Phillip. Don't be late."

EIGHTTEEN

Dear Sergeant Johnson,

Your sweet Paloma is adjusting well and growing stronger with each passing day. The money you sent for her care is appreciated and is being put to good use.

I had the chance to read Paloma your missive and it was ever so good for her soul. She keeps asking for her "Pip" and wants to know when he will come for her again.

She's quite smitten with you, Sergeant Johnson, and looks forward to the day when the two of you will be reunited of which I am working tirelessly on.

Phillip swallowed back the lump in his throat. Although it was the letter he was waiting for, it was also something that he wished he was rid of. Hiding this very situation from Libby not only placed an enormous amount of guilt on his mind, but it taxed his body and his heart.

He wanted to do more. He wanted to make everything right again. But his hands were tied. The country was only just healing from a financial depression and a costly war. No amount of money he could send would erase this circumstance from his soul.

Hearing the post office door bell jingle, Phillip quickly put away the letter and finished addressing his reply envelope. Once more, he placed ten dollars in the envelope, hoping the amount would cover another month's care for Paloma.

Glancing around at his surroundings from the corner of his eye, Phillip sealed the envelope and stood his turn in line to wait for the postmaster. As he did, he scanned the room. Not one soul in this room was familiar to him. It was for the better. He didn't need attention from one of the town's busybodies inquiring of his business. That was one advantage of coming home to a new town.

The postmaster looked up and gestured to Phillip as a suited customer in front of him left the counter. With a tip of the businessman's fedora, Phillip returned the favor then placed his envelope within the postmaster's reach.

"Just one stamp, for this one."

"Sure thing, sir." The clerk licked a clean stamp and placed it on the envelope.

Once again, Phillip was glad to rid his pocket of another letter.

He paid his bill and grabbed his bowler. "Thank you and good day, sir."

Main Street bustled with afternoon traffic as dinner time neared. Men and women walked briskly down the sidewalks—the men dressed in their slacks and suit coats, the women dressed in their suit jackets. Occasionally, female factory workers from the town's brewery passed by, wearing slacks or coveralls as the final weekend shift ended. It still seemed a strange sight to him, women in pants. He was used to it on the battlefield, but in town? It seemed unconventional. Aside from workers and shoppers, children skipped, ran, or trotted their way down the sidewalks. Not a care in the world. If only life were that simple again.

In his mind, Phillip tried taking it all in. Life just didn't seem normal, or real, or same at all. Too many things had changed. *He* had changed. The war, with its bloodshed, its surprises, its sucker punches—it had left permanent scars against his skin. Each one a stark reminder of the man he now was. And then there was Paloma…

Honk! Honk!

A deep-throated horn blared in his ear, startling him as he walked.

"Hey there, Johnson! We're headin' down to Oscar's for our afternoon *tea*. Care to join us?"

It was Peter Glowaski, his co-worker, and several of the fellas from the job site. It didn't take a genius to figure out what kind of *tea* Pete was referring to. Phillip glanced around and stepped toward Pete's parked and beat-up pick-up.

"Hiya, fellas." Phillip leaned his palms against the door window's frame. "Oscar's, you say?"

"Yeah. Y'know…" Pete made a swigging motion with his right hand. "Downin' one before goin' home to the missus. Saw you out walkin' and thought you'd like join us."

The offer was tempting. Incredibly tempting. What a week he'd had. It'd been so long since he sipped long and hard on a draft. After the great measures he took to send another message out to Paloma, he sure could use something to relieve his tension about now.

Visions of Libby filtrated his mind. He'd left her all alone at the house—something else he wasn't all too proud of. Why did he keep messing up? Making those same mistakes over and over again.

"So whaddya say, Johnson? Meetin' us down there or are y'all dried up?"

Phillip's fingers curled tightly around the window's frame then his fist knocked against the pick-up's hood with a hollow thud. "All right, fellas, I'll meet you there."

∽ᢙᢛ

Smoke hazed the small hole-in-the-ground pub and curled around Phillip's head as he removed his bowler. His eyes took a moment to adjust to the dim lighting before spotting Pete and the fellas at the bar. The bartender took their drink orders as he wiped down a fresh shot glass with his bar towel.

"What'll it be, fella?" The bartender casually leaned his hands across the bar counter.

"Make it Cream of Kentucky, bourbon."

"Right up!" The bartender crossed the aisle behind the counter and Phillip leaned into it.

Pete's eyes cross-examined him and he sensed it. "Hittin' it a little hard this afternoon, eh, pal? I didn't think you had it in ya."

Phillip's glass slid down in front of him and he took the shot, never wincing back its bitter taste.

"I'm sure there are a lot of things you don't know about me."

Another gentleman took the stool beside Phillip and dipped his chin in acknowledgement, to which Phillip returned. Then he twisted his glass in his fingers and signaled to the bartender for another round.

"Geez, man, you don't fool around, do ya?" Pete downed the rest of his alcohol.

"Three months training. Six months travelling. Three years fighting to stay alive and killing everyone else who jeopardized it. You tell me who's foolin' around."

From the corner of his eye, Phillip caught Pete's raised glass as he mumbled, "Here, here," and downed his next glass of whiskey.

Phillip swallowed his second shot and waited for the ache to subside. For the pain to decrease. For the memories to fade.

Sometimes they had to get worse before they got better. Sometimes the memories rushed back like a movie reel, ticking across his mind's eye, replaying every painstaking moment spent on those islands. And Paloma…

Sweet Paloma. He hadn't meant to encounter her. It had only been a mistake to stumble upon that hideout. But when he did, he knew he couldn't leave her there alone. Someone had to look after her. She had clung onto him ever so tightly. He knew she looked at him as her hero, but he didn't feel like a hero in the least. He only felt like a barbarian stained in the blood of all those he'd killed, confirming the horrible atrocities he was accused of doing by the enemy. Somehow, she'd seen through all that. Through large, scared, black eyes, she looked up at him, held out her hand and trusted him.

Truth of the matter was it terrified him. Everything he knew that was pure, gentle, kind, and right with the world suddenly was not. There were murderous kings with no regard for their own people. There were poor folk driven to suicide because of the fear instilled in them by their lords and rulers. At the epicenter of all those lies, all the deceit, and all the violence, *he*, Phillip Johnson, was the monster.

But not to Paloma.

A stinging slap to the back brought Phillip back to the present. Back to the room tainted with alcohol and stale cigarette smoke. Back to the fellas who caroused beside him.

"Heya, here's to the war—" With a wobbly hand, Pete raised his glass high into the air as his body swayed slightly to the right, bumping into Phillip. "And to Sarge here, Phil Johnson—for finishing off those cowardly barbarians and living to tell about it."

Cheers went out and alcohol splashed onto the counter. The bottoms of shot glasses tossed into the air and Phillip downed his third gulp of memories. Finally, he would find some respite.

❧ ❧

Eyes watery and glassy made it difficult for Phillip to focus on anything that stood in front of him.

Stopping at the doorway of *Oscar's*, he made a sorry attempt to place his hat on his head. He didn't care how it looked. Right now, he hadn't a care in the world…just like those children he watched earlier today in town. Nothing seemed to matter in his mind since his thoughts couldn't focus on any one thing anyhow.

His muscles were too relaxed to carry him to his motor car, so he just leaned a shoulder in the doorway of the social joint and watched as the town passed him by…two by two.

He rolled his eyes closed and his fingers attempted to rub out the double visions, but it was to no avail. He needed to get home, to his bed. He turned his gaze upward to the darkening sky then stumbled a bit when he lost his balance. Digging for his keys from his pocket, he staggered down the sidewalk toward the place where he remembered parking his vehicle.

He nearly bumped into a dark-suited man as he swayed to his left.

"Pardon me, s-sir," he managed to say.

The man regarded him, then his face lit up. "Say, Phillip Johnson, ol' buddy! Fancy running into you—literally!"

Phillip's thoughts jarred and he took a closer look at the fella who stood in front of him. He squinted in confusion.

"Harvey? Harvey Duncan! Arbor Springs High. Put 'er there, ol' friend." Harvey reached out for his right hand.

For the moment, the fog cleared from Phillip's mind and his memory returned. "Why, it's my old pal, Harvey." He met Harvey's handshake.

"Yes, I believe I just established that," Harvey joked. "How've you been all these years? I hope time has treated you well."

"I've s-seen better days." Phillip worked to keep the slur out of his speech.

Harvey's squinted eye glanced up at the sign from where Phillip just exited. Then his gaze grew serious.

"I see that, Phil." He took a moment's pause. "Say, why don't I take you home for a cup of black coffee. You can meet the missus."

"You got yourself hitched?"

Harvey took Phillip by the arm and led him down the sidewalk to his car. "Of course. You remember Sydney White? Well, she's Sydney Duncan now."

During the car ride, Harvey kept the conversation light. But all the while, Phillip asked himself over how he ended up from *Oscar's* to Harvey's car, to the Duncan home. Phillip had been so compliant that he couldn't understand how he allowed one thing to lead to the next. Now he stood in Harvey's foyer, his hat in his hands, waiting to meet Harvey's wife.

"Phil, I want you to say hello to the new Mrs. Duncan. Sydney, you may remember Phil Johnson, from high school?"

A short woman, with dashing blue eyes and with chocolate locks pulled back in bobby pins, welcomed him into her home with a heart-warming smile.

"Why, yes, I do remember Phillip. How could I forget? You two were always giving poor Mister Thompson a hard time of it in school." She reached out a hand to Phillip. "How are you, Phil? It seems it's been forever."

Tiny droplets of sweat beaded at Phillip's hairline. He hadn't expected to bump into an old high school friend, and he certainly hadn't expected to land in the middle of his friend's living room, ossified, and meeting the fella's wife. Why had he made the choices he had? Why couldn't he be a better man than that?

But he had to make good of the situation. He dipped his chin in regard to Sydney. "Pleasure meeting you again, Mrs. Duncan." His mouth just didn't want to work right. He tried with his best effort to cover up the fact that alcohol was in his system, messing with his head.

"Oh, please, Sydney's the name. I'm not an old woman yet. Our schooling years weren't all that long ago." She laughed as she jested.

Harvey interjected, and not a moment too soon. "Sydney, uh, Phil and I are going to catch up a mite in the kitchen over a cup or two of coffee." He glanced back at Phillip. "Maybe three."

"Oh, I see. I'll get a fresh pot brewing right away and leave you two to talk."

"Wonderful. Thank you, dear." Harvey pressed a kiss to her cheek then Sydney busied herself in the kitchen with preparations.

Phillip followed Harvey into the quaint farmhouse kitchen where two cups of steaming hot coffee sat on the table for four. Sydney set a tray of creamer and sugar between the two men and Phillip and Harvey both thanked her for it.

"You boys enjoy yourselves. Harvey, honey, I just finished baths with the children so they'll be sayin' their prayers and heading off to bed."

With that, Sydney left the room and Phillip found himself seated across from his old friend.

Like most men his age, Harvey sat in the comfortable silence of his home, sipping on black coffee while a folded newspaper sat at his right side. Harvey pushed the creamer and sugar away from Phillip.

"I don't think we'll be needing these tonight."

Harvey's pause seemed painfully long but Phillip knew he wasn't through talking. To prevent the questions Phillip was hoping wouldn't be asked, he took charge of the conversation.

"I'm, uh, surprised to see you're still in this town. I thought you had bigger, better plans." Phillip took a long swig of his coffee, wincing back its bitter bite.

"I thought so, too, until the war happened. Seems life got put on hold not just for me, but for many of the fellas around here."

"You enlist?" Phillip asked bluntly.

"I did." Harvey held his cup to his lips, keeping his eyes averted as he answered. "Married Sydney just before shipping off. Came home once on pass then I was off again across the Big Blue."

"So you're a Navy man." It was a statement, not a question posed by Phillip.

Harvey touched the tip of his finger to his nose then pointed toward Phillip. "Hot dog," Harvey answered. "And you?"

"Marines. Second Marine Division. Saipan and Tinian."

"Saipan. Tinian…Nope, never heard of them."

"You and most others. Unless you've been there…It's a far cry from civilization." Phillip's head dipped and he let his fingers tap against his mug in an effort to rally back those terrible memories threatening to invade his mind. A change in subject was needed. "What are you doing now that the war's ended?"

Harvey playfully lifted his left leg into the air, revealing shiny, new loafers.

That Harv—always the goof to make one guess.

"Shoe sales?"

"That, I am."

"Shoe sales, eh? You're a better man than I. Are you the travelling type?"

"That all depends on sales. When that dries up in one place, then I'm off to another. You know, a man's gotta provide for the wife and kids. Whatever pays the bills. It's not one's dream occupation, I know, but that's where I'm called for the time being. What about you? So, you got yourself a girl? A wife? Kids, no kids?"

"Got myself a wife. You remember Libby?"

"Yeah, sure. Sweet Libby Taylor. I remember."

"No kids. Otherwise, I might be in your shoes." Phillip's brows furrowed and he glanced back at Harvey. "Sorry. Didn't mean to…well, shoes and *shoes*."

"No offense taken. In my line of work, you learn to take those jabs with ease."

The air went silent between them for several moments.

"So, no kids. Must've either just got yourself hitched or just returned from the front lines."

"Say, I forgot how nosey you were." Phillip winced when he glanced up from his coffee cup and placed a hand to his temple.

"What are you doing, Phil?"

For the first time, Phillip really regarded the man sitting across from him. Dressed in a fine, dark suit, clean shaven, and with a fine pointed chin, Harvey Duncan certainly seemed the shoe salesman type. Of course, he'd come a long way since his boyhood days of slacks and striped tee-shirts and practical jokes. Today they sat across from each other as grown men. Men who'd prematurely seen the full circle of life itself.

Phillip shifted in his seat, and took a deep breath. "That all depends on what you mean. Right now I'm sitting with someone who I honestly didn't think I'd see again, talking about things I hadn't planned on talking about. And I'm sitting in the very town I hadn't planned on returning to—and that's right here." He drove his forefinger onto the table, accentuating his words.

"C'mon, Phil. That's not what I meant and you know it. You've got yourself a wife sitting at home and you're here in my kitchen drunk as a skunk."

"I didn't ask to be sitting here, Harv. I don't even know how I ended up right here at the moment."

"Which is why I came to your aid. I couldn't let you go home to Libby like this. Boy, you probably couldn't have even found your way home."

Phillip knew his bluff was called. Letting a sigh escape his mouth, he leaned into the table, placing his head into his palms. "Then why'd you go through all this trouble if you knew?"

Harvey lowered his voice. "Because you were my friend. And if there was any chance you had a wife and kids at home, I didn't want your reputation compromised. This isn't you, Phil. At least not the Phil Johnson I grew up knowing. What happened?"

"You said it yourself, Harv. The war happened. It changed you. It changed me. It changed all of us."

Harvey sat quiet for several moments and Phillip wondered where their conversation was headed next...if there was even any more to it. But Harv just sat patiently, staring down into his coffee mug. Then his hand slid to the folded newspaper and he reached under it, pulling a small, black book from underneath.

"You're right about the war changing us, Phil. But what I disagree with you on is that it changed all of us for the worse."

Phillip's head jerked up. What could Harvey possibly mean by that? Was the guy off his rocker?

Harvey pushed the small, black book toward the center of the table.

"It changed me for the better, Phil."

NINETEEN

Dark, black lines stained Libby's face as she picked herself up off her bed and carried her broken heart into the bathroom. Her eyes, red and swollen, revealed the pain she'd suffered.

Why? She asked herself over and over again. Why should she feel this way?

Her eyes lifted to her reflection in the mirror. "What have I done?" The woman staring back at her didn't have an answer. "All I wanted was my husband back. Now that he's here, I still don't have him."

Loneliness engulfed her soul. A pain that she'd never encountered thrust its ugly stinger through the center of her chest. Things hadn't been the same since Phillip's homecoming. *Phillip* hadn't been the same. His moods were odd. His lack of communication was so unlike him. And he was further from her than he'd ever been. Why, at times it was as if he was closer when he served across the Pacific Ocean.

Libby had kept his stack of letters from the last four years. She kept them hidden in a hat box tucked securely and secretly beneath their bed. Whenever she felt the need to hold onto Phillip, she'd pull the hatbox from its place and read through his letters, one by one. It was the closest thing she had to holding him in her arms. Many tears stained the parchments, but they were all out of love. Today, however, those tears were salted with an ache so deep, she couldn't put her pain into words. If she could, she would have found the courage to confront Phillip about her feelings.

Stumbling shoes bumped from downstairs.

Libby quickly brushed away her tears, patted down her face with a hanky, and pinched her cheeks. Another stumble sparked curiosity. If that was Phillip, she wondered why he bumped around so.

Sniffing back her tears, Libby walked down the hall toward the stairs and spotted Phillip's feet kicking off his shoes.

"Phillip?" she called down to him.

"Libby?" His head swiveled around to meet her gaze. "You're still awake?" He stood to his feet as she confronted him.

She came to a halt a few steps from where he stood at the foot of the staircase. She stood there watching, waiting, wondering if he was still angry with her.

"Where have you been?" Her voice quivered only slightly as she posed her question. She hoped she was prepared for his answer.

His eyes held remorse as his gaze rested on her. He looked her up and down briefly as if he hesitated giving up his reply. Finally, he found his words.

"I—I'm sorry, Libby. I don't know what came over me. I got angry for no reason and took it out on you. I'm sorry."

She noticed only the slight drag of his *L*s, but dismissed the perception when he held out his arms inviting her into the warmth of his embrace.

"Ohh, Phillip," she drug out the sentence as she stepped into his hold. Her head fell against his chest and she inhaled deeply the scent of his cologne, but her eyes popped open when the spice of something mixed with his aftershave wafted to her nose.

A sickening lump roiled her stomach.

He couldn't be...

Dread stabbed at her heart.

It was one thing to expect it from her father, but from her husband? A man good to his word and gentle in manner? Never in all her life would she have imagined her strong-hearted husband to stumble into their living room punch drunk.

Disbelief froze her body to the floor and clamped her tongue.

Phillip's strong arms wrapped around her small frame. He nuzzled her neck and pressed kisses against her jawline. The stench emanating from his breath turned her nose, but she bit her tongue and tried to close out the sickening aroma. She'd done it many times before, as had her mother.

She was speechless. Dumbfounded. In so many ways, he didn't seem real. Yet it was all too real. All too familiar. She'd married Phillip to run far away from a lifestyle of alcohol and everything that came with it. And somehow it had chased her down, engulfing Phillip in its bitter pool as it came for her.

Quiet tears rolled down her face and she stood cold as a statue. Phillip pulled back, then took her chin in his hand as he pressed his lips against hers. For the first time since his homecoming, his kiss was gentle, pure, and held every emotion she longed to receive from him.

She didn't want to let it go. But in the back of her mind, she knew it wasn't coming from his heart. It was the alcohol that she tasted in his kiss—that was behind the passion of his affection.

Despite her resentment toward liquor, and of no control of her own, her arms encircled his neck, locking her fingers so as not to let him go. Libby allowed herself to fall into his embrace. She'd been starved of his love for so long, that it no longer mattered what type of package it came in. He may be ossified and probably wouldn't remember this moment come tomorrow, but she would cherish each intimate minute she could share with him.

❦

A gentle breeze tapped at the window pane. Across the darkened room, the shadowed fingers of the maple trees' branches swayed against the wall. Dull moonlight slanted through the window as its crescent waned. It was just enough to send blue rays through the branches of the trees, creating shadowy dancing figures in their room.

Libby ran a hand over Phillip's chest, her round, coffee eyes staring lovingly up at him. His warm palm covered her fingers, and he returned her glance. She could just make out the lines of his half smile, but his eyes stood out from the glassy haze that covered them.

"I've missed you so much." Her voice rang softly in the darkness, just above a whisper.

"You don't deserve a man like me, Libby, but I do love you."

Libby considered him. His voice was gentle, his words, kind. His tone, sincere. But again, this wasn't the man who came home to her just weeks before. It was the first time he'd been this affectionate toward her since his homecoming, which reminded her of his current mental state.

She'd ignored the smell of alcohol. She overlooked his slurred speech. She didn't let on that she knew. Instead, she relished in the moment and took advantage of the situation. Now, he was ready to talk. So now, she would communicate her feelings…

"Don't tell me that I don't deserve you, Phillip. Let me be the judge of that. It's foolish to say such things."

"It's true, darling. I've done some terrible things—"

She plugged his lips with her finger. "Shh…no more talk of this. Let's talk about now, Phillip. About our future. I want to move past the war and everything that goes along with it. I want to return to life with you—just me and you. And I want to talk about adding children to that life. Starting our own family, our own traditions."

"I wouldn't be a good father, Libby. I'm barely a good enough husband to you."

"That's something we can work through together, Phillip. One day it's bound to happen and we'll have to make that walk together. I'm ready for that."

"I...can't."

Libby's hopes dashed like a flame snuffed out by a cool breeze. "Darling, what do you mean?"

TWENTY

9 April 1946

Thousands of possibilities rushed through Maggie's mind as she raced out the post office's doors. Her pounding heart seemed to send Morse Codes from her chest to her brain, each one sending separate signals. What rested in her hands would be a defining moment. So many questions would be answered. Or perhaps the letter that she pinched between her fingers would open up a swell of new questions. Maybe heartache? Above all, hopefully, joyous news.

Each afternoon for the last two weeks, Maggie had faithfully come to the post office hoping to find Walt's letter waiting for her. Finally, it had come. However, now wasn't the time to read it.

Maggie glanced both up and down Main Street as she prepared to cross the street. Baby sprigs of green tinted bare tree branches that arched across the double lane roadway, lining both the street and the sidewalk. In just a few short weeks, those naked branches would be blossoming with beautiful pinks and foliage. Once again, winter had come to an end. The promise of new life and sunnier days were approaching. For this town, and for so many others, the healing process would continue.

It seemed strange at times. Standing in the here and now, looking back on the war. It seemed that service on the front lines was a lifetime ago. Or a vivid story told in a book. There were instances Maggie found it hard to fathom that she had served on the front, dodged bullets, witnessed terror in full color, stared death in the eye as the hospital she stood in was bombed from above, and lived to tell about it. It was strange to think that it all had happened just a little over a year ago. Especially when she stood in the middle of her quaint little town, watching people go about their everyday business like nothing had happened at all. Suddenly, Germany and all the little towns and villages she'd visited seemed so far away.

A motorcar's horn blared in her ear and Maggie jumped.

For Pete's sake! She'd stopped in the middle of the road as she reminisced!

Embarrassed, she skittered to the sidewalk.

"C'mon, lady!" the car's driver hollered from his window.

"Sorry!" She shook her head. "Sure, Maggie," she said to herself. "Live through bullets and bombs only to get yourself killed by a motorist. Way to go."

Finally, she happened upon the familiar spot she often frequented with Grace. The small café, nestled between the hardware shop and the bank Luke worked in, was always warm and ever so inviting. Maggie missed the days of walking up Main Street with Grace just to sit and drink a cup of tea or coffee from inside the café's walls. A few evenings after her shift at the hospital and Grace's shift at the Ladies of Liberty Aide Society, this was the place to sit and unwind from a long day's work.

Maggie entered the café's doorway and immediately inhaled.

Ah...that wonderful aroma of baked bread mixed with coffee and warm sandwiches warmed her soul. Removing her gloves, she found a seat at one of the booths facing the street and set herself down. After the waitress took her order for hot tea and a slice of jellied toast, Maggie glanced around. Reminders of days past appeared before her eyes. She remembered when enlisted men home on leave would filter through the doors and glance her way. How flirtatious she had been in those days. But not anymore. These days her thoughts and her heart were continually on her new husband, Danny.

How thankful she was for him. Every day she awoke to thank God for the man she almost lost for good. A man who loved her without reservations despite the rocky turf they stood on just one year ago. He was a man who deserved everything she had to give him. And if she could—if *God* allowed—she hoped to give him one precious gift this year.

Her tea and plate of toast spread with jelly was placed before her. She thanked the waitress, whispered a prayer of blessing over her food then sipped her tea as she pulled Walt's letter from her clutch. Once more her heart picked up in rhythm as she considered what its contents might be. Inhaling deeply, Maggie pried the envelope's lip open and pulled Walt's words from inside...

Dear Maggie,

Your letter arrived in yesterday's post, and I might add we were quite surprised to hear from you so soon after your wedding. However, as always, it's good to hear from you.

Peggy and I are doing well. We arrived stateside two months ago for an overdue honeymoon. Both of us continue to serve with the Army, Peggy with the hospital, of course. I, however, put in for a promotion. Something to put Peggy's mind at ease for the time being that would keep me from the front lines. Those few months at the front were the most terrifying of my life. After Peggy and I wed, I saw that same look of fear and dread in her eyes. Knowing what she's had to endure in the past, I decided it wasn't fair of me to put her heart in that kind of danger again. You can imagine the elation on her face when I told her I put in for a promotion that would keep both of us stateside permanently.

That brings me to your request. For the time being, I have returned to communications, but for how long, I am unsure as I wait for the approval of my request. I cannot promise you anything as of right now, but as I've done in the past, I will do my best to help you. Please know that some Missing in Action persons are not traceable and that may interfere with any possibility of finding the gentleman you speak of. But I promise you, if my search turns up anything, I will wire you immediately.

My best to you and Danny. May you be blessed with love and laughter.

My Regards,
Walt

That Walt. Always so sweet and kind.

Maggie weakly smiled as she slipped the letter back into its envelope. The answers she hoped for weren't written in ink, but the promise of Walt's help was.

It may take more time than she thought to track down Abe's whereabouts, but no matter how long it took, Maggie was determined to find out.

The bell in the café jingled. Maggie hardly noticed until a shadow darkened her table.

"Is this where you womenfolk hide out during the day while we menfolk bring home the bread and butter?"

Maggie looked up, a smile spreading across her face as she

recognized that voice.

"Hello, Luke! And whether we womenfolk hide out here all day or not is nothing to worry yourself over. Especially, since you are also here most likely doing the same thing as I." Maggie winked.

Luke held up his palm. "All right. I call a truce. I won't tell if you won't tell."

Maggie giggled and sipped her tea. "How are you doing, Luke?"

"I think I've gone from shooting bullets to sweating them."

Maggie knew Luke's concern over Grace's impending delivery weighed heavily on his mind.

"Aw, don't fret over the baby coming. It's a very natural thing. Women have babies all the time. Everything will be just fine."

"That's what my aunt keeps telling me."

"That Mrs. Sullivan—she's a smart woman. And one who knows."

"She keeps pretty close tabs on Grace. Calls the house at least once a day now."

"And a fine nanny she'll be when that little gal or fella arrives. You just wait and see. You and Grace will be in good hands. And besides, Danny and I are not too far away. If you need anything, you know my door is always open."

"Appreciate it, Maggie. Well, I best be getting on. Lunch break is only so long."

"Bye, Luke."

Maggie watched as Luke made his way to the counter. Even he had changed so much since the night Grace met him. Not just the physical, but the emotional changes as well. Grace said he worried about his handicap and how it would affect their children.

As Maggie observed Luke place his order, she took notice of the things she'd taken for granted. Like how he paid for his meal. He kept his money in the pocket closest to his good arm. As he flipped through his bills, one of the greenbacks fell onto the floor. It was just one of the difficulties Luke had to face being one-armed.

Maggie felt for him. She didn't run to his aid. She dare not humiliate the poor guy, but she wanted to tell him to get fitted for that prosthesis. That it would make his life so much easier as a wounded veteran of war.

But that wasn't her place. That was something he and Grace would need to talk over and decide together.

From the outside looking in, Maggie wished she could swoop in and make everything better for Luke. His close friendship with Danny had been a saving grace for them both. It was the least she could do to put their minds at ease. But again, it wouldn't be right of her to place her nose in her best friend's life and business. She could only pray and hope for the best.

TWENTY-ONE

Arbor Springs Movie Theatre
12 April 1946

In the midst of street lights, neon signs, and strolling couples, the spring, starlit night resembled those of when Libby and Phillip had gone steady.

As Libby looked ahead up Main Street's lighted way, with its quaint little townhomes and shops nestled along the street side, she drew a little closer to Phillip's side. How glad she was that he kept his promise to take her out to the showing of *Road to Utopia,* starring Bing Crosby and Bob Hope.

Although the atmosphere still held a slight chill in the air around them, Libby's insides were warm. Her smile hadn't faded from her face since they left the house nearly a half hour ago.

Phillip held her hand like they were dating again, squeezing her palm gently and stealing glances from the corners of his eyes. His childlike smile gave away his impish and playful mood that put butterflies in the pit of her stomach.

His attention focused solely on her. He was happy. *She* was happy. Somewhere in the last twenty-four hours, a bridge had formed over the gap she felt between them. She hoped—no, she'd prayed—that the good Lord would work a miracle and bring her husband out of his melancholy and back to her.

The flowers sitting on her nightstand when she awoke this morning was a startling inclination that her prayers were being answered.

Even as the morning faded into the dusk of night, Phillip's familiar gentleness made known the fact that he still possessed some part of his former self. His soft touch and longing gaze proved that he still loved her as much as he once did, and he still desired her in every way.

The sentiment moved her emotions and gave her a sense of safety.

Even now as she stood in front of the theater surrounded by a hundred strangers.

At least until a light tap on her shoulder startled her.

Together, Phillip and Libby turned, coming face to face with Maggie and Danny.

Bouncing on her heels and wearing a broad smile, Maggie greeted them.

"Just the couple we were looking for! Hiya, kids."

"Maggie, Danny. You two were able to make it after all," Libby said with surprise tingeing her voice.

Phillip shot her a sharp glance.

"Turns out the hospital didn't need me tonight, and boy am I glad. A night at the movies sounds grand!" Maggie's knees bounced again as she clung to Danny's arm. And Danny, as easy-going as he was, just stared at Phillip and Libby with a knowing smile plastered to his face.

"She's been like this all evening." Danny put his hand out to Phillip and the two shook. "As soon as Libby called with the invitation, she's been bubbling with this—" Danny made a crazy waving motion with his hands in mid-air to make up for his loss of words.

Maggie and Libby giggled at his gesture, but Phillip, however, remained unusually quiet.

Libby glanced up at him mentally asking if he was all right.

His head lowered and he whispered, "Libby, I thought this night was for the two of us?"

Unease pinched her chest and her confidence faltered. "Well, Phillip, I—I just thought it would be nice if your sister and Danny joined us. You know, like we used to do at the soda fountain during high school."

She glanced up at Maggie whose smile had faded and was replaced with confusion.

"Phillip," Maggie began. "If we're intruding…"

He held up his palm to cut off her words. "You're not intruding, Maggie. I just didn't realize my wife had made other plans."

Moisture stuck to the insides of Libby's palms as tension hung thick between them. Why had she gone and run her mouth to Maggie anyway? She should have kept tonight's date between herself and Phillip. Embarrassment flushed her cheeks.

"I-I'm sorry, Maggie. Phillip, I don't know what I was thinking."

Before anyone else could reply, two more cheerful voices sauntered up to them.

"Hey there, Danny-boy!" Luke's strong hand jostled Danny's

shoulders.

Surprise mounted in Libby's eyes as she wasn't expecting Grace and Luke to show up on the same night at the theater, especially now that Grace was so far along in her pregnancy.

"Luke! Glad you could make it, buddy," Danny answered.

Phillip's eyes darkened as he glanced down at Libby and growled.

"You invited the Bradys too? Why would you do such a thing? You know how I feel about—"

"Phillip—" Libby was shaking her head—"No, I didn't. Maggie must've—"

"Yes, Phillip, *I* invited them," Maggie hissed. She took Phillip by the arm and side-stepped their small group. "I didn't realize this wasn't an open invitation or I'd have never agreed to it. And I certainly didn't think there was any harm in inviting the Bradys."

Libby had to intercede. This was her doing and she wouldn't allow her mistake to cause bitterness and bickering.

"This whole thing is my fault, Phillip. Maggie, I'm sorry to have ruined the evening for everyone. Phillip, I thought it would be fun to get the gang together and have a good time tonight."

"Which is something I'm really not all that worried about, Libby. Especially sitting alongside *them*." He jerked his head in Grace and Luke's direction. Both Maggie and Libby followed his gesture, and both girls looked at each other, speechless.

For only a moment, Libby hesitated. She was afraid to press him, but what was done was already done.

"Well I can't very well go and un-invite them now, can I? What have you against Luke Brady anyhow?"

"Plenty."

"You're just being fickle now, Phillip."

"Yeah, Phillip. What's the big idea? What has Luke Brady ever done to you?"

⮜⮞

Phillip

Between the ache in his head and Libby's challenge of his character, anger ignited in his chest. Once more, she'd managed to dig deep under his skin and go against his wishes.

"What has he done, Maggie?" His voice rose with sarcasm. "How can everyone here expect me to accept every change made in this stagnant town? Do you realize the last time I stepped foot in Arbor Springs was the day Jack was laid to rest? And don't you remember how broken Grace was that day? She couldn't even look me in the eye, yet today, here she stands all smiles and happy as if Jack never existed. That's what I have against Luke Brady." His hands flew through the air and dropped at his sides in pure frustration.

As his eyes rolled of their own control, then they rested on the stunned faces of five people. His chest heaved up and down as he stood there on the sidewalk. Raking a broad hand through his dark hair, he puffed.

The secret was out.

In his angst, everyone standing in front of him had heard every word of his outburst.

The sheen in Grace's eyes tore at his heart.

"Grace..." His voice came out cracked.

But Grace quietly turned her back on him and Luke followed, his expression just as confused and somber as the rest of them.

Phillip looked to Maggie, whose lip quivered. But not out of hurt—out of anger.

"Maggie," he tried.

Sharply, she held up her hand and cut him off. "Don't." With that, she turned and ran down the sidewalk after Grace and Luke.

"Come on, man." Danny was next to condemn him. With his arms spread wide in question, he backed down the sidewalk. "Whatever your problem is with Luke, get over it." Then Danny rushed off with the others.

With his hands resting on his sides, Phillip hung his head and sighed deeply. He dared not look at Libby. He already sensed her anger reaching out to strangle him.

But quietly, Libby spoke in her soft voice. "I suppose I shouldn't have expected you to keep your word. Would it have been that hard, Phillip? Just a movie sitting next to the people who love us most?"

When put like that, it sounded even more pitiful.

He'd done it again. He'd messed up. He'd broken another promise. He'd disappointed Libby for the umpteenth time and now he'd alienated his own family and Jack's old fiancée. What kind of a heel was he anyhow?

Libby rushed away from him, her heels driving into the sidewalk with enough force to stamp its imprint into the cement.

If he was ever going to make amends for his actions, he had to go after her.

The car ride home was dark and lonely. Libby may have sat only a foot away, but her soul was as far away as the sun. Upon returning home, she never waited for him to get her car door. Instead, she bolted from their motor car and scurried into the house, tromping up the stairs and finally closing herself in the privacy of their bedroom.

From his spot on the porch, he sank lower, deeper into his despair and retreated to his workshop in the backyard to lock himself further away from the world.

❧❧

10 April 1946

Dark eyes glared back at him from the looking glass. He saw a man so different from the person he used to be. Only a mere second did he pause and look deeper at the person staring back at him, then dropped his gaze to the black and white photo of himself and Libby on their wedding day.

The face of a man so young and innocent looked entirely different than the façade of who he'd become. Looking at those young faces in the photograph, he saw youth and happiness. It was a direct opposite of the life they now lived.

Feelings of regret and remorse moved his insides, but along with those sentiments came a sense of fear…a sense of caring.

He'd stopped caring long ago. He's stopped *loving* long ago. Once his care led to love, then love evolved into fear, into pain. It had happened to him twice. He couldn't stand for it to destroy him all over again.

…or at least to destroy what was left of him.

"Phillip?"

Libby entered the room. Quietly, cautiously, she stepped around him…as she had the whole day.

He couldn't understand why, but his body tensed under her presence. His shoulders grew straight and square. He waited for her to turn and walk away, but she didn't. Instead, she stood off to his side, staring at him. At first, he tried to ignore the fact that she stood over his shoulder, but the longer she waited, the more uncomfortable he became.

"Can I help you with something?" he asked in his rigid tone.

Through the mirror, he captured her round, brown eyes. For the first time in a long while, he really *looked* at them. So large. So round. So cute were they. In fact, she did look awfully grand in her blue gingham, sailor-style dress with the scooped neckline. It sure did bring out the lovely shape of her torso, the length of her neck. And its capped sleeves accentuated her shoulders perfectly. She looked stunning.

"What is it, Phillip? Why are you looking at me that way?"

He half blinked back his admiration as he shook out of his awe of her. "It's just…" His hands reached out for her waist. As he did, her eyes cowered back in unease, and he knew he'd created that in her. "You look so beautiful today."

And he meant it.

All his anger, all his irrational thinking melted away as he gazed longingly into her eyes. He hoped she saw that, and he hoped she would forgive him.

Her eyes blinked back in confusion and surprise.

Her hand smoothed down her dress as if suddenly self-conscious. "I-I do?"

"Yes. I'm sorry I hadn't noticed until now."

"What's with you lately?"

Her tone shifted in an unpleasant manner. What had he said to make her cross?

He shook his head in misunderstanding.

"One minute you're cold as ice, then the next, you're making all over me like some love-sick puppy dog. I never know what I'm walking into, Phillip. Don't try to smooth talk me. I watched my mother fall for Daddy's shallow words all too often. I know it when I hear it."

Phillip sensed her insecurity. He remembered the unspeakable things that went on Libby's childhood home. He was supposed to bring her out of that, not plunge her from one atrocity to the next.

He reached for her. His eyelids closed over his eyes, and his forehead gently fell against hers as he pulled her close. Her back muscles were stiff beneath his fingertips, but her soft sigh gave away that her defenses were slowly crumbling in his grasp.

"I'm trying, Libby," he uttered. "Do you believe me?"

"I want to," she whispered.

She may have only spoken three words, but those three, tiny words cuffed him like a sucker punch to his gut.

Why couldn't she see that this wasn't easy for him? When would she realize that coming home from bloodshed and death had altered his image? Would she ever see how much his love for her and his friends had cost him?

"Can you give me time, Libby?"

"I've given you four years, Phillip."

"Just a little bit longer? Please?"

Slowly, gently, she pulled back from him. Keeping her eyes diverted from his, she barely nodded. He'd take what he could get. He knew they stood on shaky ground. And if he didn't step cautiously, it would all give way beneath him, plummeting him to a deep, dark pit below, where no one could ever pull him out.

TWENTY-TWO

Grace wished she was anywhere but here. She should have listened to her instincts and stayed home to rest. Tonight's dreadful meeting had stolen the rest of her energy from her body.

As Maggie assisted her to the corner of the small café, silent tears fell down Grace's cheeks. Nothing she did could hold them back. Not at this point.

She slid onto the booth seat and closed her eyes as she hid behind her hands. Maggie's apologetic touch told her that her friend was there and she understood.

"Oh, Grace. I don't know what to say. I'm so sorry. I don't know what's gotten into Phillip lately. I-I'm just flabbergasted at his behavior. Is there anything I can do to help? Anything at all?"

Of course there was nothing Maggie could do. Words may hold no weight of their own but they could cut deep and hurt worse than any physical injury.

Grace took a few silent moments to dry her tears and recollect herself.

She stole a glance at the café's breakfast bar and spotted Luke and Danny hunched over in quiet contemplations.

How could Phillip do this to her? How could he humiliate her so and put Luke down in front of everyone?

"Grace, won't you let me get you something? Are you hungry, honey?"

Grace shook her head. "Thank you, Maggie, but no. Luke should be back with that drink he promised me. Why don't you and Danny go see the movie? Luke and I will be fine here. I'm awfully tired anyway and will probably head home soon."

"No. I'm no longer in the mood to see a picture tonight. Besides, Grace, you're my dearest friend, and you're well-being matters more than some dumb ol' movie reel." Maggie drew back and crossed her arms over chest. "I'm so angry with my brother I could just spit. Why, I oughtta pay him a visit tonight and give him some of my mind."

"Let it go, Maggie." Grace's demeanor screamed she gave up. It wasn't worth the fight and she was so tired.

"I can't just let this go, Grace. He's insulting the dearest, closest friends I have. I won't stand for it…I just won't, I tell ya."

"I can't tell you what to do, Maggie, but I will say this—I think maybe it would be for the better that Luke and I steer clear of Phillip for a while. At least until he figures things out. It's obvious his loyalty to Jack is as strong as if Jack were still here. I'm afraid that as long as Jack is still living in Phillip's mind, he'll never accept my marriage to Luke. That is what it's all about, isn't it, Maggie?"

With all sincerity, Grace lifted her eyes to Maggie's, whose almond gaze now glistened with pools of water.

"I don't know what this is all about, Grace. But I plan to find out. Maybe Danny can talk some sense into the man."

The girls glanced over at the fellas, who still stood at the counter lost in conversation. If Grace knew Danny, he likely was giving Luke a pep talk. And Luke sure did need that right now.

Her gaze fell on Luke. How she loved the man so. But secretly, in the depths of her heart, fragments of their first meeting haunted her mind. The memory didn't frighten her by any means, but at times, she'd close her eyes and remember back to that starry, summer night when Luke's arms encircled her waist and they danced to the tune of *Moonlight Serenade*. Briefly, she only knew the pre-injured Luke Brady, but the extent of his injuries would leave an everlasting impression on their life together. Not that it changed the way she could ever feel about him, but watching him struggle in everyday tasks pained her. It pained her for him, knowing that he would have to live with this handicap for the rest of his life. And now he would have to live with the weight of being the other man in Grace Campbell Brady's life. It wasn't at all what she wanted for her husband. Luke was the one she loved with all her heart. The last person she thought about at night and the first person to cross her mind in the morning.

Warm tears gathered in her eyes, and she quickly swiped them away.

When she glanced back up, Luke watched her intently. Then he turned toward the counter and retrieved her cup of tea from the waitress and started for her.

All over again, the memory of just a mere year ago washed over her. What a sweet and beautiful year it had been. Full of love and devotion and the promise of a new life to bring into their cocoon of happiness.

Luke's mouth formed inaudible words. Her eyes fell on his lips as she caught the formation of what he was trying to relay to her.

I love you, his lips said.

Her mouth curled upward and silently replied, *I love you, too.*

As he took special care in placing her cup in front of her, she took hold of his hand and gently squeezed. She never wanted to let go of this man ever again.

TWENTY-THREE

This last night was the loneliest she'd experienced yet.

As Libby awoke with the first break of sunlight, she hoped her stirring wouldn't arouse Phillip. She wasn't ready to see him. Not after last night's shenanigans.

All night long, nightmares plagued her dreams, making daylight all the sweeter. Her eyes may weigh heavy with exhaustion, but her mind was sound and ready to face the day.

As she slipped on her house dress and buttoned up the front, she glanced back at the bed where Phillip lay. But only an empty impression was all that was there.

Her brows furrowed together and she peered out the bedroom door, listening for any sign of Phillip. Maybe he was downstairs on the couch reading the morning newspaper.

But as she descended the stairs, her eyes caught no sight of his form on the couch. She searched the house and glared out the windows for any sign of him.

"Phillip?" she called several times.

But there was no answer.

Finally, she opened the front door and ran her eyes across the driveway.

The car was gone.

She sighed and slid her eyes closed.

It was just as well. She wasn't ready to face him yet this morning anyhow. Obviously, he had felt the same way.

Stepping back inside and closing the door behind her, she made her way to the kitchen to prepare coffee and eggs. But before she put the final touches on the eggs, Maggie's voice echoed through the living room.

"I'm here, Maggie. In the kitchen," Libby called back.

Maggie's heels tapped against the wood flooring until they stopped just short of the kitchen entryway.

"I'm not intruding, am I?"

Annoyance pricked at Libby. She was glad that her back was still turned to Maggie. "Don't be silly, Maggie. It's not me that has the problem, remember?"

Folding her eggs over once more, she pulled the hot pan from the stove and spread them over two plates. Adding two slices of bread to the meal, she took the plates in her hand and turned to set them on the table.

"Here. Have some breakfast. I don't mind the company. Tea and coffee are there on the table."

Keeping her eyes from meeting Maggie's, she plopped onto the kitchen chair and dabbled her fork into her eggs. From the corner of her eye, she spotted Maggie's hesitancy, but her sister-in-law accepted the abrupt invite and poured herself a cup of blackened coffee.

"Where's Phillip?" Maggie asked.

"Out, I assume. The car's gone." Libby shoved another forkful of eggs into her mouth.

She sensed Maggie's eyes probing her, but she chose to act as though she didn't notice.

"What do I owe the pleasure today, Maggie?"

Her sister-in-law sipped on her coffee then gently set the cup and saucer on the table.

"Well, I admit I came to see Phillip. To talk about last night. But...I wanted to talk to you, too. I wanted to ask if you were okay."

"How kind of you." Libby's eyes swung downward as she took a long sip of tea, ignoring the probing question.

Suddenly, Maggie pushed her plate away. "Libby, don't go MIA on me. I just want to get to the bottom of Phillip's situation and work it out. I can't do it without you. Please let me in, Libby. I'm just here to help."

Libby contemplated Maggie's words. Finally she resolved that she was acting no different than she had acted toward Maggie several years ago. Hadn't she put all that in the past? Hadn't she moved past the jealousy and smoothed over her relationship with Maggie? Did she really want to regress now, when she needed someone?"

Libby's shoulders slumped and she leaned her elbows against the table as her head rested in her hands.

"I'm just as confused as you, Maggie. I don't know what's going on. I really don't. But you've noticed it. So that must mean that I'm not going crazy." Libby's eyes darted to her sister-in-law's face.

Libby not only sighed in her heart, but outwardly as well. Her hands rubbed together and her shoulders shrugged inward, as if shielding her heart from more uneasiness.

"I keep trying to tell myself everything is okay. Or at least it will be okay." Her eyes followed the grain on the hard wood floor. Like those grains engraved into the planks, branching off in other directions, or suddenly halting, it seemed she found those same characteristics etched into her marriage. Her road was either coming to a halt, or chasing after some other rabbit trail.

The first grain on her heart came to a sudden stop when Phillip had left for boot camp. A new one started as she took on a job of her own. It didn't take long before another branched off as she moved herself and all their belongings to Arbor Springs and took on a new job at the cannery, all the while, working her fingers to their cores to make their dilapidated house a warm home.

Yes, she was just as worn as that plank of hard wood. Exhausted, tired, and wearing down with each day of use.

She shook out of her pensive reverie and looked to Maggie.

"He's not the same, Maggie. Phillip is not the same man as when he left. I wasn't sure if anyone had noticed his subtle comments and his unusual outbursts."

She waited for Maggie's reply, watching as Maggie's eyebrows rose and fell again, her mouth opening and closing.

"I—we, well...Libby, not everyone comes home a whole man. You know that. You've seen it with Luke, Danny, and many of the fellas here in town. You've heard people talking...those committed already and others struggling. I'd say Phillip is fairing much better than those poor souls, wouldn't you? What concerns me is his anger toward Grace for marrying Luke."

And there it was. The overlooking of one's problems to emphasize on the other. Wouldn't anyone see how they all fit together? How Phillip's discourse was not caused by Grace's marriage at all, but by some unforeseen characteristic that had yet to show its ugly head?

"Of course. I know things could be far worse off, but I thought by now after adjusting to time changes and heartier meals I would start seeing more of the man I married. What I'm seeing is more of his aggressive side—a side I've never known before."

Maggie's experienced hand patted Libby's knee.

"Perhaps Danny could talk to him. I don't know what I'm doing, Libby. I just want everyone to get along. A close knit family is all I ever wanted."

"Me too, Maggie."

TWENTY-FOUR

14 April 1946

*H**ypocrite!*
Nothing could quell that small voice from screaming out the truth of what he really was.

Tormented by his own soul, Phillip sat in the church pew alongside Libby, hoping his inward battle wasn't playing out for all to hear. Because inside his mind, the war raged on. Each attack on his character weakened the walls of his integrity—but, no, his integrity had left him long ago.

A cold surge ran through his hand, followed by tiny prickles. Looking down, he released the unintentional fist his fingers made, ceasing the blood to flow into his extremity.

Libby's gentle touch to his hand chased away the clouds. Taking a quick side glance, he gave her a weak smile. She returned his regard, but her smile failed to reach her eyes.

Of course it wouldn't reach her eyes. Ever since Friday night's ordeal, she'd hardly breathed a word to him.

So far, Libby had said nothing of his late night carousing. He hoped she hadn't noticed the smell of liquor on his breath, or the stench of cigarette smoke on his collar. Above all, he hoped her assumption of him hadn't been marred by his unruly behavior. But he was sure it was.

He glanced down at her gloved hand resting in his.

She still loved him. Otherwise she wouldn't be sitting next to him like she did. So why had he created an unseen barrier around his heart?

He cringed at the thought of someone loving him so. He was nothing, a barbarian to some, an enemy to others. How could it be that after living years as the opposition, someone would welcome him into their arms, into their heart, and not display an ounce of hatred toward him?

It seemed impossible. Yet, it wasn't.

While his mind battled back and forth, the preacher continued preaching...

"The LORD hath appeared of old unto me, *saying*, Yea, I have loved thee with an everlasting love: therefore with lovingkindness have I drawn thee."

How can Libby love me after all the pain I've caused her?

"...And we have known and believed the love that God hath to us. God is love; and he that dwelleth in love dwelleth in God, and God in him."

But I was the enemy. People died by my hand.

"Who shall separate us from the love of Christ? *shall* tribulation, or distress, or persecution, or famine, or nakedness, or peril, or sword?'...'If we confess our sins, he is faithful and just to forgive us our sins, and to cleanse us from all unrighteousness"

It's impossible to have a full pardon for all I've done, for all I've witnessed.

"'For with God nothing shall be impossible."

Phillip glanced up at the pulpit. It was as if God Himself was speaking to him directly. But as his eyes swept across the small church congregation, he convinced himself it wasn't so. God had stopped talking to him long ago. Why would He start now?

Phillip glanced down the church pew from the corner of his eye. When was the last time he remembered his father, mother, sister, and himself sitting together in church? Maybe as a twelve-year-old boy?

He wasn't sure what had taken place during his years away at war, but he knew for certain, changes had altered the family he once knew. Everyone wore pleased expressions on their faces, love emanated from their smiles, from their embraces—at least on the outside. It was hard to tell what was being said inside their own hearts toward him. But as he watched the exchanges among his family, a sense of peace seemed to have healed all past wounds.

If he could only experience that same peace.

Love had expanded the family. Libby and Maggie had grown exceptionally close, and no one could miss the pure happiness that emanated from Maggie's eyes when Danny was at her side. The family was now mended.

With the exception of him.

Libby's eyes made contact with his, and he smiled as he wrapped an arm around her petite shoulder, acting as if nothing was amiss. She looked so pretty with her dark hair curled and pulled back to reveal her soft cheekbones and jawline. Her black ladies hat sat perfectly atop her crown, making her look cute as a button to him. She relaxed into his side as they listened to the preacher preach from the pulpit.

Sunlight radiated from the church windows, giving the church a cheery glow—perfect for a beautiful Sunday morning spent with his wife.

He missed the last four Christmases and Easters with his family, including his first Christmas with Libby. In a sense, it was as if they were starting over again.

The Marine Corps had done a swell job of breaking his will, building him up, and teaching him to stay focused on the job at hand no matter what the situation detailed. However, memories of those four Easter Sundays away from Libby crept into his mind as the preacher continued his sermon. Phillip's mind travelled back to his botanical home—a place anything but serene—the only place where he could be surrounded by hundreds of souls and yet feel so alone.

So many times while laying against the hard, mucky jungle soil in the late of night, he found himself staring into Libby's photograph. Although the moonlight was mostly blocked by dense tropical foliage, and the use of lamp light was forbidden for fear of tipping off the enemy, Phillip didn't need illumination to see her beautiful, round face. He'd memorized every contour, every tone of her facial structure. The adorable round shape of her brown eyes, the sweetheart sculpt of her lips. Every inch was burned into his mind's eye, making the urge to be near her that much stronger.

He often wondered what she was doing back home. How she was coping without him. Did she think of him while he was away?

But his letters became far and few because of those unanswered questions. Libby had not been too happy with his decision to join the Marines. Therefore, their parting was blemished with anger, hurt, fear, and uncertainty of the future. He could tell by the tone of her letters that even after a year from his deployment she was still harboring hurt feelings. Reading the sadness in her words became too much to bear, because he'd done that to her. He knew he'd hurt Libby, maybe even made her feel abandoned. But how was anyone to know the Japanese were planning a surprise attack on American military bases? Someone needed to fight off the United States' offenders. Someone needed to avenge Jack's untimely death.

And that made this whole argument justifiable.

Phillip's eyes drifted across the aisle. They rested on Harvey and Sydney. Seated in the spot once reserved for the Gregorys, Harvey and his wife sat close, their two children nestled comfortably, one on each side of them. They were a picture of perfection. The all-American family—the picture of the Gregorys twenty years earlier.

All over again, the pain of losing his best friend swelled in his chest. Phillip and Jack had been childhood friends. Nearly brothers. When news of Jack's death made it to Phillip's ears, a cannon-sized whole seared through his chest. Not even his own bullet wound had hurt as bad as losing his best friend.

And poor Mr. and Mrs. Gregory. Jack was their only son.

His eyes fixed on the couple. Phillip thought back to the night before when he sat across from Harvey. The small, black book that Harv claimed changed his life sat between them on the table. Phillip had eyed it, knowing fully what it was and what it contained, but blocking out any hope that what was in it was true. So he left Harvey's house with a clearer mind, but a clouded conscience.

Then there was Grace.

Sitting a few rows in front his own pew, Phillip spotted Grace and Luke Brady. The two sat closely together, nearly straight across from the Duncans.

He sneered at the picture.

Phillip couldn't picture Grace without the company of the Gregorys—a people who would have welcomed her warmly into their family.

How could Grace do that to them? How could she flaunt her new husband around town? Everyone knew she and Jack were engaged to be married. How did she allow herself to forget everything about Jack and leave him to his grave?

Tightness clenched around Phillip's gullet and he quietly cleared his throat. Sensing Libby's quick glance, he gave her shoulder a squeeze, letting her know he was all right…even if inside, he wasn't. He'd learned that from the military as well. Bluffing, hiding his emotions. Making everyone around him believe he no longer felt fear, sorrow.

The preacher concluded his sermon with a hymn. Together, the congregation stood and sang *The Old Rugged Cross.*

Libby stepped closer to his side and he reached an arm around her waist. Her soft, brown eyes looked up at him and her lips forced a smile through her song. Her wide eyes extracted a grin from him, a distraction from deeper sentiments that only moments ago were racing through his mind.

❧❧

After the service concluded, it seemed the welcome wagon of church members would never end. With Libby clinging tightly to his arm, Phillip greeted church patrons as Libby introduced them. The people of this town were warm and kind, but they looked at him as if he were some kind of war hero, as if he had popped from the pages of a comic book and was a living, breathing superhero who had saved the world from utter destruction.

The beautiful tranquility he'd experienced in Libby's eyes now escaped him as the image of who he now was shone through. Everyone greeting him knew he was a Marine. They knew he'd served in the Pacific. And somehow, with smiling faces, they looked up at him as some sort of champion, a conqueror. He choked out his words as people thanked him for his service. Women gleamed at him with pride and wonder, happy that he survived. The men, with their hats in hand, firmly shook his hand, telling him they understood, that what he did *over there* was brave and heroic.

What was he supposed to say? How was he supposed to act? According to his personal part in the war, he was not the hero these fine people thought him to be. In the world he fought in, the real heroes had come home with the American flag draped over their bodies, marched to the tune of *Taps* while uniformed men stood straight and tall and snapped a somber and respectful salute as tears glistened in their eyes.

The air around him became thick as images of the dead shrouded his mind. He gasped for fresh air. With a sharp jerk, he pulled away from Libby and their arms separated. She reached out for him, but he pushed his way to the back of the church.

"Phillip? Where are you going?"

Libby's alarmed voice echoed as she called after him, but the longing for oxygen was greater than the need to answer her at the present time.

The large double doors came within reach and he shoved them open. He gasped for the crisp air that hit his face. Beads of sweat gathered on his forehead. He wasn't sure what just happened, but the need to survive had taken over and pushed him over the edge.

In and out...

Clean, clear oxygen filled his lungs, releasing panic from his chest.

His fingers pried loose his tie and collar to allow neck room to breathe as he inhaled.

The church doors behind him creaked open and Libby's small voice soothed his ache. "Honey? What's wrong? Are you all right?"

He didn't want to alarm her. Clearing his throat, he stretched his neck and wiggled his tie back in place. A forced, weathered smile pushed across his lips and he placed one arm around her shoulder. "Yeah. Just needed some air. It was getting stuffy in there."

Her worried brow told him she didn't believe him, but her words said otherwise. "I figured by now you'd be used to those kinds of conditions."

"It doesn't mean I like it." He gave her a reassuring smile as she reached her fingers up to adjust his collar and crooked tie. "I'm feeling better now. Let's go back inside before you catch a chill out here, shall we?" Giving her cheek a peck, he opened the door for his beautiful bride.

Phillip and Libby strolled hand in hand to meet up with his parents, and Maggie and Danny.

His mother smiled warmly. He knew she was proud to have her only son home from years of fighting, however, Maggie shot him a curious glance. He shrugged and her features softened, giving him a slight smile as other church members passed them. He pasted on a stony façade and smiled when the older ladies of the congregation bid him well.

When the last church goer had greeted him, he subconsciously let out a breath of relief. Moments later, while Libby still conversed with the organ player, a whiff of a familiar, floral perfume enveloped his senses. He didn't have to look over to see that Maggie had strolled up to his side.

"So what was all that about back there? Why'd you run out like you'd just been told to retreat?"

One thing he'd noticed about his sister was that she still had a hard time leaving the war behind. In the first few months he'd been home, she often spoke in war metaphors.

"A Marine doesn't retreat." He may have spoken a little too sharply in reply to her question so he toned down his next phrase. "You know how it is on the battle front, Maggie. Going from extreme vastness to a room full of people gets a little overwhelming."

"Seems you're doing a lot of that lately. But hey—" Maggie gave his arm a jab—"You're a Marine, right? So you can handle that, no sweat."

He was unsure how to take Maggie's curt tongue. "Yeah. Sure. No sweat."

Silence befell them and Maggie's expression, pitted with uncertain concern, grew serious.

"You're sure you're all right?"

Whether she was angry at him still or not, he wasn't sure. But if he was ever to put his sister at ease, he would have to do a marksman's job of playing his cards. Pasting a slick smile on his face, he placed his arm around Maggie's shoulders and squeezed her close to his side in a one-sided hug.

"You know, you always were annoying," he teased. "Now get, and leave me alone." He hoped he'd done a swell enough job of convincing her with his light-hearted jesting.

"Annoying or not, I still know you better than anyone else." With a wink of her eye, Maggie smiled, then turned back to Danny, who was finishing his conversation with another fella from the church.

Deep down, Phillip knew Maggie's training as a nurse had caused her to spot the look of panic in his eyes as he left the church sanctuary a little while ago. He may be able to fool a lot of people, but Maggie's keen sense of trouble had always seen through his thickest of fronts.

But what had happened to him back there? How did friendliness and kindness turn the tables on him and push him past the point of coherency? It was as if his body had taken orders from someone other than himself, ordering him to flee. Flee from anyone who could wound him, or cause him to remember the brutality he'd suffered and witnessed.

Once again his mind flashed. He was back on Marpi Point with the scared and wide eyes of desperate people staring back at him, some reaching out to him for help, others turning from him in fear, children emerging from caves, and then...

His eyes shut out the memory and all of those horrible images that were branded into his mind.

"Hiya, Phil!"

Harvey Duncan's voice sliced through those thoughts and chased out the images, keeping them from emerging.

Quickly clearing his throat, Phillip turned toward the sound of Harvey's tenor voice, placing him face to face with his old buddy and his wife.

"Hey there, Harv. Put 'er there."

As he exchanged a handshake with Harvey, Libby sidled up next to him and roped his left arm.

"Glad to see you, today, pal. Ah…and here's the missus." Harvey turned to Libby. "Libby, dear, how've you been?"

"Just fine, Harvey. Thank you." She glanced to Harvey's wife who hung on his arm." Sydney, you're looking lovely as ever."

"As are you, Libby. Why, it's been so long since school…how lovely to run into the both of you again."

"Hey'a, look, you two love birds," Harv pointed his gaze in Phillip and Libby's direction. "Sydney and I wanted to invite the both of you over for Sunday dinner. You know, catch up on old news and rekindle old friendships. Whaddya say, huh?"

Phillip glanced down at Libby, his heart wanting to say yes, but his conscience wanting to run away from the thought. "Gee, uh, I don't know, Harv—"

"Why I think that sounds like a splendid idea!" Libby exclaimed. "Can we, Phillip?"

Her eyes smiled up at him. Oh, how they sparkled, and he wanted so badly to make her happy. Perhaps a Sunday dinner with old friends wasn't asking too much from him.

TWENTY-FIVE

Happiness sprouted in Libby's soul, causing her to sit and stare with wonder in her eyes.

From the moment she and Phillip entered the Duncans' small suburban home at Belle Grove Square, an unfamiliar warmth enveloped her.

But it ignited envy within her also.

With her back straight and her eyes alert, Libby sat at the dining room table alongside Phillip, watching her host and hostess display a different type of affection toward each other.

Harvey and Sydney waltzed around as if they were the perfect American family. Sydney, short with chocolate colored hair and a pert little nose, sashayed through the kitchen with her perfectly tied apron around her dainty waist like the model wife of *Good Housekeeping Magazine*. And Harvey, neatly put together with his strawberry-blond hair combed to the side, seemed to enjoy helping his wife with dinner preparations as he carted hot plates of meat and side dishes from the kitchen to the quaint dining room. The two seemed a perfect fit for each other. Never had Libby thought the two would end up married, much less Harvey—the class jester—would become anything more than just a good fellow. In all the years she'd attended school with the trio, Harvey's personality and wayward attitude had not impressed Libby in the least. If anything, she found Harvey Duncan's character nothing short of a delinquent, incapable of becoming anyone greater than a mere drifter, moving from town to town, marring his name, and moving on again. But clearly, she'd been wrong.

Then there were the children.

Two precious tots, ages two and four, toddled around the house in their Sunday bests. The eldest, Nathaniel Scott, sat content in his high chair, shoving what was left of his cookie into his mouth. His adorable plump cheeks bobbed up and down as he worked to chew it down. He looked so much like Harvey. Strawberry blond locks fell over his forehead, and that grin…yes, spittin' image of his daddy. From across the way, Holly Faith whimpered and rubbed her eyes.

"Yes, sweetheart," Sydney comforted her. "Another busy day and you're tuckered out. Momma just needs to put these leftovers up in the cupboard and then we'll get to cuddle before naptime." Sydney glanced up at Libby. "I'm terribly sorry. You must think I'm a poor hostess. I've barely had any time to sit and talk over a cup of tea. Sometimes it takes a little longer to get settled in with two young toddlers under foot."

"Please don't fret on my behalf, Sydney. I think you're doing a splendid job. I can only hope to one day be half the mother you are."

"In due time, I'm sure of it." Sydney batted an eye in Libby's direction and Libby smiled.

"Oh! Where are my manners…can I help you take these dishes into the kitchen for washing?"

"Thank you. I just need these two side dishes soaking in the tub a while."

Libby grabbed up the plates and followed Sydney into the kitchen where the two worked together to clean the supper plates and dry them.

Holly was growing more fatigued and hugged Sydney's leg. But Sydney didn't seem to mind at all that sweet little Holly Faith clung to her skirts and followed close behind her momma. Holly's small, pudgy little fingers plugged her sweet tiny mouth as she slurped on them as only a wee one would do.

"Up you go, precious." Sydney whisked up little Holly Faith in her arms as if she was light as a feather pillow. "Now that dinner is over, it's time for your nap."

They strolled back into the dining room where Nathaniel Scott now sat on the floor with his tin soldier.

"Come, Nathaniel. Off to bed with you." Sydney glanced at Libby. "I'll just be a moment to lie them down."

"Take whatever time you need, Sydney. I'll just sip on my tea."

Libby drew her tea cup to her lips and sipped on her warm cup.

She watched as Sydney waddled up the stairs, Holly Faith in one arm and Nathaniel clinging tightly to her other hand. Libby couldn't help but picture herself dressed in that same yellow cotton, long sleeved dress with two children on either side of her. Why, Sydney was no older than she and already well into motherhood. Somehow, Libby felt cheated out of that beautiful arrangement.

Phillip.

If only he hadn't left her shortly after their wedding...if only he'd been more willing to listen to her, to hear her out. He was becoming increasingly difficult to talk to. In fact, he hardly spoke at all. He seemed perfectly content to sit out his evenings in utter silence. As long as he had his wicker chair to sit in and...and *sulk*.

Deep laughter entered the dining room. From the living room, it sounded as if Phillip and Harvey were engaged in a very lively conversation.

Studying the tone of his laughter, Libby rested her elbows on the table and allowed her tea cup to tickle her lips as she listened. It boggled her mind that conversation seem to come so easily to Phillip when he spoke with his old friends. Up until this afternoon's dinner with the Duncans, Phillip seemed quiet and somewhat distant. His odd behavior at church took her by surprise, but she reminded herself that his homecoming had barely been three months compared to the time he spent away from her.

Their new life together seemed brand new all over again. They were now in a new town—Phillip's childhood community—and he was reconnecting with his family and old friends all over again. She was sure it was overwhelming for Phillip. So she resolved to take it in stride and make him as comfortable as possible. But even that was becoming harder to do.

Several times throughout the meal she reached over to squeeze his hand, his arm, or his knee. Just a gentle sign telling him how much she loved him.

But to her disappointment, Phillip hadn't reverted back to his old self—the Phillip who would have responded to her touch. Who would have given up all else to hold her in his arms, or gaze lovingly into her eyes. In a sense, she wanted her protector, her one and only.

"Terribly sorry to keep you waiting, Libby." Sydney pranced into the dining room, combing through her dark strands with her fingers. "Whew! I feel like I need to freshen up after a meal like that and children to take care of."

"You look simply amazing, Sydney. I really don't know how you do it. You wear motherhood gracefully."

"Why, thank you. I've been blessed." Sydney rested her hands on her hips and let out a quick sigh as she her gaze swept over the dinner table. "Well, after a day like this, I say we deserve ourselves some quiet time with our tea on the porch. The air may be a bit crisp, but the western sun is shining and should give off a nice warmth before that nighttime air blows in."

"Tea on the veranda sounds marvelous," Libby replied.

Grabbing their shawls and overcoats, the two friends made their way to the front porch, where just as Sydney predicted, a beautiful evening sun rained down warmth and sunshine on them. Each woman took a seat on either side of the small side table and set their teacups down on its topside.

Cool, crisp air filled Libby's lungs and she closed her eyes in satisfaction. Then looking out over Belle Grove Square, her view glanced over the beautiful landscape of Belle Grove's quaint park. Harvey and Sydney's small community consisted of exactly what it was named—a *square*. Gingerbread-type houses and large, three-story homes of red brick aligned each side of the square. Sydney's house was one of five facing the west side of the park. Young trees reached upward across the way. Now barren of any vegetation, Libby knew, come spring, those young trees would produce a blanket of shade over the park, giving park-goers adequate shield from the sun in warm months.

Situated at the center of the small grove, was a beautiful three-tier cement fountain. Although it currently did not run with water due to cooler temperatures, Libby could imagine the beautiful glisten it gave off as water trickled down its bowls.

And the rose bushes…

How beautiful would they look in the month of June when everything was in full bloom?

Libby stood to her feet and slowly walked to the white railing. Resting her palms on the handrail, she took in the inviting view.

"I could wake up to this little town every single morning. Look at how the sun shines through the tree branches. It's like you live in a village completely separate from the world. Everything seems perfect here. Like no wrong could be done. As if love flourishes and rains down from the tree tops onto your beautiful home."

"I'm not sure I know what you mean, Libby."

Realizing how silly she must have sounded, Libby turned, leaning her backside against the rail and rolling her lips between her teeth.

"Forgive me, Sydney. I must sound like a silly fool." Warmth flooded her cheeks and she blushed against her own musings. "I don't mean to sound like an ungrateful hen."

A flicker of understanding sparked in Sydney's eyes as she considered Libby. And Libby offered up no explanation. At the moment her own mind was filled with such nonsense she couldn't separate her own dreams from reality.

Drawing her shawl closer around her shoulders, Sydney set her teacup on the side table and glanced back in Libby's direction.

"What's going on in that head of yours, Libby? I haven't seen that look in your eyes since the summer after graduation...just before you left Arbor Springs."

"Which would be the summer before Phillip and I wed."

Sydney's eyes narrowed. "Something's not right at home, is it, Libby?"

It seemed more a statement than a question, as if Sydney had glared right into the transparency of Libby's soul. Libby could only glance down at her nerve-stricken feet, afraid to answer Sydney honestly.

"You can tell me, Libby. We were once good friends."

"You know how things are, Sydney. Life becomes complicated. Things aren't always easy to fix as they once were."

"So something *is* broken."

Libby's eyes met Sydney's. The threat of tears welled up inside them and Libby had to look away.

"He's so different, Sydney."

"Who? Phillip?"

"Yes. How was Harvey able to come home and just jump back into his normal life again? It seems something has changed in him. I think he may be a better man now than before he left for war."

"Oh, he is, Libby. That, he is." Sydney patted the chair cushion beside her. "Come. Sit."

Needing to rest her weary body, Libby accepted Sydney's invitation, and Sydney patted her knee.

"You think my life is perfect, don't you, Libby?"

She nodded. "Yours and Grace Brady's—you ladies seem to live lives unmatched."

"Well, I can assure you that from where I stand, my life is not perfect, but it's not awful either. Actually, things are going very well for Harv and I, but it wasn't always this way. We walked through the deep. We endured our own battles. And we nearly lost each other in the fight."

Libby glanced up at Sydney, surprise shrouding her eyes. "What do you mean?"

"It's no secret—even you said so—Harvey was not the most suave or gentle fella to come knockin' on any girl's door. How do you think my parents' reacted when he came calling one night? One thing led to the next and before I knew it, we were walking down the isle. Then the war happened and that's when everything changed."

Smoothing her skirt, Libby added, "It seems the war changed things for everyone in this town."

"Well, you're right about that. But you see, Libby, my marriage to Harvey hasn't been a picnic in the park. No, not in the least! Harvey only wanted a cook, and a maid, and someone to sleep in his bed. He sure made that clear in our first year of marriage. I was his little side show, his trophy, to show off to his friends. While my friends were tending to their babies and taking their honeymoons I was stuck at home, cleaning, while Harvey was off carousing with his old buddies."

It sounded a lot like Libby's life at the present time. Her eyes widened as she listened to Sydney tell her story.

"Oh, my, Sydney. Honey, how did you ever manage?"

"It was difficult, I'll tell ya. I didn't think I could take any more of his shenanigans, then the war department came knocking at our door. But before the draft picked him off, he'd done gone down and enlisted on his own. I could have killed the man for doing that to me, but I knew it was inevitable. If he hadn't gone and enlisted, then Uncle Sam would've dragged him off anyhow."

"I know exactly how you felt, Sydney. Phillip enlisted two weeks after our honeymoon. Imagine me, thinking I was starting the best chapter in my life, then all at once, it was as if someone had ripped that chapter right from its spine. Those years are gone. Like missing pages to a book I'll never get back."

Sydney's teacup clanked on its saucer and she uncrossed her knees as she leaned forward and sympathetically looked at Libby. "Those years may be gone, Libby, but you still have a lifetime to write in your future. Don't base your tomorrows on your yesterdays. Each day is a brand new gift from God. Each sunrise is a beautiful reminder that there is still light shining through the darkness."

Tears sprung to Libby's eyes. A watery canvas shrouded her perfect, pictorial view. "I wish I could see that light," she whispered through unshed tears.

Sydney grew concerned and her voice softened to a low whisper. "Libby, honey, won't you tell me what's going on?"

Her head shook back and forth and she choked back a sob. "I can't, Sydney. I just can't."

TWENTY-SIX

The Brady Home
15 April 1946

In just a few short weeks everything would change. One sweeping moment would alter the Brady's life forever.

Grace stepped back from her new and completed nursery. Yellow and white glowed like fresh sunshine on the walls of the tiny room. Cross stitch patterns of nursery rhymes adorned the spots above the baby's crib and buffet. Everything was in place—that is everything but a tiny little newborn kicking and whimpering in her arms.

Glad for the final touches fulfilled, Grace slowly lowered herself onto the old wooden rocker that Mrs. Sullivan had gifted her. It felt wonderful to rest her weary feet and aching back. Fatigue settled behind her eyes, and as she gently rocked back and forth, her eyelids grew heavier until they gave in to exhaustion. A contented sigh escaped her chest.

Finally, all was right with the world.

She could rest easily knowing everything and everyone she held dear to her was safe and sound in Arbor Springs. All that she anticipated now was that long awaited arrival of her precious little baby. That, in itself, was enough to lift the burden of her late pregnancy from her shoulders and allow her body to relax in the comfort of the nursery.

At least until the slightest creak of wooden floorboards caused her to startle awake.

"Oh. Grace, dear, I'm so sorry to wake you. I was just checking in to see if you were all right."

Grace couldn't help but smile warmly at the sight of Mrs. Sullivan, Luke's beloved aunt, standing in the nursery's doorway. She'd been checking in a lot lately on Grace, and for that she was ever so grateful for the watch care of cherished family.

"I must have dozed off. I only sat down for a moment. Seems I can't get enough sleep these days." Grace attempted to push out of her chair, but Norma Sullivan jumped to her aid and stopped her.

"Oh, no, dear. If you're weary, then you must rest. Don't make a fuss over me. I'll just make myself useful downstairs. Now, you tell me what there is to be done around here." Norma pulled a quilted blanket from the closet, unfolded it, then softly draped it over Grace's form. Then she pushed up the sleeves of her blouse, ready to go to work.

"You're too good to me, Aunt Norma. I don't know how to repay your kindness."

"Ah, see now, I've already thought of that." Aunt Norma's eyes danced with pleasure and glistened with adoration. "Allow me a few precious moments with my new great niece or nephew and all is fair."

Aunt Norma's aged hands patted against Grace's fingers that peeked out from beneath the quilt. Before Norma could retract her hand, Grace clasped it tightly in her grasp.

"Aunt Norma?"

"Yes, child?"

"I have somewhat of a confession to make."

"Heavens, dear. What's bothering you?" The older woman pulled up the wooden stool from the corner of the room and settled in next to Grace.

Only lately had Grace experienced a particular anxiety. Unable to put her fears into words, she hid them. But now, with only herself and Aunt Norma in the house, the time seemed right to voice those apprehensions.

"It's funny in a way," she began quietly. "Luke makes such a fuss over me and I tell him I'm all right, that everything will be okay. But deep, deep down, I have my own fears, my own doubts and worries."

"Let me take a gander at this, Grace. Is it the delivery of the baby that frightens you?"

Meekly, Grace nodded.

"Oh, my sweet Grace."

Aunt Norma reached out and wrapped her able arms around Grace's shoulders as best as she could with the chair's arm separating them. No matter what obstacles, Aunt Norma was always there to comfort her, to guide her, and calm her fears—even when they seemed to get the best of Grace.

"What you're feeling, dear, is completely natural. I think every woman has experienced fear of that unknown at some point and time in her life. Whether it's with her first baby's arrival or her last. It's all new territory to you, and I'm sure unpleasant thoughts of something going terribly wrong has crossed your mind at some point these past nine months. But, sugar, I promise you, the good Lord has His hands upon you and that precious baby you're carrying. That child is His, and it's the Lord's gift to you and your husband. You have to trust Him, Grace, and know that the Father loves you and that little baby more than you'll ever know and understand. That alone, should give you all the comfort you'll need. It's more than I can give you, and more than Luke can give you."

Grace's eyes squeezed closed. Aunt Norma's embrace was just as close as her own mother's. "I want that assurance that the both of us will be all right."

Gentle strokes smoothed back her hair. "Ah, Grace…it will be. My prayers are sent up every night for you, Luke, and that little child growing inside you. God's given me peace about it, and now I'll pray He bestows that same peace on you too."

"You always know what to say. I don't know what Luke and I would do without you."

This moment reminded Grace of those past days when Luke was off at war. When her feelings toward him were young yet strong. When all she had to hold onto was Norma Sullivan and God's promises. Well, the Lord had brought her through those difficult times when the situation seemed dire. She had to believe and trust that He would see her through these next few weeks.

Before she could completely still her nervous energy, a loud crash ripped through the air around them.

Both Grace and her aunt startled with a jerk and sharp intakes of breath.

"What in heavens…" Norma gasped.

"Oh, I hope that wasn't my shelf of good china." Grace threw the quilt off her body and jumped from the chair faster than she had in months.

"Grace, let me tend to whatever it is. You need to rest."

"Aunt Norma, I assure you I'm—" Just as Grace rounded the banister at the bottom of the stairs she stopped suddenly when she saw Luke's unexpected presence in the hall. Gasping, her hands covered her mouth and her eyes collided with his. Then they bounced downward…

What she saw stole every word from her mouth. Speechless, Grace couldn't move a single muscle. This moment in time stood still, and she couldn't believe what appeared before her eyes.

∽ઐ̃

Tears pooled in Grace's eyes, blurring her vision of Luke. Silently, they slipped down her cheeks as she stared at Luke in utter astonishment.

Slivers of glass littered the hard wood floor at his feet.

"Grace," Luke finally breathed. "I—I'm sorry." Shaking out of his daze, Luke stooped to his knee and frantically reached down for the broken china.

Grace, still unable to move her feet, took an inward breath. Two strong hands squeezed her shoulders. She'd forgotten Aunt Norma had followed her down the staircase.

"Dear nephew," the woman began. "Do you want to explain the meaning of—of all this?" Her arms spread open, palms upward.

Luke never moved his eyes from the floor. Instead, he continued to struggle cleaning up the shards of glass with only his good hand.

With a new breath of wind cleansing her lungs, Grace rushed to his side.

"I'll...I'll fetch a broom and dust pan." Mrs. Sullivan fled the room.

However, in Grace's heart, Grace knew Luke's aunt was giving them time alone—to talk things out.

Stooping down to her knees was no easy feat, but with Luke's well-being on her mind, she couldn't care less for her own discomfort. Slowly, she reached her hand out to touch Luke's arm—

But it wasn't his left arm that she felt beneath the tips of her fingers. In fact, she didn't reach for his left arm at all.

Shiny, smooth, metal cooled her fingertips as she ran her hand up Luke's *arm*. But hesitation pulled her hand away as it shook in shock. Then, ever so carefully, her hands cupped Luke's leather palm and she pulled it closer to her body, staring at it through water-filled eyes.

A single tear dripped from the slope of her nose and pinged against the metal.

"It's a sight I didn't think I'd see again." Her voice wavered through her tears, but she chose to look up at him even though she felt her strength diminish under the circumstance.

"Do—do you...like it, Grace? I haven't made any promises to anyone. I'm just trying it on for size—"

"When did you find time to consult with the doctor about this?"

"On my lunch break. For the last three months."

China fragments slipped from Luke's other hand to the floor, clanging against the hard surface with a clatter.

"Your china cup. I'm sorry. I know how much you love this set. I'll find a way to make it up to you." Luke pulled his artificial limb from her grasp and worked with great effort to gather up the shards that still lay strewn on the floor at their knees.

Grace blinked back her unshed tears as she watched him. He was trying so hard, and she saw that deep inside he wanted to return to a normal life unabashed by war's scars.

Life had been difficult for him. All the things he had to relearn minus one limb. The simple things, like tying his shoes, buttoning up his shirt, shaving, cutting his food, it all became Luke's greatest obstacles. But he'd learned to cope.

When her eyes cleared, Grace's instincts kicked in and for the first time she really saw the mess that lay before them.

"I should be cleaning that up for you." Gathering her skirt, Grace strained to stand to her feet. The weight of her abdomen worked against her, and Luke came to her aid.

The strength of two hands enveloped her, effortlessly bringing her to her feet. She stood face to face with her husband, and for the first time in their marriage, for the first time since that August night in 1943, Luke embraced her with two arms.

Every moment of that night came rushing back to her. Like a dam unable to hold back the weight of all that pressed behind it, the flood doors to her heart sprang open.

Pressing her face into his shoulder, she cried. Her tears stained his shirt, but she didn't care. For months she'd suppressed her worry and concern for Luke, pushing those thoughts deep down where even she couldn't find them. She held them at bay for his sake, and to be that strong crutch to keep him going every day since he returned to Arbor Springs. But she couldn't hold it in any longer.

Luke's hands smoothed back her hair and held her close.

"It's okay, Grace. It's been a long road, I know," he whispered into her ear. "Please tell me, do you like it?"

The uneasiness in his voice told her that he wanted her to like it.

"It doesn't matter what I think, Luke. I would love you with arms or no arms just the same. What really matters is how *you* feel about it. Why didn't you tell me sooner?"

"Because I was unsure myself. I know you've been trying to make it seem that you're strong enough to handle all the chores in this house and take care of everything I can't. But that's not how it's supposed to be. And when I look into your beautiful eyes, I can see how it's wearing down on you. I realized I needed to stop being selfish. Pride or no pride, it's my duty to take care of you."

"Luke, you do a fine job of taking care of me—"

"But it's not enough!"

Grace winced. Then Luke's eyes softened.

"I've learned to accept my incapability, but this prosthesis has given me so much freedom again. Grace, you should see all the tools that can be attached to this arm. I feel as though I can do anything just the same as before. That's important to me." He paused, blowing out a heated breath as moisture gathered in his eyes before going on. "I'm about to be a father, Grace. That's made me do a lot of thinking lately. I want to be able to cradle our baby in my arms, to look down at him or her and make promises I'll be able to keep. That baby is going to look to me for protection and provision. I want to feel like I'm able to give our child that."

She swallowed back the lump in her throat and fought hard to hold the rest of her tears at bay. In silence, she nodded.

He was a man. A man who knew no limits until the day one devastating moment changed his life forever. Since then, she'd shielded him from further hurt and pain, not realizing that she was only shielding him from a reality he would need to face. In that moment, she understood that past sorrow and heartache were two elements that made them who they were today. That those struggles and obstacles were in fact no obstacle at all, but building blocks vital to the foundation of their marriage, of their spirituality and growth as a family. For her to take that away would be wrong.

In love and determination, Grace smiled up at Luke.

"Then let's take this next step together in faith and without regret."

Twenty-Seven

"You'll be home on time tonight, right dear?" Libby rested her palms against Phillip's chest as he reached for his lunch tin off the occasional table in the living room.

"As long as the boss doesn't work us through the evening again."

"All right. Dinner is at six sharp. I don't want to be sitting at the kitchen table all alone again tonight."

She tried her best to catch his eye, to let him see how badly she longed for that familiar side of her husband to return to her.

So far, he hadn't.

But tonight she hoped that would change. From now on, she'd decided to do everything in her power to make herself irresistible to her husband. She would give nearly anything just to have him look at her the way he used to. With that adoring, tender gaze accented by his longing sigh. Oh, to have those precious moments and young days back again.

"Phillip, there's a dance coming up this weekend at the hall. Just about everyone we know is going. I thought it would be romantic if you and I attended. You know…" Libby stepped forward and fingered the silkiness of his tie. "We could fancy ourselves up like we used to, walk hand-in-hand, and dance the night away." She dared to look up into his brown eyes still crusted over with rigidity.

"A dance? This weekend? I don't know, Libby—"

"Please? Phillip…please," she whispered. She glanced up through wide, pleading eyes, meeting his gaze. "It would mean so much to me. You've been working so hard and long. I want to be selfish and spend more time with you."

In truth, she knew his late nights were spent anywhere but his job, but she continued to hide from him the fact that she knew the truth. She'd learned from her mother that confrontation did little to help the matter. It only fueled the animosity between her mother and father. As long as Libby had breath in her and will to fight, she wouldn't let his carousing get the best of her. She would stand strong and she would win this battle on her own.

She dared to press onward. "I've been thinking. Now that things are getting back to normal around here, we should be taking advantage of these special occasions. One day they may all come to an end when children start filling the house."

Glancing down at her hands, she ran her palms up the thick of his chest, resting them at the crest of his shoulders. His muscles tensed beneath her touch.

"Please say yes?"

The only noise between them was the sound of her heart ticking in her ears.

Mild satisfaction drummed in her chest when Phillip's hands encircled her waist. She could almost see his resolve dissolving within him. But then his eyes clouded over and he backed away from her.

"I—I have to get on to work. Got new housing projects going up on the outskirts of town. It'll take me a bit longer to make the drive."

With that, he turned, not even pecking her cheek as he usually did before leaving for work. The door closed behind him. Libby was left standing alone, confused, and flustered over the invisible screen that continued to separate her from Phillip. When would it end? When would his withdrawn behavior melt away? When would the haze clear from his eyes? When would her husband return from the war he chose to fight?

∽⌒⌒∼

Submerging herself in house chores was the only way to keep her mind off the issues that hunted her down. But even they could only take her so long.

From her spot on the floor, on her hands and knees, Libby sat back on her heels. Tossing the scrub brush into her pail of soapy water, the back of her hand wiped at her brow. Lassitude slowed her progress. This morning's conversation with Phillip had taxed her more than she realized. Not just that, but her ongoing inward struggle to untangle the mess of their marriage turned her stomach. Between fatigue and her unsettled abdomen, she was due for a well-deserved rest.

After warming a kettle of water on the stove, she set herself down at the kitchen table and sipped her tea while thumbing through an issue of *Good Housekeeping*. Maybe she could find a new recipe for

Phillip's dinner tonight.

A rap at the door followed by Maggie's voice became the perfect distraction.

"Maggie?"

"Hiya, sis!"

Libby rose from her seat at the table, feeling slightly dizzy as she did. But in a moment her head cleared and she started for the living room, tossing her apron on a hook as she passed through the hall.

"What do I owe the pleasure?"

"Well, I confess it's not a random visit."

"Oh? Well, did you need something? Sugar? Flour?"

"No, no. Nothing like that. I just—" Maggie stopped short. Her dark brows creased her forehead as she eyed Libby suspiciously. "Are you feeling okay, Libbs?"

Confused, Libby blinked back the sleep in her eyes.

"Why, yes. I'm just a little tired is all."

Tired of the late night carousing, tired of the stench of alcohol, and tired of living with a complete stranger...

"Are you sure? Your complexion is a mite white."

"Oh Maggie, don't make over me like I'm one of your patients. I'm fine. I just finished up scrubbing these floors. I must have stood up too quickly. Now, what is it you need?"

But Maggie wasn't finished.

"Eh..." Maggie twisted her tongue in her cheek as she tipped her head to the side. "You look a little pale to me. You sure you're feeling all right? I know a sick body when I see one."

A nervous laugh trickled off Libby's tongue. "I'll be fine, Maggie. I promise, if I start to feel the slightest bit sick, you'll be the first I call."

"All right. I'm gonna hold ya to it." Maggie's eyes gleamed as she gave Libby a quick wink. "I just hope you can handle the news."

"Whatever do you mean, Maggie? Is everything all right?"

"Yes, perfectly."

"Then land sakes, Maggie, what's the news?"

Maggie's mouth spread wide in a large smile and her cheeks glowed with a pink hue. "I'm gonna be an aunt!"

Libby's brows furrowed. "I beg your pardon?" Her hand rested against the pit of her stomach.

"Oh! Forgive me!" Maggie's hand covered her lips. "What I mean is, Norma Sullivan telephoned me this morning, saying Luke had taken Grace to the hospital early this morning. We're gonna have a baby, Libby!"

Maggie's hands snatched up Libby's as she bounced for joy right there in the kitchen.

It took an extra moment for the excitement to register in Libby's mind, but when it did, a large smile spread over her face.

"A baby? Oh, Maggie, how wonderful! Did Mrs. Sullivan say when the baby will arrive?"

"These things take time, Libby. Especially the first baby. I told her I'd wait by the telephone. She's supposed to put in a call as soon as the baby arrives. Which reminds me, I need to get back home. It figures I would have the day off from the hospital…oh, well. I'll talk to you in a while, Libby."

"Yes, please let me know when the baby comes."

With a wave of her hand, Maggie rushed out the door, leaving Libby alone to her thoughts once more.

Slowly, she lowered herself onto the kitchen chair and lifted another blouse from the laundry basket. How nice it would be to see Grace with her baby in hand. The moment that they all had waited months for was finally about to arrive at any presenting minute.

What must be going through Grace's mind? Is she frightened? Will she be all right?

A flood of questions filtered into her mind, both of concern and curiosity. Although this very moment was most likely terrifying and exciting for Grace, Libby couldn't help but mutter to herself…

If only it was me in her position right now.

TWENTY-EIGHT

He was a heel.
Libby had practically begged at his feet and he'd turned her away—again.

How he hated to see disappointment sting her eyes. Phillip still hadn't rid himself of the incredible amount of hurt he'd seen in them the day he came home with his enlistment papers in hand.

"You volunteered!" she had shrieked.

Immediate tears flowed from her eyes and she'd hid behind her palms as she sobbed.

She just didn't understand. War had clenched his country. Hatred had stolen the life of his best friend. Revenge was to be had. And it couldn't be done without the efforts of every man's strength. Avenge Jack's death, he would. So he'd walked to the enlistment station and signed his name to the ledger.

It was done.

No turning back. No regrets.

But the look on Libby's face as the train pulled away from the station...

Another painful memory branded into his collection of bad choices, bad decisions, and stupidity.

Libby really didn't deserve a man like him. She could've had her pick of any fella in school, he was sure of it. But she'd said yes to him for that Spring cotillion. That was before war had broken out in the world. Maybe he was a different man back then...wait, he *knew* he was a different man. A different man then, a different man now. War had changed him. He could feel the transformation in his bones, by the way he saw things, the way he walked. However, nothing had changed him more than the experiences he'd survived *over there*.

When Phillip had finished pulling his shoes on his feet and tying them earlier this morning, Libby drew near, her touch undoing every building block he'd built around his heart.

"I'm going to miss you terribly while you're away from me." She pressed her lips to his cheek.

His hands caught hers and for a moment, a spark ignited in his chest. He wanted to hold her as close as he could. To have no imaginary bars separating them. The wanting in her eyes repeated what he was thinking in his heart. Then logic crept in, wedging the divide in place.

Gently, he stroked her fingers, kissed them, then he placed them at her side. "I must go."

"I know." Her voice was just above a whisper.

That's when she hesitated, then jumped into her pool of inquiries. It was too much for him to take in. Too much for his mind to comprehend, too much to wrap his understanding around. The air around him closed in, and breathing became more difficult.

So he fled.

It was happening more often these days, those instances of desperation, of breathlessness. He couldn't understand it. All his mind seemed to comprehend was he needed air. Fresh air. Space.

Just like that day on the mountain…

Smoke blanketed the air like a screen. Both sides engaged in open fire, raining live bullets down on them. More men lay beside him, their eyes cold as ice, penetrating him, screaming at him—he should have been able to save them, to kill the enemy before they killed his friends. He'd tried to push their faces from his mind, but they just watched him with those cold, blank stares.

He needed to move. To get out of there. He couldn't take it any longer. They kept watching. They kept screaming at him. They kept dying.

The jungle closed in on his consciousness and suddenly, there was nowhere to run, nowhere to hide. Panic swelled in his throat and breathing became difficult. His rifle slipped from his grip and Phillip had turned on his back, gasping for clean air. His chest pumped up and down. Bullets pelted the ground. In one swift sweep, he curled into a ball on the jungle floor, his hands covering his head.

It wouldn't stop.

The bullets…the enemy…the faces of the dead…they wouldn't stop coming, stop staring, stop screaming.

His fingers clawed at his scalp, his eyes. He couldn't erase the images, he couldn't stop the bloodshed. He couldn't stop *anything*. He was losing control.

"Hey, man! You okay, you okay?" his fellow soldier yelled to him over the sound of screeching bullets as he belly crawled to Phillip's side.

Phillip couldn't answer. He only drew himself into a tighter ball, unable to move.

"Hey! You hit?"

"No!" Phillip finally answered.

"Then what are you doing?"

"I don't know! I can't move."

More enemy fire pelted the damp ground around them and they both ducked their heads into the dirt. Phillip was sure he heard both their hearts beating through their chests.

"Hang on! I've got your back," the soldier assured him.

The guy covered Phillip's back with his own body and opened fire on the enemy. Phillip tried with all his might to pull out of the panic he was in, but he couldn't force himself to move.

What was happening to him? Why had he lost control of himself?

His limbs shook in fear, uncontrollably. Cold droplets of sweat cooled his body immensely as if a cold northern wind rushed over him. When would it stop? When would he snap out of it?

Then...

Then everything *did* stop. And when his eyes opened for the first time, he stared up into the cold eyes of the man who saved his life.

A heart-wrenching moan bellowed from deep within his soul. What had he done? He'd choked. And his own failure to perform his duty had killed another man...a man who bravely came to his aid and took over. It wasn't fair! It should have been him...

Phillip struck the steering wheel as the vision cleared from his mind.

Never was Phillip Johnson a man to retreat from his enemy. It was head first, hand-to-hand, both feet in the water to survive, to cinch the victory. But even here at home, in the span of three months, that all had changed. And he hated it. Even within the walls of his own home, he wasn't safe from his demons—those horrible disquiets that haunted the depths of his soul, of his mind. It plagued him. It now *owned* him.

Phillip had become a prisoner of his own flesh. As he glanced from side to side in the familiar place he once loved, there was no escape from the spindly fingers that gripped his soul. It sought to destroy him. So far, it had succeeded.

TWENTY-NINE

Pacing the floor wasn't relieving Maggie's jitters. There were too many scenarios charging through her mind as she anxiously awaited good news. As she turned on her heels for the umpteenth time that afternoon—while pacing in front of the telephone—she folded her hands and prayed once more for her dear friend.

"Dear Lord, please be with Grace at this time. I pray that You would allow this precious new baby to be delivered safely and healthy. And please allow my sweet friend to be okay in the end. In Your name, Father, Amen."

As Maggie opened her eyes, she glanced down at the black radial telephone. "Ring. Tell me something."

She glanced at her wristwatch. It was nearly five o'clock. "It's been all day and I haven't heard one word."

Of course she knew how long a woman's first labor could take. But this was different. This was Grace, her dear friend. Fidgeting with her fingers, Maggie contemplated. Should she leave for the hospital? No. It wasn't her place. This was Grace and Luke's time. But still…Luke was probably sitting all alone and Grace's parents couldn't possibly get to Arbor Springs before tonight. That meant, aside from Aunt Norma, Luke and Grace were at the hospital on their own.

Grace was like a sister to her. They'd been through thick and thin together. They'd witnessed death. They'd overcome the odds when they were stacked against them. Her friend needed her there. She should go.

It didn't take much convincing. Maggie snatched her overcoat from the coat hook and bolted out of the house, just in time to meet Danny as he pulled into the driveway.

"Hiya, sweetheart!"

"Hey there, sugar. Come on, we're heading to the hospital." Maggie wasted no time scurrying to the passenger side door and flinging it open before Danny could put the vehicle in Park.

"What's going on?" Concern flooded Danny's eyes and tone.

"We're having a baby!"

"Huh?" Danny's brows rose high into his forehead and his jaw slackened, nearly causing him to look sick to his stomach.

Laughter bellowed from Maggie's throat. She leaned in to kiss his cheek.

"Why, Danny, I don't think I've seen you that shade of green since Germany. Relax, I'm not talking about you and me…it's Grace. Now c'mon. Drive."

෯෯

"Good afternoon, Maggie. I thought today was your day off."

As Maggie rounded the corner of the white-wash hall she was met by Gloria, the nurse manning the information desk.

"Hello, Gloria. I *am* off duty today. However, my dear friend is in the maternity ward. Danny and I are headed to the waiting area.

Gloria nodded in understanding. "Oh, go right ahead. We're not very busy in the ward today, so there's plenty of room for visitors."

Not wasting any time, Maggie took Danny's hand and together they rushed off down the hall toward the maternity ward.

"I'm so nervous, but at the same time, my stomach is bubbling with excitement." Her slender hand gave Danny's upper arm a squeeze. He'd come such a long way from that scrawny, sickly man he'd become while a prisoner in the German camps. How thankful she was that Danny's only side-effect from his injuries was occasional absent-mindedness.

"You think *you're* nervous, think of how Luke must feel right now," Danny added.

"Just think, Danny, this is only our first walk toward the maternity ward. Just wait till Grace and Luke have more children, or when Phillip and Libby start having babies, or when…" her cheeks warmed. "When it's our turn to start a family."

Danny's eyes glanced down at her, a hint of teasing twinkled in them. "What's with you ladies and babies anyhow? One enters the world and the whole community goes batty."

"Oh, stop. This is quite the ordeal and you know it, Daniel Russo." She tucked herself closer to his side. "Take a left here."

The hallway ended, leading them to the left where a whole new room opened up to them. Another nurse's desk greeted them at the corner. Once more, Maggie took the lead, exchanging hellos with another co-worker who gave them passage into the waiting area.

"This is where the anxious fathers wait." Maggie gently turned the knob and pushed the door open. As she turned to enter, three heads perked up, their eyes wide with expectant expressions plastered on their faces. One familiar face she recognized.

"Luke, hello."

"Hiya, buddy," Danny drove forward. "How's it goin' in—"

Danny stopped mid-way as he stretched out his hand toward Luke, who was already standing to greet them. Maggie, too, halted, cupping her hand over her mouth as she stared at Luke in bewilderment.

She didn't know what to say.

Uneasily, Luke adjusted his prosthesis with his left hand, tipping his shoulder slightly upward. "Well, what do you think? I really hadn't had time to make the announcement."

"Boy, oh boy, do you have a lot of explaining to do." Danny's hand landed on Luke's back with a hearty slap. "When did this happen?"

"Just yesterday. I haven't really had too much time to adjust to it yet."

Luke seemed cautious. Maggie gathered he still wasn't sure what everyone else would think of his fake limb. However, unknown to Luke, Maggie thought the idea to be a wonderful one. She couldn't help herself—she stepped toward Luke, throwing her arms around his neck and squeezing tightly as if she hugged her own brother.

"Oh, Luke, I think it's just dandy! Just imagine all the freedom you'll have now. I'm so happy I could cry. What did Grace have to say?"

A half-smile spread across his face. "Well...she cried. I couldn't tell if she loved it, hated it, or if it was just her condition." He chuckled as he said it.

The door opened and cut through the joyous reunion. Every breath in the room stilled. One of these three awaiting men was about to be told he was a father. A nurse in her very best white uniform peeked her head in the room and called, "Mr. Ownby." A very proud papa standing in the far corner of the room with his elbow against the wall and a cigarette between his lips seemed to leap as he scurried across the room and followed the nurse through the doorway. Now, just two men in the room were left waiting for any news on their wives and forthcoming children.

Luke let out a long breath and slid his palm down his pant leg as he lowered himself to the chair.

Danny was right there for his long-time friend, taking the seat next to him. "How ya doin', buddy? You hangin' in there okay?"

"Honestly, I'm a ball of nerves, Danny. As soon as we got here the nurses rushed Grace off. I barely had time to peck her on the cheek and she was gone. I've been waiting here for hours on end, just sitting. I haven't heard anything yet. I just want to know she's okay."

Maggie stood at Danny's side, but she didn't offer up any comment. Luke was Danny's friend and right now, he needed a man to talk to. So she let her husband do the talking.

"I'm sure if anything wasn't okay they'd let you know. I mean, I don't know what you're goin' through right now, but you know the good Lord...He's gonna watch over her, and that little baby of yours."

Luke nervously nodded his head, but kept his eyes lowered to the floor as he leaned into his knees. "Ahh...Danny, I've got so many things running through my head right now. I'm worried about my wife, my child. Am I really ready to become a father? Will I be a good one?" Luke ran his left hand up his prosthesis. "That's the whole reason I chose to do this. Well, that, and Grace deserves more from me. She's been doing everything I can't. It shouldn't be that way."

It seemed so strange to see two arms at his sides. One arm natural and indifferent, and the opposite appendage completely unlike the other. Maggie tried hard to refrain from staring, but she was intrigued, and still stunned. Now that the war was over, it seemed life had bolted forward in a flash.

Things were changing. Lives were being molded. Hearts were healing. New beginnings were at hand.

Maggie's eyes fixated on her husband and Luke. Two best friends who'd seen the worst the world had to offer and still managed the fight to come home alive. Thankfully, friendships had stayed the same.

Danny's firm hand lightly jostled Luke's shoulder. It was a man's way of saying, *I understand.*

"You'll do good, Luke. I have faith in ya. Grace has faith in ya. And God believes you're the man for the job. Otherwise, you wouldn't be here right now."

"Mr. Brady."

In the intimacy of the moment, no one had heard the nurse enter the room. But all at once, every head turned and every person left in the room stood. Maggie glanced over at Luke, a broad smile spreading across her face and goose pimples dotting her skin.

Luke stood stiff as a board, all color draining from from his face. Maggie took his arm, her nursing instincts kicking in.

"Remember to breathe, Luke," she said with a giddy laugh.

When Luke still didn't move from his spot, she ushered him toward the door to the waiting nurse. Her attempt to stifle her laughter failed. She'd never seen Luke like this.

"Well, are you going to meet your new son or daughter or not?"

Shaking out of his stupor, and finally seeing the nurse for the first time, Luke stuttered, "B-b-boy? Or girl? How is my wife?"

✧✦

Exhausted, but in complete awe of the moment, Grace reached out for the small bundle swaddled in ivory blankets. The day had been long, hard, and miserable, but that first glimpse into her baby's tiny, round, perfect face chased away all her pain and all her fears.

Gently, the nurse laid the baby in her arms.

"Congratulations, Mrs. Brady. You're the mother of a beautiful little boy."

"A boy," she breathed.

Grace drew the baby in close and stared down into his precious little face. Tears filled her eyes as she lowered her head and pressed a mother's kiss to his forehead.

"My baby. My precious baby boy. How I've waited and waited for you."

She couldn't take her eyes from his beautiful form. With the tip of her finger, she stroked his plump cheek. His small mouth opened in response to her touch, and a squeak of a cry escaped his tiny lips.

"You're perfect in every way. Your daddy will be so proud."

Softly, her words were meant for her little boy alone. The one she'd waited nine long months for. She sniffed back her joy and touched his baby-soft skin. Her fingertips smoothed down his tiny hand and she counted five fingers.

How happy Luke will be to meet him...

"Can I see my husband now?" she asked as the nurse came by her bed to update her chart.

"He's on his way, Mrs. Brady," the nurse answered with a smile.

Within seconds, heavy footsteps echoed off the floor. Grace glanced upward expectantly, knowing it was Luke's eyes that she'd meet.

His face was a mixture of emotions—concern, worry, excitement.

"Grace, sweetheart." His arms reached out for her—a sight she wasn't accustomed to seeing. "Are you all right?" He stooped down at her side, smoothing back her mess of hair then pressing his palm to her cheek.

"Luke, I'm so happy to see you. Yes, I'm just dandy."

His warm lips pressed a tender kiss to her forehead. "I was so worried about you."

"I'm fine, honey. We both are." She glanced up at him with loving eyes and he met her lips with his kiss.

"Do you want to meet your son?" Gently, Grace lifted the blanket and pulled it away from the sleeping baby's face, revealing him to Luke for the first time. "You're a daddy now, Luke."

Luke's breath let out and his eyes drifted closed. "My son," he whispered. A contented smile spread across his face as he reached his hand out to touch the baby's head. "What do we call him?"

"Well, I always thought that if we had a boy we'd name him LeRoy. After your father."

Grace watched as his eyes misted over and he blinked them back. She could tell he was trying to hold back the emotions that flooded him. Perhaps it was more than he could handle at the moment.

"Of course, if you don't like it, we can change—"

"No. LeRoy. LeRoy it is. I like it. My mother would've liked it too."

"All right, then. LeRoy." Grace joined Luke in admiring their new son. "Isn't he perfect, Luke? Look how tiny he is."

"He's beautiful," Luke answered.

"I'm sorry to have to interrupt this moment, Mister and Missus Brady, but it's time to take this little bundle to the nursery."

"Oh, so soon?" Grace asked.

"Afraid so, Missus Brady. The doctor will be wanting to examine this little fella."

"If you must." Reluctant to let LeRoy go, Grace kissed him once more on his cheek and Luke stroked little LeRoy's hair with the back of his finger.

"Mister Brady, you may stop by the looking window at the nursery anytime to see how he is doing. Nurses will be there at all times if you should need anything."

"Thank you." Luke glanced down once more into the baby's face. "I guess I'll see you soon, little fella."

The nurse lifted LeRoy from Grace's arms. "Now, Missus Brady, you take this time to rest. You'll need your strength. So be sure to sleep when you can. And Mister Brady, you have five minutes."

After the nurse left the room, Grace glanced up at Luke. "We're a family now, Luke. There's three of us." Lazily, her eyes fluttered, fatigue now sweeping over her.

With his good arm, Luke smoothed back her hair from her forehead, admiring her face.

"I must look a mess."

"No, you're absolutely beautiful."

His eyes confirmed he was telling the truth. He loved her. And their love had only grown in the time they'd been together. Now, with little LeRoy's arrival, their bond was strengthening.

"Is this how you felt, Grace?"

Her brows furrowed together in confusion. "What do you mean?"

"All day long I worried about you. I prayed God would—" he choked back the words—"that everything would be okay. Not knowing what was going on back here was killing me. The tables seemed to have turned from just a few years ago. Once upon a time, I was the one confined to a hospital. Now you're the one lying in a hospital bed and I'm the one waiting by your bedside." His beautiful brown eyes pierced hers. So much love, so much concern lay within them.

Now she understood what he was trying to say. For so long she'd been the one waiting on him. She was the one who'd prayed and hoped Luke was still alive. Now she knew Luke was saying he understood *her*. He knew the fear of the unknown, of being completely helpless, and completely alone.

Weakly, she smiled as she rested her head back against the hospital bed. "I would've waited forever for you, Luke. You were worth all the worry and I'm so thankful God allowed me to keep you."

"Me too."

Fatigue overcame her, and in the comfort of that moment with her husband, Grace found pure contentment and peace. Her eyes fluttered closed and rolled beneath the dark of her eyelids.

Luke's warm lips pressed against her cheek once more and he whispered in her ear before sleep overcame her.

"Get some rest, Sweetheart. I'll be waiting for you to come home."

THIRTY

One explosion after another pounded like a hammer against Phillip's forehead with shear force. He winced at the pain stabbing his right temple.

This morning's awakening had not been at all too kind to him. His carousing from last night had surely caused him to pay his dues this morning.

Bringing his tin to his mouth, he sipped on the black of his coffee and fixated his eyes on the shell of a new dwelling that stared back at him.

With each detonation of haunting recollections, Phillip's mind traced back over his childhood instances—an intermittent collection of past merriment and post-war horrors.

His mind couldn't seem to decipher which was good and which was evil. All he knew was both flashbacks led to bad memories.

Jack's death, that dead Filipino girl, and Paloma.

It was that—*that* was his reason for his late night drinking fits, and for his sudden intermittent attention span.

The clang of metal against metal caught Phillip off guard as he reached down for another handful of nails. His body flinched as the echoing sound of carpenters' hammers shot through the air, its sound reminding him of those sudden gun shots fired in the jungle. He took a short moment to compose himself from the mild startle the clatter gave him. He'd been doing more of that lately—jumping at the mildest of sudden noises, or feeling his heart rate rise rapidly at the backfire of a vehicle. Sometimes those unexpected clamors catapulted him right back to the thick of battle. The trickery it played on his mind made it difficult to decipher what was real and what was a figment of his overworked imagination.

A slight glance over his shoulder reassured him that it was only Pete driving a metal stake into the ground with a sledge hammer.

Phillip shook his head in disgust over himself. Here he was, a fine Marine, and petty sounds were scaring the heebie-jeebies out of him. Of course, this morning's conversation with Libby didn't help matters for the better.

With extra force, he drove a nail deep into the grain of wood before him.

He'd only been home for a few short months and already Libby was wanting a baby—a baby!

Bam! Another nail dug deep into the slab of lumber.

Couldn't she see that he was still adjusting to life here at home? All he was looking for was a job to support his wife. The thought of providing for a family had not even crossed his mind! In fact, children was the one thing he had forced away from his concentration altogether. He'd never make a good father. Not when his head was full of so many tormenting memories. Adding a houseful of children to the mix would surely send his tensions rising beyond what he could handle considering...

Using his forearm, he wiped sweat from his brow. It may have been April, and the air may have been cool, but his battlefront flashbacks were enough to keep his blood flowing warm inside his veins. Some days, his reflections were so vivid, he could feel the steamy humidity sticking to his skin. But when his eyes refocused to his surroundings, it was just the cool, spring mist hitting his brow.

"Hey, uh, Phil, what's eating you, man?" Pete dropped a stack of new boards at Phillip's feet. "If the boss catches you snoozin' on the job, he's gonna send ya packin'." Pete threw his thumb over his shoulder.

"I know," Phillip replied in frustration. "I'll do better. I just got a lot on my mind right now, you know?"

Pete crossed his arms over his chest and sized him up. "Come on, fella. What's a guy like you have to worry about? You got yourself a dame, a good payin' job, food on your table...what else could possibly be playin' on your mind?"

Phillip straightened his back, his hammer still in hand. "You got a gal at home, Pete?"

"Well, yeah, sure."

"Tell me this...you got a couple of kids?"

"Two. Say, what're you getting at, Phil?"

"Libby wants a baby." He waited for Pete's reaction, but Pete seemed unaffected by his statement.

"Yeah, so what's the big deal, Johnson?"

"What's the big deal? Come on, Pete. You know more than I do what that entails."

"So the little woman wants some kids. So what? Don't they all? It's what makes the world go 'round my friend."

Maybe Pete wasn't getting the big picture. Phillip bent down and lifted another board of lumber from the stack and laid it down across the saw horses. Picking up his hand saw, he thrust the saw forward and started with the back and forth motion of cutting through wood. He paused when his thoughts formed words.

"Well, maybe I don't want a family. I just crossed half the world, Pete. I haven't seen my wife in almost four years. What's wrong with it being just the two of us anyway?"

"Gee, fella, it sounds like this is a personal matter."

Yes, it was. It certainly was a personal matter. One that he probably shouldn't be bringing to work.

"Say, what you got against kids anyhow?"

Harder and faster Phillip pushed and pulled his saw against his wood board, digging and gouging away at the grain. Bits of saw dust fell at his boots. With each granule that fell, a little more of his soul flaked. A little more of his mind's eye gave him glimpses of what he was forced to endure back on the island.

The zipping sound of his saw blade against the wood resonated deep within him like the whiz of machine gun bullets splitting the air.

His veins pounded in his head.

With each pull of the blade, he could hear the deep boom of a mortar shell detonating on the ground, sending bodies and limbs catapulting through the air.

Phillip's heart thumped harder in his distress.

He couldn't turn back. He couldn't run from the disaster coming straight for him. The only thing to do was to plow forward.

Don't turn back.

No hesitation.

His saw cut through splintered lumber, dropping the remains at his feet with a thud—just like the blast of his gun and the corpse of his enemy falling at his feet.

Phillip stared down at the ground, just beyond the toe of his boot. His eyes lied to him, displaying fresh blood that seeped from his enemy's temple as the remains of a ghost soldier laid at his feet.

He'd done that. He'd taken the life of a walking, breathing man and finished him off.

He squeezed his eyes shut, trying to cut off and suffocate the brutal reminder.

Anger stirred within him. His surroundings became clear again, the body disappearing from sight. He gave the excess wooden board a quick kick of his boot, sending it hurling across the lawn.

With a sharp jab, he threw the saw to the ground and leaned his hands against the saw horse.

A high whistle blew from Pete's lips. "Look, you don't want to talk about your problems, that's fine with me, fella, but don't go inquiring of things and getting' yourself in a tizzy over something *you* asked me about."

Pete walked off, leaving Phillip to deal with his angst and thoughts. He'd done a good job of that lately. He'd become a master at driving people away from him. And he couldn't figure out why.

Phillip retreated around the corner of a nearby building, making his getaway secret. As sweat trickled down his face from anxiety, he worked to steady his breathing. Once he rounded the corner, he leaned his back and head against the coolness of the hardware shop's block wall. The alleyway provided perfect seclusion for him to work through this recent spell.

Phillip thought back to the days when all seemed normal.

When he boarded the east bound train for Arbor Springs, everything seemed right. He'd sat on the train car with Libby's photograph pinched between his thumb and forefinger. He was going home…to her. He'd left all his baggage in San Francisco. He'd left the war in the Pacific. All that was good and safe had stood in front of him across miles of rails. It felt good to be on the safe road home.

But his homecoming had not been what he thought it would be.

For reasons unknown to him, he could not untangle the web that he'd somehow become caught up in. Why had unhappiness entered his soul? Why had the nightmares and flashbacks come back with a vengeance? Why did he continue to push everyone away from him?

Why…had he lost control?

❧❧

Whomever said time heals all wounds was mistaken. There were some hurts that simply could not be mended.

All afternoon Phillip tried without success to suppress and ignore his mental wounds. But the harder he fought against his hauntings, memories continued to gush over the walls he'd built up inside. Reminders too ghastly to dwell on pushed up between the cracks of his hardened heart. Like vines, they reached upward, grappling his soul and slowly tightening its crippling fingers around his chest.

Pain seeped its way into his chest cavity.

Libby wanted a child...a baby. But every time he closed his eyes since that day on Marpi Point, that sound—the whimper of a child—echoed through his head. It may be a sweet song to a mother's ears, but to him, it was a clamor of udder destruction, of death.

He'd known death all too well the last four years. The first that he'd encountered, none other than the death of his dear friend, Jack Gregory.

As Phillip drove up the road leading to his neighborhood, his mind continued to wander without permission to those forbidden territories in the darkest corners of his heart. How he hated it. But no matter what tactic he tried, they would not abate. He'd lost all control of his own mental state.

It angered him.

All in one swift stroke, his hand struck the steering wheel of his vehicle.

Jack should have never died!

He was a good man. An honest man. A decent man. One engaged to the finest woman in the world—and he was gone.

No warning. No good-byes.

It wasn't fair!

That familiar red brick house came into view. The Gregorys' home.

How many times had he been in that home? Played in that yard as a child? Walked this street alongside his best friend?

The memories were everywhere. Like souls of the past lurking about in plain sight.

Phillip pulled his gaze from the Gregorys' house as he turned into his own driveway. As he dragged himself from his car, more echoes of the past whispered to him.

"Johnson, have yerself a swig. It gets rid of those flashbacks real quick-like."

More than once, the bottle was handed around the camp. One by one, each soldier tipped the bottle up and swallowed a gulp of intoxicating relief.

Never before had he allowed himself a drop of alcohol, but after the sights and battles of that particular day, he'd do anything to erase the images.

Gripping the bottle's neck, and before he had time to think twice,

Phillip had given in to the temptation. Bitter liquid stung his tongue and burned his throat as it trickled down into his belly. But sure enough, after a few more rounds, his body eased, his muscles relaxed, and his mind cleared. Finally, his body knew peace and contentment— at least enough for a few hours' sleep.

Now, as his sluggish body soldiered up the stairs of his porch, he wished for a bottle of that soothing pick-me-up.

THIRTY-ONE

"That's wonderful news, Maggie. I'm happy to hear it…take care now, bye-bye."

Ever so gently, Libby rested the phone receiver on its jack. A half smile tugged her lips upward as she mulled over the joyous news.

Grace's baby had arrived.

And just like that, the anticipated moment had made its grand entrance. The Bradys were now a family of three.

Libby stared blankly down at her hands as she stood at the occasional table in the living room soaking in the news. But as happy as she was for Grace, the same joy pitted her stomach. Libby and Phillip had been married a few years longer than Grace and Luke…so why hadn't she been blessed with that same miracle of life?

Her hand rested against her middle. The longing to start a family of her own had only increased in the time since Phillip returned and as she watched Grace transform into a mother-to-be. Her eyes squeezed shut as she willed back tears. She couldn't let them fall. Not now. It wasn't her time. She should be happy for the new little life that entered the world, not wallowing in her own pity for what she didn't have.

"Who was on the telephone, Libby?"

From the corner of her eye, she glanced at Phillip. He lay on the couch, hidden behind the newspaper. He hadn't bothered to peer out from his reading to look at her. And she so desperately wanted him to look at her.

"Your sister." She paused to clear her throat. "The Bradys have welcomed their son into the world."

Phillip's disinterested mumble almost sounded like an acknowledgement.

Flipping her hair over her shoulder, Libby took the armchair adjacent to the couch. "Maggie says they named him LeRoy—after Luke's father. She also said Missus Sullivan was quite delighted over it. I can only imagine how she reacted." Libby's hands clasped together in excitement.

"Probably like any other grandmother in this country would react."

A sharp glare narrowed Libby's eyes. Phillip's short, insolent remarks were becoming more an everyday occurrence. His whole demeanor had changed, little by little, each day ever since his homecoming. And slowly, Libby was coming to the conclusion that something was not well with her husband. But like the good wife, she chose to keep silent and cater to his needs. However, it still didn't cause him to stop and really look at her—the way she wanted him to. She had a husband, but not a companion.

And she so desperately wanted his companionship.

She smoothed out her skirt with her hands—a habit she often resorted to when her nerves got the best of her—and tilted her head as she worked up the words to carry on her conversation with Phillip.

"Maggie also tells me Missus Sullivan is planning to move in with the Bradys for a while until Grace is back on her feet again. I think the idea of a live-in nanny is lovely. Missus Sullivan certainly has taken on the mothering role for Luke. I'm quite certain she'll make a lovely grandmother to little LeRoy. I'm glad to hear Grace will be in such good care during her recovery. Luke certainly loves her. I see how he—"

"Libby, darling, slow down a bit. I can't focus on this article with all your babbling."

"Babbling?"

It was as if he'd hit her chest with a concrete board. The sting that reverberated within her ate through her heart. Did he really think her to be annoying and irritating? All the years she spent alone in their flat in Pennsylvania and the months she stayed here at the house waiting for his return, waiting for the one person whom she could talk to, the one who could understand her...and he'd cut her to pieces with one sharp swing of his words.

"Is that what you think of me, Phillip? Do my *babblings* irritate you?"

His eyes peered out from around the corner of his paper.

"Well, I'm sorry if my conversation bores or—or annoys you." She stood to her feet. "I'm sorry if our life together is not as exciting as some tropical island or the firing of a weapon. Because from what I see of you, it seems as though you were happier living on an island thousands of miles away from everyone while you faced and killed off your enemies."

With a stomp of her foot, she turned to stalk out of the room, but firm pressure squeezed and jerked her arm as Phillip's grip twisted her around to face him. The sudden, swift move surprised her. Stunned, her words escaped her as Phillip's dark eyes, glinting with anger, pierced her. His height seemed to tower over her—something she'd never noticed before—making her feel ever so small and inferior to his stature.

"You listen to me right now, Elizabeth. You have no idea what I went through over there. You don't know the evils and the torture that raged across those fields and mountains. You know nothing of what I saw or what I did!"

"You're right, Phillip," her voice wavered. "I don't know what you saw or what you did because you never talk to me about it. You don't speak of anything to me. You never wrote it in your letters. Instead, I had to listen by the radio to piece together where you might be. Do you know the torture I went through?"

Just as the throbbing in her arm intensified, his other hand came up and gripped her opposite shoulder. Just when she thought he might shake her as her father had done to her mother, something in Phillip's eyes sparked.

The room grew eerily quiet. Only the sound of her quick breaths was heard between them.

She kept one eye on him, but her face she kept turned at an angle. She knew all too well what a man was capable of doing to his woman if he became angry enough.

But Phillip's ire hadn't reached that point.

Instead, she saw something different. The clouds of rage disappeared from his eyes and the stiff lines in his forehead dissipated. His eyelids blinked hard as he broke away from her scrutiny and his hands slowly released the stronghold he had on her.

"Libby...I...I'm sorry."

He'd suddenly gone from an angry, authoritative soldier to a stuttering, confused man. The change was uncanny in Libby's eyes, but it still didn't help stifle the fear that grew inside her.

With his hands now free of tension, the blood resumed its flow down her arms. Gently, his hands ran short strides up and down the upper part of her arms and shoulders.

"I—I didn't mean to..." Seemingly stunned by his own actions and words, Phillip couldn't finish his sentence.

Large tears worked their way into Libby's eyes, spilling onto her cheeks and running down her chin. She found the courage to say what she needed to say, although not without a shudder in her voice.

"All I wanted was to share my thoughts and dreams with you. And my hope was to finally build our life together and move forward like we both wanted."

With that, she turned, free of his grasp, and walked up the stairs to their bedroom.

THIRTY-TWO

Inexplicable darkness overshadowed the hollow room around Phillip. A deep void burrowed through his chest wall and settled on his heart. An ache so cavernous throbbed inside him. All he could do was collapse on the couch and bury his head into his hands.

Within the confines of his palms, his head shook from side to side as he tried to wrap his mind around his actions. Sharp breaths flared from his nostrils as the ache intensified.

Libby's wounded expression and grieving eyes continued to replay through his mind. He once again succeeded in damaging his marriage.

Broken shards of their relationship seemed to pile up at his feet with each passing day. Somehow, he'd managed to become the offender in their union, guilty of sins past and present with no clear answer on how to fix this brokenness.

The door to their bedroom clicked shut.

Libby had shut herself in for the night. He knew this because this was how it had been for the last few months. She'd come to him, wanting to talk, telling him about the new motor cars the neighbors were purchasing, the new washing machines her friends were acquiring, and babies…Phillip was sure he would never hear the end of it now that Grace Brady's baby had arrived.

Parenting had once been a dream of his too. But that was four years ago. Before marriage. Before war. Before Saipan. Before Paloma.

His calloused fingers pressed into his forehead, seeking to alleviate the tension and anxiety building up inside him. Like a hammer, his heart beat harder against his chest cavity, making it difficult to breathe.

Two girls had stolen his heart. Neither one knew the other existed. Neither one had understood his circumstances. To both, he made promises. For himself, he'd made a catastrophe.

Tremors shook his hands. His body was telling him to resort to alcohol. It was the only way to make everything disappear.

❧❧

Two hours was enough time to drive to *Oscar's*, down a few glasses of hard liquor, and stagger out the doorway onto the street. Phillip saw two of everything. Two of the same houses, two lights in every window, two telephone booths at the corner, blurred and swaying.

His eyes rolled beneath his eyelids and squinted against the lights shining through a canvas of black. The night had grown late. Late enough that the sun had long ago hidden behind the western horizon.

As he strained to look into the windows of nearby dwellings at the square across the street, he realized that everyone seemed to be tucked away safely within their homes. The outlines of men's and women's faces cleared momentarily as he peered from his place on the street's side. Yes, everyone was home, with their families, where they should be—where *he* should be.

"Hey! Hey, you!"

Stumbling to the right, Phillip's head took a spin as he swung it around to the voice calling out to him. He blinked hard, opening one eye and then the other as a figure walked toward him.

As the man neared, Phillip could make out his uniform.

"Yes—ss, Officer?" Phillip straightened. He may be inebriated, but he was still conscious enough to understand the acuteness of the situation. He stood a little straighter, albeit difficult to keep his body from swaying to one side.

"You do realize, sir, it is after nine o'clock, and town curfew is precisely at nine o'clock tonight?"

"No, Officer, I did not realize it had gotten quite that late in the evening."

The uniformed gentleman stood for a long moment, sizing Phillip up. The man's eyes carefully considered his state. Finally, he lightly nodded his head.

"I trust you are heading home to the missus straightway?"

Phillip's eyes travelled across the street to the square.

Harvey.

"Y—yes-s, s-sir. I'm heading up yonder to Belle Grove Square. Just over the hill there."

"Very well. You best get some sleep." Then the officer added under his breath. "You're gonna need it, fella."

Closing his eyes, Phillip released his breath. That was all he needed was to lose his wits about him and end up in the stockades, err the city jail.

As soon as the policeman rounded the corner, Phillip entered his car and started for Harvey's house. It was just a small skip across the street and up the hill to the grove, but trying to drive a straight line proved to be difficult in his intoxicated state of mind.

He wasn't sure what had overcome him to resort to Harvey at that moment, but he knew Harvey was the person he needed for help.

Slowly, he made it up the steps only to miss the last one and crash to his knees on the front porch. Within seconds, the porch light had come on, blinding him with a killer headache.

"Ah! Can we kill the lights?" he shouted to no one but himself.

Then the front door unlatched and opened, a large figure darkening the doorway.

"Phil?"

"Hiya, Harv."

"Phil, what are you doing on the floor of the stoop?"

"I must've missed that last step."

"Well, here, let me help ya up."

As Harvey said, he assisted Phillip to his feet.

Phillip, his head still throbbing, was glad for the extra hand. His head twisted and swayed as the blood rushed from his forehead to his toes.

"Give me a minute, will ya, Harv?"

"Hey, fella, you're not okay are ya?"

"I will be."

"No. No you won't. You best get inside. C'mon, Sydney will put a pot of coffee on for us."

"No, no. Don't make a fuss over me. I'm just passing by. I...I really should get home to my...my wife."

But Harvey ignored his plea. Instead, his friend led him to the kitchen and set him down at the old, wooden chair at the table.

"Sydney, we have company. Put on a pot of coffee, will ya, and make it strong."

Light clapping of heels clicked against the kitchen floor as Sydney entered the kitchen. Her hair had been let down and it bounced against her shoulders. It seemed as though the couple was winding down for the night. And why shouldn't they? It was past nine o'clock.

"Why, Phillip. What brings you by this time of night?"

"Uh, honey, Phil isn't feeling all too well. Can you get that brew going, please?"

Harvey's uneasy interruption seemed to speak volumes to Sydney. Without hesitation or question, his wife nodded and made quick work of fulfilling Harvey's request.

"You know, Phil, we really need to stop meeting like this," Harvey teased.

Phillip placed his aching head in his rough hands. "I know. I don't know how I got here, Harv. For some reason, I had to come."

"I see."

Harvey sat across him, just as he did at their last late night meeting and stared into the smoothness of his kitchen table. There, in same spot as before, to the right of Harvey's elbow, lay the black book Harvey had slid in front him.

"You know this matter is only going to get worse from here if you don't put a stop to it, Phil. It's going to eat at you and eat at you until it's devoured your whole being. Then it'll be too late. When are you going to say enough is enough?"

"I've already said it's enough!" Phillip winced at the height of his own voice. "I'm sorry." He lowered his tone, reeling back his anger. "I didn't mean to snap like that. I don't mean to do anything that I say or do. It just happens. I somehow lose control of everything I once possessed, and it all comes crumbling down in tiny shards that fall through my hands. The only way to lessen the pain is to drown it out."

"That's not the only way, Phil."

Phillip glanced up, his hand falling to the table, and he matched Harvey's glare.

"Then what's my alternative?"

THIRTY-THREE

The Dance
27 April 1946

Nothing Libby did could wipe the long frown from her face.
      She'd spent all afternoon dolling herself up for this evening's dance—the dance Phillip had promised to take her to. She'd pulled the pink dancing dress from her closet, the one Phillip liked best on her, and sat at her vanity to curl her hair and powder her face.

Red lipstick stained her lips. Although she wished she could find the genuine smile that came so easily to her when all was right in her world, she found even the slightest of artificial happiness difficult to display.

Things between her and Phillip remained shaky. Twice today she almost called off their engagement to the dance, but no, she would stick it out and act as though everything was peachy. At least, that's what Mother did to ward off any suspicion.

Libby stilled as she stared at her reflection in the mirror. Her eyes had become sunken and dark. Circles had formed beneath them, adding a depth so deep it scared her. This wasn't who she was. But it was who she'd become.

Nonetheless, she would walk with her head held high and march forward. Things may be disturbed in their household, but no one needed to know.

The click of the doorknob pulled her attention from the mirror to the doorway. Phillip quietly entered the room, dressed to the nines in his black slacks, crisp, white collared shirt and freshly polished dancing shoes.

The slightest hint of a smile pulled up one corner of her mouth. With his hair slicked back and his tie on straight, it was a subtle reminder of the attraction that drew her to him so long ago. To think about it, she was still just as attracted to him as she'd always been. She couldn't help but stare in awe of him.

Time seemed to stand still as she watched him splash aftershave over his face and neck. Strong was the desire to go to him and hold him in her arms, but after the last week of rejections and reprimands she refrained from all those feelings.

"Libby? Is something wrong?"

Blinking out of her musing, she shook her head. "N-no. Not a thing, dear. I was just thinking how handsome you look tonight."

To her surprise, Phillip started for her. He reached down for her hands and pulled her into him.

"I promised you a night out and a night out is what you'll get." He paused, pressing his lips to her forehead and lingering a moment longer. "I know things have been strained here, and I'm sorry. I'm trying...to figure everything out."

"Tell me when you do, Phillip. I just want you back. That's all I ever wanted."

"I'm here."

"No...you're not. Not really."

She wasn't sure if she should have said it, but it was already out in the open. She prayed her words wouldn't ignite his sensitive attitude and anger.

Forlornly, his tightened muscles loosened, releasing her from his embrace. Her sad eyes rose to meet his face and she searched for any sign that he might be angry with her. But he didn't respond like she anticipated. Instead, his arms dropped to his sides as he took one step back. His jawline tensed and he gave one nod of his head.

Strange how he never once offered up any rebuttal. Although relieved that her words didn't spark an uproar from him, Libby was now left with confusion. Confused as to who this man was and what he'd become. She didn't really know him anymore. She couldn't see through his thick exterior and into his heart and mind like she once did. She didn't know what thoughts were running through his head.

And that scared her.

☙ ❧

If ever a song had more meaning to her, it was this one.

From beneath closed eyelids, Libby absorbed the melody to Dinah Shore's new hit, *Laughing on the Outside, Crying on the Inside*. The words to the song resonated within her soul. Why? Because it was as if the song was written for her.

As Libby sat at her place at the round table, swaying to the music, everyone else in the dance hall vanished. Even though her hope in her marriage was diminishing, there remained a small thread of hopefulness within her.

If only she could turn back the sands of time. Back to the day before the Pearl Harbor incident. Before Phillip came home with those dreadful enlistment papers in hand. Before the war had stolen her husband.

A single tear seeped from her eye. Her eyelids opened as she remembered where she was. Brushing away at her leaked emotions, she sniffed and sat a little straighter in her chair. Blinking hard, she subtly dried her eyes. She only hoped her mascara hadn't left a trail down her cheek, staining her face for all to see. Grabbing her compact from her clutch, Libby checked her make-up. Aside from a slightly red-tinted nose and watery eyes, she appeared to look all right.

The compact clicked shut between her fingers and she breathed a sigh of relief.

"Hiya, Libbs!"

Sucking in a surprised breath, Libby shook out of her pensive moment to find Maggie standing in front of her with her arm hooked over Danny's elbow.

"Maggie. Danny. Well, hello."

"Sorry we're late. It took a little extra time to get ready tonight. I think we're all a little pre-occupied with Grace's baby."

Phillip chose that moment to return to their table with two cups of punch in hand. Carefully, he set Libby's down on the table, making momentary eye contact with her. Inside, she knew that look. Perhaps the only thing about him that she did recognize. Pain dwelled behind those brown eyes of his. She remembered it so well. It was the same morose expression he wore after Jack's funeral.

"Hey there, big brother." Maggie's voice nearly squealed out of joy.

Libby weakly smiled. That Maggie. Always so jubilant with gaiety. At least something was going right in someone's life.

"There's my little sis and the best man." Phillip reached out to shake Danny's hand.

"Hey, fella, good to see ya," Danny replied.

The gang sat down together. Phillip sipped on his punch while Maggie placed her belongings under the table. Danny rested his elbows on the tabletop, something Libby had grown accustomed to after her proper upbringing.

After Maggie got herself situated, she let out sigh of relief. "What a way to ring in springtime. First a brand new baby then a spring dance." Maggie's red-stained lips smiled with a boldness about them.

"Speaking of baby. Have you any news on Grace?" Libby asked.

"I was able to look in on her today. She's doing just wonderfully. A little tired, which is to be expected, but she's just swell. And that little LeRoy...he's just darling."

"Hang on to your hat, Phillip. Now that these two are together and the baby talk has begun, that'll be the end for us."

"Daniel Russo, I resent that!" Maggie nudged Danny's arm.

"I'm afraid it's true, sis," Phillip joined in. "We've lost the both of you to infantitis."

"Infantitis?" Maggie questioned. "I beg to differ. Now you two go on and have your manly talk in your corner of the table. Leave us ladies be."

"Gladly," Phillip sighed. "Children are a nuisance anyhow. I'm sure Grace and her new beau will find that out shortly." Phillip sipped on his glass as if nothing about his callous attitude phased him at all.

Libby, as well as Maggie and Danny, sat in stunned silence. None of them knew what to say or how to react to his insensitive opinions.

Swallowing hard and taking in a shaky breath, Libby's nerves stood at the edge of ruin. She could only imagine what thoughts were racing through Maggie's and Danny's minds. Perhaps a change of subject was necessary, however, Maggie was the first to break the silence.

"Anyhow...before we were rudely—" her eyes darted to Phillip— "interrupted, I believe I was answering your question on Grace's condition."

Libby's eyes switched between Phillip and Maggie, unsure if she wanted to continue this conversation any longer. Weakly smiling, she only nodded.

"Well..." Maggie patted Libby's hand, excitement bolstering from the broad smile on her face. "She's expected to stay on the labor and delivery floor for at least another four days. But she's already telling me how much she wants to go home to Luke. Isn't it just dazzling, Libby? Grace and Luke are now a family of three!" Maggie paused to clap her hands together.

"It *is* exciting, Maggie. It makes me want for my own baby even more now."

At that moment Phillip cleared his throat, causing Libby to stop mid-sentence and glance over at him.

"Are you all right, dear?" Her brow rose into her forehead and her conversation dropped off.

Grumbling, Phillip lifted his glass of water to his lips and sipped before answering. "I'm fine, darling." He pasted an easy smile onto his face and gave Libby a reassuring glance. "Couldn't be better. I'm surrounded by all the people I love."

"Isn't this just lovely?"

All heads jerked around in surprise to see Mrs. Johnson standing behind them. And just behind her, was Mr. Johnson, looking spiffy in his black suit and bow tie.

Libby was not expecting her in-laws to make the occasion tonight, but she was grateful for their sudden appearance as her tensions were mounting.

Mr. Johnson moved to the only two empty seats left at their table. He pulled one chair from under the table, allowing his wife to be seated, then took a seat of his own.

Mrs. Johnson set her clutch against the white of the tablecloth and beamed at all of them, thankfulness radiating from her glowing smile. "I feel as though my world is complete. My family is back together again and gathered at our table. We have much to be thankful for this year."

Libby's eyes wandered around the table, moving from person to person as her mother-in-law spoke about the tragedies and triumphs through so many sufferings of the past four years.

As she looked from Mrs. Johnson to Maggie, Libby took a deeper gaze into the woman Maggie had become. The flirtatious, self-centered girl she once knew when she married into the family had now blossomed into a fine, mature woman. But not without consequence.

As Libby examined Maggie's smooth complexion and dancing eyes, she could hardly believe the girl had suffered loss, been sought after and shot at by the enemy, and strung between two men whom she loved. Not to mention the displacement and rejection she'd endured at the hand of her parents...and by Libby herself.

Truth of it was, Libby was jealous of Maggie. Her sister-in-law's fun personality drew people to her in a way Libby had never experienced. Maggie strolled into crowds and affairs with ease and made friends quite effortlessly. And Phillip talked about her all the time. Too much. In fact, so much that Libby forbid him to mention her at all after they were married.

Reminded of her own awkwardness caused great dissention and envy to take root in Libby's heart. *She* was the woman in Phillip's life, *she* should be the one Phillip talked about, thought about, and loved most.

However, when Phillip left with the rest of the men on the westbound train, it didn't take long for loneliness to burrow into that hollow hole in her chest. Not only was the love of her life gone, but she had pushed away everyone else who could possibly be there for her.

Night after night, she cried into her pillow. Day after day she walked with her head down and her spirits crushed. She hadn't spoken to anyone after Phillip's departure. That is, until she learned of Maggie's shocking decision to join the Army Nurse Corps and volunteer to serve overseas. Only then did Libby's heart take a sharp turn. Suddenly, she understood what was truly at stake. Phillip and Maggie both had put themselves into harm's way to avenge, to save. So Libby took the plunge into waters uncharted and asked God for forgiveness then sat down at her maple desk to write the longest apology of her life. An apology that would take nearly 3 months to cross an ocean and foreign land to find its way to a sister-in-law lost to her.

She hoped her sincere admission of guilt would build a bridge spanning thousands of miles to connect her soul with the very person whom she pushed so far away. And miraculously...Maggie had forgiven her.

Now, sitting in the present, so many months after the close of war, Libby looked at Maggie through new eyes of understanding and curiosity. Maggie didn't live life for her own gain. She lived life to enjoy each moment gifted to her. She lived each day serving others by using her healing talents. She lived life with no regrets.

While Libby recognized those traits, she wondered how Maggie could put so many eventful and tragic memories behind her. She'd lost so many to war. She'd survived bombings and air raids, and yet, the woman sitting across from Libby Johnson looked as common and poised as any other woman in this town.

Libby's skin pricked as she wondered how she could ever measure up to a woman of Maggie's kind. What an inspiration Maggie had become.

Then there was Danny. The fun-loving Italian man who'd stolen Maggie's heart...and nearly broke it in two. A man who experienced death not once, but practically twice. How thankful they all were to learn Danny had not died in the D-Day jump as the War Department initially reported.

Libby watched as the couple across from her exchanged loving glances and clasped each other's hands. Words didn't need to be said, for Libby could see the gratefulness and joy that emanated from their faces.

And Phillip...

Libby clutched his upper arm tightly, so thankful he was home and so thankful he'd survived the war in the Pacific. Yes, her mother-in-law was correct—they had so much to be grateful for this year.

Her attention fell back to her mother-in-law. Mrs. Johnson reached for her glass and raised it in the air. The soft glow of lit candlesticks danced across her face as she smiled and took a moment to acknowledge each of her children.

"To our blessed life and the love we share between us. May we never lose sight of what's important. May we never become torn apart again. And may our Lord bless us throughout our whole lives."

Such a wonderful thought, to think that nothing or no one could ever divide this family again. But in the depths of Libby's heart, she somehow knew a wicked storm was brewing on the horizon of the Johnson homestead.

THIRTY-FOUR

*C*hildren are a nuisance?

Guilt shamed Phillip as soon as he'd said it. Now his own mocking voice echoed back to him as his mind replayed that line over and over again.

He knew everyone at the table glared at him, either surprised by his outburst or appalled by it.

He didn't really think children were a burden. But for reasons he was still trying to untangle, he'd pushed the thought of ever having children of his own as far away as he could. After Saipan, he couldn't look at another child the way he once did. At least, not without the accompaniment of those horrid and grizzly images. Images he could no longer control and put out of his mind. No, these images refused to be abated. They found their way into his deepest of sleeps, into his eardrums, as mental recordings of their screams played back like a broken record. There was no way to stop them. So he chose to forget the idea of children altogether. If he couldn't see them, then they couldn't cause him any more grief uncontrolled by his own body.

But that didn't mean that anyone else would understand him. The only way to avoid their questioning was to create the false façade that he'd changed his mind. That he no longer wanted children of his own, let alone he would be interested in anyone else's children—especially Grace Brady's.

Tightening jaw muscles ground his teeth together.

He wanted to be happy for Grace, but after all the years of growing up, all the years of knowing Jack and Grace would one day marry, he still couldn't picture her without Jack.

Jack was like a brother to Phillip. When Pearl Harbor was bombed, Phillip couldn't believe his best friend had perished. Not Jack. He was too strong. He was too full of life. And he had so much more of his life to live.

Jack's good-humored smile still haunted him. The smile he gave everyone as he boarded the train bound for San Francisco. Little did they all know that in just four months' time, Jack would be lost to all of them.

It never occurred to Phillip that Grace would find someone new. That once he returned from war, she'd be married to someone else. Perhaps it shouldn't bother him like it did, but he couldn't help it. Grace was the last person in this town who was Phillip's tie to his best friend. Even Jack's parents had soon moved away after their son's funeral, leaving behind every memory.

That was why he chose to sit in his chair on his front porch and stare. Libby often asked what it was that he gazed upon day after day. Perhaps his parents hadn't told her, or maybe she knew the truth. Either way, nothing or no one could change the fact that Phillip awoke every single day to the taunting reminder of what he'd lost. Because every day, he walked out his front door and his vision collided with the sight of all his childhood memories—the memories he'd created with Jack.

…because Phillip Johnson now lived across from Jack Gregory's home.

⊰⊱

Dancing.

Yes, dancing would be the perfect distraction from his intense thinking.

"Libby, darling, how about a swing around the dance floor?"

Her eyes perked right up as he held his outstretched hand to her.

"I'd love to, Phillip."

The band struck up lively and engaging tunes, all new to Phillip. Living in the jungle over a half a world away meant the latest jazz and swing tunes didn't travel to his ears until months later.

A few songs in tribute to the late Glenn Miller were announced from the stage. Those songs were some of his greatest hits to reach the airwaves. As the numbers slowed in rhythm, Libby's steps matched the tempo, and she leaned in to his chest. He hadn't found the words to tell her, but the closeness of her proximity and the touch of her cheek against him, created an overwhelming sensation inside him.

He really did love her.

He hadn't shown it lately—not like he really should—but he truly loved and adored Libby.

But he also loved Paloma.

Paloma had stolen his heart with her large, chocolate eyes and bright, beautiful smile. He knew he shouldn't have saved her from that underground cave, but he couldn't let her die all alone in there. He'd never forgive himself.

The idea was to never allow himself to feel anything for her. He was just a soldier doing his job. But when those beautiful black eyes stared up at him and tears spilled down her cheeks as he left her in the care of the Red Cross, he knew he'd never be able to let her go.

But he had.

His efforts to save her got him as far as San Francisco. From there, the Red Cross became involved and would not permit her passage.

Phillip's eyes squeezed shut as tears flooded them in the middle of the dance floor...

That day he left San Francisco for the east coast was the hardest day he could remember in his life. He'd held on to Paloma as long as he could, before the aid workers pulled her away from him. He never felt more the villain than that day. With tears streaming down her face, Paloma cried out to him, but there was nothing he could do. He was forced to leave her there. All alone. In a strange land with strange people. He hoped and prayed that the aid workers would take as much care with her as they promised him. And that's why he made those frequent trips to the post office. To ensure her good care, he paid a considerable amount to Paloma's caretaker month after month, until he could figure another way to bring her back to him.

"You seem a million miles away tonight."

Libby's soft voice rushed into his ears. He'd nearly forgotten where he was.

"I'm sorry. I suppose I got myself absorbed into the music."

"It's beautiful, isn't it, Phillip?"

"That it is." His hands reached up to where hers rested against his shoulders and his fingers intertwined with hers. Sincerely, he gazed down into her eyes to tell her the truth that rested on his heart. "It's beautiful just as you are. I don't believe I got around to mentioning that earlier."

"No, you didn't. But thank you."

There was more she wanted to say, he could sense it, but instead of voicing it, she pressed her lips into a tight smile.

Sensing the canyon growing deeper between them, Phillip didn't know what else to say or how to say it. Instead, he pulled Libby into his chest and continued their dance. As their bodies swayed to the slow rhythm of the soft music, his eyes swept across the room of dancing couples.

Mother and Dad danced gingerly as the spark of their re-kindled love for each other illuminated their faces. Both exchanged looks of love and adoration. It was a sight Phillip was unaccustomed to seeing.

But that's what he had envisioned for his marriage.

Yes, long before his trek to the Pacific and the islands, Phillip had wanted that close connection with Libby. He wanted more for their marriage than his parents ever had. And so did Libby. Her broken home had been the farthest from stable and loving. Her living conditions had thrust Phillip's desire to marry her further than he could have ever told her. He wanted to protect her from her drunken father's fury and his abrasive language. So they married quickly and without fuss.

Those past memories caused his arms to hold her a little tighter. He shouldn't have let her go as he did, but the reality of it was his number would have been called sooner or later regardless of his actions. He was here now. And he should be the protector she deserved. Not the rotting mess he'd become.

The quiet moment passed and the next tune picked up tempo. Couples matched the cadence of the music and hopped to the beat.

As if no cares burdened her heart, Libby pulled away and took his hands. A broad smile revealed her pearly whites and they jived.

The song moved them across the floor and they laughed and carried on as they bumped into Danny and Maggie.

Phillip and Libby continued their glide around the dance floor. Libby squealed with laughter as their feet fell out of rhythm with each other.

"Looks like I'm out of practice!" Phillip shouted over the music.

"Perhaps we both are!" She responded.

For once, Phillip's heart felt light. He was able to forget everything else as he struggled on the dance floor and when Libby's giggle tickled his ears. The harder he tried to find the right dance steps, the worse his dancing became. Giggling without reservation, Libby finally took both his arms and stopped him.

"Watch," she said as she started up the dance steps once more.

This time he was able to recover and together they continued their lively waltz.

Their laughter lasted until half-way across the dance floor when they bumped into another couple.

Phillip's eyes, jubilant and easy, turned to apologize.

"Excuse us. Seems we have two left fee—"

He nearly choked on his words as his feet came to an abrupt halt. The face staring back at him triggered the same response he was trained to react to.

"What's your problem, buddy?" the man asked in annoyance.

"C'mon, Phillip." Libby tugged at his elbow. "Let's continue our dance."

Phillip was staring into the face of a Japanese man. His fury ignited and before he had any time to think, his reflexes reacted on their own.

In one bound, Phillip lunged for the man, knocking both of them to the floor. With Phillip pinning him down, the man begged for mercy.

"You're a Jap!" Phillip shouted.

Sharp intakes of breaths and screams bounced off the walls of the hall as the crowd became aware of the situation.

But Phillip hardly noticed.

The only thing registering in his mind was the fact that the enemy was standing in his hometown.

Rage blinded Phillip as he prepared his fist for the punch. Hand-to-hand combat was taught for this reason alone. Phillip had no weapon and the encounter had taken him by surprise. No worry to Phillip, he knew how to fight to the death.

His fist drew up tight and he went for the punch. But two other men tackled him to the ground, saving the Japanese man from a brutal attack.

"Come on, fella! What's your problem?" Phillip's assailants asked. "If yer comin' here for a fight, you're in the wrong place."

Both men held him by the arms and pulled him to standing, but he wasn't through with the fight.

Freeing his arms, he shoved the men back, triggering retaliation.

Screams echoed throughout the hall and more men jumped into the middle of the brawl, separating the opposing parties.

The Japanese fella stood, wiping blood from the corner of his mouth.

Phillip eyed him, hate radiating from his glare.

When the fog cleared, Phillip became aware that Danny, his brother-in-law, was one of the fellas who held him back.

"Phillip, what's wrong with you, man? Johnny, here, ain't no enemy. He's just as much an American as you and I." Danny pointed to the Japanese man.

"Stay out of this, Danny. I know who I'm dealing with."

"Phillip, get a grip on yourself! Johnny ain't the bad guy. The war's over."

Danny stood in front of Phillip, his eyes piercing him.

When Phillip glanced at Johnny he was met with sharp, precise words. "I oughtta report you to the authorities, I should. Bad enough I fought alongside you boys for the duration, but now I have to listen to your discrimination? Go on and get outta here before I do call the cops."

His breath coming quick, Phillip refused to back down. However, the entire hall now had their eyes on him. He glanced from face to face, his pride faltering. Finally, his eyes rested on Libby.

A pitiful sight.

Her hands covered her mouth. They trembled as large tears spilled down her cheeks, one after another.

"Libby…" he muttered.

Instead of coming to his side, she turned and bolted out the door, her sobs echoing in his ears as she left. And in Phillip's heart, he knew he'd fixed another nail in his coffin.

THIRTY-FIVE

Waves of nausea roiled in Libby's stomach. Horror gagged her throat and bound her to unspeakable mortification. Never had she been more humiliated, more disgraced...

Sharp breaths ballooned her lungs, dizziness and a sense of weakness languishing her strength with each breath. Her shaking hands wrapped tightly about her arms as she shivered in the dark of night. It wasn't the cool night air that caused her bones to tremble. No. It was Phillip's ridiculous behavior. His revolting actions were unpredicted and bewildering. Every soul in that dance hall had stopped and stared with gaping mouths. Tomorrow, she and Phillip would be the talk and laughing stock of the whole town of Arbor Springs.

It was too much for her to bear. Standing in the hall's courtyard all alone, her knees buckled and hit the slab floor. Not caring at all that her dress would be smudged with dirt and mud, Libby cowered by the stone wall, her tears falling like lead onto the courtyard floor beneath her.

What had she done to deserve this? What had caused her husband's sudden change of character? And why did God seem to be so far away?

For months she'd been asking Him to fix their marriage, to put it back together, but day after unrelenting day, her situation remained the same. No—her situation had grown worse. Now, Phillip's anger was affecting more than just her home.

Poor Johnny Hatayama.

As American as anyone in that hall, he was there to have a good time, dance with his wife. He wasn't looking for a fight. If anything, everyone there was looking to put the fighting, the war, behind them forever.

Libby's sympathetic thinking forced more tears, more trembling sobs to wretch her body.

"Libby!"

Swift, ladies heels rushed behind her, soon accompanied by strong, feminine hands on her shoulders.

"Libby, dear!"

"Leave me alone, Maggie. Let me be," Libby cried as she crouched her head to her knees.

"I won't. You need to tell me what's going on."

"It's no use, Maggie. What's done is done. I can't fix it. You can't fix it—no one can fix the brokenness." More sobs shook her shoulders and more tears streamed down her face and dripped to the ground.

Maggie's hands rubbed at Libby's arms. "Sweetie…I knew something was wrong. I knew from the very beginning. I should have listened to my instincts. Please tell me what's going on. Mother, and Dad, and Danny are inside with Phillip trying to sort out this mess. Let me be there for you, Libby."

"I don't know, Maggie. I just don't know."

Maggie's hold slackened. "Then how can I help? If you and Phillip don't give me answers, there's no way I can help you."

"It's not your problem, Maggie."

"Maybe not, Libby. But Phillip's my brother."

Inside Libby's head, she knew she needed to reach out to Maggie's invitation, but her mother's words constantly echoed back in her mind.

It stays in the home, Elizabeth. Outsiders only make it worse. They'll laugh, ridicule. At least we can retain our dignity by making them believe that all is well in their eyes.

Her friends' marriages were picture perfect. Maggie, Grace, Sydney, even Mr. and Mrs. Johnson's. No one could possibly understand her situation.

Wait…

No, there was someone.

"Take me to Sydney Duncan's home, Maggie."

⊰∾⊱

"Are you sure you don't want me to go inside with you, Libby?"

Maggie asked her the same question for the third time as they sat in front of the Duncan home at Belle Grove Square.

Libby sat a little straighter, however, with her eyes lowered, and sniffed. "I'm sure, Maggie. Thank you for driving me here."

Trying to regain composure, Libby squared off her shoulders and dabbed her hanky at her eyes. Reaching for the door handle, the passenger door popped open and Libby slid her legs from the vehicle's interior.

"I'll see to it that Harvey drives me back. Tell Phillip I'll be home later tonight."

It had been years since Libby used her rigid tone with anyone. The last time she remembered hearing such stringency in her voice was when she demanded Phillip stop all talk having to do with Maggie. And yet, here she was again, pushing Maggie out of her life.

"I'll be praying for you and Phillip, Libby. I'm sorry I can't be of more help to either of you."

With that, Maggie shifted the vehicle into drive and pulled away from the curb.

Libby knew her sharp tone and refusal of Maggie's aid had hurt Maggie's feelings, but her sister-in-law was the last person who could lend assistance in Libby's peculiar situation.

As the sound of Maggie's car faded in the background, hidden by the rows of town houses and businesses, Libby found strength to push her way up the porch stairs and rap on the Duncan's front door.

Behind her eyes, the sting of threatening tears pushed their way forward, putting her on the verge of another breakdown. Shuddering in her own skin, Libby willed herself to remain calm.

When Harvey opened the door, she bit her lip and only stared at him.

In the foyer of their home, Sydney's soft complexion peered over Harvey's shoulder.

"Libby!"

Her friend rushed forward, but Libby couldn't find the energy to move from her spot on the porch. Her hands clenched her upper arms as if cold had swept in to overtake her bones. But as Sydney came near, pushing past her husband and taking Libby into her embrace, Libby couldn't fight back any longer. All at once, her tears fell, and sobs shook her entire being. And through it all, Sydney just held her.

"Honey, I know all about it. Why don't you come inside."

Gently, Sydney led Libby into her home.

With no fight left within her soul, Libby complied, her muscles now loose with fatigue and exhaustion.

Harvey quietly leaned into his wife and whispered, "I'll put on a pot of coffee for you."

"Thank you, dear," Sydney replied as Harvey rushed off into the kitchen. Then Sydney glanced at Libby. "Harvey's going to get us fixed up with something to warm you up."

Sydney tried to smile, but Libby knew it was a ruse to lighten the mood. However, Sydney was being a friend—a true friend.

Libby's eyes drifted close as moisture seeped from them. Another whimper hiccupped from her throat and Sydney's arms came around her shoulders once more.

"Delores called me, Libby. I won't pretend that nothing happened, sweetie. She told me all about the incident at the dance. Are you here to talk about it?"

Without answering, Libby plunged into it. "I don't know what's happened to him, Sydney. He's changed. He's changed so much, I don't know him anymore."

"Phillip?"

"Yes. One minute we were dancing, and he held me so tightly in his arms. Much like he used to. Then, a moment later, everything about him had changed. I've never seen him act like this. Never. My husband has never laid a hand on any human being before. Why now, Sydney? Why?"

"There are some things we just can't understand, Libby. Especially in light of the recent events surrounding the country, nothing seems to make much sense anymore. Our world is changing and it's changing fast."

"I want it to stop," Libby whispered.

"It's overwhelming, isn't it?" Sydney's eyes looked softly on her. "But you know what I can promise you, Libby?"

"What's that?"

"The good Lord remains the same. He remains faithful. He remains steadfast. And He hasn't gone anywhere."

"I try to believe that, Sydney, but for the past four years it seems like He's never been more silent."

"And sometimes He is. But not for the sake of causing you misery. It could be that God is trying to show you something. Maybe for the past four years, He's been molding you into something beautiful for His good will."

Libby glanced up, pulling her attention from her hands to look into Sydney's blue eyes. "How did you and Harvey ever get through your troubles? Right now, I don't know if I can bear another day in that house with Phillip."

At that moment, Harvey entered the room with a heaping tray of coffee and sliced jelly bread.

"Here you are, ladies. Take all the time you need, and if you need a refill on coffee, just ask. I'll be in the other room."

"Thank you, dear. We may be a while."

Harvey leaned down to press a kiss to his wife's forehead. "I'll be waiting no matter how late."

It was just another awful reminder of how much love and devotion Libby was starved of. And she wondered, was Phillip thinking of her at all right now?

THIRTY-SIX

"Libby!"

Phillip's booming military voice broke through the walls of his home as he shoved open the front door and marched into the house. One by one, he glanced into all the downstairs rooms, searching frantically for her.

"I told you, Phillip, she's not here."

He turned to Maggie, who stood in the doorway alongside Danny. They'd followed him home after his exit from the dance hall.

"Where is she?" he snapped.

Maggie opened her mouth to answer, but was stopped by Danny's upright hand.

"Hold on." Danny interrupted. "I'm not sure you're in the right mind of knowing where she is at the moment."

That statement only fueled Phillip's anger. Who was Danny Russo to tell him what he could and could not know about his wife?

Stomping forward, he placed himself nose to nose with Danny.

"Phillip…Phillip, stop." Maggie pleaded.

He dismissed Maggie's plea and shot Danny a deadly glare as he dueled him in an intense match of stare-down.

"Where's my wife?" he growled.

"Let her be, Phillip. After the stunt you pulled tonight, she needs time."

"Danny's right. If you would have taken her feelings into consideration, you'd understand why she left the hall. Now stop this nonsense."

Maggie's petite hands pushed against his brawny chest in attempt to put space between him and Danny, but Phillip refused to back down. A Marine didn't back down from a fight.

So that's how it's gonna be, then?" Phillip snarled. "Fine. Stand in my way, why don't ya."

In one quick sweep, Phillip's fist collided with Danny's jaw, knocking his brother-in-law back. Maggie's shriek pierced his ears as she backed against the wall.

"Phillip, stop!"

But Danny was the next to throw a punch as his fist hammered into Phillip's gut. Danny's momentum pushed the both of them back and to the ground. Blunt force sent shards of pain up Phillip's spine and through his abdomen.

"Danny! Stop! Both of you! Nothing will get solved this way."

Maggie weaseled her way between the two of them. Once his sister stood between the fight, Phillip could do nothing but halt.

Wiping the back of his hand across his lip, Phillip's breath came hard and fast. He glared at Danny, angry with him for keeping Libby's whereabouts a secret. In fact, he was angry with the world. The globe had shown him nothing but cruelty. If he couldn't find help within his own family, then benevolence didn't truly exist.

"Let us help you, Phillip." Maggie stepped forward, her tone softening. "You can get through this. *We* can all get through this, but you have to allow us the chance to help."

Phillip considered her a long moment. His anger still boiled within him. Heat rose from his face as he struggled to keep his wrath caged. How could he speak to either of them? They were against him. They were *all* against him. And hiding Libby's whereabouts were about as low as family could get. So much for love, loyalty, and trust.

"You best go on and get. Both of you. There's nothing here to see."

☙❧

At quarter past ten, with the lights low in the living room, Phillip sat with his head in his hands amid the three distractions that had altered his life.

With his knees buckled against the coffee table, he rubbed a rough, calloused hand over his eye. A hiccup thrust its way up his throat, but he continued to reach for his flask. He'd made too big a mess of his life to quit now. He might as well finish what he started.

Tonight was proof that he was incapable of living in the sober world. Flashbacks of a war torn jungle plagued his mind at every turn, with every blink of his eye. The disease had only grown worse after his arrival home. And that homecoming hadn't gone at all like he hoped. Coming home was supposed to help him, to relieve him, to cure him. Instead, coming home had been the beginning of his undoing.

With an unsteady hand, he set the flask back on the small table and reached for the parchment lying open and exposed in front of his eyes. For the third time tonight he re-read Miss Howard's letter.

Dear Sergeant Phillips,

I hope my latest missive finds you well. Thank you for your generous donation in light of Paloma's care. I'm sure you will be enlightened to know that her health has improved immensely. I assure you that the monetary gifts you are sending are being put to good use as it has helped to clothe and provide adequate staples for her.

In reply to your inquiry, at this time, please be advised that the organization's process is somewhat extensive in bringing Paloma home to you. Your interest in becoming her legal provider must be reviewed by our board. Upon that, our counselors will also confer with Paloma about the possibility of becoming a United States citizen. All ducks must fall in a row for this process to be legal and binding. Please try to understand and have patience.

Before closing this letter, I thought you'd also like to know that Paloma speaks of you often. I overhear her talking to her friends about the great American soldier who came to rescue her from fire and ash. It is very noble what you did for her, sir. I'm sure there are many who would not have bestowed the same kindness toward her or her people.

Sincerely,
Adeline Howard

Allowing his eyes to roll beneath the dark of his eyelids, Phillip leaned back into the couch. His heart ached for the chance to see Paloma once more. So much time had spanned between holding her on the ship and his arrival home. What if in time she would forget about him all together? His heart would break in two.

A lone tear seeped from the corner of his eye. A show of emotion was never tolerated in the service. Sure, many of the men had breakdowns, but were later chastised for it. Sometimes severely. But this was different. Tonight he was home. Home alone, in the quiet of an empty shell.

He was losing everything.

His sanity. His sobriety. His marriage. How did he manage to take such a beautiful life and turn it into a shambles? Now, one by one, everything he once held dear to him was sifting through his hands like the island sand.

The clock chimed the half hour.

Libby still had yet to return. Would she ever come back to him? Never had she been out so late into the night.

As his thoughts continued on their path, his irritation festered all over again.

Libby was his wife. No matter what, she should be here, alongside him—

But, then again, why? He hadn't exactly held the door of love and kindness open to her. Instead, he'd shut her out completely.

As the two voices raged on and on inside him, his body became wrought with distress. The only way to make the voices stop was to keep drinking. Drink until they abated. Drink until the feeling stopped. Drink until the world went dark.

THIRTY-SEVEN

Steam rose from Libby's coffee cup as she sat across from Sydney, her eyes fixated on the heat escaping its pool of dark liquid. Slowly it rose and disappeared into thin air.

In a way, she wished she could do the same.

As much as Libby wanted to break away from her internal thoughts and allow herself to relax, her mind was tortured. Tortured with unspoken issues that insisted on replaying over and over again inside her head.

Her face continued to flush with humiliation at the thought of Phillip lunging at Johnny Hatayama. All those horrified faces staring between the two of them. The punches that were thrown. The words that were said...

Unable to silence them, Libby's hands squeezed her head between her arms and she doubled over to her knees.

"Libby, sweetheart." Sydney's voice barely cut through the recurrences. But the gentleness of her hands were warm and notable.

"I can't stop them, Sydney. The voices, the images...they keep replaying over and over again. It was awful, just horrid. How could Phillip do such a thing?"

"I don't know, sweetheart. My best guess is Phillip is dealing with something much bigger than we can understand. Start from the beginning. Perhaps we can shed some light on this predicament."

Sydney placed Libby's coffee cup in her hand. Accepting it, Libby sipped and relished in the warmth entering her chest. She took in a shaky breath and whispered in her heart, *I'm sorry, Mother. But this time I can't keep it to myself.*

Libby took the plunge and poured out her feelings to Sydney Duncan. It felt so good to finally talk to someone about her problems instead of hiding behind them. No wall was high enough to cower behind the evidence that Phillip had changed. He no longer loved her.

And she told Sydney just as much.

"Libby, I think he does love you," Sydney replied. "I know for a fact that he was here several nights ago talking with Harvey. From what I gathered after talking to Harv myself, Phillip is confused. But he loves you."

"Phillip was here?"

"Of course. Didn't he tell you?"

Libby's eyes trailed off across the room. "No," she said flatly. "He never tells me where he's going at night. But I always know where he's been when he comes through that door." Coldly, her eyes stared straight ahead, not seeing anything but the image of Phillip stumbling up the staircase. "He doesn't know that I know. But I lived too long in a broken home to not notice the slurred speech, the staggering, the babbling, and the stench on his collar and his breath. If my father taught me anything it was the look and putrid smell of an alcoholic. I could spot it from a thousand yards away."

Sydney grew quiet, her eyes downcast and sad. "Yes. Phillip has come here a few times ossified. Thankfully, the children were all in bed at the time and Harvey knew what to do."

Libby's eyes squeezed shut.

"I'm so terribly sorry, Sydney. I'm sorry that I can't control my husband's actions. I'm sorry that he's landed on your front stoop more than once in an inebriated state. And I'm sorry you're the one who has to put up with our problems."

Sydney glanced at her, a spark of hope twinkling in her eye. "I'm not sorry, Libby."

Sydney's statement surprised her. "What do you mean?"

"I mean, I'm not sorry at all that Phillip ended up at our door."

"I'm afraid I no longer follow you, Sydney."

"Remember when you once asked me how I was able to cope with Harvey's carousing and the such?"

"Yes."

"Honey, whether you know it or not, you are precisely where I was two years ago."

"I can hardly see you and Harvey at odds with each other."

"But you know it's true, Libby. You remember how Harvey was in school. It was no secret that his ways were far from gentlemanly."

Libby nodded in agreement and Sydney continued.

"What everyone doesn't know it that his foolhardy ways became worse. His time in the service didn't offer up any help either. Once he was injured and returned home, the homecoming was anything but sweet. At that time, we'd only had Nathaniel Scott. I thank the good

Lord every day that he was too young to see his daddy drunk and abusive."

"Abusive?" Libby's eyes widened.

"Shocking, I know. But you know how it goes, Libby. Those things aren't spoken of. A man and a woman—you know, are supposed to stay together."

Oh, she did know. She knew all too well the silence that went on in her own home as a child.

"What did you do, Sydney?"

"What did I do? Well, I had a child to look after so I packed little Nathaniel up and told Harvey I would be spending the summer with my parents. Many city folk do the same...the wives pack their things and take the children up to New England somewhere to visit the grandparents. So in the community, no one would think anything of it. But Harvey needed time. And I needed a safe place to stay."

Pausing, Sydney wiped at her eye. "I still get emotional over it sometimes. It was the hardest decision I'd ever made in my life, Libby. I loved Harvey. I didn't want to leave him. But I couldn't go on having him hurt me the way he did...and I certainly didn't want Nathaniel to become affected by it either. But praise God, Harvey woke up that summer. A few men from the church came to the house and presented the Gospel to him. By that point, Harvey had hit solid rock bottom. He was tired of living in misery. And he missed his family. Realizing he couldn't save himself, he asked God to save him. The Lord changed my husband, Libby. And He changed my life forever. When Harvey called to tell me the news, I didn't want to listen. I didn't want to believe it. But he asked to visit me at my parents' home. After thinking about it, I agreed. I had to see the change for myself."

"What did you see, Sydney?"

"The first thing I saw was a sense of peace on his face. Harvey had cleaned himself up. He'd bought a new dress suit. His hair was combed to the side, all neat and proper-like, and he wore a nervous smile on his face. But what I remember most was the new look in his eyes. They were clean and clear. And then he spoke to me. *Hello, Sydney,* he said. It wasn't his greeting though, it was the softness in his voice. The sincerity that held a deeper meaning in his tone. I knew right then and there that our life would be changed forever. It took months for me to fully trust him and for him to prove his sincerity to me, but we managed. In a way, it was as if we were dating all over again. But eventually, God gave me peace, too, and I was able to forgive Harvey."

Libby blinked back tears and her fingers fidgeted together in her lap. "Something like that seems so far away for someone like me, Sydney. Those things don't happen for everyone. I've prayed to God every day that Phillip's heart would change. That he would become the man he used to be."

"No, Libby. You can't do that."

Questions filled Libby's eyes as she glanced up at Sydney. Why shouldn't she pray for her husband's restoration? She waited for Sydney to explain.

"Libby, what I learned from my experience, is the proper way to pray. If you pray for things the way they used to be, you'll end up in the same spot you are trying to move from. Instead of praying for Harvey to return to the man I once knew, I prayed for him to become the man God wanted him to be. And instead of praying for restoration of our marriage, I prayed God would give us a marriage like we'd never known. A marriage based on the foundation of godly principles. After all, God instructs a man to love his wife as Christ loved the church. Christ gave his life for the church. The Bible also gives us godly examples of how to live our lives. The fruits of the spirit for example. Love, joy, peace, longsuffering…it was a learning experience for the both of us, but together we walked into our newfound faith and together we've grown alongside each other. My life has been so sweet since."

"I want that, Sydney. I want our life to be beautiful."

Then let me take you through the Bible and show you, Libby. And together we'll pray that the Lord works a miracle in your life. We'll pray that Phillip's eyes are opened and that his demons are snuffed out for good."

THIRTY-EIGHT

"Hold still a minute. Land sakes, Danny, you get shot by a bullet and nearly die, but let me give you some cold meat for that shiner on your face and you turn into a child."

Danny winced as Maggie dabbed at the swelled bruise over his eye. Still bewildered by tonight's sudden turn of events, all she could do was shake her head at it all.

"All right, all right," Danny answered. "I'll behave." With a crooked smirk coming over his face, Danny settled back against the couch and gave her a coy look. "Fix me up, nurse. I ain't feeling so well."

"Now, that's the Danny Russo I know." On her knees couch-side, gentle hands ran their fingers against the lump on his forehead. Her eyes prodded her husband's minor injuries caused by the fight.

Danny's touch followed her finger's trail alongside his temple, catching her hand in his.

"Bring back a lot of memories?" he asked softly.

"Too many bad ones," she replied as she met his eyes.

The want emanating from his gaze pulled her into him and their lips met, but still, her mind was full of too many distractions, too many questions to allow herself to let go and fall into Danny's embrace.

She broke away from him.

"I don't understand what's happened to them, Danny. I can't figure out what possessed Phillip to start a fist fight at the dance, and I can't figure out why Libby refuses to talk to me. It's almost as if they're purposely pushing me away."

"Maybe they are." Danny pushed himself upright, patting his knee for Maggie to sit.

"What?" Maggie took his offer and rested on his lap, leaning back into him as his hands encircled her waist.

His face snuggled near hers and pressed a kiss to her ear. "C'mon,

Maggie, you know how it is in society. Whatever the problem, it's obviously between the two of them."

"Tell that to your black eye, why don't ya." Tapping her fingers against the back of Danny's hands, Maggie paused and considered the situation. "Libby was pretty adamant that she didn't want to come home. And she didn't want Phillip to know where she was. Doesn't that seem odd to you, Danny?"

"Perhaps it's a bit over exaggerated, but—"

"No...something's not right. Remember Mother's welcoming home party? I sensed it then too. And remember the remark he made to Luke about being *the replacement*? I've never known him to make such a brazen comment. Phillip wasn't right that night. There was something in his eyes. Something going on inside him that I couldn't pinpoint. Something's there, Danny. I just don't know what it is."

The air between them grew eerily quiet. In the still and dark of the aging night, Maggie sensed both their minds probing the possibilities. Tension hung in the atmosphere of the town, in the troposphere that spanned the space between their home and Phillip's home. Especially after the awful fight that ensued at the dance. Everyone was left speechless, stunned.

"Johnny Hatayama is Japanese, right, Maggie?"

"Yes, I believe so. But he's been an American citizen his whole life. He was born here."

"That's beside the point."

"What are you getting at, Danny?"

"Johnny *looks* Japanese. Phillip went to war with them..."

Maggie loosed herself from Danny's grasp and turned to look at him with intrigue and irritation.

With cautious consideration, Danny continued. "Maggie, could it be possible that Phillip is battling some form of shell shock?"

The inquiry itself and the mention of the term slammed into Maggie's gut. The tiny hairs that covered the middle of her back stood on end as an unnerving chill ran down her spine.

"No." She pushed herself off his lap and stood in the middle of the room. "No. There is no way my brother is suffering from that horrible disorder."

Danny came to her side and reached for her, but Maggie slighted him.

"My brother is too strong for that, Danny. I can't believe you would make such a preposterous suggestion."

From behind closed eyes, Maggie pushed the thought away. That wasn't it. It couldn't be. How could Danny even offer up such an idea?

"Sweetheart," Danny followed her through the living room. "You said yourself that something isn't right there. What else could it be other than that?"

The pieces to the puzzle fit, but she couldn't bring herself to accept it. It had to be something else.

"No, no, no. It's not shell shock. It could be a wide array of things, Danny." She paced while counting off her fingers. "Like malaria. Malaria for one can do so much damage to the brain and the body."

"But Phillip hasn't come down with the fever. Nor has he said anything about it," Danny replied.

"Well, what about Schistosomiasis?"

"Maggie." Danny looked at her with an expression of disbelief. His hands came to rest on her shoulders as he looked her in the eye. "You're a nurse. You know what the signs are to Schistosomiasis, and you know Phillip is not suffering that parasitic disease."

One large tear slipped from her eye. "I know a lot of things, Danny! Probably too much for my own good. But my brother is not going crazy! You're implying he's a basket case! Well, he's not, Danny! He's not!"

"Maggie, calm down." Danny's hands came around her back as he pulled her in close to embrace her. "I wouldn't even bring it up if I didn't think it had anything to do with what's going on right now. Think about it, Maggie. Both of us were on the battlefield. Both of us have seen it firsthand."

With tears filling her eyes, Maggie met his gaze. "But only one of us has seen what happens to that person after they come home."

THIRTY-NINE

S itting in the Duncan's motor car and driving home with Harvey at the wheel was the longest car ride of her life. The trip was only fifteen minutes, but the road stretched on forever.

Libby's hands grappled with the skirt of her dress the whole ride home. Her nerves bubbled illness in the pit of her stomach. She didn't want to go home. She didn't want to face Phillip after the chain of events that had ruined their evening together. And she certainly didn't want to engage in another argument as she returned home late in the night.

"Everything will turn out fine, Libby."

Harvey's voice broke through the silence as if he'd been reading her thoughts. But she wasn't so sure things would be all right when she walked through the door of her home.

"I'm not so sure, Harvey."

Silence carried them the rest of the way home. When they reached the driveway and Harvey parked the car, Libby couldn't move. She knew she had to go inside and face whatever state her husband was in, but just for another moment, she wanted to relish in the safety of the Duncan's vehicle. To soak in the peace and tranquility that lingered in the air inside it.

"I'll walk you inside, Libby, to make sure everything is all right and look in on Phillip."

"Thank you, Harvey. Thank you for everything."

After assisting her from the passenger side, they walked up the small pathway that led to the porch, but before Libby could reach for the doorknob, the front door flew open.

Libby froze and her eyes widened as she took in Phillip's sloppy state. His shirttail hung half way out of pant waist. Several buttons had been undone at his collar. His shirt cuffs were also undone, and his hair was a mess. Then she saw the glassy haze in his eyes and she knew he'd been drinking again.

A sense of fear grappled with her heart as their eyes collided with intense force.

"Do you know how late it is?"

Her skin pricked at his low growl. She didn't answer.

His sight shifted to Harvey as Phillip was sizing him up.

"So this is where you've been?" he snarled. Then he pointed his words at Harvey. "Some backstabber you turned out to be, Harv. What's the idea of taking my wife?"

"Phillip, you're drunk." Harvey spoke up, taking the lead and stepping closer to Phillip. "I didn't take your wife. She came to us for help."

His gaze moved to Libby. "Is this where've been all night while I sat in here wondering where you were? I've been waiting for hours, Libby!"

"Hey!" Harvey jumped between Phillip and Libby, putting himself in the path of Phillip's anger and rage. "She's your wife, Phil! Is this really how you want to treat her? Look at yourself. You're a sloppy, drunken mess. Isn't that what you tried saving Libby from in the first place?"

Tears spilled down Libby's cheeks. It was an awful reminder, but she knew Harvey was right in bringing it up. The words needed to be said. But they still stung.

"Who are you to tell me what to do with my marriage?"

"I'm your friend, Phil, that's who I am. And a real friend is there to slap you with the truth."

"Get out."

Phillip's low rumble stopped all conversation. Seeing his muscles tense and feeling the tension mounting, Libby knew she had to put an end to this. She turned to Harvey with urgency.

"Harvey, you go on and get home to Sydney. Please. Before any more harm comes to anyone."

"Are you sure, Libby? I can stay a little longer—"

"No. I'll be fine." She glanced from Harvey to Phillip and back to Harvey again. She spoke with more courage than she felt right now, but she couldn't bear the thought of her husband throwing a punch to a dear friend. Not again tonight.

Squaring her shoulders, she held her chin high and walked past both men. Finding the strength to be bold, she tried to overcome the inferiority she felt within.

"Say good-night, Phillip. And close the door before the midnight pests come in."

৶৻৵

It took a lot of courage and much strength, but somehow Libby had managed to control her overwhelming flood of emotions and bottle them up for the sake of tending to Phillip.

He hadn't been happy with her at all, but somehow her take charge attitude had thrown off his balance of order and he complied. It was well into the next morning when she'd finally succumbed to sleep. However, Phillip, overcome with alcohol had no trouble finding slumber of his own.

It didn't seem fair.

He'd been the one to commit the wrongdoings and he was able to find rest. It was as if he saw no wrong in his actions or his manner of words. He didn't seem to care who he pushed away as long as he was right in his own eyes.

And that wretched stash of alcohol that she'd found in his footlocker…

The sun rose high into the morning sky. Phillip still slept with no signs indicating he was ready to awaken any time soon. Taking into consideration the humiliation of last night and the stench of alcohol emanating from their house, they wouldn't be attending church this morning. So she went about her chores and housework.

Phillip's dress suit from last night still reeked of alcohol. Quietly, she tiptoed through their bedroom picking up his clothes and dirty laundry. His suit coat from last night peeked out from behind their closet door. Relieving her arms of the laundry load, she quietly set them on the floor and carefully opened the closet door. She retrieved his coat without making a sound and threw it on the pile. She finally took a long breath of relief when she exited their bedroom without waking her husband.

Downstairs, she filled the wash tub with water and began the daunting task of laundry. She couldn't help but groan about the fact that Phillip still hadn't made good on his promise to fix her with a brand new washing machine that would take the extra work out of washing clothes. It was just one of the many promises he failed to keep since his homecoming.

Harder and faster Libby scrubbed on the wash board, taking out all her frustrations on the innocent fibers in the grips of her hands.

He should have come home to her. He should have been a whole man, not a broken fraction of the man he used to be. Time and distance was supposed to bring them together, but it had only separated them further and further. The only thing that now tied them together was the gold band around her finger.

Catching the shine of her wedding ring, Libby's hands slowed their task until they stilled. She stared down at the band on her ring finger for a long moment.

For better, for worse.

Never had she imagined that she would have to make true on the vow she made to stick with Phillip for worse. Marriage to Phillip was supposed to make her life better, to bring her out from the bad situation she had lived in prior to their wedding day.

Deep down, she loved him though. She'd seen the best of him. She knew there was so much more to him than what he allowed her to see.

After wringing out his dress shirt, Libby reached for his suit coat. As her usual habit when doing laundry, she searched the pockets for loose change. Surprisingly, no change jingled in his pockets, but her hand did stumble upon a folded piece of note paper.

Her brows furrowing, Libby pulled the paper from his pocket and sat down at the kitchen table as she unfolded it.

As soon as her eyes read the name in his handwriting, her heart took a sudden drop to the bottom of her stomach.

"Adaline Howard?" she breathlessly asked. "W-what is this?"

Nausea roiling within her, she read on…

Dear Miss Howard,

I received your last missive concerning Paloma's well-being and I thank you for caring for her until I am able to bring her home…

Libby had to stop. Swallowing past the lump in her throat, she bit back the need to vomit. Her heart pounded against her chest and the room began to spin. But she had to know. She had to continue.

Please proceed with the necessary actions to help with this. Until that time, I will continue to post payment for Paloma's care.

Please send my love to her.

Sincerely,
Sergeant Phillip Johnson

Her breath came fast and heavy. Tremors shook the steadiness of her hands, and tears pushed upward into her eyes.

This couldn't be true.

What she was seeing wasn't real. Phillip couldn't be in love with someone else...could he? Was this the reason he'd been so distant? The reason for his cold shoulder? Could it be that he didn't love her anymore?

"What are you doing?"

Libby startled and jerked when Phillip's voice sounded behind her. Squeezing shut her eyes, she waited, for she didn't trust herself to answer.

"Libby?"

She heard him shuffle forward and halt when he came closer to her.

Opening her eyes, she stared up at him and stood to her feet. Hurt clogged her throat, but she found her voice anyway.

"What is this, Phillip?" She held the note up for him to see. "Who is Adaline Howard and who is Paloma?"

Her voice rose with each accentuated syllable.

Shades of white paled his face as his jaw hinged open and his eyes spied the letter in her hand.

"Answer me, Phillip! Who are they?"

"Libby...let me...explain."

His voice was soft, quiet. All the more reason for her tears to fall. There was no reason for him to become angry because it was true. He'd found someone else to love.

Nausea rolled its way into her belly. So overwhelming was it that she clamped a hand over her mouth and leaped forward. But she didn't make it far. Before she could round the sofa, her head spun with uncontrollable dizziness. Losing her balance, her body tipped to the left, but then darkness swallowed her whole before she landed on the floor of the living room.

FORTY

As Libby's lifeless frame toppled to the side and hit the floor, Phillip's insides plunged to the soles of his shoes. Flashbacks of his brothers-in-arms replayed in front of him, falling with the spray of each opposing bullet. But this was Libby. *His* Libby. And she now lay lifeless on the floor in front of him, her face drained of all color.

He lunged forward and knelt at her side.

"Libby!"

Gently, he turned her onto her back and cupped her head in his hands. Stroking her hairline with an unsteady hand, his voice wavered as fear gripped his throat.

"Libby, come back to me. Wake up."

He didn't know what happened. One second she was standing, and the next, her body seemed to give out. There was no warning. No signs. Just as it had been on the battlefield. There was hardly ever a warning signal. But when men began dropping, they knew danger lurked in the jungle.

And right now, fear and danger lurked within his own home.

With tears springing to his eyes, his head lowered to hers. She had to be all right.

"Libby, darling, wake up."

It was all he could say, over and over again. Then his medical training came back to him. In one sweep, he slid his arms under his wife and carried her limp body with ease to the couch. Laying her flat, he placed a pillow beneath her legs and feet to elevate them. It would hopefully rush the blood back to her brain.

He checked her pulse. With relief he let out a long breath. Her heart was beating, albeit faintly. It was a sign that her blood pressure had dipped too low.

Kneeling on the floor at her side, all drunken haziness had somehow chased itself away. His eyes could see clearly. His thoughts were in order. All he could think about was Libby and hope she was okay.

His warm hand cradled her clammy cheek. Ever so gently, his thumb caressed her temple.

She was so beautiful. So perfect for him. And his lies and secrets had finally found him out. He'd done this to her. And he'd never forgive himself.

As he admired her face, and wallowed in his misery, he caught the slight furrowing of her brows. He held his breath, hoping she was coming out of her spell.

The slightest squeak of a moan rattled in her throat. He leaned in closer to her face, pressing his warm lips to her cheek and whispering, "Libby, wake up. Everything will be fine."

Her eyes rolled beneath her closed eyelids and he knew she was fighting to regain consciousness.

She turned and attempted to sit up, but Phillip held her down. "Not yet, sweetheart. Just lie there until you feel better."

Slowly, her eyes fluttered open, but her mind seemed absent from them.

"Thank heaven," Phillip breathed.

"Ph-Phillip?"

When his eyes lifted, he met her glassy gaze. Her voice was weak, but he was happy to hear it.

"Darling. Thank goodness you're all right."

As if he'd fallen into his old habits, gentleness took over. Once more he pressed his forehead against hers and cupped her face in his hands. He wanted to hold her in his arms, thankful she hadn't been seriously harmed in her fall.

"I've a horrible headache."

"Then you stay right here, darling. I'll bring you a blanket and a glass of juice. You do have a jar of my mother's grape juice on hand, don't you?"

"In the pantry."

"All right. Stay put. I'll take care of you."

With haste, Phillip hurried to meet every one of Libby's needs. When he stopped to think about it, when was the last time he'd done anything like this for her? He couldn't remember. For the first time since his homecoming, he realized just how much love and affection he'd starved her of.

He'd been a rotten husband, unworthy and undeserving of Libby's love. Perhaps he'd been better off dying in the jungle.

After fetching a blanket and a glass of juice for his wife, Phillip knelt at her side and helped her sip on the cup. She never said one word, only accepted what he offered up to her.

"Does that help, darling?" he asked.

Nodding her head, she closed her eyes and rested against the pillow Phillip placed beneath her neck.

Phillip chose that moment to lay the blanket across her body. Standing over her, he watched. There was so much he could do for her. And so much he could give her. Why had he chosen to withhold all that from her?

As his thoughts rambled on, Libby grew increasingly tired. It was still early in the day, so how could she possibly become so overly exhausted in such a small amount of time? Perhaps it was all the stress he'd put on her. Everything he *hadn't* done for her. She needed rest. She needed the comfort of her own bed.

Not wasting any time, he scooped her up into his arms and started for the staircase.

"What are you doing?" she asked, urgency clenching her words.

"You need your rest. So I'm taking you up to bed."

Her brown, questionable eyes prodded him, and it seemed with reluctance she relaxed into him.

"But it's not even lunch time yet."

"Shh. It's all right. I'll take care of everything."

He settled her into the warmth and comfort of their double bed.

"You just get some sleep now. And don't worry about anything."

He gave her a kiss of his deepest affection. How long it had been since he'd given it so freely. By the look in her eyes, she hadn't expected it either.

Only after a few moments of her considering him did she finally close her eyes and drift off to sleep.

A burdening sigh blew from his chest. He'd been so harsh that his genuine kindness seemed a stranger to his wife. Her hesitancy of him told him that. How did their marriage come to this point?

Throughout the day, he piddled in the house. Sweeping the floor, washing the dishes, tidying up the place, while Libby slept. Every strike of the clock, he lifted his gaze up the staircase, listening for any muffled sound indicating that Libby was awake.

But the house remained quiet.

He never remembered Libby sleeping so much.

As the day wore into evening, Phillip prepared a bowl of soup for himself and an extra for Libby. When she didn't emerge from their bedroom promptly at six for dinner, he knew something wasn't right.

He finished his soup with haste and in silence—like so many nights he'd left Libby alone at their table. So this was what it was like to sit and wait for someone who was never going to join him.

His appetite stealing away from him, he dropped his spoon with a *plunk* into his bowl and pressed his fingertips to his forehead.

"I don't deserve her," he breathed. "Not a wretched fool like me."

Glancing toward the living room and the staircase, he stood, taking Libby's soup bowl in his hand. He may not deserve a woman like Libby, but he wouldn't let that stop him from trying to make amends.

Once at the foot of their bed, he couldn't bring himself to wake her peaceful body. He didn't remember a time that she slept quite like she did right now.

Right now, her eyes didn't hold that look of disappointment, of hurt. Right now, her muscles weren't tense and stiff like she'd come to wear them. And right now, the slightest hint of a smile played across her lips. He missed that smile—the smile of an angel.

As he watched over Libby like her guardian, he knew she deserved more. But it was more than he could give her. As she lay peacefully in their bed, breathing evenly, he knew he couldn't lay next to her. Not tonight. Not after what he'd put her through. She deserved to lay in complete peace as she did at the present moment.

Tonight, he belonged in the room down the hall.

FORTY-ONE

The Brady Home
1 May 1946

Beads of sweat trickled down glasses of iced tea. Even with the windows open the cool breeze couldn't push the warmth from the Brady home. It wasn't an unbearable warmth that sheltered itself beneath Grace and Luke's roof—it was a quite pleasant atmosphere that surrounded the home.

Soft coos rattled from Little LeRoy's mouth as Norma Sullivan spoke gentle tones to the baby's face. The woman's laughter at his questioning facial expressions and mocking *coos* caused Grace and Luke to chuckle at their guest's musings.

"I do declare that child is the spitting image of his father." Norma gleefully glanced at Luke then turned to Grace. "With eyes as dashing as his mother's."

From his seat next to his wife, Luke gazed down into Grace's deep blue eyes. They shone brightly of sapphire and danced as she smiled up at him. "He's one lucky fella. Baby blues like those don't come a dime a dozen."

"Oh, Luke," Grace gave him a gentle nudge.

"No, I'm serious. I had to give my right arm just to get to see your beautiful blue eyes again."

There was teasing in his voice, but deep inside, Grace's heart pricked…because his statement was all too true. But God had given them a beautiful love story and a strong marriage that had been formed from the molds of tragedy. Now, as she sat there admiring her new little family, her heart danced in the wake of sharing this wonderful life and precious moment with the two men she now loved most.

Nothing could have prepared Grace for LeRoy's entrance into their world. Love she thought she had experienced was nothing compared to the love she felt for her own child. And by the way Luke gazed down into their son's face, she was sure he felt the same way.

"It's wonderful to be home again," she said, mostly speaking to herself.

Aunt Norma quickly glanced up and placed her palm over Grace's hand. "And my dear, it's good to have you back where you belong. My nephew nearly drove me mad while you were away. You'd have never known that man lived on his own before, let alone in a war zone."

"Gee, Aunt Norma. Give me a break, why don't you? At least try to make me look half-way decent in front of my wife," he winked.

Soft giggles trickled off Grace's tongue. My how she loved her family.

"Grace, dear, it's so nice to hear that beautiful laugh of yours." Mrs. Sullivan scooted forward onto her heels and lifted herself off the chair, LeRoy still cradled in her arms. She spoke softly with animated expressions trailing off her face as she gazed down at the sweet baby. "Now, it's about time for me to go into the kitchen and whip up something for lunch." Kissing LeRoy's forehead, she placed him in Grace's arms. "Off to your mamma you go, and off to the kitchen I go."

Grace smiled as she snuggled into the couch with her baby in her arms. How tiny was his form. How little were his features and fingers. How perfect he was.

Luke had grown silent. When Grace glanced up at him, she caught him staring at her.

"What is it?" she asked.

"It's you."

"What about me?"

"I'm just thinking about how beautiful you are. How wonderful you are. And how wonderful it is to look over at my wife and son together."

Her cheeks warmed and all she could do was smile at his tender words.

Luke gathered himself together and stood, his prosthesis glistening in the sunlight as he passed through the window's rays. Grace watched as he positioned himself next to her on the sofa and gazed lovingly down on LeRoy.

He was completely smitten. She could see it written all over his face. It even emanated from the soft touch of his finger against LeRoy's cheek. Luke had found a whole new love, and Grace was part of it.

"Isn't he just wonderful?" she whispered as Luke's head neared hers.

"He's an angel. I've never felt this way before. I mean, there was you, which was the greatest feeling in the world, but this...this is something different. And just when I thought I couldn't love you more, I did—I do."

"Me too, Luke. I feel the same way. It's amazing."

"It sure is."

"Would you like to hold him? I *am* getting a bit tired. I should rest before his next feeding."

Before Luke could answer, Grace placed LeRoy in Luke's arms, with his good arm supporting the baby. He stared down in awe of his son, and Grace could almost hear Luke's inner thoughts.

But he hesitated.

Unsure of himself, Luke lifted his prosthetic hand but it lingered alongside LeRoy.

"It's okay, Luke. You won't hurt him."

"It's not that, Grace."

"Then what is it?"

His chest heaved upward with a longing sigh, his eyes never leaving the child.

"I want—I want so badly to reach out and touch his face. To feel his soft skin with fingertips that are no longer there, y'know? I want to feel like I can protect him from anything."

Grace leaned in close and rested her cheek against Luke's upper arm, nodding her understanding.

"Do you think he'll look at me with disappointment one day?"

Grace sat up, pointing a surprised expression in Luke's direction. "Luke Brady. Why no, I don't think that at all. I think one day LeRoy will look at you with great admiration as I do. I think one day when he's out playing ball with his friends and his daddy comes to take him home, he's going to smile proudly and say, *that's my dad*. Luke, don't let one handicap become your biggest downfall. This is who you are now. I love you. Aunt Norma loves you. And LeRoy is going to love you too. This is us. Our family. And I don't want difficulties to come between us. We're going to work through them. And we're going to overcome them...just as we did through the war."

FORTY-TWO

There was nothing more refreshing than waking up to sunshine slanting through her windows and sweet song serenading her from the bluebirds perched on her maple tree branches. It was the promise of a new day. The awakening of a new dawn brimmed with hope for a bright future.

As Libby's eyes fluttered open, the first thing she noticed was how quiet the house seemed. Reaching to Phillip's side of the bed, her hand touched emptiness—a vague reminder of the lonely mornings she spent four years of her life waking up to. It was enough to dash her hopes.

"Phillip?" she called out into the room.

But there was no answer.

Scanning the room from side to side, she looked for any sign of him. The bedroom door was closed. The closet door, closed. The window, opened a crack.

"Did I open it last night?" she asked herself.

Straining hard to think back, she couldn't remember getting into bed. Her brows furrowed together and she rubbed at her forehead with her fingers. Questions now bubbled in her mind.

Then the faint smell of bacon and eggs drifted to her nose.

Phillip's downstairs, she thought. But that didn't make sense. When was the last time Phillip made breakfast for her?

She smiled.

It was four years ago. On their honeymoon.

With new hope bursting in her chest, Libby swung her legs off the bed and slipped her feet into her bedroom slippers. Then just before leaving the room, she grabbed for her robe and wrapped it around her slender shoulders.

Perhaps last night was just a bad dream. A dream that felt so real, she had nearly believed it. It was a beautiful morning, complete with warmth and sunshine. Today was surely a turning point in her life, in her marriage.

But as Libby rounded the staircase and rushed into the kitchen, every want and expectation came to a crashing halt.

"Maggie?"

Libby's chest constricted as she breathed her sister-in-law's name. There Maggie stood at Libby's stove, an apron tied neatly in place around her waist, and a spatula fitted in her hand.

"Libby! Good morning. Would you like some breakfast?"

Confusion drove Libby's head in circles. Feeling lightheaded, she took a seat at the kitchen table.

Maggie stopped short as she turned to place a plate of bacon, eggs, and toast in front of Libby. "Why...Libby, are you all right? You look a little pale."

Why did everyone keep asking if she was all right? No, she wasn't all right. Every little stem of her life had been uprooted, left to thirst and hunger for everything she couldn't have. Suddenly, every moment of the night before came flooding back to her.

"Where's Phillip?"

She watched Maggie swallow hard before carefully placing Libby's breakfast plate on the table. The uneasiness lingering over Maggie's face seemed to say it all.

Folding her arms over her chest, she leaned into the table. Libby sighed and blankly gazed at her over-prepared eggs.

"He's not here, is he." Her words fell flat as the sole of her shoe.

"I-I don't know where he is, Libby. Honest." Maggie's thumbs twiddled together before she abruptly pulled the kitchen chair from under the table and sat. Placing her hand along the smooth surface of the table, she leaned toward Libby. "I came over after he telephoned me this morning. He asked if I would look after you while he ran some errands. He said you had a bad spell late last night."

Libby sighed her irritation. It all really had been real. All too real. And she wanted to forget every second of it.

"You fainted?" Maggie asked. "What's going on, Libby? Why won't you tell me?"

The pleading in Maggie's voice was so worrisome that Libby couldn't keep up the charade any longer.

She'd lost everything. Phillip was gone. Now that she knew all about Phillip's double life, the decision he'd apparently made to leave her had been easy...or so she thought.

As if she never heard Maggie's plea, Libby scooped the fork up in her fingers and pushed her eggs around her plate, but the aroma turned her stomach as soon as it entered her nose.

Sitting back in her seat, she dropped the fork and pushed her plate away from her.

"Won't you eat something?" Maggie urged. "Please, Libby...I-I don't know what to do anymore."

Libby shifted her burning eyes to Maggie. Maggie, too, was on the verge of tears. As Libby studied her sister-in-law's face, she realized that Maggie had no more answers than she did.

Libby's shoulders drooped. "He's not coming back."

Maggie's eyes peered through slits. "Who? Phillip?"

Libby nodded. "Maggie, you'd never believe me if I told you the whole story."

"At least let me be the judge of that."

"That's what I'm afraid of."

≪∂∂≫

"If you won't confide in me, Libby, then please say you'll join me in visiting Grace today. She and the baby are finally home and I was hoping we could put last night's incident behind us and focus on something positive."

Visiting Grace Brady was the last thing she wanted to do today. Exhaustion weighed heavily on her bones and the sting of last night's awful discovery still blistered her heart. Her outward showing of love had been smeared through the mud, and her emotions had been drowned in an ocean of hurt. Not to mention her queasiness still had not let up by the early afternoon. But here she sat on the couch in her living room with Maggie at her side. At the present time, she had nothing else to aspire for. No matter if Maggie, or Phillip, was here or not, she'd still exist in a hollow bubble. Alone and feeble.

Perhaps accepting Maggie's invite was as good as any for the time being.

Reluctantly, she nodded. "All right, Maggie, I'll go with you, but please don't bother me with a barrage of questions. I'm just not ready yet."

Libby knew without a doubt that Maggie wouldn't understand. For years, Libby watched as her mother sank deeper into depression as she treaded these very waters, barely keeping her head above it.

More than that, Libby had seen the denial offered by her father's family when her mother had turned to them for help.

Excuses.

Excuses and blame is what her mother received from Pa's family. Not one member of the family would listen. Instead, they told Mother that is was all her doing. That she was the cause of his misconduct and disorderly behavior. So with a heavily burdened heart, Mother had taken Libby back home. From then on, Mother had given up. She'd lost all hope.

As Libby rode down the road in the passenger side of Maggie's car, she reminded herself that spilling all of her problems at Maggie's feet would likely accomplish nothing. Maggie would surely find the good in Phillip and refuse to believe anything different about her brother. It was best for all of them that Phillip's secret remained a secret from all.

⊰⊱

From the moment Libby walked through the door of the Brady home, an atmosphere of a different kind emanated from the air inside.

Mrs. Sullivan greeted both girls with a warm hug and a smile large enough to light up the entire house.

"Come in! Come in! Look at the two of you…my gracious, it's good to see you ladies. Come have a seat. Grace will be thrilled to see you. She's just awakened from her nap."

Exuberant, Mrs. Sullivan nearly skipped as she showed them into the living room. The woman's excitement extracted a smile from Libby.

As they entered the quaint room, an adoring sigh slipped from Maggie's mouth.

"Oh, my! How beautiful is that baby boy!"

"Maggie!" Grace's tone was both soft and surprised. "I didn't know you'd be joining us today."

Maggie rushed over to embrace her best friend, while Libby looked on.

"You know I couldn't stay away. I had to come see this darling little face again." Maggie's hand gently cupped the crown of LeRoy's tiny head. "My land, he's so small and fragile. Oh, goodness, where are my manners? I brought Libby with me."

Grace's eyes shifted to Libby. Offering up a weak smile, Libby waved. "Hello. Congratulations on your precious little boy, Grace."

"Thank you. I'm so glad you came to visit. Would you like to meet LeRoy?"

Without answering, Libby forced her feet to move forward. Slowly, she inched to where Grace sat in her rocking chair. Nausea roiled once again in the pit of her stomach as her eyes fell to the baby—the baby that she had so desperately wanted.

This was all she had hoped for in life. A family of her own had been her heart's desire since the day Phillip proposed marriage to her.

But not anymore.

Not after the appalling discovery Libby had made of Phillip's unfaithfulness. How could she even entertain such thoughts anymore?

But Grace, and a handful of others, were watching from a distance, waiting to hear of what she thought about the newborn.

Finally, Libby found the courage to gaze upon LeRoy. Grace uncovered the blanket from his little face, revealing a perfectly rounded head on a healthy body.

Tears sprang to her eyes and stung her nose, but she held them back.

"He's beautiful," she whispered.

Then right there in her heart she knew that she hadn't completely lost all hope.

FORTY-THREE

"Hey, look at that." Maggie pointed to Libby's tea cup. "Beverly Donahue—you remember, my nurse friend who served in the Philippines—well, an old Asian saying goes, if steam rises straight up from your tea cup, good fortune is coming your way." Maggie gave Libby a reassuring wink of her eye.

Libby immediately understood it was a ruse to perk her up.

However, Libby couldn't concentrate on the words said in front of her. Aside from her taxing relationship with her husband, her mind and eyes drifted to the beautiful Grace sitting sidelong from her.

The woman had it all. A loving, caring, and giving husband. A beautiful home. And a precious new life resting peacefully in her arms. From Libby's perspective, Grace Brady lived a charmed life, a flawless life.

She wanted that too.

Libby sipped on the warmth from her cup and allowed it to soothe her throat and chest. Maybe today's visit wouldn't suppress all those inner longings and hopes like she'd thought. How could she not think of having a family when a woman who had just given birth sat in front of her?

"What's it like, Grace?" The question seemed to bolt from Libby's mouth without permission, surprising herself. "Becoming a mother. Holding your very own baby?"

A broad smile broke out on Grace's face and her eyes softened. "There are so many emotions. Disbelief. Joy. And a tad bit of fear. I feel like a barrel of emotions right now. One moment I'm happy as a June bug, then the next, I'm crying into my hands and I don't know why. Even when I'm overjoyed about something, tears seem to fall on their own. It's all quite confusing. But the doctor says that will all dissipate soon."

"Yeah, you should've seen her the other day, trying on a new pair of shoes Luke had bought her. When she threw out the old pair, she balled like a baby," Maggie laughed.

"Oh, my," breathed Libby.

"I'll have you know, Margaret Russo, I'd had those shoes since the beginning of the war. I was sort of attached."

"Honey, that was a relationship you needed to end years ago."

As Maggie and Grace bantered on, Libby wished she could put herself in the comfort of their shoes. Small talk came easy to the two friends, and although distance had put a wedge between them for the remainder of the war, they still picked up where they left off as if not a minute had passed between them.

If only she could find some way out of the dark corner she hid in, stuffed away like a lost and forgotten book. Why had she pushed Maggie away for so many years? If only she would have let go of her envy and embraced the sister she needed for so long instead of allowing jealousy to grow bitterness towards her. Maybe she, too, would have that same connection with Maggie as Grace did.

Even if she did have Maggie, she still wouldn't have Phillip. Somewhere, time had stopped between her marriage to Phillip and his return from the Pacific. Those new chapters she'd looked forward to writing together with him, stalled on blank paper. Unwritten.

Loneliness wriggled its way back into her soul and Libby found herself cowering back into her dark hole. The sun shone everywhere except in her heart. Two lovely friends sat in her presence, but she was alone.

"What about you, Libby?"

The call of her name registered and she blinked hard. "I'm sorry, my mind went wandering off on me. What was the question?" Embarrassment warmed her cheeks. This wasn't the way to win friends.

But Maggie and Grace just laughed it off.

"I see you're still in the newlywed state also." Grace laughed.

Apparently, Grace was none the wiser to the events of last night, and certainly unaware of what went on in the confines of the Johnson home, but she was aware of Phillip's resentment toward Luke. And somehow, she still managed to overlook that and welcome Libby into her home.

"I—why, I suppose. I mean, technically I've only seen my husband for a little over six months of the four years we've been married. Yes, of course, we're still like newlyweds."

So she lied.

Not everyone needed to be aware of her marital affairs and

misgivings.

Libby spied Maggie's probing gaze. Maggie knew it was a lie. Maggie was there at the dance. But Grace wasn't, and so far, Grace hadn't mentioned any of the town's talk. Flashing Maggie a warning look, Libby subtly shook her head. She didn't want her sister-in-law spilling the beans about her crumbling marriage. Maggie's head tipping upward affirmed she caught Libby's unspoken words.

"Ah. Marriage. I tell ya, girls, never in a million years would I have dreamt it would be this sweet." Wonder and haze settled over Maggie's eyes as she spoke as if nothing was amiss. "And to think it almost didn't happen...how blessed I am." She glanced around the table at each of them. "How blessed *we* are. And now we all have the rest of our lives to look forward to as we start families of our own."

Maggie's ruby lips turned upward in her beautiful broad smile. No wonder people were drawn to her. Libby had never had an alluring smile like that.

Sweet.

That was how people described Libby. Just plain sweet. Always the one lost in a crowd. Always the quiet one. Always the one to wish she were someone else.

Enough, Elizabeth. This is the same disastrous path that led me to hatred before. Let's not revisit it amid my marital status.

"Say, Libby," Grace spoke up. "What about you? Are children in your future now that the war has ended?"

Suddenly, all eyes were on her. Warmth filled her cheeks and a tingle prickled down her spine. She hoped she could mask her discomfort.

From the corner of her eye, she sensed Maggie's demeanor tense.

She could handle this though. She'd watched her mother play the masquerade for years. She had surely learned how to dance around those probing questions more than once.

"I'm afraid that hasn't happened for us yet." Folding a napkin between her fingers, Libby turned her attention to the table setting and fidgeted with the various items. "But honestly, like you said, Grace, Phillip and I are practically newlyweds all over again. It's good to have some time alone before we start filling our home with crying babies."

Only after she said the words did she realize how that last phrase sounded.

"Oh, I'm sorry, Grace. I didn't mean for that to come across as smug."

But Grace's eyes didn't show the least bit of offense. Instead a laugh escaped those perfect lips.

But then, as if Maggie was now the naïve party, she offered up her unfitting advice as she gazed dreamily into nothingness. "I think this is an exciting time in our lives. Finally, everyone is back together where they should be and we are moving on with life. I look forward to the day when Danny and I are raising our own children. And I even look forward to the day I become an aunt." Maggie nudged Libby's arm.

Libby's irritation grew increasingly uncomfortable. Maggie knew things weren't well between Phillip and Libby, and yet she persisted on as if nothing was wrong.

But wasn't that what Libby was doing also? Isn't that what she wanted?

No. This was different. It was just like she'd witnessed in the past. The wrongdoings of family were always swept under the rug—which is why she couldn't tell Maggie just how awful life had become for her and Phillip. So she let Maggie talk.

"Isn't that right, Libby? Why, I remember how much Phillip talked about a family of his own just before he proposed to you."

Yes, Libby remembered those days too. She remembered how many nights they sat on her parents' front porch dreaming about the rest of their lives. Children had certainly been in the future.

But that was before tragedy. Before Jack Gregory's death. Before her marriage to Phillip. Before Phillip's enlistment.

Everything had changed. Her dreams dashed. Her hopes crushed.

But no one had to know.

"Yes. Phillip often spoke of our future family. I'm sure one of these days we'll find ourselves coddling young of our own."

"All in God's perfect timing, Libby."

The touch of Grace's hand patting hers comforted and stung her all at the same time. The small part that brought consolation gave her a smidge of hope that one day all would return to normal and this rocky time would be but a small memory. But of course it was something Grace Brady could say easily. She hadn't known what it was like to live with a husband who'd turned cold all at once. Or find it hard to please him when his irritation began to boil.

Again, those things weren't spoken of. *What goes on in the home stays in the home*, her mother's voice rang back.

As for Libby, what went on in her heart, stayed in her heart.

FORTY-FOUR

The minutes ticked by. Libby's body grew tired and all she wanted was to go home. She'd had enough visiting for a day.

Keeping up appearances had been more work than she anticipated. No wonder Mother never left the house except for those errands of running to the market or the dry goods shop for needs.

However, Libby didn't want to seem rude after the kindness shown by Grace, Mrs. Sullivan, and even Maggie. So she patiently waited until Maggie was ready to leave.

When Grace started showing signs of fatigue, Maggie was the first to speak up and urge her to get some rest.

As Libby and Maggie gathered themselves to leave, Luke walked through the door.

"There's my girl!"

"Luke! You're home early," Grace said happily.

"The boss let me off early. I couldn't wait to get back to see you and LeRoy."

"I'm afraid we'll keep you in suspense. He's down for a long nap and I believe I'll be taking one too." Grace slowly stood to her feet.

"Just take 'er easy. Let me get there to help you." Luke jumped to Grace's aid.

"Aw, look. My knight in shining armor." Grace looked back and gave the girls a wink of her eye.

Smiles of adoration exchanged between husband and wife. Libby's longing now yearned for more than just a baby. Phillip hadn't looked at her like that in ages. Or at least since that moment he stepped off the 2:10 train on the day of his homecoming.

She watched as Luke took Grace's hand, assisting his wife up the stairs and to their bedroom.

Would that one day be her and Phillip? Would having a baby possibly change the way he felt about her? Would he lovingly help her up their set of stairs at home? Would he fuss over her well-being? Would he give her any attention at all?

They all said their farewells and soon, Libby and Maggie were homeward bound.

"I didn't realize the time," Maggie said as they backed out of Grace's driveway. "I need to get home. I told Danny I'd make his favorite dish tonight. Meatballs."

"Meatballs, huh?" Libby inquired. "I never thought you were the homemaker type, Maggie."

"Strange, isn't it? It's batty what a woman will do for her man when she loves him. Thankfully, Danny is very forgiving of my bad cooking." Maggie side-glanced at Libby. Her eyebrow quirked upward. "Home economics wasn't exactly my best study in school."

"No. More like shop class was your best interest, wasn't it? Only instead of putting motorized cars and machines together, you put bodies back together."

"And some He made the hand and others the foot."

Libby's brows furrowed in confusion. "Pardon?"

"It's taken from the Bible. *'But now are they many members, yet but one body. And the eye cannot say unto the hand, I have no need of thee: nor again the head to the feet, I have no need of you.'* It means God has given each of us a specific job in this world. Some are the hands—the doers. Some are the head—or those in authority. Not everyone can be in charge, nor does everyone have the skill to work with their hands. But no matter what job we have we are reminded to *'do it heartily as unto the Lord'*."

"Your skill required the hands, I take it." Libby's fingers dug into the skirt of her dress. Theology wasn't her strong point in Bible class.

"You're correct. However, at times God chose to use my feet as well. I'll never forget that day at the airstrip. I still don't know what came over me, but I ran as fast as I could against Army regulations to that ambulance to try to save those airmen. I don't know if they would have survived if Bonnie and I hadn't disobeyed orders and ran past those gates. I guess some rules are meant to be stretched as long as God is the one urging you to do the right thing."

"I don't think God has called me to be a hero of sorts like you, or Danny, or Luke. Really, I'm not sure what my place is right now."

"What do you mean, Libby? Your place is in your lovely home, supporting and taking care of Phillip—no matter how difficult he is—and one day, you too, will be blessed with a brood of your own. That's a fine task to be given."

The view from the outside was always a lovely picture painted for everyone else, wasn't it? No one really knew what went on inside the four walls of her home. Even if anyone did know, they'd say it was her fault. That she wasn't doing enough for her war hero husband. That she wasn't good enough at what she did. She'd heard it all before. She'd seen the damage first hand.

"You're forgetting what you saw last night, Maggie. While those dreams sound wonderful and perfect, they couldn't be further from the truth of reality."

From that moment on, quiet settled between them. However, Libby knew a whole conversation was still carrying on inside Maggie's mind. She'd love to ask what Maggie was thinking, but then again, the same thought terrified her.

What goes on in the home, stays in the home.

❧❧

Her lovely afternoon was quickly giving way to a stormy evening. Darkening skies grew in the western sky and the hint of rain hung in the air. Just as the skies overhead grayed, Libby's demeanor also darkened. As Maggie's car pulled into the driveway, Libby unexpectedly spotted the reason for her discomfort.

There Phillip sat in that rickety ol' wicker chair, staring across the way at that ill-fated home across the street.

Why was he back? She'd thought for sure that he'd left her for good for those names in his letter.

Dread quickly replaced apprehension as she studied him from the car. She instantly became aware of Phillip's agitation. Even from the car she could see it cloud his eyes.

"Thank you again for the wonderful afternoon out, Maggie." Libby opened the car door and briskly stepped out.

"It was a pleasure. We'll have to do it again sometime soon. I'll ring you up next time I have the day off."

Libby glanced back at Phillip with eyes filled with concern. She tried to politely rush Maggie off before Phillip began his rantings.

"Please do," she said from the driver window. "I'm sure Danny is waiting on those meatballs. So go get started on them. I'm sure this time they'll turn out splendid."

"I sure hope so. See you later, kid."

"Bye!"

Libby waited until Maggie backed out of the driveway to turn and rush up the front porch steps.

With a sweet melody to her voice, she tried to greet Phillip with happiness, as if nothing plagued her heart or her mind.

"Hello there, dear. How was your day?" She bent down to kiss his cheek, but he moved not one muscle nor did he flinch.

"Where have you been? I left you in Maggie's care, and I come home to find you gone." His voice was rigid and stern.

"What do you mean? I was with Maggie and Grace for a visit." And what was the meaning of him questioning her of her whereabouts when he was the one to leave her all alone in the house with no one except his sister to care for her?

"Do you know what time it is?"

She checked her wristwatch. "Dear, it's just a quarter till four o'clock."

"Precisely. I've been sitting here for fifteen minutes waiting for you. I was hoping to come home to a rested wife and the smell of supper cooking on the stove. But what do I smell instead? Nothing." His voice then lowered to a mumble. "The thanks a fella gets for trying to take care of his wife."

"I'm sorry, Phillip. You were the one who suggested Maggie come to the house this morning, were you not? You were the one who left the house early before I awoke without even a word left to Maggie of *your* whereabouts. What was I supposed to do? Besides, don't you have your mistress to run to?"

Her words dripped with scorn as she said them.

"Paloma is not a woman of the night, Libby! Perhaps in my absence you grew more accustomed to living the life of a single woman rather than my wife."

"Oh, hog wash! All of it is hog wash! Then who is she, Phillip? Tell me!" His words had pricked through her chest, stinging like needles to her soul. But she longed to know the truth from him. Who was Paloma and who was the woman he wrote to?

"First of all, married women don't go frolicking around town when they have husbands who work their fingers to their cores to provide for their families and wait at home for dinner to be put on the table."

"Well, we don't exactly have a *family* now, do we?" Libby pushed past his chair and thrusted open the front door. With swift, deliberate steps, she raced to the kitchen and threw on her apron. Anger seared her skin, rattling her fingers as she reached into the oven for her pots and pans. They clanked against the range, but she didn't notice the loud clamor over the pulsing of blood rushing through her ears.

"Libby!" Phillip boomed.

"What!" She turned with a sudden jerk and was met by forceful hands grasping her wrists. Phillip's grip startled her and her sharp intake of breath stole away her words. The pan slipped from her hand and clanged against the hard kitchen floor with a crash.

Dark, dark eyes pierced her. Never had she seen such anger in his gaze. His fingers tightened around her wrists and his strength shoved her back against the kitchen wall.

A sudden pang of fear struck her chest and pitted her stomach. For the first time in her life, she was afraid of what the next few minutes would hold.

A slight cry escaped her lips. Everything moved in slow motion and she still couldn't believe the situation she was in—even as Phillip spoke to her, she only half heard his words.

"With an attitude like that, maybe you don't deserve a family. When you learn to be happy living here in the house, maybe *then* you'll be ready to raise a brood."

His eyes large, and wide, and angry pinned her to the wall, but instead of backing down, she met his gaze. Anger, hurt, and fear mixed within her chest. She wanted to lash out at him. She wanted to cry. And she wanted to run. But his grasp on her wouldn't allow her to leave and crying wouldn't do her any good. The only tool she had was her tongue.

"Phillip, I have *lived* at that tiny in-town flat and this house *alone* and worked my own hands to their cores to make this place a home—*your* home—and I did it all the while living in complete isolation from you! And you have the audacity to tell me I'm not content living here? Phillip, I endured painful lonely nights here without you. It's not fair to say I live as a single woman when I cried myself to sleep almost every night missing you. It's not fair of you to say such things. And you're hurting me."

Pain clogged her throat, constricting it, and she choked it back. Tears stung her eyes and nose, and she blinked hard to fight them back.

He seemed to respond to her emotional outburst. His eyes bounced back and forth, finally lowering to where his hands clamped hers. His grip loosened and he took a step back, sweeping his hand behind his neck to catch the sweat beading on his skin.

"And now that I'm here?" His arms spread wide, his voice became hoarse, but he wasn't about to give up his fight. "I come to an empty house. I hardly see you when I am home."

Libby had heard enough. Her anger and hurt bubbled to the surface and she couldn't take another cut from him. Her chest rose and fell and she worked to keep her anger grounded. But the longer he argued with her, the more he fueled her temper.

"You hardly see me?" she shrieked. "Day after blessed day you come home and set yourself in that stupid chair, staring off into some unknown abyss completely detached from me, from life. So you tell me, Phillip, what is it? What is it that draws the life from your body and away from me?"

Libby waited, hoping to hear his answer, and yet too afraid to listen. But without another word spoken between them, Phillip turned, his anger tossing the kitchen chair across the floor.

The crash it made as it hit the table and wobbled against the cabinets caused Libby's skin to jump and tingle with goose bumps. Her eyes flitted closed, tears seeping from beneath her eyelids. But the slamming of the back door was like the nail in the coffin.

Why, Phillip? she asked herself. *Why do you torture me so?*

FORTY-FIVE

Even as he walked out the door, slamming it behind him, he knew he was wrong. Why he wasn't running back to her and covering her with kisses and apologies he wasn't sure. His feet continued to carry him further away from her.

What was he thinking? What had come over him?

The incident replayed over again in his mind. How could he touch Libby in such a way? Never—ever—had he put a hand on her. What had caused him to act in such an awful and sickening way? The look in her eyes shadowed his mind. He'd scared her. All the years of loving and knowing Libby, his own wife, and he treated her like this? With forceful behavior? With uncontrolled anger?

Nausea roiled his stomach as he stomped to the car. His shaking hand reached for the keys to the ignition as he threw open his car door. After sitting inside, his forehead rested against the steering wheel. Exhaustion and overwhelming nausea weakened his muscles.

What was wrong with him? Why did his anger and emotion get the better of him and mistreat her? As it always did after their quarrels, guilt chipped away at the callouses on his heart. He wanted to do what was right, but something continued to cloud his judgement and ignite his anger. Only instead of extinguishing the flames, he allowed his ire to target his beloved wife.

He knew he wasn't himself. He knew his treatment of her and their marriage was all wrong, yet he couldn't bring himself to make right what his anger was damaging.

Opening his eyes and lifting his head, he glanced up at the two-story house they called home. Its façade showed it was still in need of some tender loving care. Libby had done so much to prepare for his homecoming, even spending her hard earned money to make the necessary repairs to the broken down house. All he was doing was tearing it down, piece by piece.

With a sharp blow, his hand struck the steering wheel.

He was an idiot.

Glancing back up at the house, he spotted Libby's small silhouette in the front window. She peered at him from behind the curtains.

He should go to her. He should take her in his arms like he used to and tell her he was sorry, that everything would be okay.

His left hand gripped the door handle.

All it would take was his feet to waltz him back up those steps and run to her.

But he was a different man now.

Allowing himself to get too close to her would only bring back all those horrid retentions.

If only Libby knew the truth…

Why couldn't he bring himself to answer her questions? She knew about Paloma. So why did he continue to hide her?

He could never allow himself to become the soft-hearted man he once was. And he could never give in to Libby's request for a family.

He released the door handle. The car's engine hiccupped to a start and he backed out the driveway.

∽❦❧

Jazzy tunes bounced off the piano as the pianist banged against his ivory keys. Loud voices seemed to swallow his train of thought, making it easy for Phillip to forget the exchanges going on in his head. Hazy cigarette smoke did more than cloud his sight. Along with the shot of hard liquor in his hand, both worked together to calm his nerves and pacify his irritation.

Another column of smoke left his mouth and his eyes sank deeper into their sockets. He flicked the ash from the end of his ciggy, his eyes now staring down at the bar counter.

This had become his life.

This—he looked at his hands full of filth and bitterness—*this* had become his escape.

Why was it he couldn't be fully relieved of his evils, his plagues, like all his other brothers in arms were when they touched this stuff?

Why was he the exception?

He'd never been this low before. He never once touched alcohol or dirty cigarettes in his life. But here he was, in a downtown Gin Mill, drowning his troubles in a pool of grime.

More than once he'd sat on this same bar stool asking himself the same question…why?

Every time, he knew why, but he refused to admit to himself that *it* had affected him. That *it* had stolen his life completely away from him…and from Libby.

"Hey, Larry," he called to the bartender.

"Yeah, Phil?"

Phillip dropped his cigarette onto the ash tray and leaned forward, sliding his shot glass across the bar top. "Another round."

"Say, you's hittin' it sort of hard tonight, aren't ya, Phil?"

Pale liquor curled into his glass. In one swig, Phillip tossed it into his mouth and swallowed hard. "I guess you could say that."

"What's the deal? You got girl troubles?"

"I have a heck of a lot more than girl troubles right now."

"Is that a fact?" Larry, the bartender, wiped down a clean glass.

Phillip's shoulder slumped and he hunched over the bar counter. "Tell me, Larry, have you ever seen the crater a shell leaves after it hits the ground?"

"No, can't say I have. Army deemed me 4-F."

Cold and depleted, Phillip's eyes never strayed from the counter where he looked deeply into a place far from where he sat. "Well, it's deep. It's wide. And completely barren of anything living." He glanced up at the bartender through glassy eyes. "It's a lot like my life right now."

❦

What had happened to the man she loved?

The same question repeatedly stalked Libby's mind. For the last three months she stood by, watching a man she hardly recognized.

The glimmer that once shone in his eyes when he looked at her was no longer there. Instead, hollow sockets stared into what seemed like a world invisible to her. But Phillip saw it. Something held his affections captive, hiding his love away from her.

Hearing the clock chime 11, Libby's attention turned back to her cleaning. A pile of reading littered the hall table. With haste, she lifted the stack of *Good Housekeeping* magazines from the side table and rushed past the place where her photographs sat. Out of habit, her eyes turned to the very thing she'd held on to for so long…

Her wedding day photograph.

But Phillip was home now, she didn't need to mull over a picture when her husband was physically within arm's reach.

Or did she?

She stopped and closed her eyes. No, she *did* need to stop and long for that man.

Setting the magazines down, she gazed at the photograph for a long moment then gently lifted the frame into her hands. Phillip was most certainly here in the flesh and safe from danger, but his soul was void in her life.

She loathed that. Deep down, her confusion evolved into a burning ache. A sense of anger ignited in her chest, burning a hole into her heart. Why was he holding back from her? Why was *God* allowing her to bear such sorrow?

She thought of Grace and Luke and the tragedies that brought them together. Her mind raced through the events that led Danny back to Maggie.

Everyone had come home. And now those same people were moving on with their lives. Marriages were being laced together, and families were being created.

So what made her and Phillip so different from everyone else?

Suddenly, the photograph that once brought so much hope and peace to her soul now sowed seeds of hurt and angst.

She replaced the wedding photograph back to its rightful place on the side table with force, causing the rest of the photographs to clang together. Sliding her fingers onto the bridge of her nose, her eyelids closed, and she willed herself to calm.

Where was her peace? What was it that caused the ground beneath her marriage to quake? Even if Phillip couldn't sense the foundation of their lives being shaken, the tremors were there…Libby glanced out the front window to the place where Phillip's empty chair sat…

"And he doesn't even care," she whispered to no one but herself.

14 June 1946

Creaking hinges and stumbling shoes told Libby that her husband had finally come home. It was the same sound she'd become accustomed to listening for every weekend for the last two months.

From her cold spot on the bed, she pushed herself up, listening for his voice or any indication of his current condition.

Every muscle in her body stiffened and she hoped she wasn't in for a doozy of a night.

All her inner strength was exhausted. In no way was she ready to venture into another heated argument with Phillip. Not tonight. She was through. Emotionally and physically, she was wearied. And more than once, her exhaustion, her emotional pain had landed her in the bathroom to empty her stomach's contents. Tonight, nausea tore through her stomach.

Another crash sounded from downstairs, this time causing her to startle. With a sigh of dread, she pushed up off her bed and forced herself to walk the seemingly long hallway to her husband's aid. When she reached the staircase, she spotted Phillip half slumped over the railing.

She shook her head and started down the stairs.

Her light footsteps jarred Phillip and he attempted to straighten.

It was a pitiful attempt on his part, but he put on his *I'm-doing-all right* mask just the same.

"Honey, I'm home," he said through slightly slurred speech and glassy, red eyes.

"Cut the lines, Phillip. Let's get you up to bed." Not giving in to his sweet talk, Libby clenched his arms without compassion and empathy and guided him up their staircase.

Just who did he think he was fooling anyway? Of course he thought he'd hidden his foolishness from her. But she'd known. For a very long time now, she'd known everything. And still, he came home every weekend ossified and thinking she was completely oblivious to all his tomfooleries.

She'd known for months now that his vehicle had made more than one appearance at the bar in the next town over. She'd also learned that he made frequent stops at Harvey's after his nightly revelry. And more times than she could count had Phillip shown up at the house in his inebriated state.

Sweet-smelling cigars and cigarettes were woven onto his clothes and tainted his breath. The stench of alcohol also stained his shirt sleeves and collar.

And each time, she would take his garments and vigorously wash them to get rid of the filth that polluted them. Maybe she hoped it would also rid them of whatever else it was that tainted Phillip.

When they reached their bedroom, Phillip plopped onto the bed. Libby gave his knee a rigid pat.

"Here. Let me have that button-down. I'll need to wash it right away." She held her hand out for his shirt.

Slowly, his hands worked the buttons on his shirt.

"You know you are the prettiest girl in my life…even when you're hopping mad?"

"I'm not mad, Phillip." Just saying those words made her nose sting with tears.

"Yes. Yes you are. I left you all alone again."

"Yes, you did." Why was it like talking to a child when he came home like this?

"I didn't want to."

"Then why did you leave…again?"

His eyes, glossy and drowsy, rolled, then met hers . Hesitation rested on his lips for several noiseless moments.

"Libby, I'm sorry."

Though she wanted to hear those words, she knew it wouldn't be enough. Not last time. Not this time. And most likely not in the near future. Through her tears, she shook her head, averting her eyes from his face. "No. No, you're not."

"Yes, darling, I am. Please. Won't you look at me?" He tried for her hands and reached out to touch her cheek, but she stiffened and jerked them away, the reminders of what he'd done to her wrists still tainted her skin.

Just like their friends and family, he'd pushed her away from him. To the point that she now flinched when he reached for her.

"Phillip, I'm tired. Tired of all this."

"Darling, I know. And it's all my fault. I just don't know what comes over me sometimes."

"Then—you best figure it out."

FORTY-SIX

Peace.

It was nowhere to be found. Even beneath the darkened backdrop of his eyelids, Phillip's soul wriggled and writhed in fitful slumber. Shadows and voices moved across the airwaves of his subconscious mind. Mounting tension was the cause for the inner war raging in the confines of his intuitive thinking.

Recollections of his quarrelling with Libby replayed through his dreams. Through a watery canvas, Libby's tears fell from her eyes. He reached out for her through his dream, but as he did, the farther away her silhouette moved from him until she faded into a smoke-filled sky. That's when the first burst of dropping shells scattered abroad the skyline, shattering his home and the very woman he loved.

In the next moment, he peered down from atop the tallest cliff of a lush, green island—the place of his imprisonment.

Sweat beaded on his forehead and his lungs drew in and released shaky breaths as his unsure footing inched closer to the bluff. The constant rush of ocean waters crashing against robust rock filled the salty island air. Echoes of screams, of crying, seemed to come from every direction. But as Phillip turned his head from side to side, panic struck his chest. They seemed to be coming from behind every rock, every palm tree, from every large leaf that grew on the mossy, rocky earth, but not a soul was to be seen.

Then it was the nauseating splash of something plunging into the ocean that drew his attention back to the cliffs, back to the very place he stood. As he gripped his rifle a little tighter, his breaths grew short. His heart pounded harder within his chest, and his throat constricted with dread. Slowly, ever so slowly, did his eyes wander over the bluffs to the island shore below. And slowly, did his knees buckle under the grizzly scene his eyes witnessed.

First it was a leg. Then it was an arm. Next it was a body, followed by many, many more. They all stared up at him, their eyes wild, piercing, and yet cold. They looked at him as if they condemned him. He was, after all, their enemy.

Stumbling backward, his foot caught in a foxhole and Phillip fell on the flat of his back, knocking the air from his lungs. Twigs and dirt cut into his sides and he spat on the ground.

From behind him, a tiny whimper cried out. Holding his breath, he cautiously turned his head to the sound of the small cry.

That's when he spotted two large, round eyes peering at him from the dark of an abandoned foxhole. They belonged to those of a girl, a frightened girl.

Reaching out his hand, he coaxed her out, and stared into the prettiest black eyes he'd ever seen. But as he wrapped his arms around her to shield her from the bombardment of raining ammunition, something tore her from his embrace.

Crying out, he ran to catch her, but her image faded just as Libby's had. Falling to his knees, he buried his head into his blood-stained hands. Faces of the dead appeared before him. Wiping his brow and rolling his eyes beneath their lids, his attempt to smudge out their daunting images was futile. Panic seized his core, gripping his soul and crushing his insides with terrifying force. Suffocation dropped him to his knees where his lungs ached for air. Slowly, the world around him blackened. Fading skies marred his view of a once beautiful sunset over the ocean.

It was much like his life. His once beautiful life, complete with Libby as his bride and a heart full of dreams for a perfect future, had been tarnished with the blood of the dead and the soot of destruction. The picture perfect castle in the air he once desired now seemed like a shack built on sand.

And that sand was sifting beneath his feet.

Life post-war had not been the cure for his mental evils. Even while asleep, his conscience still reasoned and debated his case.

Why was he locked within a corridor of his mind that continually plagued him with vivid recollections of images he was forced to face on the front lines? Why couldn't he put those horrific experiences behind him and move forward? Why did they invade his home and wreak havoc on the life he so desperately wanted to live?

Throughout his nightmares, throughout the night, Phillip's body twitched and writhed as he was forced to relive those atrocities. His body protested against it, but the attack on his mind was stronger.

Phillip Johnson may have left the battle far behind him, hidden past an entire ocean, but the war had followed him. And that war had commandeered his very home.

FORTY-SEVEN

Sleep hadn't come easily that night. Libby's stomach rolled back and forth as if she were being tossed on stormy sea waves. At times she squeezed her eyes shut, hoping she didn't have need to run to the restroom sink. It didn't help that Phillip tossed and turned on his side of their bed.

Her heart ached. A crater-sized hole hollowed out her insides. Emptiness. Every ounce of her strength and willpower had been exhausted when Phillip stammered through the doorway drunk as a sailor.

Silent tears seeped from her closed eyelids as she begged for sleep to claim her body. If she could just close her eyes for a long, long time maybe she would wake up one day to find Phillip at her side ready to be the husband she needed him to be.

As the clock ticked under midnight shadows, somehow, somewhere, Libby drifted off to sleep, her pillow still damp from her shed tears. As soon as her body gave in to the rest she desperately needed, all the hurts, and broken promises, and fears that lay heavy on her heart faded away into a dark abyss...

If only that peace could have lasted all night.

Waves of restlessness jerked her body. At first, the bed tossed her only once or twice, but still in the twilight of sleep and consciousness, her mind chose rest.

Once more, the bed shook and she rolled from her right to her left side. An occasional moan resonated with her and crept its way into her dreams.

As she sailed closer to the harbor of her dream, rocks pushed upward and she reached a hand into the water to paddle away from them should they sink the small vessel she sailed on. Frantically, she paddled harder, faster, but it seemed it was all for naught.

Suddenly, a large boulder pushed up from the sea beneath her boat and capsized it, spilling her into the raging ocean waves. As her head sank below the water, she gasped for air. There was no air. Violently, her arms and legs kicked and treaded, but it was no use, she could feel her life leaving her...

Libby gasped for one final breath and her eyes burst open. As her surroundings cleared, her lungs did not. Then she realized what was happening to her.

Something clenched around her neck. Her hands, shaking and frantic, reached for her throat. Her eyes, large and bulging, stared ahead. Just above her, with his legs straddled around her waist, Phillip loomed over her. His eyes were black and unseeing. And he was...choking her.

She swiped and clawed at him, not understanding what was going on other than the fact that she couldn't breathe.

Just enough air filled her lungs to scream out his name. Her legs kicked from beneath the quilt and she attempted to turn to throw him off her. He was so much larger than she and it took every ounce of effort to fight.

"Phillip! What are you doing? Get off of me!" She was able to yell.

He mumbled something back to her. She couldn't make out his words over the ringing in her ears, but she caught his military slang.

Again, she clawed at his wrists, fighting for her life. Tears now filled her eyes. With one final jerk and turn of her body, she was able to throw him off balance. She took advantage of that and fell to the floor of their bedroom.

With each deep breath she took she coughed, but she could breathe again. But Phillip's stumbling footsteps and towering shadow caused her to look up. Terror filled her chest as she glanced up to find his rifle in his hand. Her entire body shuddered with dominant fear. What was wrong with him? What was he doing?

Libby stumbled to her feet and backed toward the doorway. With each step she took, Phillip matched it.

"Ph—Phillip...what are you d—doing?" Each word quivered on her lips. A fear unknown to her coursed through every vein in her body. "You—you're scaring me. Stop it!"

He continued to step closer. His hands gripped his rifle. It pointed upward to the ceiling, thankfully, but the bayonet was fully intact. How would she ever fight him off if it came to that? And what was going on? She needed to get away. She needed to get far, far away from here. Creaking floorboards moaned with each step she took down the hall.

She was almost to the stairs when Phillip made his move. The sharp edge of the bayonet slanted toward Libby and she let out a blood-curdling scream just before her foot slipped off the top step. Before she could catch herself—but before the bayonet could catch her—she tumbled down the staircase. Stabbing pain pierced her side, wrists, cheek and back. For a moment she lay at the bottom of the staircase on the floor in a daze as to what just happened to her. Had Phillip actually stabbed her? Or had she suffered bruises and injury from the fall?

She was still comprehending it all when Phillip's voice rattled her ears.

"Libby! Oh, Libby, darling, are you hurt?"

"Get away from me!" She cried out in pain and fear of him. Her arms, as sore as they were, found strength to push her weight up off the floor and away from him.

She spotted his form in the dark coming toward her. Instinctively, she retreated from him.

"Libby? Libby, are you all right?"

"You just stay away from me! Don't you come near!"

She limped away, rubbing her shoulder.

"What happened? Did I—?" Phillip's eyes darted around the room, when they settled on his rifle, they grew wide with seeming surprise. "Oh, no...what did I do?"

"I've had enough, Phillip." Not taking her eyes off him for more than a second at a time, Libby reached for her shoes and shoved them onto her feet. "I can't stay here another moment." With haste, she grabbed her overcoat and started for the door.

Phillip glanced from his rifle to her. "Honey, I—I don't know what happened. One minute I was in the jungle, the next moment, I'm waking up here...and you..." He glanced at the spot that throbbed on her cheek. "Oh, honey...you're hurt."

His speech was still slurred. Alcohol still claimed his mind. She was tired of it all. As his hand reached out to her, she flinched and drew back.

"Don't touch me. You've done enough already. I'm leaving, Phillip. And I won't be back until you've cleaned yourself up. You hear?"

Not giving him a moment for rebuttal, she walked out the door and out of his life.

The air was cool but she hardly noticed. In fact parts of her body burned. Her cheek throbbed with pain. She touched the spot, and sure enough, a small knot had formed on her cheekbone where it bumped against the railing of the staircase. Her back also stung with each step she took. The nasty fall did a number on her, but it also saved her from worse. Phillip's bayonet most likely would have—she shuddered to think what it would have done to her.

She dared not look back.

It may have been the dead of the night and she may have walked with a limp, but her legs carried her farther down the street.

Where too?

She had no idea. She just let her legs do the walking and the carrying of the load. At this point it didn't matter where she ended up. Anywhere was better than on the end of a bayonet.

FORTY-EIGHT

The Russo Home

Maggie curled her body up close to Danny's as she slipped in between the sheets. A soft, summer's breeze hooked the curtains and blew across her skin. The glow of the full moon slanted through the window pane, and cast a blue hue over Danny's profile. Why didn't anyone ever embellish on marriage being so sweet?

It was the perfect distraction from her reading and the issues that wore heavy on her mind. For weeks she's been reading all she could on the shell shock disorder and its cure. But it seemed that the more reading she did, the worse the end result was. Tonight, she needed a break. No more reading. No more worries. Just a beautiful moonlit night with the man she loved.

Her fingers reached up to smooth away a curled tendril that hung over Danny's forehead. He caught her hand before she could pull it away.

"Don't stop."

She smiled in the darkness. "There are no more curls to brush away."

"I can help with that." With one swoop of his hand, Danny tousled his hair into a dark mess.

"What am I going to do with you, Danny Russo?"

"At the moment, I don't care."

"In that case..." She stretched her neck to plant a kiss on his earlobe. He reacted by cradling her in his arms and covering her mouth with his in slow, passionate kisses.

Thump, thump, thump.

"What was that?" Maggie whispered in between breaths.

"I think it came from the front door."

"A caller?"

Danny sat up in bed and listened. Another knock sounded from the porch. "Someone's at the door."

Maggie's heart thundered. Pulling the covers up close to her chin, she shuddered. "Who do you suppose it is?"

"I don't know. It's awfully odd for someone to call after midnight."

He swung his legs over the side of the bed and grabbed his undershirt.

"Danny be careful. Wait. Let me go with you."

"No, stay here, Maggie. I'll take care of it."

Danny walked from their bedroom toward the direction of the foyer. Maggie threw the covers off her body and grabbed her robe to toss over her shoulders. Tying it closed, she padded quietly through the house. She reached the living room just in time to see Danny throw open the door to a meek little woman whose face was blotched with contusions and a shiner on her cheekbone.

"Libby?" Maggie raced for the door and pulled her sister-in-law inside. But before she could set Libby down on the couch, the girl's legs gave out beneath her. Danny's arms caught her before she hit the floor.

"Libby, honey, what happened to you?"

"Maggie?"

"Yes? What is it, dear?"

"Maggie. Hide me. Don't let him find me, please. I don't have anywhere else to turn."

"Who, Libby? Are you in trouble?"

"Libby." Danny bent down beside her. "Who hit you? Where's Phillip?"

Agony tortured the poor girl's eyes. A mix of blood and tears intermingled on her cheeks and added a sheen to her complexion. But the girl looked famished and sickly. Something was very wrong.

"Libby, you can tell us. Danny and I will protect you."

"He's not the same anymore. He's a monster. You have to believe me."

"I believe you, Libby. But you have to tell me who it is."

Her eyes lazily rolled upward to meet Maggie's gaze. Before Libby's eyes drifted closed, she managed to whisper, "Don't you know? Phillip."

⋘⋙

Maggie had always known nursing was her calling, but she never imagined her calling would require her to aid a family member in the dark of night.

As Maggie rinsed out a cold cloth in the basin on the night stand, she studied Libby's still form. Her sister-in-law had long ago entered her deep sleep. It wasn't a normal night's rest that claimed Libby, however. And deep down, Maggie knew it had everything to do with Phillip—her only brother.

Slowly, Maggie wrung out the cloth and folded it over. With gentle strokes, she dabbed away at the abrasions on Libby's face, arms, and legs.

What had happened to her? Where had the bruises come from and why were they there?

Placing the cloth back in the basin, Maggie leaned an elbow on the night stand as she sat in a chair with her chin in her hand. A strong sense of dread bubbled in the pit of her stomach. Could Danny be right? Was it possible that Phillip suffered from a mental disturbance? Even though she'd succumbed to entertaining the thought, she couldn't bring herself to say the term, even in her head she couldn't think it to herself.

She'd seen the devastation. She'd seen the lack of communication in affected soldiers. She'd watched perfectly healthy men turn into cowering beings that no longer were able to function in the real world. Then she'd witnessed the doctors sign their names on the line…sentencing those poor souls to a life outside of the living.

No!

Not Phillip. Her brother was stronger than that. He was a better man than to allow the war to get to him and tear him apart from the inside.

Warm, painful tears welled in her eyes. Her brother wasn't ill.

But then she looked at Libby's sad state.

Libby wouldn't do this to herself. Someone was the cause of these awful injuries. Who else would do her harm in the middle of the night?

The dreadful truth smacked Maggie in the face, causing her unshed tears to slip quietly down her cheeks. Her eyes closed in surrender. She knew it was true. The signs were becoming clearer with each passing day. Phillip was suffering with shell shock.

"Sweetheart," Danny's soft voice whispered as his hands rested on her shoulders. "How's she doin'?"

Nonchalantly, Maggie swiped at the tears on her cheeks and silently cleared her throat. "It seems as though she's sleeping like she hasn't slept in months. As for her injuries, she's very bashed up. I'm not going to deny it…I'm worried for her, Danny." Maggie reached up and grasped the hand that Danny held against her shoulder and squeezed. "Her coloring is pale. She's a bit on the thin side. I hadn't noticed that until now. And her eyes…look at the dark circles under them. I knew she seemed tired recently, but I assumed she and Phillip had yet another quarrel. I keep recalling that morning that Phillip telephoned for me to come by the house. I should have noticed all the signs then. Phillip's not well. Neither is Libby. She's so weak. I just don't know, Danny. I'm thinking perhaps I was foolish and you were right. I keep replaying Libby's words over in my mind. What did she mean? Phillip, a monster? He did this to her?" Maggie's fatigued fingers smoothed over her brow. It was all so difficult to comprehend. "I don't understand all this. But I'm slowly starting to see some truth. Something's not right with Phillip, and you can bet I'm going to find out."

❧❧

Although the sun began its ascent into the sky, the graying clouds prevented its cheery rays from reaching the room where Maggie sat with Libby. It had been a sleepless night as she kept watch over her sister-in-law and chased differing scenarios running through her head.

Danny had already left for work, promising Maggie he would return at noon to check on the situation. If anything, Danny was ready to speak with Phillip concerning Libby's condition. It was one of the ideals Danny thought strongly about. Maggie knew that and she knew Danny felt strongly enough about it to confront Phillip on the matter of Libby's bruises. But Maggie had asked him to wait until she had the chance to speak to Libby about it first. It didn't do anyone any good to go on assuming things.

Libby's stirring form let a slight sigh escape her nostrils. Maggie pushed upward in her chair. The quilted blanket that hung over her chest and shoulders slipped to her lap. She couldn't sleep anyway. Gently, Maggie pushed out of her chair and padded softly across the room. Pulling back the floral curtains, Maggie gazed out the window to the gray world outside.

The skies seemed to match the mood of the day. Morose. Melancholy. Drab. It only needed to drop rain to match the tears that fell within Maggie's heart. For her heart was breaking in two.

This wasn't supposed to happen. Life was supposed to get better now that the war was over. Never did she imagine the rippling effect war would have on her family.

"Maggie?" Libby's soft voice called out to her.

Turning, Maggie answered. "I'm here, Libby. How are you feeling?" Maggie's bedside manner took over. Attending to Libby as if she were one of her hospital patients, Maggie stood at her bedside and checked her pulse and vitals.

"I've got one doozy of a headache. And I'm afraid my stomach is quite ill."

"I do hope you haven't suffered a concussion, Libbs."

Stillness hovered between them, but Maggie sensed the conversation spinning within the walls of Libby's mind. Maggie offered up no questions. As much as she wanted answers, she knew Libby wasn't ready for her line of questioning.

"I'm sorry, Maggie."

Maggie's head tilted in uncertainty. "For what, Libby?"

Libby's arms spread wide. "For all this. For intruding in the middle of the night. For dropping my problems on your doorstep."

Maggie didn't answer. The long moment that passed between them was filled with Maggie's unanswered questions. As she sorted them out in her mind, wondering which to ask first, her mouth decided to act on its own.

"Libby, from the beginning…what happened?"

FORTY-NINE

It wasn't easy to break down the walls surrounding her heart. But block by block, Libby removed each stony surface, revealing every bruise, every graze of her broken heart.

The wounds had grown so deep, and she'd suppressed them so far down, that even she hadn't seen the full destruction imputed on her spirit. But as she sat there and bled out her soul to Maggie, those wounds revealed their severity to her. Tears fell like ice crystals down her cheeks. Hard, cold and razor sharp, they pushed from her soul and out into the open. So much damage had Phillip done to her.

Maggie must have empathized. It was either that or Maggie didn't believe her at all. She sat stone-silent as Libby told her story from the beginning. The look of exasperation on her face was of both disgust and disbelief. But Maggie continued to listen to her. However, when Libby had finished spilling the depths of her soul, ending with last night's grapple, it was Libby who had the questions.

"Maggie, please say something. You do believe me, don't you?"

Libby watched as Maggie's lips sealed together and her jawline tensed. Libby was afraid of Maggie's answer as her sister-in-law found it hard to swallow.

Maggie's eyes closed, revealing droplets of tears on her eyelids.

"As much as I don't want to believe Phillip could ever possess a destructive bone in his body, I do believe you, Libby. I think I've known all along, but I chose to ignore the signs. And I'm sorry, Libby." Maggie moved to grasp Libby's hands. "I'm so terribly sorry. I should've acted on my intuition when I first noticed his change in behavior. I could have prevented all this from happening."

Tears seeped from Maggie's eyes and Libby knew she was telling the truth. A sense of relief warmed Libby's insides despite the cold flow of emotion sliding down her cheeks. Finally, she'd found a harbor for every lost vessel that had sailed from her heart. Maggie seemed her last hope. But that didn't answer the mound of questions billowing on the inside.

"Maggie, what did I do? What wrong doing have I committed to be sentenced to this life?"

An embrace of warmth and understanding surrounded her with Maggie's arms. Libby relaxed into Maggie's embrace and allowed its soothing nature to pacify the ache inside.

"Nothing, Libby. Nothing. It's not your fault. I'm going to take care of you. And I'm going to get Phillip the help he needs. Until then, you stay as long you need, but first, I suggest you make a call to Doctor Cole."

⊰⊱

Just the thought of bringing Doctor Cole into the situation caused a shudder to run down Libby's spine. Surely, he'd want to know about every marking on her body. She wasn't sure if she was ready to bring a third party into her quandary. But Maggie insisted, informing her that she'd worked closely with the doc and that they could trust him.

"Everything will be fine, Libby. I wouldn't suggest it unless I was certain. Trust me, this is all unmarked territory for me too."

Bile rose up Libby's throat. All morning she'd fought back the need to purge. Weakness had settled in her bones and all she wanted was to close to her eyes and to not wake up for a very long time. But as she stood at the mirror in the guest bedroom, attempting to reel back her sentiments, Maggie's voice gently called in to her.

"The car is ready, honey. Are you doing okay in there?"

Inhaling and releasing her breath, Libby knew she had to go through with it. Perhaps the doctor could prescribe her some pills to help her sleep. Or at least give her a concoction of something to ease the nausea growing in her stomach. Either way, she had to go, and at the moment there was no turning back.

Libby wrung the handles of her purse as she sat in anxious silence. Although Doctor Cole's office was inviting and painted pale blue with white ornamental trim outlining his waiting room, the comforting shades of pastel couldn't ease her apprehensive mind. She sat, tense and barely breathing, with a heartbeat that could have matched ol' Man O War's speed at the Pimlico Race Track.

Libby tried to wrap her mind around her situation. She tried to put all her fears to rest and calm her insecurities. But she couldn't hide truth.

Her hand rested against her midriff to quell the butterflies flittering about it.

"Everything will be all right," Maggie whispered to her.

Drowned in her own apprehensive state, she'd nearly forgotten Maggie sat at her side.

Giving Maggie a slight half-smile, her heart nearly lurched when the nurse shadowed the doorway.

"Mrs. Johnson. Doctor Cole is ready for you now."

Libby's eyes grew wide, the deep pulse of her heart hammered loudly in her ears as she stood. Lightheadedness seized her senses, and she groped for the nearest chair.

"Mrs. Johnson, are you all right?"

"Libby?"

The echoes of ladies' voices rang back, but she was able to hold on to consciousness by barely a thread.

∽ઠ૨ళ

Libby's eyes closed as she waited in tormented silence. If it wasn't bad enough she'd nearly fainted in the waiting room, she now prayed the doctor's suspicions were nothing more than a bad case of the flu.

The doctor insisted she lie down on the examining table until he returned. It was like a jail sentence. Every fiber within her wanted to run as fast as she could out of the office and to her bedroom to cry out her frustrations.

But reality and common sense forced her to stay put. Her heart was torn between two valleys. She wanted nothing more than to go home and live a life of happiness, to build her dreams on a firm foundation with the man she loved more than anyone else. But Phillip's dark, angry state wouldn't allow room for that in their home. If the doctor's diagnosis was correct, the entire being of her life would change drastically—and she wouldn't know where to go from here.

She didn't know the future. She couldn't predict tomorrow or the next five minutes. She remained feeble, helpless.

When Doctor Cole entered the room, her heart's pace sprinted and she attempted to sit up.

"No, no, Mrs. Johnson. Let yourself be for just a few more minutes."

She eased back down, eyeing the physician as he walked to his desk and lowered himself onto his chair.

Folding his hands on the desk, he glanced at her. The seconds that ticked by seemed an eternity.

"It's as I suspected, Mrs. Johnson. Good thing your sister-in-law got you in here when she did."

The beat of her heart stilled and the queasiness in her stomach returned, tightening into a ball and washing a sense of nausea throughout her entire body. Lightheadedness caused the room to spin round. It was good she heeded the doctor's orders and rested on the table.

"Ar—are you sure, Doctor?"

"Quite. There's no mistake in what the examination found. You can expect your baby to come mid-January."

She wasn't sure if she should laugh or cry. Laugh out of complete hysteria or cry because of the dread that now burrowed within her. Either way, her heart ached—it ached because she couldn't go home. Because she feared Phillip's disappointment. It ached for the joy she so desperately wanted to possess for this new little life, but couldn't because her marriage had crumbled from the foundation they'd once built.

No matter how badly she'd wanted to hear those beautiful words from the doctor and feel that wondrous joy bursting within her chest, she couldn't. Not even the sting of a bee could burn into the numbness she felt. Every ounce of joy she could possess had been stolen somewhere between the Pacific Ocean and Arbor Springs, Maryland.

FIFTY

At her bedside, Maggie kneeled. With her forehead resting against praying hands, she asked God where to go from here. She'd honestly thought that with the ceasing of war, their lives would continue. That new and wonderful experiences were ahead of them. But that joy was completely destroyed the night Libby stumbled onto their doorstep.

Now she had new challenges to face. Libby would not be able to handle the circumstances on her own. Not now. Not after the doctor's surprising news.

Poor Libby. She'd sobbed the entire car ride home. The hopelessness that weighed heavy on Libby's shoulders soon fell hard on Maggie's as well. Libby was her sister-in-law, family. Phillip was her brother, flesh and blood. But blood lines couldn't stifle the anger that swelled in her chest at the present time. How could he do this to Libby? How could he treat her with such a callous attitude...and while she carried his baby?

As soon as she and Libby arrived back at the house, Maggie saw Libby into the guest bedroom and brewed a cup of hot tea. Libby's eyes hung so heavy, that it didn't take long for the girl to fall asleep. Maggie was thankful. Libby would need all the rest she could find.

As Maggie stepped into the hallway, she gazed at Libby's still form. She refrained from showing her worry. The nasty fall Libby took surely put her and the baby in danger. Maggie only prayed that no internal damage was done to either of them. Prayer. That was all she had this time.

On second thought, aside from her prayers, she had lips and a tongue. Perhaps both had gotten her into a great deal of trouble in the past, but this time was different. Phillip was her brother and it was time she set him straight.

∽❧∾

When Phillip didn't answer her knock, she'd let herself in. The house was eerily quiet as she stepped into its dark interior.

"Phillip?" she called sharply. "I came to talk."

Her voice echoed through the hall, calling back to her. The stone silence sent an unnerving shudder down her spine, raising the hair on her arms.

Something wasn't right.

Eyes wide, she scanned the floor of the downstairs. When no sign of Phillip turned up, she turned to the stairway. As she glanced upward, her stomach roiled with a great wave of nausea.

Phillip's rifle lay haphazardly across the floor.

Pressing her fist into her abdomen, Maggie pushed her legs up the staircase. Her mouth opened to call out Phillip's name, but only hollow air pushed its way upward. The tremor in her throat prevented words from forming on her tongue.

Lord, prepare me for whatever my eyes are about to see. And please, Lord, save my brother.

"I pray I'm not too late," she whispered to herself.

With a jerk, her chest sucked in a sharp breath as she reached the top floor. Slowly she crept down the hall toward Phillip and Libby's bedroom. As she passed each doorway, she stopped to scan the rooms.

Her feet stopped short when Phillip's combat boots caught from the corner of her eye.

There. There he was.

Mustering up her courage, she ventured inside the guest room. Slouched over his green foot locker, Phillip's still body lay in an incoherent state.

"Phillip?" Maggie rushed to his side and jostled his shoulders.

A deep groan vibrated from his chest.

"Come on, Phillip, wake up."

When his head lifted, it fell back against the closet door. Glassy eyes coldly penetrated her. That's when the stench hit her nose.

"You're drunk! Oh, Phillip, how could you?"

All at once her greatest fear gathered into roiling anger.

"I'm sorry, Maggie."

Phillip's lips barely moved as his words rushed out in a whispered sigh. His eyes hardly lifted to her face. Haze screened his outward appearance in his ossified state.

Pacing the floor, Maggie's palms pressed into her cheeks and ran across her forehead. What could she do? Reasoning with him would do no good. He'd surely forget she was even here by morning.

"What's happened to you?" she finally breathed.

"She doesn't deserve me. You don't deserve me. No one deserves me. Look at me, Mag-gie. Look at what I've become."

"Phillip, I feel as though I don't know you anymore. And Libby doesn't know you either."

"I hurt her, Maggie. I hurt her real bad."

"Well, she's safe for now. Danny and I are taking care of her, and we'll continue to care for her until you come to your senses and be that man she needs you to be."

"She doesn't need me."

"Yes, she does, Phillip. Do you hear yourself? You're talking crazy."

"Do you hear them too, Maggie?"

She stopped. Dumbfounded, Maggie stared in confusion at her irrational sibling who somehow cracked under pressure.

"Do I hear what?"

"Their screams. Their cries. They don't stop. Day and night they yell and holler. They don't stop. They don't stop."

He was becoming agitated. His body writhed on the floor of the guest room, his hands pressing against his ears, in what seemed to be an attempt to silence his demons.

For the first time in her life, she didn't know what to do. Her skills were not trained for the human mind. But it was clear that Phillip suffered from the condition she dreaded most—shell shock.

Gulping back her dread, she swallowed hard, suppressing the bile that rose up her throat. If she couldn't help him mentally, then she would help him in the only other way she knew how—spiritually.

"Have you tried faith?"

"How will that help me now? What's done is done. How will faith erase the images? The screams? The dying children?" On his last word Phillip's voice gave out, and his body collapsed to the floor.

Curled up on the floor, his hands clawed at his hair. His sobs grew louder with each gasp of breath.

Maggie stooped down, her own tears falling over the crest of her cheeks and onto the floor as her heart ached for her grieving brother who suffered torture by something more than just war.

She didn't recognize him. Once headstrong and solid, Phillip always knew who he was and where he was headed in life. Now, as she stooped down at his balled up form on the floor, she realized he wasn't the invincible man she once knew him to be.

She had to get to the core of the problem. As much as the thought of knowing the truth caused her neck hairs to stand on end, Phillip wouldn't be able to get the help he needed if she didn't press him for answers. Her curiosity budded, not recalling him ever mentioning anything about children before now.

"What about the children, Phillip?" she asked in a soft voice, masking her tears behind her carefully trained nurse's voice.

"No...no!" In an obvious attempt to ward off the memories, he covered his face and ears with his palms.

But Maggie wasn't going to let up so easily. Her hands—firm and strong from the years of field nursing—carefully maneuvered Phillip's arms from his face.

"You have to confront the phantoms, Phillip, or you'll never be able to move forward. And I've seen what happens to those who don't deal with their pain. You're my brother, and I refuse to let you give up and have this war drag you to the underworld." Her sharp, brown eyes penetrated his soul. She waited until his gaze locked onto hers before continuing. "So tell me—what happened to the children? What happened to you?"

Trembles shuddered through his arms. Her eyes swept across her hands, which still held onto his wrists. His face grimaced and she feared he was already too far gone for the survival of his mental state.

"Don't leave me, Phillip. I still need you here. I need you to hang on to the fine thread that your soul is dangling from. Don't give up now. Please talk to me."

And that's when she allowed herself to show her brother her tears. Two large droplets fell from her eyes, but she refused to let her gaze drop with them. Her fingers tightened around his palms, testing his senses by stimulation.

Finally, after what seemed like an hour, Phillip's voice cut the silence between them. Broken, his first sentence relayed the anguish he'd been living with.

"Maggie...I just...I just want to forget." His eyes cast downward, his head shaking from side to side. "No one understands. The children—they keep...keep visiting me. At night. During the day. I can still hear their voices, their screams. They won't let me be. They won't go away."

As if too much for him bear, Phillip pulled his hands from Maggie's and cupped them around his sideburns as he rocked back and forth, back and forth. He was a man in despair—no, more than that. He was a man who'd had his life cut from him, in bits and pieces. Maggie couldn't help but wonder if all that remained was a small fraction of a man whose only shard spared was his ability to *feel*. He was barely a shell of a human being. All strength and skeletal function chipped away by the horrors and atrocities of living as a war time soldier. But she couldn't allow that to be his crutch to lean on for the rest of his life. She knew all too well what happened to the men who refused to return to society, and her brother would not become another casualty of war.

Clearing her mind of her brother's current state, she imagined her brother as he was ten years ago—the boy who teased and made fun of her. The boy who also cared for her after her father's harsh words. The brother who loved with everything he had. That's who Phillip Johnson was. And who she hoped to find once again.

"Phillip." Her tone was firm, unyielding. Her touch to his hands, as she pulled them from his face for a second time, would not allow him to cower behind his fears any longer. "Look at me. You are stronger than your problems. *God* is stronger than the evils you're facing. Stop allowing the devil's work to shadow you, Phillip. Reach out and anchor yourself to the all-powerful God who has brought all of us together again. He loves you, Phillip. And He's casting out His life preserver to you right now."

His eyes, brimming with unshed tears, glistened under the evening rays. "Then why is He punishing me?"

"Is He punishing you, or is He trying to show you something bigger? For Pete's sake, Phillip, look around you." Her arms swept around the room as if showing him something big and new for the first time. "Look at the beautiful life God brought you home to. A warm home that a loving wife slaved over to make perfect for you, a family that has miraculously been brought together again, friends who are here, who want to be your support, and a baby to call your own. *Your* baby, Phillip. Your flesh and blood. Do you really want to leave it all behind? Don't you care at all what your son or daughter will look like? Don't you want to be there when Libby looks up at you for the first time as a mother, and you a father? Don't you see? God's given you a wondrous gift. And it's yours. So why do you keep pushing it away?"

"Baby?" His eyes suddenly registered coherency.

"Yes, Phillip. A baby. *Your* baby. Libby didn't know until today. And she didn't know how to tell you."

His eyes darted from hers, almost as if he were running away from her words.

"No. No!"

She was losing him again.

"Phillip, why can't you see how beautiful a life the Lord has given you? Why are you running away from your own wife, your own family? Why won't you give Libby that family she wants?"

"Because I don't want be anywhere near my own kid!" His shout startled here, and she jumped back. "You hear me? The last time I got close to a kid, she jumped from the side of a cliff. You know why? Because *I* was the enemy! She chose death rather than trusting a dirty American G.I. Because I was the *bad guy*, they told her. That's what they told them all." He stood to his feet. In a flash of rage, his anger overturned the side table in the guest room.

Maggie froze in place. She was a hospital nurse, not at all trained in the profession of psychiatrics. Had she pushed him too far? A cold shiver filtered down her spine.

"There were more, you know! We tried to stop them. We tried to help them. They were innocent people hiding from the Japanese, yet not fully trusting our intentions. So they hid from us. As we closed in on them, another native told them we were there to kill them. To hurt the women. It wasn't true. But they didn't know that. Next thing we knew, women and men started to emerge from the caves. Some women clung to babies. They held the children tightly against their chests, as if we were going to rip their babies from them. At first we thought they decided to trust us and let us help them. But as we drew closer, the refugees edged closer to the cliffs. That's when..."

He broke off, sweeping a deep intake of breath into his lungs. His eyes, squeezed shut, his pain visible from the outside.

"Then...they jumped."

Maggie's mouth hinged open, her heart dropping with dismay as she listened in horror to Phillip's recollection.

"But then, the children...we tried to stop them, but the fathers...they—" A sob hiccupped in his throat and seemed to lodge itself there, cutting off his words. It was a long moment before Phillip could compose himself. "The fathers, they threw their children off the ledge, too overcome with fear of what would happen to them in our care. It got worse from there. And all I could think was, *if I wasn't here, these people might have had a chance.* They plunged themselves into death because of me and my orders. I'm the one who killed all those people...all those children." His gaze shifted to Maggie. "I can't look any child in the face without seeing that day on Saipan all over again. I just can't. So you see, Maggie, how will I be capable of caring for a child of my own? How will I ever be able to look at Libby while she holds our baby in her arms and not see those women clutching to their babies as they jumped off that cliff? I can't do it. I just can't."

Tears streamed down Maggie's face. Her hands cupped against her mouth. She was unable to speak. Unable to comprehend the burden that was just laid out in front of her. It was a horror even to her own mind. What a burden for her brother to carry on his shoulders all this time. Her heart ached with an incredible pang.

"I'm sorry, Phillip. I'm so very sorry." It was all she could say in a breathless manner. In answer to his very question, she asked herself, *how* can *he?*

FIFTY-ONE

Dark, sad eyes stared back at Libby. For the first time in her life, she was truly unhappy. Not having the unconditional love of her husband was far more damaging than living in a house where her ossified father lived.

Dropping her gaze to her left hand, she glared at her wedding band with disgust. She was bound to Phillip by the sacred vows she repeated to him on their wedding day. He was a different man then. Loving him came so easily. And it seemed loving her came easily for him as well. Somehow, all that had changed when Phillip left for war.

The most painful tears she'd ever cried pushed up into her eyes. As they spilled down her cheeks, a violent sob hiccupped from deep within and escaped her. It was followed by another. Shuddering hands covered her face. Her knees wobbled, and slowly they gave way, slinking her to the cold floor beneath her feet.

She couldn't prevent those cries of desperation. For too long she'd tried to go about finding her true Phillip on her own. But it was all for naught. The man she once knew, the man she'd married, was nowhere to be found.

It hurt. The gut-wrenching pain balling in her stomach was enough to empty it of its contents. But that was nothing compared to the crater-sized hole boring into her heart. Like an arrow shot straight through her chest, every emotional bond she held for Phillip seemed to spill from the wound it produced. And today had only intensified the pain with the knowledge that a new little being was growing within her.

Phillip no longer wanted a family. He no longer wanted her. So how could she break the news to him?

"Why me, Lord?" she cried out. It came as quiet as a mouse's squeak. "Why is it that my life has turned to dust time and time again? What have I done to lose the love of my father and my husband?"

Waves of profound emotion wavered her words and stung her throat. The anguish of her hurt bent her over until she could no longer sit up on her own. Slowly, ever so slowly, her body fell to the floor. There, her knees pulled in close to her chest and her arms clung tightly around them until she lay in a tight ball. Her cries shook her body and her voice trembled. Words she could not say, ask, or speak to anyone finally found their escape from the dark interior of her soul. And those words cut as sharp as a two-edged knife.

"Why am I not enough?"

⤜⤝

It could have been hours or days that Libby lay on that floor, huddled in the protection of her own anguish, it wouldn't have mattered. But somehow, a small voice beckoned her. It was inaudible to her ears, but her heart made out every word.

As if someone had reached down and dried her eyes, her tears stopped their flow. Her mind emptied of all hurt and confusion. Could it be that her body was drained of all emotional extracts? Or had some invisible being touched down into her core and gifted her with renewing strength?

Tidbits of Maggie's conversation with her slowly came back to mind. Maggie knew something wasn't right. Deep down, Libby knew that Maggie held the answer to the lingering questions in her mind.

Phillip wasn't well. He hadn't been well since the war effort. The secret lie across the ocean and inside Phillip's head.

If only she could extract those answers from him. Who was Adaline Howard? Who was Paloma? And why did Phillip still choose to live here in Arbor Springs with her if another woman waited for him elsewhere?

Libby pushed up off the floor of the bathroom and rubbed a hand against her temple.

Today was the day. The day she would make changes in her life. The day she would stop playing the victim and get some answers. The day she would stop running from everyone and everything and allow God to take over.

For the first time since the day she decided to leave her parents' awful house to marry Phillip, Libby really prayed.

Father, I know it's been a long time since I've come to call. I know I've been stubborn and tried to fix things my own way, in my own time, but right now I'm asking for help. I've been foolish to think no one else could help me. You can, Father. So that's what I'm asking. Because I can't go on like this, not on my own. My strength is spent. My heart is broken. My spirit is crushed. I'm tired and I'm weak.

Please show me the way, Father.

I want my husband back. I want our relationship restored. I want a life...with Phillip. I want to raise our child together. Lord, if there's anything I ask of You in my lifetime, it's to see my husband come back to me, to come back to You. Show us...me...the way, Lord. In Your name, I ask. Amen.

As if Jesus himself sat down at her side, peace washed over Libby. She could feel her Lord's tender embrace and could almost hear His words, *Lo, I am with you always*, whispered into her ear. Tears of comfort—something she hadn't experienced in years—strolled down her cheeks and she knew everything would be okay.

An hour later, Libby sat on the bed of Maggie's guest room, staring down at a leather-worn Bible. She'd been meaning to read it for months, but working at the cannery, and fixing up the house, and Phillip's homecoming had caused her to put it off longer than she intended. Looking back, she regretted every moment she didn't open God's Word, even to read just one or two verses.

She could do it now. Her mamma always said there was no time like the present to make a change. Mamma never lived by her words, but that shouldn't allow Libby to follow in her mother's footsteps. Libby *could* make a change. And that change would start today.

The gals had given her many Bible passages to consider and ponder. Although they didn't know it, their encouragement was branded into her mind and she would read over every passage she could to learn how to be a better wife to Phillip, and a virtuous woman for herself and others.

Her fingers reached down and lifted the cover of the Bible.

"Proverbs chapter thirty-one, verses ten through twelve. *Who can find a virtuous woman? for her price is far above rubies. The heart of her husband doth safely trust in her, so that he shall have no need of spoil. She will do him good and not evil all the days of her life.*"

Surely, she'd done Phillip nothing but good since the day they were married. How could he not see that in her?

Listen, Libby...

That still, inaudible voice reminded her she was here to learn, not to judge her own doings.

"All right, Lord. I'm listening. Help me, Father."

Then it dawned on her. Before she could become a good wife—a godly wife—for her husband, she first needed to change her own heart and become a godly woman in her own self. Perhaps Phillip wasn't the only broken part of their marriage who needed fixing. Perhaps the trouble laid between the two of them. They had shared everything as part of their unity. Even so, they shared responsibility for what their marriage had become. But somewhere in the mix of emotional bondage and anger, she'd forgotten to pray for him, for his soul.

Her fingers thumbed through a few more pages until she stopped at Proverbs chapter fourteen, verse one.

"Every wise woman buildeth her house: but the foolish plucketh it down with her hands."

That's what she needed to do. Libby Johnson had need of building her home on a firm foundation of godly principles. No more wallowing in self-pity. No more hiding behind her insecurities. Although her heart was damaged and severely burned, she would not allow it to destroy her home and steal it away from her. Every waking day from this moment forth, she was a new woman. And she would fight with every last morsel of strength inside her small body to win back her husband's love, his heart, and help him heal. She would no longer play the foolish woman and continue to tear down her marriage, her home, in spite of her own hurt feelings. It would cost her. Oh, yes, it would cost her more tears, her pride, and sleepless nights, but she was not going to give up on the man she loved the most.

Only death would end her love for Phillip—even if it cost her the very life she lived.

Libby found new resolution within her. Unlike any feeling she'd felt before, something strong stirred within her soul. A burning kindled inside her chest. Newfound strength that she'd never experienced before built up within her. Like concrete, her feet stood sturdy. Upright legs held her spirit high as the trunk of a solid and mighty oak tree. And a faith rooted deeper than the love of her very own self gave her the courage she needed to go on. Loving Phillip in his current mental state was going to be difficult—more difficult than she imagined. But he needed her to love him. Whether or not he reciprocated that love, she would have to be the giver of undying, unconditional love. She loved him, and love meant sacrificing the luxuries of one's own self for the sake of another. Her husband was worth the fight. Perhaps one day he would return fully to her and they would know a love and marriage that they had yet to experience.

❧☙

Hunger rumbled in the pit of her stomach. Libby couldn't

remember her last meal. Then again, she'd been too distraught to think about eating. She needed to take care of her herself. She no longer could live in her own selfish world for she had another being to think about.

She called for Maggie, but her sister-in-law didn't answer. When Maggie was nowhere to be found, Libby assumed she had errands to run. So she helped herself to the pantry and toasted some bread. Smoothing homemade jelly over her toast, she sat down and indulged in its creamy sweetness.

Then a knock sounded at the door.

Libby padded to the living room and peaked out the window. With relief, she smiled. Sydney Duncan's lovely face greeted her on the other side.

She turned the knob on the door. "Sydney!" Libby reached out to her dear friend and pulled her into a grateful embrace.

"Maggie telephoned and said you were here. I hadn't heard from you for some time now. Say, what's that?" Sydney reached out toward the bruise staining Libby's face. "Are you all right?" Sydney's hands grasped Libby's arms in a light hold. "Maggie sounded urgent on the telephone, and well, now I can see why."

Unsure of how to answer, Libby only stared blankly. Shaking out of it, she nodded, then shook her head, then nodded again.

"I don't know, Sydney. It's a long, long story. Won't you come in?"

"Well, don't mind if I do," Sydney replied as she side-stepped Libby and entered the living room. "I think I'll have a seat."

Bit by bit, Libby told Sydney everything leading up till today's doctor visit. More than once, Sydney's jaw hung open and she set her teacup down mid-sip before lifting it back to her lips. Pure bewilderment had registered on her friend's face.

"Libby, I—I don't quite know what say to all this. I'm perplexed to say the least." Her mouth clamped shut as her shoulders drooped in a heavy sigh. "I'm very sorry for all you're going through. I have been praying."

Libby reached a hand out and rested it on Sydney's wrist. "Please keep praying, Sydney. I can't do this alone, but I've come to a conclusion while reading through Maggie's Bible. I'm going to fight for my marriage. I'm going to fight for Phillip, no matter what's ailing him. No, I may not be able to go home right now, but if I'm going to love him, be his wife, then I need to love him unconditionally, without reservation. After all, what is love without forgiveness?"

Sydney watched with admiration in her eyes. "This, Libby...this is what you were meant to see through all the heartache. The Lord is going to use you, and He's going to use you in a big way."

"I don't know what tomorrow holds, Sydney, but one thing I do know, my husband needs help and I won't rest until we've figured this out together." Libby gathered their teacups and placed them on the tray. Standing, she spoke over her shoulder. "Maggie has offered to let me stay here a while until Phillip has calmed down. However, I must go home to gather a few things in my valise."

Sydney held up her palm, face forward. "Say no more. I'll drive you there."

❦

Maggie

Phillip's broken state had bewildered Maggie. Her brother, her once fearless protector, had crumbled right in front of her. His fragmented soul seemed to sift between her fingers as angst-ridden thoughts ran rampant in his subconscious mind.

As a nurse, she knew what had to be done. As a sister, she didn't know what to do. Now she knew what all those families had felt as doctors told them the ill-fated prognosis of their sons, husbands, brothers, and fathers.

But in merely minutes, his fractured spirit had taken a sinister turn.

As if unable to cope with his own behavior, Phillip jumped off his spot on the floor and staggered past Maggie.

"Where are you going?"

"Leave me alone, Maggie."

"No! You're unstable, Phillip. Let me take you to the hospital, or the church, or somewhere where you can talk to someone for help."

Phillip ignored her plea and stumbled down the staircase.

Running after him, she retreated from the guest room and followed him down the staircase. She glanced in the hall corner and gasped.

"Phillip, where's the rifle?" Sheer fright clenched her heart.

Refusing to answer her, the front door slammed shut and Phillip's rigid form plodded down the porch steps and rounded the corner.

Where was he going? Not waiting for an answer she trailed him. His strides were long and purposeful, but she didn't understand what his intentions were until the glare of his rifle reflected in the sunlight.

She gasped as her hand flew over her mouth. With her eyes wide and wild, Maggie put her feet into motion, screaming Phillip's name.

"Don't you do it, Phillip! Come back here! I won't let you!"

But his long steps were too far ahead of her and he reached the shed before she could reach him. Once inside, he slammed the door and bolted it shut.

With as much force as she could muster, Maggie rammed the door with her side and shook the rusty knob. As hard as her strength would allow, her hand flattened against the aging wood with a thud. She banged on the shed walls, hoping the ruckus would jar his thoughts.

But the inside was deathly quiet.

Panic seized her whole being. Her body shook with tremors so great, her knee caps ached. The fear of spraying bullets was nothing compared to what she felt right now, at this present time.

"Somebody help me!" she called out.

She closed her eyes and the flood gates opened. She didn't know what to do.

FIFTY-TWO

Madness had taken over, blinding all sense from his ravaged mind.

Through wild eyes, the scenes of the night before replayed before him. Everything that lead up to this moment of him sitting alone on a dirt floor with nothing but the company of his pistol and rifle. He watched in horror as the image of Libby's frail body rolling down the steps flashed before his eyes. The vivid recollection was followed by the frightening look she flashed him just before declaring her leave. Although the house was dark, he'd seen every contour of her face, every angry and hurt wrinkle in her brow.

He'd not realized what he'd done until his eyes scanned the area. His rifle sat against the angle of the staircase as if it were ready for action. Why had he grabbed it in the middle of the night? Then the dawning truth sucker punched the air from his lungs.

His sickness had gone too far. This time, it had pushed him over the edge of sanity. And his wife had been the target of his mental ambush.

Frantically searching the shed, Phillip snatched his shovel from the nail on the wall. Feverishly, he took the spade and thrusted it into the ground, chipping and digging away the earth. He would bury his past. That way it could do no harm to anyone else.

He ignored Maggie's screams and the pounding of her hands against the door as he worked. Once the hole was dug, Phillip reached down for the rifle, and gripped it, as if choking the life from its barrel. Clenching his teeth together, he threw the weapon into its grave where he worked tirelessly to bury its memory. Once he'd stomped on the spot and packed the ground good and hard, he collapsed against the shed wall and huffed as sweat dripped from his hair.

Great waves of remorse thrust his head into his hands. Violently, Phillip's sobs shook his body. He'd lost every single part of his life.

Libby was the only thing left to hold onto in his world, and he'd cut the rope. He'd never get her back.

What was left of his life now? The empty shell of his house provided mental defeat, sending his already war-torn mind into a craze. He couldn't take the silence. He couldn't take the vivid memories. He'd lost everything. His best friend. His wife. His family. His mind. His will. There was nothing left for Phillip Johnson in this world. Every menacing echo in his mind chanted the same line over and over again.

An eye for an eye. For every man you killed, for every child that died in your presence, so shall you die a thousand deaths.

It was the only answer.

He could no longer live with the guilt. He couldn't drown his miseries with alcohol for they would resurrect with the morning light. He'd wronged Libby and every friend he'd had in this world. He'd alienated everyone from him. Surely, they wouldn't miss him. And his nightmares...they would finally come to an end...

He was tired. He was miserable. And he just wanted it all to end. He had the power to stop the madness, to stop the pain, to stop the hurting, to snuff out the constant stirring of voices in his head. Peace. It's what he longed for most. But he was not going to obtain it while he still had breath within him.

He reached for the pistol that he'd slipped into his belt. Feeling the weight of its burden, he stared into the coal black of its purpose.

He could make all his afflictions disappear.

Out of sight from the world, he could end all his sufferings, all the anguish in his troubled heart. Ultimately, he'd loose Libby from the tormented abyss she'd been bound to live in as his wife. He'd held her to his prison long enough. It was time for the undoing.

FIFTY-THREE

Light conversation helped alleviate Libby's tensions as Sydney drove her home.

Now that Libby's new resolve had put her in a place of peace, she no longer dreaded walking through her front door and facing Phillip. And for the first time today, the thought of having a baby of her own placed a smile on her face.

"Okay. Here we are," Sydney breathed as she eased onto Libby's street.

As Libby glanced up, the blur of a familiar vehicle rushed past them. Libby glared over her shoulder.

"That was Maggie. Where is she going in a hurry?"

It seemed odd that Maggie was on her street. Maybe she thought to gather some of Libby's things that way Libby wouldn't have to make the trip back to the house. Or maybe she was checking on Phillip. That Maggie, always the one to take care of others.

"Perhaps she's on her way back to her house to check on you?" Sydney offered.

"Perhaps. Well, nothing I can do about it now. I'll just have to catch up with her when I get back."

Phillip's car sat in the driveway and Libby gazed up into the house. The inside was dark. Not even the tiniest illumination of a desk lamp burned inside. Seemed strange that Phillip was home, but the lights were off. Even in the daylight the porch did much to hide the light from reaching indoors.

Libby sat a moment and stared blankly at the house.

"Everything okay, Libby?"

Libby contemplated. "Phillip's home. Or at least he appears to be. I wonder if he's drunk and passed out on the floor again. That would explain the lack of lighting inside." Libby gathered her purse and opened the car door. "Well, if he's out like a light, I'm going to have to help him into bed."

"I'll come with you."

Once inside, Libby's brows furrowed in confusion. Phillip's sleeping form was not inside the foyer as she expected. Nor did the downstairs smell like the interior of a bar. Removing her gloves from her hands, she gingerly and cautiously stepped up the staircase.

"Wait here a minute, Sydney."

But Libby's search for Phillip turned up nothing. After making her way back downstairs and glancing in each room, she stood in the middle of the room with her hands on her hips.

"Where could he be?"

"Where does he usually go when he comes home from work?"

"That's what's odd. He normally places himself out there on the wicker chair." She pointed to the front porch.

"Maybe he's out for a stroll."

Libby half-chuckled. "He's not the type." After a few more contemplative moments, Libby shook her head. "Well, I don't have all day. Maggie will surely expect me for dinner and I still need to freshen up. I'll just leave a note for Phillip here at the desk, telling him I was here and where he can find me."

As Sydney stood close by, Libby sat down at the oak scroll top desk in the living room and switched on the lamp. Taking a sheet of note paper from the drawer, she picked up an ink pen and began a short note to Phillip. But before she could finish, the slightest rap at the door interrupted her thoughts.

"Now what is it?" she said as she stood to her feet.

After crossing the room, she stood at the door and opened it, expecting to see the postman or perhaps Maggie returning. But the person who stood on the other side was not who she expected at all.

"Can I help you?"

A tall, thin, and neatly put together woman stood with perfect posture on her doorstep. But as Libby opened the door the rest of the way, the woman's hand held tight to a dark-skinned little girl.

Libby's eyes bounced from woman to girl, and back again to the woman.

"I'm looking for Sergeant Johnson."

The woman's crisp words were precise and clear, but Libby still had trouble comprehending the woman's words.

"Pardon?"

"Sergeant Johnson. This is his home, isn't it? We had an arrangement. He's supposed to meet me today." She checked her wristwatch. "Right now, in fact."

"I-I'm sorry. He isn't here at the moment. I'm not sure when he'll return. I'm Missus Johnson. May I ask your name and give him a message? If you'll tell me where you're staying I can have him meet you there, or you may call again."

The woman sighed with annoyance blowing. "I'll only be in town for another night. He knows this. My name is Adaline Howard. Please be sure he gets the mess—"

"What did you say?"

Libby nearly choked on her own tongue. The woman's name nearly knocked Libby to the floor. She found it difficult to take her next breath, but she forced herself to breathe.

"Libby, honey? Is everything all right?" Sydney's hand rested on her shoulder.

"I-I'm not sure."

Libby stared back at the woman.

"I'm sorry, ma'am. I'm on a very tight schedule. I just came from the train station after a weeklong trip from San Francisco with this child in tow. Now, please be sure to see that Sergeant Johnson gets this message." Adaline Howard thrust a small square of note paper into Libby's hand. "He must see me before I leave town tomorrow morning."

"I'll be sure he gets it."

Libby finally took a few breaths, but her eyes blinked hard and fast as this sudden visit blurred before her. Too overcome with emotion to make any legible mention, she only stood there at the door and looked on.

The little girl who clung tightly to Miss Howard's hand looked back at Libby, her sad, brown eyes looked as though they nearly pleaded with her. Like…she wanted Libby to rescue her. The red bow in her hair bobbed as she made her way down the steps. She was maybe five, six years old at the oldest.

"I want Pip," the young girl cried.

"Wait! Miss Howard?"

"Yes?"

"The little girl. Who is she? And why have you come?" Libby started for them.

Miss Howard glanced down at the tot then back to Libby. "Oh, forgive me, Missus Johnson. I assumed you knew. This is the reason I've come. This is Paloma. I'm to deliver her to Sergeant Johnson. He's been paying for me to keep her in my care until the papers were signed to allow him custody of her."

Libby's mouth hung open and all blood drained from her face. She stammered backwards, reaching for the wicker chair.

"Sydney?"

Sydney rushed forward, taking Libby by the arm and lowering her to the chair. "Deep breaths, Libby."

"You didn't know anything about this, Missus Johnson, did you?"

Unable to speak, Libby shook her head.

"Oh, dear. This does pose a problem."

Before Libby could take another breath, gravel popping beneath fast moving tires drew everyone's attention to the driveway. In a flash, three individuals emerged from the vehicle, one of them screaming at her.

"Hurry, Danny!"

Libby's stomach churned for the hundredth time that day. Maggie's hysterical sight pinched her insides as Maggie's voice called out to her too.

"Is he okay, Libby? Did you stop him?"

Something in Maggie's voice was unnatural. Fear gripped Libby's chest and she stood to her feet.

"What are you talking about, Maggie?"

But no one stopped to answer her questions. Instead, Maggie led Danny and Luke to the backyard.

"Excuse me, Miss Howard."

Brushing past the woman and Paloma, Libby skipped down the steps, Sydney calling after her.

"What's going on, Libby?"

"I don't know."

They rounded the back of the house where Danny used his shoulder to ram the shed door. Luke chimed in on the second attempt to break down the shed's entryway. Maggie pounded against the woodgrain and shouted into the tiny shack.

"Phillip! Phillip, can you hear me?"

Libby's feet picked up in speed as she neared the shed. The terror in Maggie's voice and the urgency in Danny's and Luke's efforts was enough to send Libby's heart into cardiac arrest.

"What going on?" she cried as she neared them.

Maggie pulled herself from the shack and ran to Libby, mascara streaming down her face and staining her eyes.

"Libby, he didn't go through with it, did he?"

"What? Who?"

Maggie searched Libby's face, and then realizing Libby was none the wiser, she broke down and relayed everything about her visit with Phillip.

Sydney's gasp was what brought her to her knees. Libby collapsed on the ground, her hand covering the screams that itched to break through her lips.

"Oh, my heavens, Maggie! What are we going to do?"

"Pray that Danny and Luke can get in there before it's too late."

The deafening sound of a gunshot cut through the air, causing each one of them to startle and lower to the ground.

Screams of despair sliced the silence as Libby, Maggie, and Sydney crouched down in a huddle together.

Danny and Luke recovered, this time forcing their way into the shed.

"Is it too late, Danny?" Maggie cried. "Libby, stay here. I'm going to help."

"Maggie, please, no. Stay here, please?" Libby pleaded with her through her sobs, reaching out her hand for some form of help.

It wasn't Maggie's touch that responded, but rather, Sydney's. It was Sydney who wrapped her arms around Libby and held her close.

"Heavenly Father, Lord, please intervene. Please save. Please help us that need helping." Sydney's prayer breathed into Libby's ears. Tightly Libby clung to her friend's arms, and her prayers for help, hoping that God would work a miracle.

FIFTY-FOUR

One Year Later
June 1947

L ibby stood at the window of her bedroom window and squinted into the morning light.

As the dawn of a bright new morning showered down on her skin, so did the hope of God's promise.

With so many ugly memories now behind her, Libby had finally found peace. It seemed this day would never come. That its shadows were always just out of reach of her fingertips.

But then God chose to work a miracle through mishap.

She'd learned to love again. And through that, she'd also known a love she'd never experienced before.

"Libby? It's time." Maggie's voice softly filtered into the room.

As Libby turned her gaze from her window to Maggie, she was suddenly back on the train platform the day Phillip had arrived home—thinking...*Today so much would end. Today, so much would begin...*

The church seemed to glow in the morning light as Danny's car pulled to the front doors. Quickly, Maggie came to Libby's aid and walked her inside the church's entryway.

"I'm a ball of nerves, Maggie."

"Don't be. Everything will be perfect. The way it should be."

"Do I look all right?" Libby's shaky hand came to the tendrils of hair that hung over her ears.

"Beautiful. Now let's get going before the groom sees you."

Libby smiled.

Her groom. She would finally have the marriage she always wanted, the one she had dreamed of. Now she could stop living in the past and look forward to the wonderful life she had yet to live.

"Libby, there you are." All eyes turned to Luke Brady, who

sprinted his way up the isle toward Libby. "Here. *He* wanted you to have this."

Libby took the small envelope from Luke's hand and scanned its contents. A quaint smile spread over her lips.

"He's asking for me."

"But the groom can't see the bride before the wedding," Maggie protested.

"Who says?"

"Tradition."

"Well, tradition did nothing for luck the first time around, so I'm throwing the rule book out the window."

Picking up her skirts, Libby dashed out of the church and across the church lawn to the little white gazebo where her groom requested she meet him.

As the gazebo came into view, Libby slowed and stared ahead at the tall, strong man standing with his back toward her.

Her heart hammered in her chest.

It had been so long. So very long. And she'd waited for this moment her entire adult life.

With each crunch of the grass beneath her feet, one more step placed her closer to the man she loved.

With his back still turned to her, she stopped just short of the gazebo's first step and watched him. Gone was the rigidity. Gone was his uptight demeanor. In place of it all, his stature displayed tranquility. There was an easiness about him. It was a peace that only God could give, and that peace had been bestowed on him the day he chose to give his life to Christ. Libby wanted nothing more than to stand there and relish that tranquility for the rest of her life.

But she would have the rest of her life to do that. Today, they had an engagement to fulfill.

"I got your note." Her tone was soft, even as it broke through the silence of the morning.

Without turning around, he answered her.

"I had to see you, but tradition says it's bad luck to see the bride before the ceremony."

"Those silly traditions. I don't put much stock in them. Do you, Phillip?"

She stepped under the gazebo and stood close to him, waiting for his body to turn toward hers. His head lowered and his jaw tightened as if he weighed out her words very carefully. But then, all at once, he twisted and met her gaze.

He was as nervous as she felt.

His hands took hers in his, and tenderly, he brought them to his lips.

"I want to get this right, Libby. I made a promise to you and I'm going to make good on that promise. I know I spent the last five years making you miserable, and I'm so sorry for every hurt I've caused you."

"Phillip, I told you at counseling I've forgiven you."

"I know, but I need to tell you this before we go inside and renew our vows."

"All right."

His cheeks deflated as he blew out a long sigh. "I'm promising to be the man God has called me to be. I've quit my old ways, my old habits, and I no longer hold any secrets from you. I've completely given my life to God and to you...and our family. That doesn't mean I'm not scared to death, but I'm not going back to the man I was a year ago. I'm promising you this, Libby."

Libby's eyes softened with the sincerity of his words. Nodding, she lifted a hand to brush back a strand of hair that had fallen over his brow. As she combed it back, her fingers brushed against the scar where the bullet had grazed his skull just one year earlier.

"And I also ordered that washer you had your eye on at the department store. It arrives in three weeks."

Tears sprang to her eyes at the memory, and a smile spread over her lips. "I love you, Phillip," she whispered through a shaky breath.

Her hands came around his neck and he pulled her in close.

"I love you, too. So very much, Libby."

It was the beginning of a new life. For twelve months, Phillip had been confined to a convalescent for his alcohol and mental disorder. For twelve long months, Libby had agreed to undergo the necessary counseling needed to heal her heart and mend their marriage. It wasn't easy, especially when Phillip Junior made his arrival into the world. She wanted her son to know his father, but his father was still in no condition to come home to his family.

Those were the hardest months Libby had faced yet. Tears had fallen like rain down a window pane. The days spent as a single mother were the loneliest she'd remembered. She'd taken every odd job she could handle to pay the bills on her own. As time wore on, progress was made, and Phillip's condition improved.

She couldn't have done it without the help of her family and friends. Every day someone had come to check on her and the baby.

Even Mrs. Sullivan offered to stay at the house as Phillip Junior's nanny until his father returned home.

Thankfully, the Bradys and Phillip had mended their differences when Phillip made the trip to their home to apologize for all his wrongdoings. Now, the trio of families were bonded stronger than they'd ever been.

Phillip had also had that talk with his parents—the one that was long overdue. He finally understood what had changed his parents' lives, making their marriage stronger, unbreakable. Phillip could now possess that same love and understanding.

And Paloma...Libby had it all wrong. Paloma hadn't been some mistress Phillip kept hidden away. And he had never planned on leaving Libby at all. His plan was to bring Paloma into their lives by adoption. But those wretched war reminders had blinded all sound thinking on his part.

They'd nearly lost Paloma after the day Phillip attempted to take his life. It had taken months to convince the orphanage and Adaline Howard that Phillip's recovery was under way and that he'd make a full one. Eventually, Ms. Howard agreed to make a second trip to Arbor Springs where she approvingly signed the paperwork to leave Paloma in the Johnsons' care.

The child made a lovely addition to their family and Libby had fallen in love with her as easily as she did the day Phillip Junior arrived in her arms.

Today would seal that family's love.

Libby looked up into Phillip's gentle eyes. How handsome his face was. Gentleness and kindness had replaced the darkness that once shrouded it.

Clear eyes sparkled as they stared down at her, not a cloud to canvas them.

"The war's over, Libby. I'm ready to come home."

The Rest of the Story....

60 years later

Grace

Never did she think that she would one day set out on the same trail her husband once embarked on.

With butterflies twittering around in her stomach, Grace looked onward toward the towering bluffs just ahead. Her sunglasses did little to fight back the sun glare as it reflected off the channel. Using a fragile hand to shield her eyes, Grace squinted as she examined the French coastline.

"Oh, my." As if on cue and as if he read her very thoughts, Luke's wearied voice breathed a response of awed reverence.

With the turn of her head, Grace studied his profile. Although his skin was worn with age and the visor of his veterans cap shadowed his face, she still looked at him as that young, strong, capable man she had fallen in love with sixty years before.

As the boat pressed onward through the calm waters of the English Channel, Grace reached out her feeble hand and rested it over Luke's. Without glancing at her, he grasped it and held tight. After sixty-two years of marriage, she'd come to understand every gesture, every look that flashed in his eyes. And today...well, today would be an emotional time for both of them.

Luke stared ahead at the coastline, no doubt every minute of June 6th, 1944, replaying in his mind. She sensed it. She could see it. No cap or dark sunglasses could hide the sentiments from playing across Luke's face.

As the boat slowed and made its way over the building swells, Luke leaned toward the right, eyeing the distance between the boat and the shore.

"This is about where we jumped into the water. The operator told us he couldn't go any farther and we had to jump into the water here. It was much deeper than we anticipated…because the sandbars had pushed us back further. The storms had done that a few days before the operation. None of us were prepared for it…any of it…they didn't cover that in training."

"Did the German soldiers know you all were in the water at that time, Dad?"

Grace turned to where LeRoy was sitting in the row behind them. The family had joined them on this momentous trip. All their kids, LeRoy, Annabelle, and Claire, along with their spouses, had pitched in to allow Luke this final visit to the place that forever changed his life. But it also allowed their children to see and hear, firsthand, the accounts of that historic and tragic day.

"Well, sure," Luke answered impatiently. "Danny and the other paratroopers had already made their landing before daybreak. With all the cargo planes that crashed into the countryside, they knew something was coming. The only other place for them to look was the water."

Grace couldn't help but chuckle at Luke's abrupt answer. He'd grown old, and was a no nonsense sort of guy. But underneath the years of wear and below the sunspots on his skin, he was still that same, gentle, sweet, and caring man he'd always been.

After the boat had docked, a car waited for them. Both Grace and Luke sat silent as their chauffeur taxied them to their next destination. And Grace knew the next stop would be especially difficult for Luke.

Before they had time to open their car doors, LeRoy, Annabelle, and Claire were waiting to help them out of their vehicle.

"Take your time, Dad," Grace heard LeRoy say.

"Watch your step, Mother." Claire, the youngest of their children, grasped Grace's upper arm to help steady her.

"I see the rocks. Thank you, dear," Grace answered in her still sweet, soft voice. "Now help me get to your father before he wanders off and leaves all of us behind."

Her girls chuckled at her teasing. Even after all these years, she still knew how to get a giggle from them.

Together, the family walked alongside Luke as they carefully made their way up the wooden planks surrounded by lush green foliage. Sweet song echoed through the dome of trees and leaves as songbirds sang from overhead branches. Luke had grown silent long ago and Grace wondered if he was fighting back his own emotions as they neared the place where he once met death face to face.

Taking slow shuffles, Luke walked up the footpath, stopping occasionally to glance up, then he'd stare down at his feet and walk a little farther in the sand.

The rush of waves grew louder and their feet padded on sand. Tall sand dunes stood over them on both sides, and the beach slowly came into focus. Finally, Luke came to a stop on top of the dunes. Placing his unsteady hands on his hips, he stopped and just stared in somber silence.

After a few moments, Grace shuffled to his side and placed a hand around his waist.

"It doesn't look quite like it did in forty-four. I don't recall it ever looking so beautiful."

"Time heals all wounds. Even on the earth. It is breathtaking." Grace glanced out over the shoreline, watching waves crash over another, drawing back, then rolling in again.

The beach was wide. From where they stood at the edge of the dunes, it still seemed the ocean was a mile away.

"Do you remember the shore being this long, Dad?" LeRoy asked. "Or does it seem like it's been altered?"

Luke took a moment to answer. "I think it was longer," he replied with a half-chuckle. "We supposedly came in at low tide, but remember we had to leave the Higgins boats sooner than expected." He paused to catch his breath. "The beach was estimated about a thousand feet from the dunes. A thousand feet was quite a distance if you account for fighting the waves with our heavy packs on our backs, our guns in our hands, and our water-logged boots. Then if we made it out of the water we had to maneuver past the stakes, hedgehogs, and the mines, all the while not getting shot."

Taking a hanky from his back pocket, Luke wiped at his brow then at his lip. Folding it over his prosthetic hand, he returned it to his back pocket. He glanced behind him and scaled the bluffs with his eyes. A boney finger pointed up the bluff.

"There."

The journey had been a bit exhausting for the both of them, considering their ages, but Luke took the lead as he always had as head of the family and marched up the sandy hillside as if he was twenty-four all over again.

They walked past an abandoned German bunker, now open to the public, and LeRoy stopped.

"Dad, did you want to take a look?"

Halting his steps, but never giving the bunker a second glance,

Luke answered, "No...I remember it. Let's keep moving."

The path was long, and Grace's lungs weren't as young as they used to be, but she was making this trip out of love for Luke.

Annabelle stuck close, assisting her mother along the pathway. Claire, the daddy's girl she always was, made sure her father took careful strides up the bluff. Grace whispered a prayer of thanks to God for blessing her with such a beautiful family.

Once near the top, Luke stopped amid a shrub-lined path. Thankful for the rest and shade, Grace watched her husband.

"Where are we now, dear?" she asked through her deep breaths.

Without answering, Luke glanced over the footpath, peering through the foliage, looking overhead, and back again. Grace watched with dread as his leg swung over the rope barrier.

"Dad, what are you doing?" LeRoy and Claire rushed to his aid.

But Luke shook them off.

"Daddy, you're going to hurt yourself. There's nothing to see there." Claire urged him back to the wooden path.

Grace held up her hand, stopping them. "Let him be a moment," she whispered.

With his good arm, Luke wiped at his eye and Grace moved to his side.

"This is the spot," he choked out. "This is where I laid and thought I'd never see you again."

Silently, a tear swelled and seeped from Grace's eye. She remembered that day so well. She remembered the uncertainty of that dreadful morning when she woke up to pray with her landlord, Mrs. Shepherd. She remembered the same thought running through her head—would she ever have the chance to see Luke Brady again? Thankfully, the Lord had answered every one of her prayers. Not only did she see him again, but she was gifted with Luke's precious love, and the blessing of a family together. A family that now stood with them as they reflected on a day that did change the course of their lives.

"The good Lord knew what he was doing with us, Luke." She found the words to say, even though they came out shaky. "He wasn't through with you. And He knew we'd make it back here today to tell our children about it."

Luke's left arm—his good arm—came around her waist. Just as it had over the years together, his love and protectiveness enveloped her. Their outward appearances may have changed, but the love they shared inside still remained as fresh, new, and exciting as it had the day they sealed their love for each other with the exchanging of vows.

"Over there." Luke pointed out over the growth of greens to a grove nestled alone. It seemed forgotten over the years with the overgrowth of trees and bushes and grass, but to Luke it was of great importance. "That's where the shell hit. It threw me all the way over here. And about thirty feet from me is where…"

Grace glanced up at her husband when his words stopped short. The skin of his throat bobbed up and down and he choked back the sentiments pushing their way from his heart.

"It's all right, sweetheart." Grace soothed him with her words.

He pulled his hanky from his pocket and wiped at his nose. "This is where I held that boy in my arms as he took his last breath."

"Tommy. I know, honey."

Leroy's hand rested on his dad's shoulder and he squeezed, knowing how difficult the memories would be.

After a few moments of weeping together, Luke sniffed and dried his tears.

"I—I just wanted…to see this place one last time. Just to remember…and for closure."

Grace's fingers wrapped around his arm and she leaned into him.

"We've made it through many difficult circumstances during our lifetime. Many of which I would never want to face again, but our life together turned out the way it should be. And I wouldn't trade any of those hard times for anything else. Luke Brady, you have been the love of my life and though our days now are numbered, I still wake up each morning thanking God that He gave me you."

Luke's teary smile enlightened her heart.

"And I thank God for all those letters from you…my saving Grace."

⊷৵

Maggie

It seemed that the effects of war had taken years for the undoing. Not in the good it established, but in the lives of those who lived through it.

As Maggie squinted out the window of the tour bus, the countryside seemed to come alive before her weathered eyes.

They travelled past the landmarks of past U.S. and British

encampments. Instead of seeing the small towns and communities, Maggie's eyes visualized in black and white the scores of tents, the convoys of Jeeps and supply trucks, the ghosts of military personnel scurrying about the camps.

Returning to Germany was not an idea she had ever entertained after returning from World War II, but one phone call had changed her thinking…

"Everything has changed, hasn't it?" Danny's grayed head leaned down to peer out her window. Although not quite as thick as it once was, he'd managed to keep his hair like he'd always said he would.

Blinking back moisture from her eyes, Maggie smiled. "No. It hasn't changed one bit. Those hills are still the same. The contour of the ground is still the same. Even the bumps in the road are just as I remember."

Danny's head shook in disapproval. "You always were a troublemaker."

"But you married me anyway."

Danny clutched the travel bag that sat in his lap a little tighter. "That I did. And I don't regret it."

And even though her eyesight wasn't as it used to be, and though health wasn't at its finest quality, Maggie still gazed upon Danny with much love and admiration. But one thing that hadn't changed was their zest for life. Their bantering back and forth. Their close companionship.

The bus's wheels screeched to a halt, and Danny stared forward. Maggie pursed her lips together as she studied every wrinkle in Danny's face.

"Are you ready for this, dear?" A touch of worry hung on the tip of her tongue. They were a long way from home and this particular trip would prove to be a difficult reunion for Danny.

"Maggie, I've waited sixty-two long years for this. I survived a disastrous plane jump, and Nazi attacks, and your cooking. I'm not about to back down from this. No sirree."

Crossing her arms over her chest, Maggie's brows lifted as she eyed him. She spied the hint of teasing by the way his eyes nonchalantly casted her way from their corners.

"And what about my cooking, Daniel Russo? I learned from your mother."

"And she would be pleased, cupcake."

Just like the days when their love was young, Danny leaned in to meet her lips. Laughter flitted from Maggie as she grabbed hold of his upper arm and hugged on him.

"I do love you, Danny. And you're right. You've waited far too long for this day. Everyone else has just about left the bus, so get yourself up there and let's stretch our legs. The others will be waiting for us."

With little difficulty, Danny pulled himself up and then offered a strong hand to assist Maggie. Her legs weren't quite as strong as her younger days, but it made her ever more thankful for Danny and the help he'd been to her. Together, they exited the bus and stood with the gathering crowd outside the bus station. According to the itinerary, a car was due to meet them for the next leg of their trip.

"When are the kids meeting us?"

Maggie glanced up from her pamphlet. "For the hundredth time, Danny—Kathryn and LeRoy will meet us here. Then the girls will bring Luke and Grace and meet us at Elizabeth Islands, England."

Hard of hearing, Danny lowered his ear in close as Maggie spoke up.

Before Maggie took the last step off the bus, familiar voices greeted them from the sidewalk.

"Daddy. Mother. Oh, it's good to see you, finally."

Spotting her daughter and son-in-law, Maggie's heart skipped with joy. Not only was she looking forward to Danny's big reunion, but she was anxious to hear how Luke's visit at Omaha Beach had gone.

Together, she and Danny greeted Kathryn and LeRoy. How thankful Maggie was to have her best friend's son as her son-in-law. Kathryn had made a lovely choice in accepting LeRoy's proposal all those years ago.

"Hello, dear, how was the trip?"

"It was beautiful, Mother. How are you two holding up? I trust Sigfried took exceptional care of you?"

Maggie batted a hand. "Oh, yes. A fine boy." She turned to LeRoy, a man the spitting image of his father. "And you, there, Trouble. How did your father do on his big affair?"

LeRoy reached down and warmly embraced her. Like his father, he didn't spare kindness.

"Hello, Mama Russo. I think Dad enjoyed himself. It was a little tough for him at times, as to be expected, but all in all, I think he was glad to make it back."

Maggie patted LeRoy's chest. "Your father is a good man. He endured a great deal of—of pain during the war. But the closure is good for his soul."

"Yes, ma'am."

The next few hours were long and tiresome as their escort taxied them through German villages. After dozing off long enough to rest her wearied body, Maggie caught Danny staring off into the distance as the village passed them by.

"I remember this," he muttered. He pointed across the plain to the foot of the hills. "That's where we marched through the snow. My word, it was cold. That-that means we're not too far from the place we camped out at that night."

Like a child staring in awe and amazement on Christmas morning, Danny's weathered eyes scanned the area. Maggie, too, looked out her window, hoping to catch a glimpse of the old farm that had been branded into her mind from Danny's stories.

But Danny shook his head in frustration. "It's all changed now. It doesn't look anything like it did in forty-four."

"Well, Daddy, it's been sixty years. Things are going to change."

"Bah." He dismissed his daughter's logic with a wave of his hand.

"Pay no mind to your father, Kathryn. He'll be fine as soon as we get out of this car."

Finally, the long car ride came to a close. As its wheels slowed and turned onto a gravel driveway, Maggie and Danny both perked up. With inquisitive eyes, they strained to see the dwelling ahead of them.

A small stone house came into view. Its walls were worn with age, crumbling and moss covered, but by the look on Danny's face, it was just as he remembered it.

"It's still there."

His head swiveled around to the opposite side of the driveway where the skeletal remains of an old barn stood.

"That was it. That's the barn. Why, it's burnt up."

No one said anything.

Instead, they allowed Danny to reminisce. He was the only one to have ever seen this place before. As best as could be told, the buildings were exactly where Danny had remembered them.

Scores of vehicles were parked in designated areas on the property. As they neared the dilapidated barn, faces emerged from under tents and trees.

"Looks like the whole town turned out for this, Daddy." Kathryn tapped her father on the shoulder.

The kids helped them from the vehicle. A man dressed in a fine suit conferred with Kathryn and LeRoy. Handshakes and head shakes were exchanged before Kathryn took Danny by the arm and led him toward the crowd.

Reporters encircled them and cameras flashed as they walked.

Maggie watched Danny carefully for any sign of fatigue. His silence throughout the day was so unlike him, but then again, it was a big day for him.

Kathryn ushered them to a tent where a row of chairs sat lined up. They settled themselves down and waited. Reporters asked Danny questions and he politely answered, but the way his eyes kept darting around, Maggie knew he was not as interested in them as they were in him.

When the moment came, everyone grew silent. Kathryn leaned in and whispered to her mother, "He's here."

Maggie grasped Danny's arm and squeezed. He'd waited nearly his whole life for this moment.

Finally, a feeble, old man, accompanied by strong, young men rounded the corner of the tent.

Danny tensed beneath her hold of his arm. All at once, Maggie's husband stood to his feet, in utter amazement. Slowly, he shuffled his way toward the person he hadn't seen in sixty-two years.

"Abe? Is it you? It's really you?"

"My old friend. We finally meet again."

As Danny reached out to embrace his friend, all the reporters, all the flashes of cameras, and all voices seemed to fade as Maggie's eyes welled up with tears.

"You're a bit older than I remember," Danny added with a light chuckle.

"You're no spring chicken either, *Joe*."

Ah, Joe. Maggie closed her eyes in regard to that awful time in Danny's life when no one knew who he was, not even himself. It seemed surreal that after all these years Abe Flemming still remembered and referred to Danny as Joe, his MIA name.

"We made it out alive, that's all that matters." Danny pointed a crooked finger at Abe's chest. "For so many years I laid awake at night wondering what ever happened to you."

Abe responded by patting his shaking hand on Danny's shoulder. "And I spent many days hoping I would get the chance to thank you for saving my life."

Although Danny had never been the type to show his emotions in front of anyone, but today, not even his tough military background could stop the tears over this happy reunion.

It was a day sixty-two years in the making.

Maggie would never forget the day Walt Radford rang her telephone to tell her he'd located Abe Flemming.

Right away, Maggie had made the trip to where Danny worked to tell him the glorious news. Abe had survived. And he married the daughter of the man who owned the German farm—the very farm they now sat on.

For years, Danny and Abe wrote to one another, but time and distance seemed to keep them apart. Until the day Abe's children came to call. A special day was being set aside in Abe and Danny's honor. All those who had heard of their story came together to make this momentous occasion happen.

Just when Maggie had thought the Lord was done with her, he'd sent her out on another mission.

And today, that mission was fulfilled.

⊰⊱

Phillip

It didn't take long for that salty sea air to hit his senses and flood his mind with the fragrances of bittersweet memories. Even after all this time, and although his mind couldn't remember certain instances, he remembered the aroma of salty ocean and burning sulfur. Nothing jarred his memory quite like it.

This final journey was the trip he'd promised himself he'd make before he died. With the help of his family and the kindness of his church family, they'd made this trip possible. It was just in time, too.

Libby's failing health seemed to decline each day. But he'd promised her this chance long ago. It was the last promise he vowed to fulfill in their lifetime. He wasn't about to break it. Not after all the years of hard work he'd put into righting all his wrongs. How blessed Phillip was to have such a devoted woman at his side for the last sixty-five years.

As they disembarked from the boat, Phillip's eyes soaked in the beauty of the Hawaiian island from the very spot he anticipated standing for a very long time.

So this was the splendor Jack had awakened to every morning.

"Dad, wait up for Mom."

Phillip halted, then jogged his way back to his precious Libby, Paloma, and Phillip Jr.

"Wait, wait, wait." Phillip danced behind Paloma. "Let me take your mother."

Without wasting any time, Phillip gripped the handles and bent over to whisper into Libby's ear.

"Do you see that, sweetheart? Here we are. Just like I promised you."

Libby's thin and frail head bobbed up and down, her silver locks blowing in the light sea breeze. "It's so beautiful, Phillip."

He wondered if the wavering in her voice was from age or emotion. He stood to his feet and took over guiding Libby's wheelchair.

As they neared the entrance to the memorial, somber notes played over a loudspeaker. As the American flag waved proudly overhead, Phillip's steps slowed. He told himself he wouldn't get choked up, but it had hit him that this was the last place his best friend had stood before he died.

"Are you okay, Pop?" Phillip Junior stood at his father's side.

"Yeah. It's just—well…" He couldn't finish.

"It's okay, Pop. I know. If you want to wait a bit, we can sit by the water."

"No. No, I promised myself I would see it."

With that, Phillip pushed forward, Libby going before him as he pushed her wheelchair. Her feeble hand came up to reach for his as they entered through the gates.

So many years had she cared for him. She'd waited patiently while he took the steps to rehabilitation and then waited several more years before he finally took control of his shell shock, putting it to its death for good.

Now, his turn had to come to be there for her. To love and cherish her. To wake up each morning and tend to her needs the way she selflessly had tended to his. Time had made their love stronger and he so desperately loved her. Their time together was growing short, and as much as he prayed to God every night for just one more day with Libby, he knew their beautiful union on earth would soon end.

That's why this trip was so important to him.

Taking a deep breath, Phillip made his way to the starboard side of the sunken ship.

This was the moment he waited sixty long years for. After years of grieving, this would be the moment Phillip Johnson gained closure. He would finally fulfill his wish to say a proper good-bye to his best friend.

Standing at the wall, he sucked in a deep breath and gazed down into the clear waters of the harbor. He couldn't believe what his eyes saw.

Below him, it seemed just within arm's reach, was the ship that held Jack's body captive. It was the grave that preserved his friend as he was in 1941.

Paloma moved in close and placed her comforting hand over her father's shoulder and rubbed his back with the other. Then she reached down into her bag and pulled a yellow rose from within.

"Here you go, Dad."

Glancing down at the rose, Phillip thanked her. For a long moment, he studied it.

For doing what you were called to do, Jack. For all the years you had my back. For the laughter, the good times, and the bad. Forever, you are missed, my friend.

Unexpected tears seeped from his eyes. And as Phillip leaned over to release his rose into the water, those tears trickled down into the salty tomb —a piece of him left at the very place where Jack gave his life.

"Excuse me, sir. Did you serve here at Pearl Harbor?"

Those somber thoughts were interrupted by another tourist.

"No, son, I didn't. But my best friend did."

"I'm trying to gather information for a college paper. Would you happen to know what your friend witnessed the day of the bombing?"

Phillip gazed down into the watery grave below him. "Well, now, that's a story that's buried below us. But I can tell you three harrowing stories about lost love, a man who came back from the dead, and the story of a man who didn't know what war really was until he came home."

Author's Note

Dear Reader,

Another story comes to a close.

I hope you found Phillip's War an appropriate ending to the Love & War Series. It was not an easy book to write.

So many nights I struggled to find the words to say. Frustration was constantly at my fingertips. The emotional struggle to create Phillip's character slammed me into a brick wall more than once. I wanted readers to love him and to hope for his restoration. At times, I hated writing his character, but I knew his story must be told.

Post-Traumatic Stress Disorder is real.

Sometimes it shows up right away, but there are instances when it rears its ugly head years later.

Unfortunately, during World War II, the struggle was often overlooked and patients diagnosed with Shell Shock were often committed and put away. The YouTube videos on World War I shell shock patients are horrific to watch.

Once in this book, I make reference to Phillip in terms of a *"basket case."* While nowadays we throw that slang around in reference to someone who is very upset or crazy, it was a real term in the 1940's. Basket Case was used in the medical field for patients diagnosed with shell shock.

Certain patients were moved to a different ward where doctors found that weaving baskets calmed the patients' minds.

Many baskets were made by shell shock victims and used during the war. Today, the term is used loosely, its true meaning hidden by years of overlook. But perhaps after reading this author's note, people will be more informed of the origin of this slang.

Then there is the question of emotional and mental abuse in the home. What people don't know in today's society is that anytime abuse was ongoing inside a home in the early 19th Century, it was rarely spoken of. Women kept quiet, husbands kept quiet, and they put on a false façade that their lives were impeccable. It was taught that way to their children as it was to them. Of course, it doesn't make it right or okay in anyone's eyes.

The reason I chose for Libby to renew her vows with Phillip was for the purpose of closure, solitude, and forgiveness. While Phillip was never physically abusive in his right mind, his actions were often taken out during a shell shock spell. I chose to give the couple one year before their reunion as husband and wife. In that time, Phillip would have lived in a convalescent where he could obtain proper treatment for his illness. Libby, too, could get counseling from her pastor or doctor. But ultimately, I believe Phillip and Libby could not have fully recovered without putting Christ in the center. Just like any marriage, without Christ in the center of the union, the walk would be difficult and hopeless.

It's my hope that someone will be encouraged by Phillip's and Libby's story.

Acknowledgements

It's amazing to think this series has finally come to an end. For five years, these characters have been a part of my life and to close out this series is much like saying good-bye to an old friend.

It took many eyes and many hands to bring all three stories together. Like any project, each book had its own special team to bring home the finished product.

Above all, none of this—these 3 books, the ideas, and my writing talent—would not be possible without Christ leading me. It's because of the Lord's calling that these stories of love, dedication, and forgiveness were born.

I want to thank my family, Chris, April, Ryan, Andy, and Candace for getting behind me all the way. This book was a tough project to take on and they know the many hours I sat at my desk and stared at a blank screen. Without their willingness to sacrifice certain nights, this book would have never seen its end! Thank you all and I love you!

The undertaking of this book became emotionally challenging for me from the very beginning. Knowing I was going to take on Post-Traumatic Stress Disorder (Shell Shock, as it was known in the '40s), I wanted to make sure the book was written accurately, effectively, and yet gently. For this, I called on someone who is an expert in this field. So much of my gratitude for creating Phillip's character goes out to a long-time friend, Cindy Greenslade, Ph.D. For months we exchanged emails, historical information, and articles based on cause, symptoms, and treatment of PTSD. Miss Cindy, without your help, I would not have had the confidence to write out Phillip's character. It's because of you that this idea molded into a book worth writing. Thank you so much for your professional insight. Hugs and love out to you in sunny CA!

I hit a brick wall more than once while writing Phillip's War. Tears, frustration, love, and hate were all poured into this project. But when I thought I'd written myself into mental exhaustion, one person's phone call made all the difference. My dear friend and fellow author, Rita Gerlach, gave me the words and inspiration I needed to keep going, to keep writing, and to continue penning the words that needed to be written. Rita, your phone call made all the difference in the way I looked at this project. I will be forever grateful for your friendship and the support you have offered me since the beginning of my writing career. Thank you for being my support and encourager throughout this last year. I love you for it!

And the story is not a book without the crucial work of an editor. Anne-Marie Albaugh, I owe you the world and nothing short! Thank you for the hours of time you sacrificed for my work. I know it is no easy feat, and I would be lost without you. My books would not have been ready for the press if not for your keen eye. Any mistake caught in this book is purely of my own fault and overlooking.

One unique characteristic of this story is not just the main characters, but a few of the supporting characters. In 2015, I was asked by Carroll Christian Schools if I would donate to their annual school auction. We came up with the idea of auctioning off a character in a book! One person was the lucky recipient of that donation. The book cannot go on without mention to the real life Sydney Duncan, the recipient of the star in a book promotion. Sydney, I hope you find the story engaging and inspiring. Thank you for allowing me to use your name as one of Phillip's War's biggest support character. May the Lord bless you as you walk through this life, and may you find your purpose as I did. God bless you!

I need to make one other special mention: To Ann Ellison, a dear reader who has become a great friend. Ann, thank you for beta reading on such short notice. Your helpful insight and support is what pushed me to finish this book on time. My thanks is not enough for the kindness you've shown to me.

Two more characters from this book were taken from real life persons. The first is by special mention.

Ashleigh, thank you ever so much for allowing me to use Holly Faith's name in this book. Although the role in the book was short, Holly's memory is not. May the Lord continue to use her and you for His glory. Holly is forever in our hearts.

And to Chad and Tina Mania, I thank you for allowing me to use Nathaniel's name for Harvey and Sydney's son. It was a pleasure to create a character fitting for him in this project.

No words or ideas could have been complete without the help of all these individuals. Their love and support is what guided me through the nights when I wanted to give up. My gratitude is too full and too great to express on these pages, and I feel as though I am forever indebted. Thank you all for your help and encouragement. I am truly blessed with wonderful friends like you.

All my love and gratitude,

Phillip's War

~Rachel

<u>*Other Books by Rachel*</u>

Bring Home the Complete
Love & War Series
Today!

Praise for
Love & War Series...

"With warmth, grace, and finesse, Rachel Muller has crafted a memorable and powerful story in **Phillip's War**. *She paints a vivid and accurate portrayal of what so many faced upon returning from WWII, plunging into the gritty depths of an emotional turmoil not often broached in the genre. She has gifted the world a stunning, fictional testimony as to what God can rebuild out of utter brokenness— making* **Phillip's War** *a truly unforgettable tale."*

--Meghan Gorecki,
Author of Historical Romance, *God's Will*

"When I finished **Letters from Grace,** *I felt that I needed to learn the rest of the story. Therefore I am delighted that* **Maggie's Mission** *is now available. I found Rachel Muller's writing style engaging and heartfelt."*

--Susan Bulanda, Award Winning Author

"In **Letters from Grace,** *talented author Rachel Muller proves that nothing—fear, misunderstanding, lack of faith, not even war— can stand in the way of true love. Readers will identify with the tough choices faced by Muller's characters, and wait with bated breath for the next installment in the* **Love & War Series**. *Make room for these novels on your "keeper shelf, because you'll want to read the realistic, heart-pounding stories again and again!"*

--Loree Lough, Best-Selling Author

Is loving a man in uniform worth the risk?

Scarred from the death of her fiancé in World War II, Grace Campbell must learn to love again. Lieutenant Luke Brady could make falling in love easy…except he's going to war. There's one thing that can keep a thread tied between them—letters. But the suave Dr. William Keller enchants Grace with his charm and proposes marriage. She must choose between them. Will she settle for comfort and safety or risk losing everything on the Normandy beaches?

Phillip's War
Maggie's Mission
Book 2 in the Love & War Series

A buried vow and a broken past meet face to face on enemy territory...

While trying to prevent a war from breaking out within her own tent in Germany, Army nurse, Lieutenant Maggie Johnson, is just trying to do her job—save lives. But when the field hospital is directly bombed, it's Maggie's life who needs saving instead. In the midst of her struggle, a ruggedly handsome soldier comes to her aid and resembles the face of a man she once loved—a man who is dead.

Is war playing mind games with her or is she facing the ghosts of her past.

Made in the USA
Middletown, DE
18 December 2022

19180471R00172